TENERIFE

ANTHONY MCDONALD

Anchor Mill Publishing

Anthony McDonald

Anchor Mill Publishing
4/04 Anchor Mill
Paisley PA1 1JR
SCOTLAND
anchormillpublishing@gmail.com

.

Acknowledgements

I would like to thank my two musketeers, Roger McGeachin and Douglas Glen, for reading the manuscript with a critical as well as an affectionate eye. Also Sarah Parnaby, Pamela Hardy, Barry Creasy, and Simon Richardson.

Anthony McDonald

For Aristheo Hernández García

ONE

I met him on a park bench in the dark, a little before midnight. It was barely a bench, though. It wasn't even a park.

I'd clocked the place in the daytime. A tarmacked path ran S-wise around a patch of waste ground just beyond the edge of town. The place where the supply of hotels ran out. Within a few years new hotels would spring up here where now lay piles of rubble and rock, and clumps of weed and grass.

On the wilder side of the snaking path a swathe of bushes and small trees filled the space before a ravine opened up. There were yucca trees and small palms, many types of cactus, red-flowering aloe vera, and rambling wild spinach. Rough trampled paths wound intriguingly among the tangled trees, disappearing into the wild undergrowth. I didn't need to follow them to know that they led to clearings where the ground was littered with used condoms and innumerable stubs of cigarettes.

I found myself here again after dark. Rather drunk. I wasn't quite sure what had brought me here. Though of course you know and so, I suppose, I guess I did.

There seemed to be no-one else about. No red-glowing cigarettes pulsating amid the brush. No sound. No furtive rustling. No tramp of feet on the tarmacked path.

There were streetlamps at the beginning of the footpath. But then they gave out. Only the light of hotels a hundred yards away and a distant mountainside of twinkling houselights, gold and white, made inroads, by silvering the edges of a million leaves and fronds, into the dark. A deep darkness, whose deepness and whose darkness were made even deeper and darker by the fact of my being drunk.

The first bench I passed was empty. Nobody sat there at this late hour, in hopeful or hopeless wait. I ran my eye along the silvered unbroken lines of its parallel slats. I walked on.

The second bench was different. The silver lines of its slats abruptly stopped. So I stopped. To look. A figure sat immobile in the darkness. A slim figure, the outlines of whose legs and other features were just discernible in the distant light. He was wearing a cap, it seemed. His legs were crossed at the ankles. He was holding a can of something. Beer? Red Bull? Tear gas? I continued my walk.

Round the S-curve. Three more empty benches. The path wound uphill beside a bravely modern church. There it emerged from the wooded shadows and met a road beneath the stare of bright streetlights. I turned around and went back down the unlit path.

The return seemed even darker. Only my feet, not my eyes, could tell me where the path was. From time to time encroaching seeding grass-heads brushed at my legs like passing cats, signalling me to adjust my course.

The three empty benches were still empty. I had to peer hard at them to be sure of that. But then the fourth one… His legs still claimed a piece of pathway. Still ankle-crossed. Jeans-clad. Trainer-shod. Face hidden from the distant hotel-glimmer beneath the shading peak of his cap. I came to a stop. My eyes focused on the shiny can he was holding. After a time it gave up its secret. Dorada, it announced.

I stood where I was for a long half minute. He didn't move a muscle. I sat down on the other end of his bench.

Still no reaction from him. His silhouette continued to hold his beer can's silhouette, resting it on his knee. His face was in profile. He had a cute short nose. I sat immobile, a foot away from him. A minute passed. Then I unzipped my jeans and got my cock out. He did turn his head a little then, to take a look at it.

I laid a hand on his nearer thigh. It warmed me through his jeans: a night heater that had stored up the day's warmth.

He didn't move away or brush my hand off. So I moved it further into his private territory. I found his fly, unzipped it, and took his own cock out. *'Bonito,'* I said. It was warm and starting to fill out, though by no means to become erect. But by now mine was.

He made a snickering sound, then took a nervous sip from his beer can. *'¿Español?'* I asked.

'Si,' he said. *'¿Tu Ingles? ¿Aleman?'* It was as reasonable a guess as mine had been. Most tourists here came into those two categories: English, German.

'Escocés,' I said. Scottish. I thought it was important to get this clear from the start.

'Then we can speak English,' he said unexpectedly. 'I'm a teacher of English.'

'So am I,' I said. I felt his hand grasp my cock.

We moved closer together on the bench, wriggling towards each other till our thighs made contact down their full length. He offered me his beer can. It was nearly empty but I took a swig from it. Slowly, thoughtfully, we stroked each other's dicks.

Silhouettes of men, alone or in pairs, passed us at intervals, two feet from our knees, on the path. Their figures came between us and the distant hotel lights and made those lit windows blink. Some walked on regardless, others turned and looked. None of them spoke to us or tried to join us on the bench.

'I have a hotel near here,' I said, continuing to rub his cock. 'I mean a room in a hotel. I'm on my own here.'

'Which hotel?' he asked. I told him. He didn't seem to know it. I pointed across the dark waste ground towards the beckoning lights. 'Just beyond those,' I said. 'On Calle del Aceviño. Five minutes' walk.'

He nodded. 'We'll go there.' Without returning his cock to its hiding place he got up from the bench. 'I need to piss.'

'All that beer,' I said.

He stood by the end of the bench, slightly shielded from the path by a litter bin on a post, and hosed the ground behind it. I took hold of his dick while he was doing it and waved it about, so that he ended up watering the lower branches of an overhanging broom bush. He chuckled his surprise at that little intimacy while his flying, falling chains of water glittered intermittently in the distant hotel-light.

'*¿Como te llamas?*' I asked as we began to walk. His English would inevitably be better than my Spanish, which was meagre. But I didn't want him to think I couldn't speak a word of it.

'Teo,' he said. 'It's short for Aristeo, which sounds a bit heavy to anyone who isn't Spanish. Come to think of it, it sounds a bit heavy even if you are Spanish.' Crikey, his English was good. 'What about you?'

'I'm Jonty,' I said.

'Short for Jonathan,' said Teo cleverly.

It was also a Scottish version of good plain John but I didn't want to get into all that. Actually I didn't know why my parents had called me Jonty. The name suggested Edinburgh public schools or land-owning gentry families, neither of which was my background at all. I wasn't going to go into all that either. 'Are you...? Do you live here in Puerto?' I asked.

4

'Yes. Tenerife born and bred. Actually I was born up in La Orotava. But now I live down here.'

Down here was a relative term of course. My hotel, and the waste ground where we'd met, stood two hundred feet above Puerto's town centre and the waves of the Atlantic. But I only had to glance along the streets whose ends we walked past to see the lights of La Orotava hanging like jewels in the sky a little way inland, where the small inland town and its outskirts climbed the mountainside for a couple of thousand feet.

My hotel came in sight. I picked up the vibrations of Teo's nervousness even before he spoke. 'What will they say at reception?' he said.

'Same as always,' I said, brushing his fears aside with an outward show of confidence. *'Buenas noces.* If even that.'

'Better do our zips up, though,' he said. 'Hostages to fortune if we don't.'

'Good thinking,' I said. We had put our cocks away after Teo finished pissing, but neither of us had bothered to zip up in the dark. Now we did it as we walked.

Side by side we marched through the big doors of the hotel lobby. I gave the receptionist a nod and a smile as we swept past the desk. *'Buenas noches,'* she said.

I returned her goodnight, while Teo swept the cap from his head and said, *'Bona noche.'* If that didn't mark him out as a local nothing would. But we sailed on unchallenged towards the lifts and buzzed impatiently. Not until we got inside one and were on the way up to floor seven could we feel entirely safe.

But once we were inside the lift, the doors had closed and the liquid crystal numbers were mounting up, we felt extremely safe. We were surrounded by mirrors. We had our first chance to get a proper look at each other in good lighting. We liked what we saw. We kissed.

We had to break apart quickly when we stopped at floor six and a middle-aged man got in with us. He'd seen us in mid-clinch as the doors began to open (we hadn't actually noticed that the lift had stopped) and although he didn't say anything, and we hadn't been doing anything illegal, it was still a bit embarrassing. We were glad we were only going up one more floor before we got out.

Outside the lift was a spacious landing with chairs on it, and with paintings of a snow-capped Mount Teide on its walls. Teo looked at the paintings and asked, 'Do you paint, Jonty?'

'I didn't paint those,' I said, wondering for a crazed moment if he thought that I had.

'No, obviously,' Teo said. 'That wasn't what I meant.'

'No, sorry,' I said. 'No. I don't paint at all. Quick drawings on the whiteboard to explain a word...'

'The same with me,' Teo said. At that moment I found myself wishing I did paint. Wishing that I could. Because I would have liked to paint him. Seeing him now in the light I thought he looked gorgeous. He had the looks of a model or a minor film star. I heard him say, 'But at this moment I wish I was an artist. Because then I could paint you.' We reached the door of my room. I unlocked it with my plastic key and we went inside.

The first thing Teo did was to kiss me briefly. Then he stood back and began to take off all his clothes. I did the same.

Teo and I were the same size. Same height (about five foot eight), same lithe and slender but lightly muscular build. But then the differences began. He had a lovely olive complexion and very smooth skin. Round eyes like glossy black chocolate, and lashes that were long, thick and curly, like a gazelle's. His lips were soft and cushiony, and he had a small, dished nose. His pearly teeth made a neat and orderly but not too assertive appearance when he smiled. Which he was doing now. His forearms, like his legs and chest, were lightly furred with glossy black. On legs and arms the hair grew in tidy striation. On his chest it grew in pleasing whorls around his nipples, fountaining from a line that rose by way of his navel from his trimmed pubes. His cock, fully erect now, was the same shape and size as mine.

What of my appearance? Those looks of mine that had made Teo say he wanted to paint me. Quite ordinary, I would have said, except that I am very, very blond. With almost albino hair. On my head, that is. For apart from my pubes and underarms I had very little hair to show off. Teo would have had to mix lots of white paint with a very little rose and cream to capture the colour of my skin. And to find a very bright pale Prussian blue for my blond-lashed eyes. In short, he would be painting someone who was unmistakably northern European, very northern European; while I would be ransacking the paint-box for the colours of the Spanish and North-African south.

'Our dicks are the same shape and size,' Teo said. He sounded quite pleased about that. They weren't particularly big, even in relation to our modest overall size. Their foreskins were both half retracted at this moment of intimate comparison. Except in the matter of colour scheme they might have been twins. 'Big balls,' Teo observed, feeling my pair with one hand.

'Same as yours,' I said, doing exactly the same. Then we stopped eating each other with our eyes and embraced each other, warm flesh against warm flesh.

Teo had a backpack with him. I hadn't seen it until he'd stood up from the bench and had picked it up from the ground before having his piss. Now, naked in my hotel room, he delved into it and fished out two cans of beer. We sat side by side on my hotel bed, holding the Dorada cans in one hand while swigging from them, and fiddling with each other's dicks with the other hand. We made conversation the while.

'How old are you?' I asked.

'Thirty-four,' said Teo. 'You?'

'Same.' I was struck by the coincidence. 'Your birthday?'

'Same as Shakespeare's and Cervantes's…'

'April twenty-third,' I said quickly, to show I knew. Though actually I hadn't known about Cervantes. 'But that makes you very old.'

'Why? When's yours?'

'May fifth,' I said. 'We're very close.'

Teo gave my cock a friendly squeeze. He said, 'You're telling me.'

We took a shower together after we'd finished the beer. Soaped each other down. Paying special attention to the bits you'd expect us to. I peed on the tip of his dickhead at one point, which made him giggle, because he hadn't expected me to. 'You're hotter than the shower!' he said.

'I'm even hotter in bed,' I said, then wished I hadn't. I'd given myself rather a lot to live up to.

Actually we were lovely in bed together. We liked each other's touch and feel and smell, enjoyed the pace at which we wanted to explore. Both of us were dead keen to fuck the other, and had proved the fact just before climbing in together by each ferreting out a condom from a pocket in our jeans, which were lying together on the floor in a discarded muddle.

But since we both wanted to do it and neither would give way the result was a bit of an impasse, although a friendly one. After a little while we ended up bringing each other off by hand, belly to belly. That was very nice for both of us – we managed to come almost simultaneously, just a second between us – and at that point the impasse magically disappeared. Teo looked about him. 'It's OK,' I said. 'Stay there. I'll get one of the bathroom towels.' Ah, the luxuries of a hotel room.

I woke up briefly in the small hours. It took me a second to realise there was someone in the bed beside me and a further second to remember who it was. I looked across the pillow and received a horrible shock on seeing Teo's face in the near darkness. It was all covered in black hair. I'd gone to bed with a werewolf. Then the penny dropped sleepily. Teo was lying turned away from me. It was the back of his head I was looking at. Relieved, I went back to sleep.

We awoke at morning light and pleasured each other by hand a second time. Then Teo said it was time he went. He got out of bed and quickly hopped into his clothes. I said, 'I'll walk down with you,' got out of bed and started to hop into mine.

Picking up strangers on park benches at midnight might not be the safest of behaviours but I hadn't lost all instinct for self preservation. I checked that my wallet was still in place in my jeans pocket. It was not. Nonchalantly I moved over to the chair on which I'd left the shorts I'd worn in yesterday's midday warmth. I felt a relaxation of my tummy muscles as I encountered its small, thick bulk among the folds of fabric. Nevertheless I took it out and looked inside it. My cash was there – at least there was a wodge of notes; I didn't count them – but my debit card was not. At this point I knew I had to say something. 'Bugger. I can't find my debit card.'

'When did you last have it?' Teo asked reasonably, pausing in the act of tying the laces of his trainers.

'I didn't take it out with me when I...'

'No, obviously,' said Teo. 'I didn't take mine. Try all your pockets.'

I started doing that. I knew by now that I wouldn't be letting Teo leave my room before I found the elusive slice of plastic. And I was almost conscious of the moment, about a second later, when the penny dropped with Teo that he wouldn't be going anywhere until I did find it.

Thoughts cannoned around my mind. One was the comforting idea that fellow English teachers would not rob each other. There was honour among professionals, wasn't there? Another was the question of how I would actually stop Teo leaving if he wanted to. Overpower him physically when his fingers were pulling on the door handle? We were the same size and build. I guessed we were equally matched in strength. Perhaps he could overpower me physically? I hadn't been in a fight since I'd left school. These days I couldn't really guess how such a thing would turn out. I heard Teo saying, 'Think of every possible place.'

My leather jacket had six pockets in it. My two backpacks – a small one was stowed inside the bigger one – together notched up eight, as well as their main interior spaces. I had two used shirts with breast pockets in them and two further pairs of shorts...

My eyes lit on the paperback I'd been reading out by the pool. Something just showed an edge, jutting between the pages. I picked up the book and my card fell out of it. 'Found it,' I said, in a physical ecstasy of relief. 'It seems I was using it as a bookmark.'

'Alleluia,' said Teo, loudly and fervently, and I could hear his pent-up breath whoosh out as he spoke. Then he added, 'Yes. It's the sort of stupid thing I'd do myself.'

We kissed again in the lift going down, but even though no-one got in on the intermediate floors, it didn't turn into a major business.

'I'm here three more days,' I said casually as we walked across the lobby towards the door. 'Room seven oh one, seventh floor.' Teo said nothing in reply. I added for good measure. 'Most evenings I'm in City Bar at some point. Just along the road.'

'I know it,' Teo said. He didn't say he might see me there.

We were outside in the warm daylight now. A light breeze ruffled the palm trees along the pavement and made them clatter their fronds. I said, 'How far do you have to go to get home?'

'Twenty minutes' walk.' He didn't say in which direction. He didn't say where. We'd left the hotel forecourt and were out by the road. An airport bus was embarking a load of homebound holidaymakers, and their suitcases were trippingly everywhere. We stopped and turned to face each other. We both grinned.

'Hasta la proxima, Teo,' I said, not very hopefully. The moment did not seem to be pointing towards a next time.

Teo stuck his hand out towards me in a manly, no-nonsense way. I took it for a second only. Equally firmly. Equally manly. There would be no final kisses out here in front of the buses, the tourists and the window-eyed hotels. *'Amigo,'* said Teo. And I said, *'Ciao, Teo.'* We turned away from each other and I walked back into the hotel. I didn't stay to watch him go.

Amigo. It had a final sound to it. It rhymed almost with *Finito.* And its English translation rhymed even more strongly with The End.

TWO

It wasn't yet nine o'clock. In a way I had come to Tenerife looking for sex. Well, I'd found it. But now what?

I walked round the hotel's pool area. Scarlet petals fallen from the overhanging tulip trees littered the grass and created sunlit lakes of red. But I didn't feel like sprawling on a sun lounger yet. I left the hotel grounds and crossed the road to the terrace where I usually had my first coffee.

The German-sounding café Bei Thomas was one of a line of almost identical cafés along the Calle del Aceviño. I favoured it for two reasons. It was the only one of those cafés whose terrace offered a view of Mount Teide's snowy summit, fifteen miles distant. And I fancied the waiter who worked the morning shift.

He gave me a smile and a nod as I walked onto the terrace. *'¿Café con leche?'* he checked. I said si, and good morning, and took a seat in the morning sun. I wouldn't be able to stay there long. I hadn't put my sun-cream on yet.

I sat there, sipping the coffee through the froth on top of it, and went through in my mind all the details of the previous night. What we did. What I felt. What we'd said.

Teo had asked me, naturally, what I was doing holidaying on Tenerife all by myself. I'd recently split up with my boyfriend, I told him. He'd nodded his sympathy but had been quite unsurprised. We'd been planning to come out to Tenerife for a week this Easter anyway, I told Teo. After we'd split I decided on a whim to come out on my own. Just for… Just for what? I hadn't asked myself that question, and I didn't go into it with Teo. I still didn't know. Had I come here to cheer myself up? With a view to making a new start? Just for sex? Out of spite?

Teo's question had come in the course of the conversation we'd had while drinking beer side by side on my bed. It hadn't been a long conversation. First, there had only been one can of beer each. Second, we were both itching to get each other between the sheets. We had talked a little, but only a little, about the coincidence of our both being teachers of English. It was something we had in common, though what our jobs had in common was limited. Teo taught English to Spanish kids as a foreign language. I taught English to Scottish kids as their first. The two jobs were entirely different.

Now I found myself thinking about the things we hadn't said in the course of that beer-swigging, dick-stroking, ten minutes. The things I didn't know about Teo – and the things he didn't know about me – filled a universe. I didn't know if he had a boyfriend. Or several. If he lived on his own, or with someone else, or with friends, or with his parents. I didn't have his mobile, his FB details, his email, or his street address. He'd told me that he lived twenty minutes' walk away. So did most of the other 30,000 inhabitants of Puerto de la Cruz.

So what? You found people, enjoyed sex with them, and then forgot them. At least that was what was supposed to happen. But I found that a bit difficult. Perhaps I wasn't old enough to feel that way. Perhaps I wasn't young enough. Perhaps I was simply different from most.

I could have gone on Grindr at this point and, putting thoughts of Teo behind me, looked to see what else was on today's menu, within a handy distance. But actually I didn't have Grindr on my phone. Harry and I had agreed not to use it during our four years together, in a very pragmatic spirit of self preservation. Not that, in the end, that agreement had done us a lot of good. Grindr might have come in useful out here on Tenerife, I had to admit. Yet somehow the idea didn't appeal particularly. Really? The idea and easy practicality of Grindr didn't appeal to someone who was more than happy to pick up strangers on park benches at midnight? All I could reply to myself was that we were all full of contradictions and I was no exception to that.

I finished my coffee and paid for it. Then I ambled along the pavement, past other cafés and shops that sold beach hats and flip-flops, glancing from time to time at the grand view of Mount Teide coming and going between the palm trees that lined the little street. I turned towards a cliff-top viewing area and walked up to the parapet.

The centre of Puerto lay spread below me. Beneath the cliff a double avenue ran down – bright flowerbeds overflowing its pedestrian central reservation – towards the surfers' beach. I could see the wet-suited bodies of young surfers. Paddling out across the lagoon whose breakwater kept back the worst of the Atlantic's winter fury but still allowed the more manageable waves to race shoreward around its seaward corner. From my height and distance the surfers seemed as small as sand-shrimps.

I had actually thought about enrolling in the surf school when I arrived here. It would have been something different. But as I'd watched I'd realised that I couldn't attain much of a standard in a mere week. The island's spring weather was balmy, but the Atlantic in April was not. I'd come here for a relaxing break, not total immersion in cold and wet. Anyway I already had the looks and rangy physique of a surf dude (so people told me) if only a rather small one. If I looked like a surfer, I told myself, I didn't actually need to be one.

I looked beyond the shrimp-sized surfers, beyond the breakwater, across the sea's infinite blue brilliance. I turned away after a couple of minutes and retraced my steps to my hotel. I picked up my book (it no longer contained my debit card), applied a lot of sun-cream, then abandoned myself to a sun-lounger beside the pool beneath the crimson-crowned tulip trees, with nothing on except my shorts.

I spent a good part of that evening in City Bar. I'd told Teo I hung there and had at least some reason to hope that he'd turn up. I was on holiday from school in the wake of Easter and I'd assumed that Teo also was. But I hadn't asked him how he would be spending his day. I spent a good deal of that evening, as I threw down beer after beer, trying uselessly to guess.

City Bar had attracted me on my first evening in Puerto de la Cruz. Most of the bars along Calle del Aceviño were occupied by middle-aged German couples staring across identical glasses of beer at each other and trying to think of something new, after thirty years of married life, to talk about. City Bar was intriguingly different. It was at the bottom end of an awning-covered pathway. It was noisy with young people and dimly lit. I'd made my way down to it as if to a cellar, jostled my way inside, towards the crowded counter and ordered a beer for myself.

The bar was lit by wall-mounted ships' lights. Behind the horseshoe-shaped counter the blue lights of product displays shone enticingly through a double row of polished wine and beer glasses, while red light bled through the lines of bottles of spirits and liqueurs. Two young barmen worked the crowd at a manic pace, their movements most gracefully choreographed. When they scooped cash payments from the counter and discovered that a punter had left a tip they flung the extra into a bucket that hung from a beam just above their heads. A bell hung right next to the bucket, and the bucket's swing would make it ding each time a coin or two went into it. It happened a lot. One of the young barmen wore a T-shirt with This Is Living printed on it.

Teo didn't materialise in City Bar that evening. I left the place when it closed at one o'clock, giving the younger of the two barmen a rather drunken kiss when I said goodnight, and made my way a bit unsteadily back along the street to my hotel and bed. Teo didn't turn up the following night, or the next. And then it was my last day. My last night.

I treated myself to a dinner in one of the best restaurants downtown. That meant walking down the hundred and something steps of the Camino las Cabras – its name meant goat path – that wound its way down the cliff. There had been a storm during the night. It had left a bright sunny day in its wake but the sea below had not forgotten it, and as I went down the steps I could see that the distant horizon was no longer flat but had spikes and lumps across it.

I dived towards the Old Town. I had found a restaurant there that I liked the look of, just off the Plaza del Charco. It was in a traditional old Canarian house, all chestnut beams and interior balconies with turned balusters. I asked for a table for one and was given a cosy spot in the lee of the sweeping staircase.

I'd done a calculation on my way here. I had thirty five euros left in my wallet. If I paid for my evening meal by card I would still have enough for a nightcap at City Bar, tomorrow's breakfast, and any bits of shopping I might want to do at the airport. My holiday package included airport transfer in the morning, so I wouldn't have to worry about that. I reckoned I didn't need to find a cash machine tonight.

I had prawns in garlic oil and then braised rabbit, with a small carafe of wine, and even a chocolate mousse by way of dessert. The bill came to thirty-one euros by the time I'd added a tip. But my debit card was no longer in my wallet.

I had to stand up to go through all my jacket and jeans pockets. I came near to undressing myself. I got on my hands and knees and combed the floor with my fingers. But my plastic money was nowhere. I had arrived at the restaurant without it.

I didn't panic. I'd once seen a postcard that bore the legend, Don't panic: count to ten and then panic. I'd tried to abide by it ever since. But I'd have to count to more than ten tonight. There were more than two hundred cliff-side steps between me and the hotel room in which I'd most likely left my plastic. With a calmness that surprised me I handed over the thirty-one euros that were almost all I had, said a cheerful goodnight and see you next time to the waiter, and walked out with my hand in my jeans pocket. Repeatedly I rubbed and fingered the coins – three euros and sixty-four cents – that lodged there. I wondered what I would spend them on.

This time there was no question that Teo might have stolen my bank card. I hadn't seen him for over two days and I'd used the card several times in the meantime. I had either left it in my hotel or lost it.

I looked at the ground as I retraced my steps through the town and up the Camino las Cabras. I didn't see my slip of plastic. I was more optimistic about the hotel room. Once I had got up there I went through everything. After the dummy run I'd had the other morning I was in practice, and I searched efficiently and quickly. But there was no sign of the card.

It was still too soon to panic. My wallet had once contained a scruffy bit of paper that gave the number you were supposed to ring if you lost your debit card. Almost to my disbelief I found I still had it. At the first rummage. But to phone the number I would have to go down to the lobby. I couldn't get a signal inside my room or on the balcony.

I found the lobby full of noise. A jazz band was playing in the restaurant. There were alto sax and tenor sax and a vocalist, and none of them giving short measure. I walked out into the dark street.

I'd thought the Calle del Aceviño a quiet enough sort of place. But when you were trying to phone the UK from an island in the mid-Atlantic nowhere was quiet enough. I keyed in the number amid a cacophony of hooting taxis, shouting youths and cars grinding up and down their gear changes. I wasn't hopeful. I was Aladdin trying to summon the genie from his lamp.

But somehow there came a friendly Scottish voice announcing the name of my bank and of his department in it. I was more than happy. And the voice at the other end seemed quite happy with the sound of my voice too. For I too had – and have – a Scottish accent.

There were hoops to go through. Could I remember my national insurance number? The fourth letter of the name of my first boyfriend? (Not that my compatriot asked me that exactly. 'Memorable information' was how he put it.) Then there I was. My card was cancelled. No-one had misused it and as from this moment nobody could. That included me, in the unlikely event I found it. 'Do you want emergency funds transferred to a bank in Puerto de la Cruz?' my new friend asked.

I thought for a moment. I was going to be picked up and taken to the airport at ten. Once I was on the plane I'd be OK. I had enough British cash to eat and drink and get home with. I could sort things out at my local bank branch. 'No,' I said. 'Though thank you very much.' Then we exchanged a few cheerful sentences and closed the call. I walked back with a lighter heart. Up to a point. My bank account was secure and safe. But I was temporarily penniless.

I asked the barman in City Bar what the smallest, cheapest measure of beer was. They did a small glass for a euro: it had about the capacity of a small wineglass. I drank it slowly, then bade farewell to the two barmen with *hasta la proxima* hugs and returned to my hotel-room bed.

I had my morning coffee at the café Bei Thomas as usual, in sight of Teide's sunlit snowy peak. The coffee cost one euro forty. It always had cost me one euro forty, though before today I hadn't noticed. I now had just one euro and twenty-four cents left. Normally I didn't take sugar in coffee. It was there for the taking, though, in little sealed paper tubes that contained about a teaspoonful each. I tipped four of the things into my froth-capped cup. It seemed a prudent thing to do. I didn't know when I'd be getting my next fix.

Out of interest I googled something at that point. How long could you survive without food or drink? The general consensus seemed to be a rule of three. You could go three weeks without food, three days without water, and three minutes without air. I thought they would feel like very long weeks, days and minutes. Especially the three airless ones.

Back at the hotel I was hailed by the woman behind the reception desk. 'Mr Allen, there has been a phone-call from your tour company. They have said sorry but there is a four-hour delay to your flight. They will come here for you at two o'clock.' Instead of ten. My flight would not be taking off till six. Nine hours from now. It seemed a long time to survive on a coffee and four spoons of sugar.

I had checked out of my room and my case and backpacks were in the luggage room. As an experiment I asked the receptionist if I could have a glass of water. She told me to ask at the bar. Where they were very nice to me and gave me a big glassful with clinking ice cubes in it. I'd learnt that bars in Spain were legally obliged to give water to anyone who asked for it. I'd seen tramps avail themselves of the service. Now I had joined their number. I wondered whether that held good in Britain. Maybe it wasn't such an issue back home. We never seemed to be short of water in Scotland.

I wandered down to the town. The sea horizon was flat and smooth again today and the top of Mount Teide crystal clear. I wondered as I walked down the Cabras steps how many calories were in four teaspoons of sugar and how many were used in going up and down steps. No doubt there would be a table I could google. But I resisted the urge to get my phone out. It seemed a sad thing to want to do on such a sunny day.

I sat on the stone seats near the surf school and watched the guys out on the water for a time. By twelve o'clock my stomach was complaining, and there were still six hours to go before I could fill it on the plane. I went to the beachside bar and asked for a glass of water, although I wasn't particularly thirsty yet. They looked at me sceptically but gave me the water. Grudgingly, I thought. I noticed there was no ice in the glass. I tipped the water down inside me. I thought that might keep my stomach quiet for a bit but it wasn't fooled.

I did a bit of window shopping along the seafront parade. It's a masochistic thing at the best of times: it reminds you of all the things you can't afford. And now it was worse. I'd never before done it in a situation in which I didn't have a bean.

Money is time and time is money... I was discovering that the relationship was a complex one. The hungry hours ahead of me seemed to stretch like elastic while all around me, at sun-shaded tables on the promenade, people were eating seafood with bright lemons and fragrant crusty bread chunks, and drinking golden wine and beer.

'*¡Hola, Jonty!*' I heard a voice call. I span towards it and saw its owner, who had come to a stop among the promenading crowds. It was Teo, with a smartly dressed young woman in tow.

THREE

The three of us looked at one another. I waited for Teo to say something. After a second or so he did. Touching both of us lightly on the forearm he introduced us. In English. 'Marina, this is Jonty, an English ... sorry, Scottish friend. Jonty, my sister Marina.'

Marina and I shook hands. I said, *'Encantado,'* and she, presumably not wishing to be outdone, said, 'Pleased to meet you.'

I couldn't imagine what we would say next. Perhaps Marina knew about her brother's habit of picking up men on park benches in the middle of the night. Perhaps she didn't. The ball seemed plainly to be in Teo's court. An expression of discomfort appearing suddenly on his face indicated that he was also aware of this. 'I thought you were flying home today,' he said.

'Not till this afternoon. There's been a delay to the flight.'

'Then let's have a coffee,' Teo said, sensibly enough.

'I haven't any money,' I blurted out stupidly. Teo hadn't suggested I should pay for the coffee. There was no earthly need for me to have mentioned my penniless state.

'You haven't lost your bank card again?' said Teo with a laugh, and I saw his sister shoot him a querying look.

'Exactly that,' I said.

'Cash?' Teo asked.

'I've spent it all,' I said. 'I've one euro and twenty-four cents left.'

Marina giggled in surprise and Teo said, 'Then I'm buying the coffee. And lunch. And then we'll go to a cash machine and get some money to ... how do we say?'

'Tide me over? That won't be necessary. Though coffee and lunch would be fantastic.'

Marina said, 'Where did you two meet?'

'In a bar,' Teo lied seamlessly. 'City Bar up in La Paz.' We were all standing just a metre from a line of café tables under an awning among the strolling tourists. 'Shall we sit?'

Marina would have had difficulty pretending she was other than her brother's sibling. She had the same dark chocolate eyes and gazelle eyelashes, the same pearly smile and slightly dished nose. She had the same kiss-me lips. Not that I especially wanted to kiss them. I would have been happier – very happy indeed – kissing Teo's. But this was not the time or place.

Over coffee I learnt that Marina lived on the other side of the island, in the capital Santa Cruz. That was only a thirty-minute drive by motorway, but you nevertheless had to climb to two thousand feet before dropping down the other side of Tenerife's volcanic spine. More interestingly she was a professional clarinettist and had a job in the Tenerife Symphony Orchestra. That touched my northern sensibilities: it sounded one of the nicest jobs in the hemisphere.

We talked in English. Marina's was good, though not as good as Teo's. 'Oh no,' she said when she heard what I did for a living. 'It is enough bad that my brother is a teacher of English.' Her eyes smiled. 'But now...'

'Bad enough,' Teo corrected under his breath. It was an autopilot thing; I understood.

'Are you married?' Marina asked me, looking very directly into my eyes.

'No,' I said and returned the challenge. 'Are you?'

'She's engaged,' Teo pitched in gallantly. 'To a very handsome man who is an *aduanero* ... what's that? ... a customs officer. At the port of Santa Cruz.'

Import duties and the clarinet, I thought. Excise and Brahms's symphonies. It would be an interesting marriage.

'Teo hasn't found the right girl yet,' Marina said, leaning a little across the table towards me. 'Perhaps you can find him an English ... Scottish one.'

So Marina didn't know. And if she didn't, then probably the parents didn't either. I couldn't remember if Teo had a brother – someone close that he might have confided in. He'd told me a bit about his family when we'd sat naked on my bed drinking beer, but I hadn't remembered all the details: I'd had other things on my mind and between my fingers.

I tried not to look at Teo but of course I did. And I saw that he was trying not to look at me, with similar lack of success. I saw on his face a dark and difficult something that I was only too familiar with: the expression that appears on a gay man's face when he's taken for a straight one and is unsure whether he should challenge the assumption or not. I guessed that Teo was seeing a similar expression on mine.

'We'd better order some lunch now,' Teo said abruptly. 'Jonty, you had no breakfast I suppose.'

'No,' I said.

'Jonty's starving to death. And plus, he has to leave for the airport before very long.' Teo called a waiter over and said something to him in Spanish. The words came out so rapidly that I couldn't decipher a single one.

Mixed fried fish. Between the three of us a carafe of red wine. A ponced-up but delicious ice-cream. Teo wouldn't let me even see the bill. 'I must send you my share by post,' I said.

Teo laughed. 'Don't be a silly billy.'

I said, 'Give me your address anyway. Number at least.' We would be parting in a few minutes' time and the idea of maintaining contact was suddenly important to me. Teo wasn't allowing me my pretext of paying him for my meal. Now I'd asked him point blank, my motive exposed to the scrutiny of anyone who wanted to look for it. I got my phone out. 'Facebook?'

Teo made a jerky movement with his head. It was difficult to see whether it was a nod or a shake. He said, 'Whatsapp.' I put his number in and his name popped up. There was more of it than I'd expected. Aristheo Gonçalves Domingo.

'I'll message you when I'm back in Glasgow,' I said casually. I could give him my own contact details at that point. I didn't want Marina to see us making too big a thing of this little ritual. I didn't say to Teo (now Theo apparently) that I would want to tell him I'd arrived safely.

By now it was time for me to go. I had to climb back up the steps of Las Cabras and the Camino San Amaro in order to pick up my airport transfer from outside my hotel. We all stood up. We shook hands and said polite words. It was difficult for me – and for Theo too, I noticed – to turn off the tap of polite words and to stop looking at each other. The first signs of perplexity appearing on Marina's face were our eventual cue to stop and for me to turn away. I walked off down the promenade wanting desperately to turn around and wave and only just managing not to by the exercise of a huge amount of willpower.

I had plenty of time on the plane to ponder what had happened to me. I wasn't remotely wealthy by the standards of my part of the world. But I wasn't poor either, as anyone from a less favoured region of the planet would have been quick to point out. I seldom felt the pangs of hunger. If I did I could simply open the fridge or else go out and buy something. With the money in my pocket. Now, like someone in a morality tale, I'd been given a taste of what it might be like for the others. I'd been exposed, like King Lear, *to feel what wretches feel*. It hadn't felt very nice.

Then along had come Theo, a man I'd briefly been to bed with, like the deus ex machina, to wave the magic wand of ready money to make everything all right again. I didn't want to think ... but I couldn't stop the idea peeping into my mind ... that all this *meant something*.

As my plane climbed away from Tenerife the island of Gran Canaria came into sight some way ahead of us. A black mass of rock that was spread across the blue Atlantic. Yet one little bit of it wasn't black at all. A golden tongue protruded from the southern tip of it. I knew what it was. I'd been there. It was the golden sand-dune desert of Maspalomas. A name to make any gay European man nod his head and say knowingly, 'Ah, Playa de Los Ingles. Those naked-people dunes. The Yumbo Centre.' I peered hopefully towards the golden tongue of Maspalomas, but from this distance – thirty or more miles? – I couldn't see the naked people. Then the plane banked and turned northwards and we left the Canary Islands behind us.

I sort of knew the way back. I'd done the outbound journey after all and had made a couple of visits to the Canaries before with Harry. I knew that the first section of the homeward flight would take us over the islands of Madeira and Porto Santo about forty minutes after we'd left the Canaries behind us. But we'd only been going twenty or so when I noticed someone in front of me jerk his head towards the window. I followed his example. Below us, visible through a hole in the clouds, lay an island.

It was too small to be Madeira. Too small even to be Porto Santo. It was too far south, anyway, to be either. There was no sign of a town or village on it. No airport runway. Its surface was brown and flattish, its edges were cliffs that, since they were clearly visible from 30,000 feet, must have been enormous. It had the general appearance of an overcooked cake, made without the help of a confining cake tin.

I tried to remember the whereabouts of St Helena. Not here, I thought. But I couldn't think of any islands between Madeira and the Canaries. After all, I taught English, not Geography. Perhaps the island had remained undiscovered through the centuries. Known only to airline pilots. And now me. Perhaps I could lay claim to it. Name it Jonty Island. No, islands were always named after people's surnames. It would have to be Allen Island. Though there would probably be an Allen Island somewhere in the world already: Allen was a lot of other people's surname. Perhaps the man who'd looked out of the window a second before I did would want to give it his name. Whatever that might be.

At that point a female member of the cabin crew asked me if I wanted something from the drinks trolley. I reached awkwardly into my pocket for money.

It was dark long before we arrived at Glasgow. It was while I was waiting beside the carousel for my small checked-in suitcase that I decided to send my arrived-safely message to Theo. I reached into my pocket for my phone. It wasn't there. I went through all my other pockets. It wasn't in any of them. Had it fallen out when I'd fished for my passport at Tenerife airport? Or when I'd rummaged for English cash to pay for my on-board drink? Or at some other point? I was hardly interested. I had lost Theo's precious contact number. I'd lost Theo.

FOUR

I stood in my 'very nice' flat, the one that had been Harry's and mine, and I didn't want to be there. I left my suitcase, unopened, and my backpack, in the middle of the floor and went straight out again into the dark northern evening.

Of course I'd gone to the help desk in the arrivals area. 'I think I've left my phone on a plane.' We went through the hoops together, the woman behind the counter and I. Flight number, arrival time. She did me proud, that silver-haired airport lady. She got on a phone. Got in touch with the gate. Got somebody to go on board. My seat number? I still had the stub of my boarding card. Ironically. Why couldn't I have dropped that instead?

They checked thoroughly. The lady behind the desk relayed that information to me as it arrived via her own securely wired-down phone. I had no reason to think they hadn't done. But with no success, she informed me sadly. So where had I last seen my all too mobile phone? Um... I'd held it in my hand at the airport. Tenerife South. In the departure lounge. I didn't remember handling it after that. Although I might have done.

The lady directed me to a desk run by my carrier airline. There another woman told me the airline would contact Tenerife South in the morning. I had to fill in a form. All the time I was doing this my new confidante wore an expression on her face that indicated – it was probably a message she wasn't allowed to convey in words – that my quest was hopeless. I handed back the form and went away with the grim conviction that I would need to set about getting a new phone in the morning.

For now I took a train the short distance into the centre of Glasgow. I had nothing in particular in mind to do when I got there. Just have a drink somewhere. Just not be alone in my empty apartment. Give myself half an hour to acclimatise myself to the cold northern spring, the dark evening, the flat without Harry in it... And to the loss of someone else. Someone I'd only met four days before but who had become unaccountably important to me today when I'd discovered the loss of my phone and his number.

Theo, short for Aristheo. Of course it was pronounced the way I'd heard it – Tayo. But I hadn't imagined the H until I'd seen it. After all, we didn't write Aristhotle in English, and in English Theo would be short for Theodore. But then, that was the way with words. The name Antonio in Spanish or Italian could be Antony in English – or Anthony, pronounced exactly the same. Where had those H's come from? Perhaps I would research it one day. Someone must have written it up on Wikipedia.

I hadn't set out to go to Del's but, once I'd got off the train and left the vaulted concourse of the Central station I found my feet taking me to Virginia Street like well trained donkeys that knew their own way home. Arriving beneath the rainbow flag I pushed the big door open and walked in and the thing that happened next was instantaneous.

He was standing by the bar with his back to the counter, facing the entrance door. He looked directly into my eyes and half smiled. As though he half knew me, or was half waiting for me.

He was a little taller than me. Black, slim and handsome. As though to rub in the knowledge that I was no longer in the sub-tropics he was wearing a heavy dark winter coat with a thrown-back hood, and a grey woollen ski-hat with a pom-pom top-knot. He had Timberland-type boots, and jeans. To get to the bar and order my drink I had to approach and then stand close to him.

He turned his head and studied my profile carefully while I, equally carefully, didn't turn towards him. I ordered myself a pint of lager while watching him from the corner of my eye.

There was nowhere to sit. I took my pint and stood against a wall, facing towards the bar. The guy stayed put, but he turned his body so that he faced me full square. There were just two yards, and a few people passing or briefly standing in between us.

After a while I raised my glass to him minutely, and with his pint of lager he did the same. He didn't move towards me. I didn't move towards him. A minute later he did half smile at me again. This time, I couldn't help it, I half smiled back at him. I guessed his age to be about three years less than mine was. I thought him very good looking indeed.

I wasn't in the mood for anything. I'd known that before setting out. Even the handsome guy looking at me wasn't going to change that. I'd just got off a plane. I'd just lost Theo. I knew I would go home – however little I wanted to be there – as soon as I'd finished my beer. I drank it unhurriedly and then, being careful not to look towards the guy beforehand, went off towards the toilets for a prudent piss before the train.

I was barely halfway through when someone came and stood beside me at the urinal. I didn't need to look to know who. But I looked anyway. At his face, which he'd half turned, smiling, towards me, and at his displayed cock, flaccid but considerably longer than mine, from which he was pissing a torrent.

He didn't stop doing that, nor did he waver in his aim, as he twisted his torso from the waist and kissed me. I didn't protest, but kissed him in return, and our two tongues got involved, and all sorts of clichés came into my mind, like *you wait ages then two come along at once* and *don't look a gift horse in the mouth* and, bad-punningly, *go with the flow.*

But then another person blundered in and my neighbour sprang back from me, finished his original business, zipped up and disappeared out through the door. He was one of those people who could empty themselves out, even during a beer-drinking session, in almost no time at all. It took me a few more seconds, then I too went back to the bar.

He was back in his original position. I felt I couldn't leave without saying goodbye. I went up to him and said, 'Sorry, got to go now.'

He looked at his glass. There was just about another inch of lager there. 'Me too,' he said. 'Early shift tomorrow. I'll give you my number.'

I said, 'I've lost my phone.' I found I was rather glad of that unusual circumstance.

He said, 'Piece of paper?'

'Sorry,' I said. 'I'm not very good with those.'

'I'll write it on your hand,' he said, and took a pen from inside his coat.

I found myself unable to say no. I stood still while he scrawled a string of digits across my palm and half a dozen people watched us in the disinterested way of cattle when one of their number is doing something unusual, or being mounted by a bull.

'What's your name?' I asked. Not that I intended to call or message him. I was curious, that was all.

'Maxwell,' he said.

I said, 'Jonty,' and we shook hands. With our right hands. His number remained un-smudged on my left one.

I looked at that left hand when I got home. I had no intention of making use of the number that was written on it. All the same, without a phone to put it in, it would disappear for ever the next time I washed my hands, just as Theo's had done. I transferred Maxwell's scrawled number, with a little question mark above one of the digits, to a piece of paper instead.

I had loved the place I lived in. I had a flat in the second or third biggest building in Paisley, I forgot which. (The biggest was the medieval Abbey, which might give a helpful idea of the scale.) It had once been a factory. A thread mill. I sometimes asked older people if they remembered Anchor Thread. Of course they did. The words, and the anchor emblem, had been printed on every cotton reel they'd known in childhood. 'They were all made in the building I live in,' I would smugly say. And everybody knew the Paisley Pattern. 'Created in my home town – though before I lived there,' I'd tell them.

I thought my apartment wonderful when Harry and I shared it. It had a big front living space with two huge windows in it. They looked out, from the fourth floor, over a vast swathe of the Renfrewshire countryside, with a backdrop of distant lowland hills. The curtains must have cost a pretty penny, but we'd got them included in the price when we'd bought the flat.

We... Harry and I. There was no we now. Just a resounding I. Or a resounding me. Depending on your grammatical preference. Similarly, there was no view of rolling green countryside tonight at eleven o'clock. Just dotted farmstead lights in the distance and, immediately below, the outer filaments of Paisley's little warp and weft of lamp-lit streets. But it wasn't the same as the sight of La Orotava's lights, gold, silver and bronze like polished Olympic medals, climbing a thousand feet heavenward in the subtropical dark. I closed the curtains and went to bed. I had the rest of my life in which to unpack.

In the morning I walked round to the retail centre in the High Street and into the first phone shop I came to. I was impatient with the sales talk of the man who served me. I didn't care too much what kind of phone I got, or what kind of a deal they could offer me when it came to a payment contract. It wasn't really a phone I wanted; it was Theo.

I kept asking the same question. 'Will I be able to get my lost numbers and stuff back?'

And the young man – he was really quite pretty, and looked almost too young to know quite so much about phones – shrugged expressively and told me it would depend whether I'd saved my numbers to Google Contacts. I told him, yes I had done. At least, I said, I was pretty sure I had... But privately I was asking myself, had I – had the system – saved Theo's number?

'All you have to do,' the very young man was saying, 'is put your account details into the new phone,' he waved the thing in front of me like a carrot, 'and everything will synchronise.'

I signed the paperwork and took my new phone out into the street with me. As soon as I got home – it was barely five minutes – I did what the man had told me to. And it worked like magic. Almost everything I'd had stored on the old phone popped up almost immediately. But there was a notable exception. The very number that I most wanted to get hold of was still missing.

I tried looking for Theo – still pronounced Tayo – on Facebook. The jerk of the head he'd given me when I'd asked him if he was on FB had been inconclusive. It hadn't indicated that he was on it, but neither had it said clearly that he wasn't. Trying to find him now took a little time. I couldn't quite believe how many people shared his name – Aristheo Gonçalves Domingo. But not one of them had his birthday. The one he shared with

Shakespeare and Cervantes. In the end I had to give up on Facebook. I'd need to think about where else to look for him.

In the meantime I tried to find out what Atlantic island I'd been looking at, halfway between the Canaries and Madeira. The island I thought of calling Jonty Island, or Allen Island, if someone hadn't got there first. It wasn't in my Atlas, and I didn't know how I would go about locating a tiny dot in the middle of an ocean on Google Earth.

An idea came to me. I found a flight-tracker website, scrolled down to Tenerife and located a plane that had just left the island and was heading north. It was bound for London Gatwick. I reckoned that the route would be the same as mine had been for the first part of the flight.

I increased the scale relentlessly as the plane headed up across the featureless Atlantic. For twenty minutes the plane's radar footprint moved over empty blueness. And then I was rewarded. A tiny dot appeared just to the right of the plane's track. I homed in on it, magnifying and magnifying, until it delivered up its size and shape. It looked like a small, roughly made cake. But even when I reached the point of maximum resolution no name appeared beside it. Allen island, you are mine, I thought.

Still, it had one final test to pass. I googled 'island between Madeira and Canaries' and, oddly disappointingly, up it popped. It had a name all right. Selvagem Grande. Disputed by the Portuguese and Spanish down the centuries, it was now a world heritage site of special scientific interest. A bird watchers' paradise and inhabited only by the warden – and with luck his wife. You could only visit it with a special permit. I couldn't help thinking that if I really had discovered it I'd be able to turn it to better account than that.

A few days later I came across the piece of paper on which I'd written Maxwell's phone number. After a further dozen hours of hesitation, during which I had to make a choice about the digit that the creases on my palm had rendered difficult to interpret, I sent a text to it.

Hi Maxwell. You wrote your number on my hand in Del's a few nights ago. That was nice. When will you be there again? Jonty

A reply came half an hour later.

Looool sorry you were given the wrong number pal.

That marked the end of the chapter, I guessed. But the following morning I felt differently about things, and about the difficult digit. I'd tried it as a 4. Now I had a second go at texting the number, changing the 4 to a 2. This time my wording was a bit more cautious.

You wrote your number on my hand. Not sure I've read it right. Maxwell? When are you at Del's next? Jonty

The reply to that, when it came a few minutes later was not much more encouraging than the first one. It said simply, *Who?* But then, an hour or two later came this. *Sorry sorry. How are U this evening? Saturday.*

Encouraged, I replied, *Saturday is good for me. What time?* And he wrote back, *Between 5 and 6.* So I wrote, *Great, see you then*, and Maxwell came back, *OK Sexy.*

Next I went back to the number of the kind person who had put me wise to my mistake about the number. *Tks for messaging back. I got right number second attempt.* Unsurprisingly that was the end of that particular correspondence.

He was sitting on a high stool in a corner of the room when I entered. He had been watching the door and he smiled immediately. He was nursing a pint glass that was three-quarters empty or, if you preferred, a quarter full. I went up to him. 'Good to see you,' I said.

'You too.'

I pointed to the glass. 'Shall I get you another one of those?'

He said, 'Yes please,' then leaned up towards me and kissed me on the lips.

I was back with a pint for each of us in no time at all. There was no vacant stool near his so I straddled one of his outstretched knees and sat on his thigh, facing him, my back to the rest of the bar. Then we kissed intermittently and stroked each other's nipples through pullovers while we sipped our beer.

We didn't stop at that. We took each other's cocks out and played with them admiringly, using our big winter coats as screens. In the crowded space people brushed my back as they passed on the way to the loo. None peered over my shoulder to see what was going on. As far as I could tell.

We had to adjust our clothing when Maxwell got up to buy us another pint, but we adjusted it back again when he returned. By now I had commandeered the stool so he sat on my knee, chest to chest with me. The day would come, I thought, when one of the sixth-formers I taught in term-time would walk in here and find me thus compromised. But it hadn't happened up to now. If or when the occasion did arise I would deal with it splendidly I told myself. Though I couldn't begin to imagine how.

'Do you want to come back to my place?' Maxwell asked me after a while.

'Where is that?' I asked cautiously.

He lived in Govan, near the old docks. 'Take the Clockwork Orange,' he said. That was our local name for the underground train system that circled the city beneath the streets and drains.

'We'll do that,' I said. 'It's nearer than mine.'

Maxwell looked deep into my eyes with the beautiful dark searchlights that were his own. 'Which is where?'

'Paisley,' I said. I added breezily, 'Miles away,' as if he might not have heard of the place.

'By the airport,' he said. 'I work there.'

We sat close to each other on the subway train, our thighs pressed together through jeans and overcoats from hip to knee. But apart from that we behaved discreetly. I remembered an occasion when a friend from England had come to visit me a few years before. We'd agreed to meet inside Glasgow Central station. 'But remember this isn't the open-minded south,' I'd warned him on the phone. 'No big kisses under the clock.'

'Quite right,' he'd said. 'We'll save it till we're on the train.' We'd both laughed. The idea was literally unimaginable. Maxwell and I didn't try to realise it now.

He was a bar-tender behind one of the airport's bars. I could have seen him there at some point, I thought. In theory anyway. He might have poured a drink for me... 'I'm an English teacher,' I said. I named the secondary school I taught at. Its name meant nothing to him; he hadn't gone there.

We climbed out of the train at Govan Cross and came up into the cold evening air. I was in his hands now. He knew where he lived; I didn't. I'd hardly ever been to Govan before.

'I need a piss,' he said.

So did I. 'Is there somewhere...?'

He led me up a happily ill-lit alley near a bus stop and we did it there, up against someone's wall. Seeing his wonderfully long dick again after forty minutes' enforced separation from it was like being reunited with a handsome friend. We crossed swords and touched each other briefly before shaking and stowing away. We returned to the street and the lamp-light.

'Is there somewhere round here we can get something to eat?' I asked. He'd invited me to his place, whatever sort of a place that might be; but obviously he wasn't going to cook me a meal when we got there.

'There's an Indian,' he said doubtfully. 'We could get a takeaway...'

Vindaloo on the bed covers and the air full of turmeric and cumin in the morning. 'Or we could eat in the restaurant,' I said. 'Are you OK with Indian? I'll pay.'

'Yeah,' he said, brightening audibly. 'Be nice that will.' We each knew what the other did for a living. There was no question but that I'd pay.

He frowned across the table. 'Are prawns vegetarian?' he asked as we both perused the leather-bound menu.

'Why? Are you?'

'No.'

'Then it doesn't matter,' I said. 'But I don't think they really count as vegetarian. I mean, they're not vegetables, are they.'

Maxwell nodded gravely. I was glad we agreed.

We began to learn about each other. Maxwell was Nigerian, but had spent most of his life in Scotland... And some of it in Italy. His mother was married to an Italian entrepreneur. They had a nice house in the countryside outside Turin. I saw pictures of it – and of Maxwell in it and in its garden – on his phone.

Maxwell had a house of his own in a village in Nigeria. I saw a picture of that too on his phone. It seemed bereft of furniture of any kind except an electric fan. 'I'm the only person in the village who's got one,' he told me with justifiable pride. 'The only guy who can afford petrol for a generator.'

So he was the richest guy in his home village. He was probably the only gay in the village too. I asked him, 'Do people there know you're gay?'

He shook his head. 'It isn't easy being gay in Nigeria.'

'I imagine it isn't,' I said soberly. I looked at him across the table and if anything he seemed more beautiful.

FIVE

He was even more beautiful naked. Standing together on the floor of his tiny room we were like two entwined carvings, one of ivory, one of ebony. We both marvelled at the effect. And when we clasped our hands together, fingers interlocking, the impression was of half an octave of piano keys and we both giggled at that.

But apart from the living statuary that we'd created his room was sadly under-furnished. His bed, window-seat narrow, was the only thing you could sit on. There was a coffee table but no chair. There wasn't room for one. He had a lap-top, a music system and a TV, all crowded close at hand, and close together, around the walls. The wires that served them ran criss-cross over the floor, which was alive with junction boxes that you had to be very agile to avoid treading on with every step. Above the door a small crucifix was fastened to the wall. Beside it, less than postcard size, was what Roman Catholics called a Holy Picture. My family was Roman Catholic. I knew.

Maxwell had put a finger to his lips as he'd let us in through the shared front door. We'd climbed the stairs without speaking, and trying to sound as though we had one pair of feet between us rather than two. The six rooms in the small terraced house had been converted into six separate dwellings by the simple addition of a Yale lock to each door. There was a shared bathroom-toilet which, before we got naked, the two of us took it in turn to use. It wasn't the sort of household that would take kindly to the idea of Maxwell bringing home a fellow male to spend the night with. Govan was a roughish neighbourhood. That was another thing I knew.

There was really only one place to be once we'd done admiring each other's nakedness with hands and eyes while standing clasped together on the floor. We climbed aboard the window-seat bed and pulled the rug that served as bedclothes up on top of us.

I let Maxwell fuck me. His cock was the longest one I'd ever allowed inside. But it was a very beautiful instrument, with a gentle taper to it and a smallish conical head. It announced its entrance gently, starting with the thin end. And its owner was a gentle person anyway.

He'd rolled a condom onto it but in the end he didn't climax inside me. We came together eventually, belly to belly and cock to cock, while my insides still glowed warm from the largest thing they'd ever swallowed from the rear. We spent the rest of the night cuddling and holding each other hungrily: as if we were trying to merge our two bodies into one; just as the black and white notes on the keyboard lose their separate identities in a harmonious chord.

In the morning we drank filter coffee he had made, sitting side by side, still naked and intermittently stiff-cocked, on his narrow bed. Then I got dressed, we hugged protractedly, and Maxwell let me out. I tiptoed unchallenged down the communal stairs and let myself out through the front door.

We had talked of many things over our curry supper the previous night. Maxwell might have been unsure whether prawns were vegetable or animal but in general he was bright enough, and our conversation had ranged through politics and social questions in addition to the inevitable discussion of sexuality and sex. We'd touched in an open-minded way on immigration. 'We're very lucky,' Maxwell had said, his *we* referring to himself and me, 'to live in a country people want to come to rather than one that people want to get away from.' I mulled that over. I put it in the context of his Nigerian origins. I thought it was a valid point.

I caught a bus to Paisley. A few minutes after hopping off it I was back in my all-too-spacious flat, looking out through the big windows at the rolling countryside beyond Glasgow's fraying edge. Maxwell and I had said we'd keep in touch. We still had each other's numbers on our phones. I thought about inviting Maxwell here. To my spacious portion of the town's converted cotton mill. 'My place this time.' But if Maxwell saw this place he'd want a piece of it, I guessed. What if he decided he wanted to move in with me? That's what we were all like after all. See it, want it, take steps to get it.

No-strings sex. That was what everyone was after. Or so they said. That's what everyone promised you on Grindr and all the other hook-up apps.

But there was no such thing as no-strings sex. It hadn't been designed that way by evolution – or, if you preferred it, God. However hard you tried to make it so, however anonymous an encounter was, there were always strings attached to it. If the other person had something that you hadn't, you always wanted a bit of that. It might not be as extreme as wanting to share their flat, their lifestyle or their bank balance. But you wanted a stake in their beauty, if they had that, or in their brains or business prospects if they had those things instead. You wanted something of them, a piece of them to hold onto and make yours for ever. Even if it was just a simple swallow of their spunk.

Nothing involved in sexual transactions came without strings attached. Not even mobile phones were cordless except in the most literal, physical sense. And however hard you tried to persuade yourself it was not so, the memory of any, every, sexual adventure would keep on tugging at the purse-strings of your heart.

In spite of that... Because of that? I decided I wouldn't contact Maxwell again. If he phoned me, if he messaged me, we'd take it from there. Though for the moment at any rate I didn't want that. In going to bed with Maxwell I'd been trying to forget Theo. But it hadn't really worked. Though Theo too had been just a one-night's stand I found that in his case also there were strings attached. It wasn't simply that I couldn't forget him. There were other things. I owed him lunch for a start.

A few days later I plunged into the long dark tunnel of the school term. I always had the feeling that I was creating the tunnel as I went along it, like the driver of one of those powerful machines that corkscrew their way through the subsoil to make roads through mountains and railways beneath the sea. Weeks passed each time before I saw the daylight at the other end.

It wasn't all blackness. I wouldn't have persevered with being a classroom teacher if it had all been like that. There were flashes of light, even of happiness, every day I taught. When a pupil made a breakthrough of understanding, or found a sudden love for a classic author or poet, or confided in me something that belonged in the depths of his or her heart, or simply said, 'Thank you Mister Allen,' at the end of a long day. And like everyone who goes out to work in the mornings I enjoyed the camaraderie and the banter of my colleagues, or most of them, and would miss them if it were all to stop.

But about a month into that summer term I made a decision, or more exactly a decision suddenly came to me. It concerned the mid-term break, which would be upon us in two weeks' time. My colleagues raised their eyebrows when I told them, and tried to conceal their two-and-two-together smiles. My mother came out with it directly when I spoke to her at the weekend. 'Tenerife again? You've only just come back. Have you got someone out there now?'

'No,' I said, and laughed off her question as if it had been something absurd. Yet it was hardly a lie I'd told her. Because of my carelessness with my phone I had no contact with anyone out there at all. I hadn't even managed to stake a claim to the Selvagem islands that I'd be flying over on my way.

I had an early flight out. I bought myself a coffee and a croissant in one of the airport bars. I wasn't served by Maxwell. I wasn't sure if I was relieved or disappointed. There were perhaps ten food and drink outlets in the departures area. In the minutes before my flight was called to the gate... OK, I did peer into all of them in case he might be on duty there. He wasn't to be seen in a single one. I wasn't too surprised. He hadn't told me which company employed him but I did know that he worked a variety of shifts: some early, some late. It was probably as well I didn't have to explain to him where I was off to, in the hope of re-encountering another man.

Not much happened during the flight. It was a cloudy day. When the drinks trolley came round I ordered a gin and tonic. My dad had always insisted that was what you had to have on an aeroplane, with cashew nuts beside, and although I hadn't taken after him in much else I'd followed in his footsteps in this. So that's what I ordered now.

I was careful. As I squirmed in my pocket for the right money while trying not to upset the can and the small plastic bottle in front of me, I remembered how I'd lost Theo's address the last time I'd been in this situation. I poured my drink out and thought how unusually yellow it seemed. Refracted light from the slice of lemon in my plastic glass, no doubt. But it went on getting yellower, not to say amber, as I added the tonic. One of those new-style tonics, evidently, with added spice and price. I looked at the label on the can. Ginger Ale, it read.

The stewardess apologised. She gave me two more gins with the can of tonic water with which she replaced the ginger ale. That was nice of her. As for the gin and ginger that was sitting in front of me... Well, what did you do with that on an aeroplane? Reader, I drank it. It was a bit surprising, a bit unusual. Like a pizza made by a friend that had a topping of prawn and grapefruit. But you wouldn't complain. You'd eat it.

The gins kept me going for quite some time. It seemed almost as if they were keeping the plane aloft. Quite suddenly we were descending towards the clouds and Tenerife. I looked out. There was no sign of the Selvagem Islands. They'd become as invisible as Maxwell.

There was an element of homecoming about my return to the hotel in Calle del Aceviño, and to City Bar just a few doors along from it. Reception staff at holiday hotels and bar-tenders in resort hangouts saw thousands of visitors and met a fair number of returners. But the returners had seldom returned a mere seven weeks after their last visit. I was greeted warmly in both places. Including by the barman I'd rather drunkenly kissed one night towards the end of my last stay. He clearly hadn't forgotten the incident, and the warmth of his welcome suggested that he didn't see anything in it that required forgiveness or even forbearance.

But then he was off to deal with another customer and I was alone on a stool at the counter, re-familiarising myself with the bar's dim interior, its wall-lights and the strangely attractive neon red and blue brand logos that refracted and reflected among the glasses.

'Looks like you're well-known here,' said a voice from close by me. The bar was propped up by a number of solitary men, holidaymakers of different nationalities whose wives had retired for the night, presumably to flick through the TV channels in their hotel bedrooms. The tables against the walls, on the other hand, were occupied mainly by boisterous groups of young locals. But it was one of the solitary holidaymakers who had addressed me.

I smiled and shrugged at him. 'Second visit in two months,' I said. Then, 'Where are you from?' thinking he might have said Denmark or Finland. He looked to be a couple of years younger than me, with fair hair and blue eyes. Nice looking, though at barely thirty already balding slightly.

'Canada,' he said, which surprised me a bit. I didn't think the Canary Islands were a usual holiday destination for Canadians. I hadn't met any on my last visit. I told him where I came from and then we narrowed it down a bit, locating ourselves a bit more exactly on each other's mental map of the other's country: mine on the small side, his enormous.

Nat – that was the name he gave me – had recently split up with his wife and was treating himself to a month away from everything in response to the trauma of it. It seemed a similar story to my own. I told him I'd not so long ago split up with my boyfriend. Nat wasn't gay, presumably, or if he was he wasn't going to say so right at this moment, but he wasn't remotely fazed by the discovery that I was. 'My brother's gay,' he told me matter-of-factly. 'Younger than me. Lives in Vancouver.'

'You'll have to introduce us,' I said. I added, deadpan, 'Next time I'm in Vancouver.' It took Nat a second or two to conclude that I was joking and then he chuckled and smiled.

We enjoyed two or three beers together, chatting lightly. Then I said it was time I went to bed, although it wasn't yet midnight, and left him to it. But I didn't go to bed right away. I walked down to the patch of waste ground where I'd first met Theo. A light breeze was blowing: neither from the sea nor from the mountains, but down the coastline. From the north east. The North-East Trade Wind. As it blew along the house-lit mountainside it was picking up the scents of the spring blossom. Acacia. Lemon. Orange. Thyme.

I let the grass heads stroke my legs as I walked to where Theo's bench was. My bench. My bench with Theo. But he wasn't on it. Nobody was sitting on any of the benches. I walked up and down a couple of times. Then the moon rose groggily from beyond the mountain. The wind grew cooler. Though everything is relative. It was nothing like in Glasgow. I made my decision, turned and walked back to my hotel. I could have gone on past it, gone to see if Nat was still downing lonely beers in the City. But I didn't. It would all have been far too complicated. I simply went to bed.

The reception staff seemed to remember me fondly, which was nice. They either hadn't clocked or chose not to remember that I'd smuggled a visitor into my room for an overnight stay during the course of my last visit. They were happy to let me sit in the morning sunshine that flooded the lobby with the residential phone directory for North Tenerife on my lap, looking for the name Aristheo Gonçalves Domingo.

I had tried to do this online, from home, weeks earlier. I hadn't got very far. Now, with the physical doorstop of white pages in my hands, it should have been easier. But it wasn't. At first I wasn't sure whether you looked up Domingo or Gonçalves. I had to ask at the desk. They told me you looked under Gonçalves. I did that. No

Aristheo was listed. But, with an enormous choice of first names or initials, there were an awful lot of people who rejoiced in the name of Gonçalves. Many were here in Puerto de la Cruz. And there were many more in La Orotava. I remembered Theo telling me that La Orotava, less easily visible on the mountainside by day than by lamp-lit night, was where he'd been born.

I thought about cold-calling all the Gonçalves who were listed, in alphabetical order, and asking if they knew the address of a namesake called Aristheo. In my halting Spanish. There might have been lots of Aristheos. I might be directed towards the wrong one. And been obliged to deal with that embarrassment in broken Spanish. My nerve and will both failed me. I hadn't given up on the phone-book idea, but for the moment I returned the tome to reception.

Like a detective who travels abroad to track down a suspect I had thought through a couple of lines of enquiry before coming out here. Though a real detective would have known what he was doing, and had more and better plans. I shrugged internally. It couldn't be helped that I was a teacher and not a private eye.

Aristheo taught English at one of the schools in Puerto. He must have told me whether it was a primary or a secondary school but I couldn't remember. Nor did I know whether it was a state school or a private one. The field seemed to grow larger the more I thought about it. But at least, if I phoned a school there would be someone there who could speak English. And they'd either have an English teacher called Aristheo Gonçalves Domingo or they wouldn't. There wouldn't be any maybe about it. I borrowed the yellow pages – paginas amarillas – from the reception desk and asked if I might take them out to the poolside for ten minutes.

I caught up again with Nat, my Canadian drinking partner, late on that evening. 'So how's your day been? What've you been up to?' Those are the invariable questions that get asked in this situation and we asked them now.

'I was up in La Orotava,' said Nat. 'You been there?'

'Not yet,' I said guardedly.

'You should go. It's so cute. Steep streets that open suddenly into little squares. Flowers and trees in them. And the houses. They're old. Picturesque. Seventeenth and eighteenth century. Built by rich fruit growers and merchants. Least, that's what the info plates all said.'

I said, 'I've seen them in pictures. Those carved wood balconies...'

'Anyway,' Nat said, sliding the glass and bottle of Dorada that he'd bought me along the counter, 'how was your day?'

'I spent most of the afternoon phoning schools and colleges, trying to track down an English teacher.'

Nat peered at me humorously. 'Do you need an English teacher?'

'I am an English teacher,' I said.

'I know,' said Nat. 'I remember you told me.' We both said cheers and clinked glasses. 'So I guess you were looking for one particular teacher.' He grinned slyly. 'Want to tell me about it?'

I found that I did, and I did tell Nat about it – in as much or little detail as a gay guy usually goes into with a straight mate. 'I didn't get far with the schools, though,' I said. 'Three simply put the phone down and the others gave me a polite *sorry he doesn't work here* and wished me luck.'

'You should have come to La Orotava with me today,' Nat said. 'If that's where he comes from. You could have checked if anyone walking in the street looked remotely like him.'

'Ha-ha,' I said.

Nat shrugged. 'We coulda enjoyed a couple of beers in the sunshine while you were looking.'

'It's not a bad thought,' I said, though I wasn't even sure myself if I meant looking for family traits in the citizens' faces or simply hanging with Nat and sinking a few Doradas together. 'Actually, my next plan is to trek over to Santa Cruz and try to find his sister. I've met her. She plays in the Tenerife Symphony Orchestra and they're based there.'

'Oh,' said Nat, sounding interested. 'What's her instrument?'

'She did tell me,' I said, 'but I've forgotten.' That sounded very lame. I was clearly no Poirot, no Maigret.

'But you've got her name.'

'First name...' But it had gone. 'It'll come back to me. Her surname, though... Same as...' The obvious struck me. 'Shit. She was engaged. She may be married by now.'

'Might not be a problem,' Nat said comfortingly. 'How long do engagements last out here? Anyway, artists – performers – they usually work under the name they were born with.'

'Yeah,' I said. 'Lady Gaga. Madonna. Sting...'

'Faint heart,' said Nat. 'We could go over there tomorrow.'

When I parted from Nat a few beers later I didn't tell him where I was going to next. Well, I did. I said I was heading back to my hotel and bed; it was simply that I wasn't going there just yet.

I walked around the edge of the waste ground, peering through the darkness. Theo's bench was untenanted. So were the other benches. But there was no shortage of activity in the area this midnight. Young guys, probably still in their teens, were shambling along the path or diving rather purposefully into the tall bushes: the oleanders, palms and sword aloes. They wore hooded jackets so I couldn't see their faces. They were intently focused on the pale light from their phones, presumably checking the narrowing distance between themselves and the approaching lads whose tastes and other details were displayed on the tiny screens. In amongst the bushes I could glimpse dim lights from the phones of those who had got in there first, silently announcing their presence like glow-worms in the night. Until recently this would have been done by the red glow of lit cigarettes that would have increased in brightness when someone took a drag to show his interest in a stranger's approach. It seemed that Grindr had come to Tenerife at some point during the few short weeks since I was last here.

I wasn't inclined to shoulder my way in among the prickly vegetation. I walked to the end of the path, to where it met the lit road beside the church, and then retraced my steps. The slats of all the benches gleamed dully in the light of the far-off hotels. Until I came to one bench that showed only a foot or so of its seat and back. I slowed my walk to a loiter. The bench was no longer unoccupied. In the short two minutes since I'd last walked past it someone had materialised, as if from space, and was sitting on it, darkly dressed.

The sitting someone wore a cap, while a can of something just about reflected a little dim light. I stopped directly in front of the sitting figure, turned and faced it. With the lit hotels a hundred yards behind me I would have presented a totally black silhouette. 'Theo?' I queried. I couldn't quite believe this was happening. That I was saying this. The figure had been listening to music on a phone or something. As it realised that it was being addressed it took the ear-pieces away from its face. I tried again. 'Aristheo?'

The figure didn't move a muscle. But after a second's hiatus it spoke. 'Jonty,' it said. 'Jonty Allen.' I'd remembered the wonderful quality of Theo's English. Now I was startled to hear how Spanish his accent was. My memory had air-brushed that.

SIX

I sat down beside him. I put an arm around his shoulder and ran my hand down his back. He sat immobile, not reciprocating. Neither of us spoke.

I rubbed myself against him like a cat. Head, shoulder, thigh, knee, hip. At last one of us spoke. It was Theo. 'It's good to see you,' he said in English. Then in Spanish he said, 'Extraordinary.'

'I lost your number.' I discovered I was close to tears. I extended my arm around his slim waist and gripped him tight. And at last he put one of his arms, the one that wasn't involved with the beer can, around me.

'Why have you come back here?' he asked.

I said the only thing I could. 'I came to find you.' Corny, cheesy, hackneyed cliché. Its only merit lay in being true. I tried to burrow my head and body into him.

'You need a bit of affection, I think,' Theo said in Spanish. It came out a bit stiffly.

'Everyone needs affection,' I answered in the same language, sounding equally prim. I found myself wondering who or what he had been waiting for, sitting on his bench in the dark. Quite obviously it hadn't been me.

'But you especially,' he said. 'You more than most.'

I felt for a brief moment at the denim-covered little mound in his crotch. 'Would you like to go for a drink in City Bar?' I asked.

'Good idea,' he said. He handed me his beer can. From the lightness of it I knew that it was nearly empty. 'Want to finish that?' he asked.

Nat was no longer propping the bar up. It was past midnight now; he'd gone to bed. By chance the stool that Theo climbed onto was the one that Nat had recently vacated. I hauled myself up onto the one next to it. 'What do you want to drink?' I asked. 'I haven't forgotten that I owe you lunch.'

Theo smiled and chuckled. It was the first time he'd done that in the ten minutes since we'd met. 'Dorada,' he said. The local beer. It was what I normally drank with Nat.

In the dim light of the wood-panelled interior Theo gazed searchingly into my face. Those eyes of his; that handsome face. Theo could gaze at me for ever if he liked. 'I'm finding it difficult to believe this,' he said.

'Me too,' I said. I still wasn't sure to what extent Theo's astonishment was a happy one. A lot can happen to a person in six or seven weeks. I needed to find out. I took a risk. 'I'm very, very happy to see you.'

'I'm very, very happy to see you too.' But Theo's voice seemed to measure the words carefully. It had been the same with mine. We sounded mechanical. Polite.

Our beers arrived. We poured them. Clinked glasses. Said cheers together, then for good measure, *salud.* It was at that moment that I realised that, except for having slept together, we didn't know each other at all. 'Do you have a boyfriend?' I asked.

Theo lowered his eyes so that I had a view only of his long curled lashes. He said, 'I used to have.'

I said, 'Me too.' At some point we would talk about them. There was no need to do so now. But we knew each other better, infinitely better, than we had done a few seconds before.

We talked of easier things. My flight out here from Glasgow a few days ago; Theo's day at school. After a while I said, 'Will you sleep with me tonight?'

He frowned. 'I've got school tomorrow. We don't have a summer-term half-term like you do.'

I put the palm of my hand on his warm knee. 'Please?'

'I'll have to get up at silly o'clock,' he said. Not *would have to* but *will*. I felt my heart skip like a child.

'I love your English,' I said.

'I love words,' said Theo.

I said, 'So do I.'

The hotel lobby was dim and quiet. The night porter peered across the reception desk at us from out of his lit cubby hole but he didn't emerge. We ignored him, walking past with pretend nonchalance, exchanging a few nonsense sentences about Scottish football. A moment later we had reached the sanctuary of the lift. We hopped in and closed the door. My heart was thumping. You'd think we'd just crossed a sniper's alley in a war zone. Surrounded by mirrors we fell into a clinch and kiss quite automatically, as if from long habit, although we'd only ever travelled in this lift together twice before. But our snog was just a brief one. I wasn't on the seventh floor this time but on the third.

To be in bed with Theo again was delicious. The second time can be better than the first. It often is, because you are more comfortable with the other person and more confident in yourself. We accomplished something we hadn't managed on that first occasion. Reader, we fucked each other.

But soon, too soon, it was morning; the dark sky beyond the balcony was turning a translucent silver-grey. We showered together in the dawn and then got dressed together. All of a sudden there was a lot to say and little time in which to say it.

'I'll do my teeth and stuff back at my place,' Theo explained carefully.

'I'm supposed to be going to Santa Cruz today,' I said, remembering suddenly. 'With a Canadian guy I know from City Bar. The plan was to go and find your sister.'

Theo, halfway into his trousers, lost his balance in his surprise and nearly fell over. 'Find my sister? Why?'

'To help me find where you were,' I explained. 'I'd tried the phone book and ringing round the schools...'

Theo shot me a look. 'You really did want to find me.'

'Never wanted anything more,' I said. Though I wondered as I heard myself if I wasn't exaggerating just a wee bit.

'If you do see my sister...'

'We won't be looking for her...'

'But if you did run into her, best not to say you've seen me.'

'OK,' I said, slightly startled. I wasn't going to ask why, but Theo told me anyway.

'She does know I'm gay, but it's slightly awkward.'

'Fine,' I said. 'I'm sure we won't bump into her but...'

Fully dressed now we moved towards the door. Theo opened it and poked his head a cautious few inches into the corridor. 'Coast's clear,' he whispered and we made our way out of my hotel room.

We kissed perfunctorily in the lift. I could feel Theo's body and mind tense with the prospect of the working day ahead of him. We strode across the hotel lobby leaving the reception desk behind us. Expecting a challenge like a sudden bullet in the back of the head. Walking quickly. Not daring to look behind us.

Out in the street we relaxed a little. 'Thank you for coming down with me,' said Theo. 'You didn't have to. That was good of you.'

I said, 'Of course I had to.' Theo would walk back to his own place now, wherever that was, and collect his thoughts and papers for his classes. I said, 'This evening?' A bit desperately.

'Of course,' said Theo. 'Do you want to eat together?'

'That would be great,' I said. It really would be.

'City Bar at seven, then,' said Theo, firmly in charge now. 'We'll take it from there.'

'Right,' I said. 'See you.'

Theo said, *'Hasta luego,'* we kissed for a microsecond and then I turned around sharply, to walk back inside the hotel and face the music – if there was to be any.

I walked past the reception desk, nodding curtly to the night porter. He nodded back. There wasn't any music. I went back upstairs and lay back down on the warm bed, still with clothes and shoes on. It would be a good two hours before the local cafés opened. During that time of waiting I found a moment in which to realise that Theo and I still hadn't swapped phone numbers.

'Still up for Santa Cruz?' I asked Nat when he sauntered onto the terrace at the café Bei Thomas.

'Why shouldn't I be?' he asked.

'We no longer need to hunt down Theo's sister,' I said. 'I've found Theo.' Nat's eyebrows shot up. Surprise and uncertainty. I needed to reassure him. 'Still, a day out...'

Nat nodded. There was no reason to cancel a trip we'd both looked forward to. 'How did you find Theo?' Nat asked. 'If I'm not being...'

'You're not,' I said. 'The most extraordinary thing happened. After I left you last night I bumped into him in the middle of the street.' I didn't feel like sharing the rather complicated story of the cruising ground bench. But I told him most of the rest of it. How we'd come to City Bar but Nat had already left, and then gone back to my hotel for the night. In the middle of the story our two coffees arrived without our asking. 'This morning he's gone off to teach,' I ended. 'We're meeting up again tonight.'

'I'd better not be around,' Nat said. 'Cramp your style...'

'I'm sure he'd like to meet you over a drink,' I said. 'He knows you exist. Oh.' I remembered something. 'In the unlikely event that we do run into Marina we're not supposed to let her know I'm seeing Theo.'

Nat's eyes opened expressively wide. 'Really? In this day and age?'

'I don't know why,' I said. 'She knows he's gay. She knew his ex-boyfriend.' I shrugged. 'Maybe she's not happy with the idea of him having casual sex.'

Theo gave me a curious look. 'Casual sex? To travel two thousand miles and spend three days looking for someone... You reckon Theo sees that as casual sex?'

Nat had framed a couple of thoughts that I hadn't got round to yet, even though they were fairly obvious ones. But I side-stepped them. 'Maybe Marina would see it as casual sex.' I shrugged again. Nat let me get away with it.

Most buses that headed out of town towards the north came past the end of Calle del Aceviño and there was a stop there. Nat and I waited a while in the sunshine – it was no hardship – and hopped on the first bus that arrived bound for the island's capital. It had already come grinding up a long steep hill from the bus station down in the town centre. And after we'd taken our seats it went on climbing. Past the botanical gardens and up into the mountain countryside. Steep curves on the dual carriageway gave us long views back and down to Puerto at first, and then our route turned inland, through pine and eucalyptus, forever and forever climbing. We reached the clouds and rain eventually, passing our highest point alongside the runway of the north airport. But we stayed at that damp height for only a few minutes. Beyond the airport the road descended rapidly. The east coast and the sunlit sea came into sight ahead of us, along with Santa Cruz, its docks and shipping. We'd crossed the backbone of the island in a little over twenty minutes and were back among blue-flame flowering jacaranda and sun-worshipping fronds of palm.

Two men arriving in a strange town with no particular objective will look around them for the nearest decent looking bar and make for it. Gays and straights are alike in this, and that's what Nat and I did immediately.

It seemed a different Nat that I chatted with this morning: different from the Nat I'd got used to during the last few evenings. Different appearance, different personality, different manner. It was as if a statue or bust that I was used to seeing daily had been rotated a few degrees on its plinth and now showed me a slightly different aspect of itself as I routinely walked past it. But as we sat together, drinking ice-cold beers on a café terrace and enjoying the bright warm sunshine, watching the people pass, tourists and residents alike as they went about their business, I came gradually to realise that Nat hadn't changed in the slightest. Only I had. It was I who had been rotated on my plinth by my chance re-encounter with Theo and by having sex with him again.

Enjoying the bright warm sunshine. A banal phrase that: stale and hackneyed. But the experience was anything but hackneyed or banal. Not for Nat or me, coming from Canada and Scotland. Our morning soak in the Canarian sun was a treat to relish. Like a glass of wine so rare and expensive that we would be lucky if we ever got to taste it a second time. We didn't get this much sunshine in spring in Scotland – and nor did Nat, I presumed, in Canada. We sat appreciating it, almost purring with delight. And when we'd finished our small glasses of Dorada we got up and walked in it.

With no destination in mind, now that we were no longer on a mission to track the Tenerife Symphony Orchestra to its lair in the Auditorio de Tenerife, we wandered carelessly, criss-crossing the grids of narrow streets and occasional flower-bright, palm-lined, boulevards. We came to a park: a green space full of trees and children. We walked among its broad paths, exchanging half smiles occasionally with the people we passed. And then among those passing strollers I saw a face I recognised. It belonged to a young woman who was walking arm in arm with a well-built man a few years older, I guessed, than she was. The woman's face seemed, this second time, even more strikingly similar to Theo's. We had bumped into Marina.

She recognised me too. The two of us stopped dead, and the men we were walking with also stopped, about half a second later, like dogs on leads.

It was not quite true that Marina recognised me. It was rather that she saw I had recognised her and had to start thinking very quickly about who I was. After all, though she had been very much in my thoughts during the past hours and minutes I was very unlikely to have been in hers. But it didn't take her more than a second or two. 'You're Theo's friend,' she said. She looked Nat up and down, then turned back to me. 'Are you here with Theo?'

That threw a spanner into Theo's plan that I shouldn't mention our 'reunion'. I said, 'He's teaching today. I still owe him lunch from last time.' I was clutching wildly at things to say.

'My fiancé Alberto,' said Marina, giving the man at her side a little forward shove. Well, that answered one question. She wasn't married yet. She still had Gonçalves for a surname.

'This is Nat,' I said. 'A friend from Canada.' We all shook hands.

We had a snack lunch together, the four of us. At a small café the locals used, where you could have a sensibly small *tapa* or two rather than the unexpectedly huge and expensive platefuls that were served to unwary tourists. *Tapas variadas* looked like an easy as well as an enticing option on a menu board; it saved difficult choices and translations; but it didn't come light on the stomach or the wallet.

In the middle of our conversation over the wine and slices of omelette Marina remembered something she'd said to me and that I'd forgotten. 'I told you try find a good Scotch girl for Theo.'

'Ah,' I said, and nodded thoughtfully to her across the pavement table.

Marina smiled. 'I guess you know girls not his cup of tea.'

I found I couldn't look her in the eye for a moment. 'I do know that.'

'But that is "up to now",' Marina said. She put audible inverted commas round the 'up to now' like she was proud of knowing the phrase. 'It can be not too late for him to change.'

Alberto, who had been talking to Nat about football in an impenetrable Spanish of which Nat would have understood little, now leaned unexpectedly into our conversation. 'Theo lived with man not good for him.' That was said in English.

I had to ask. 'Do you mean the man was not good for him, or that living with a man was not good for him?'

'Live with a man OK, but the man no good for Theo. He too English.' Alberto chuckled while I tried to interpret the *He too English*.

'I'm not English,' I found myself saying. How often I heard myself coughing up those coward words, fine-tuning my Britishness when it suited me.

'What Alberto means,' explained Marina, 'is that Theo's partner was half English. Or his mother or his father was English. He was good to Theo at the commencement, but then abandon him.'

'Perfidious Albion.' I just couldn't help myself. I wanted to say that I would not abandon Theo; that I would always be good to him; but it seemed a bit soon to make such a public declaration. 'I'm sure he'll find someone,' I came out with.

'So tell me, Marina,' I heard Nat arrive with the rescuing cavalry, 'What do you play in the Tenerife Symphony Orchestra?'

'Do you mean the instrument or the music?'

'Both,' said Nat, and grinned encouragingly across the table.

SEVEN

When I got to City Bar at seven o'clock I imagined I would be the first out of the three of us. *Hora inglés* is the Spanish instruction for 'Be punctual' and although I mightn't be English I had acquired the teacher's professional habit of arriving on the dot. But there, sitting at a table together under the tunnel-like awning, were Theo and Nat, the two people I was looking forward to introducing, already in animated conversation over glasses of Dorada. I semaphored my request for a beer to the distant waiter and joined them at the table.

'How did you find each other?' I asked.

Nat answered without hesitation. 'It was easy. He looks like his sister.' He smiled at Theo. 'Though obviously more masculine.'

'Really crazy,' Theo said. 'That the two of you actually met her. Without looking.' He shook his head to display his wonderment. 'It's a big city.'

Not that big, I thought. Santa Cruz was hardly Glasgow, but I didn't say so. 'I couldn't keep my promise to you,' I confessed instead. 'I couldn't tell Marina I hadn't seen you. She asked me directly.' I thought I ought to get that out of the way at once. It was unlikely that Nat had omitted to let Theo know he'd been mentioned.

Theo gave me a look I couldn't quite decipher. 'I suppose it doesn't matter.'

'I didn't tell her we'd slept together,' I said in mitigation.

'Your sister's a cracker,' Nat said, surprising me as well as Theo. In the light of the last words he'd spoken that was an oblique compliment to the brother and Theo had the grace to smile in reply to it. 'Pity she's engaged,'

Nat went on blithely. Was that a bit un-gentlemanly? I wondered. Or was it a commendable example of across-the-Pond frankness? Neither of us Europeans commented.

Then the three of us talked happily for ages, drinking beer slowly. The Spanish drank little and talked much when they met in bars, I'd noticed. Unlike the Brits, who drank a lot and talked little. But we did it the Spanish way this evening. We'd probably only got through two small beers each by the time I noticed that it was already eight thirty. 'Right,' I said to Theo, 'I haven't forgotten I'm taking you out to dinner.' I turned to Nat. 'I still owe him lunch from last time.' Nat nodded. He already knew the story.

'Where do you want to go?' Theo asked me.

'To the Regulo,' I said firmly.

'It's expensive.' Theo frowned.

'No importa,' I said.

Theo said, 'All right then. It's the other side of town, though.'

'We'll get a taxi. My treat.' Would we be getting another taxi to bring us back here? I didn't know if I'd be smuggling Theo into my hotel again later. The end of the evening was still a mystery to me. I suspected that the same went for Theo.

The Regulo was the place where I'd discovered the loss of my debit card at the end of my last stay in Puerto. It was indeed a bit expensive, compared to most of the restaurants in the town. But it was manageable for someone like me, on a British teacher's salary. Theo and I did the same job essentially and had an equal number of years' experience. But perhaps he didn't earn the same as I did. We hadn't got to the stage of talking about our salaries and savings. If we ever did get there. Perhaps when Theo said the Regulo was expensive he really meant it was too expensive. I would need to tread carefully.

We said our goodbyes to Nat and left him with his beer and dreams of Theo's sister. Though I didn't feel too sorry for him. He was an outgoing guy and in a busy bar like City would always find people to talk to. Theo and I set out along the pavement to where, as we both knew, there was a taxi rank after just fifty metres.

I could never travel in the back seat of a taxi without having the uncomfortable feeling that I was being kidnapped, or about to be kidnapped. I had to push the idea away deliberately each time. But now it came to me more strongly even than usual. The corkscrew road that the driver took to descend from the cliff-top heights of La Paz was quite unfamiliar to me: its broad curves a kilometre and a world away from the paths and steps I took when I was making the same journey on foot. But it wasn't only that. Our taxi driver, in contrast to most that I'd encountered, was totally silent throughout the journey, addressing not a single word to Theo or to me in Spanish or in any other language.

But we were nice to him. We let him drop us at the taxi rank in the Plaza del Charco. From there we would only have a one-minute walk to the Regulo, while our driver would not be obliged to waste time and petrol threading round the one-way system to join the back of the queue of hopeful taxis. After I'd paid him and we were walking towards the restaurant I told Theo how surprised I'd been by the driver's silence.

'Yes,' Theo agreed. 'As a rule they're a talkative species. Even by Spanish standards. But you mustn't be too surprised. The thing is, he didn't know what to make of us. You are … excuse me but you are … very obviously a tourist. And I am very obviously a local.

One of each in a taxi together... Well, it isn't very usual. He wasn't very comfortable with it.'

'Do you think he thought that one of us was a rent boy?' I asked lightly.

'Yes, but which?' said Theo, and we laughed in each other's face.

OK, we'd made a joke of it. But I felt a small worry gnawing in the pit of my stomach. Puerto de la Cruz was a small society. I had little need to worry about its unwritten rules and strictures. But Theo had to live and work here. Was he defying one of his home town's conventions by fraternising (to use a mild expression) with a gay tourist? I decided not to pursue this with Theo. Not right now at any rate. We had reached the door of the restaurant.

Theo knew that I'd been here before. I didn't ask him if he had. He didn't volunteer that information, nor did he greet any of the waiters as if he knew them. We were shown to a table and a moment later were eyeballing each other across an immaculate white linen surface. A memory forced itself on me although I really didn't want it: the last time I'd sat facing a man across a restaurant table the man had been Maxwell. I pushed away the image of him by concentrating hard on Theo. He looked fantastic and I felt a rush of self-esteem at the thought that I was dating him. And then wondered, as Theo looked straight back at me, what he thought. For a second we stared into each other's eyes as if through windows. And yet it also seemed like staring into an infinite series of mirrors. I know that's how it seemed to me. I'm pretty sure the same went for Theo. That long second came to an end at last: the waiter arrived with the menus.

We opened them simultaneously. 'English or Spanish?' asked Theo.

'Spanish,' I said bravely. The restaurants here all had their menus set out in several European languages. I made it a point of honour always to read the menu in Spanish and order from it in that language, even if I sometimes had to flick over to the English page to check the translation of something unfamiliar when nobody was looking. Tonight I wouldn't even need to do that. I would simply ask Theo.

'They've got *cochinillo,*' observed Theo. 'What's that in English?'

I was delighted to be asked. For once I knew a translation that Theo didn't. 'It's roast sucking pig,' I said. I went on, showing off, 'Most menus, and even TV chefs, say suckling pig these days. But it isn't right. It's a sucking pig or, if you like, a suckling. A suckling pig would be something different.'

Theo had to think about this. He frowned as he did so; it was a knitting of his handsome brow that I'd grown fond of. Grown fond of because it was quintessentially Theo. 'OK,' he said at last, slowly. 'There's the verb to suck and the verb to suckle...' I nodded encouragingly like a teacher. Theo recognised the gesture and his eyes twinkled complicitly. 'So a suckling pig would be ... enormous. A female pig feeding its ... piglings?'

'Piglets,' I corrected apologetically. 'But yes, exactly. A half-ton sow (that's a female pig) breast-feeding her...' Now I hesitated. 'Her litter? Her farrow? I'm not sure what the collective noun is for piglets.'

'So it's sucking pig, then, for *cochinillo,* not suckling pig. But you said you could also say a suckling?'

'Think about it,' I said. 'Though you already have. When you said piglings.'

'Of course,' said Theo, and I saw his light-bulb moment shine out in the radiant smile of understanding that he gave me. 'Like duckling and gosling. It's not the

-*ing* part of a verb at all. It's -*ling*, meaning diminutive. A suckling means a little sucking thing.'

I began to say, 'Out of the mouths...'

But he finished it for me. '...Of babes and sucklings.'

We sat back in our chairs and admired each other once again. This time not just each other's appearance but also each other's cleverness.

'I love language,' Theo said. 'I love discovering more and more about it. It's probably the most important thing we learn in life. The most important thing we teach to children.'

'Hmm,' I said, wondering if I could agree with him. 'You could say that maths was also pretty essential. And in today's world, science.'

'OK,' Theo said. 'Point taken. You do need those to make sense of the physical world. To try to understand the infinities of space and time. The cosmos. But when it comes to people... Nobody has ever talked about love by using a mathematical equation or a chemical formula.'

'No,' I said. I found I'd lowered my eyes back down to the menu. 'No they haven't.' Theo had uttered the L-word. I hoped that hadn't been a dummy run for an announcement that he loved me. I wasn't ready for that yet. Yet? I wasn't sure I ever would be. Or certainly not so soon after Harry's departure.

But Theo evidently wasn't gearing up to say that he loved me, or if he was he didn't get the chance to. The waiter came to take our order. We both chose the cochinillo.

At some point one of you has to say it. On this occasion it was me. Over the dessert. 'I'd like to sleep with you again tonight. I don't know...'

'Yep,' he said a bit brusquely, though with a commendable lack of hesitation. 'But where?'

If I'd been expecting him to say, 'Come back to my place,' I now had to pretend I wasn't. Very smoothly I said, 'Back at my hotel.'

Theo gave me one of his frowns. 'Reception staff... I don't want to get you into trouble.'

'You won't,' I said. 'I've thought about this. The hotel bar doesn't close till midnight. It's usually quite busy in the hour or so before. They won't notice us from the reception desk if we go in there and it won't matter if they do. There's another exit from the bar that comes out by the lifts. Out of sight of reception.'

Theo treated me to a smile. 'Blimey, you have thought things through.' I'd never heard someone who wasn't British say blimey before.

Clearly Theo's own place of residence was out of bounds as far as I was concerned, at least for now. Perhaps he lived with his parents. I wasn't going to ask him. He'd tell me in his own good time. If he wanted to. And if he didn't want to? I could live with that too.

The plan worked perfectly. We left the hotel bar shortly before it closed, taking with us a few bottles of Dorada which Theo had had the forethought to buy as carry-outs a few minutes beforehand. I couldn't help noticing how differently Theo ordered a round from the way I did. When it was my turn the conversation went like this.

Me: *Dos cervezas, por favor.*

Barman: *Sí, señor.*

Me: *Gracias.*

Barman: *De nada.*

Whenever it was Theo's turn it went more like this.

Theo: *Hablahablahablahablahablahablahablahabla.*

Barman: *Hablahablahablahablahabla.*

Theo:

*Hablahablahablahablahablahablahablahablahablahabl
ahablahabla.*

It could go on like that for upwards of a minute, unless
the barman was called away to serve someone else
before the minute was up. I understood virtually nothing,
but I got considerable pleasure simply from listening to
him talking Spanish, just as I enjoyed watching him eat,
drink, piss or ejaculate. But I was more than ever aware
of the gulf that lay between the native speaker of a
language and the clever tourist with a phrasebook.

We drank our takeaways on my balcony with the light
off. We looked out over the blue-lit water of the
swimming pool and the two or three energetic souls who
were taking a dip at this late hour. We touched and
caressed each other from time to time, in greedy
anticipation of the moment when we'd get undressed and
go to bed and see what happened there. Like children
that lick the outsides of sweets, taking pleasure from
deferring pleasure, before putting them irrevocably into
their mouths.

And when the time did come, and we were ready and
aching to, I let Theo fuck me, gazing into my eyes while
I looked up into his. I didn't then insist on taking my
turn in fucking him. We'd both done that the night
before, proving to each other that we didn't believe in a
gay world that was unnecessarily divided into tops and
bottoms. There was no need to make the point a second
time. I let Theo coax me to my own climax with his
hand. It wasn't difficult to do and it didn't take him very
long. We continued to gaze into each other's eyes in the
reflected light that was coming in via the balcony doors
from the poolside. The first and second nights we'd been
together we'd had sex, quite simply. Tonight we did it
all a bit more thoughtfully. There's another expression
for having sex in this way but I wasn't prepared to frame

the words in my head, let alone utter them aloud. Nevertheless we slept the whole night wrapped in each other's arms; and any physical discomfort that that might have entailed was more than outweighed by the good that it did to our hearts and minds and feelings.

It was another ridiculously early morning. Theo had to get back to wherever it was he lived, then get ready for school. It went through my mind as I blearily silenced my phone alarm that part of the attraction of a holiday romance must be the fact that both of you are on holiday. I shrugged the thought off as I pushed back the duvet and put my feet to the floor. A holiday romance with someone who had to get up and go to work at an ungodly hour was better than no holiday romance at all.

I was in the bathroom two minutes later when I heard Theo call, 'Jonty, can you come here?'

'Two seconds,' I called back. I was finishing up my morning pee. I changed into a faster gear.

Theo had been putting his shoes on a bit too quickly and had managed to get one of the laces in a knot. He was sitting on the sofa in anxious exasperation. 'More haste, less speed,' I said as I knelt down at his feet. He didn't say if he agreed or disagreed.

Normally I wasn't very good with knots. I didn't have the right sort of nails, I thought, or else I lacked the skill. I usually ended up cutting my losses and cutting the laces. But desperate situations sometimes lend us superhuman powers. I worked on that knot with all my strength of hand and brain, my eyes taking in not only the knot itself but the little twin bands of Theo's tanned skin that were visible between his socks and jeans. Suddenly – and one never knows how this has happened – the knot was gone and the two ends of the lace were freed.

'All done, Theo,' I said, and looked up at his face. At the same time I placed a hand on one of those bands of skin and ran it up under his jeans a little way. I said, 'You're warm.'

He said, 'Thank you, Jonty,' very quietly, and he gave me a look, a smiling sort of look, that I'd never seen before. I realised that something very intense and intimate had just happened between us and that we'd both been deeply stirred by it.

Then it was a repeat of yesterday. Checking that the corridor was clear of human traffic, a momentary kiss in the lift, then the walk across the lobby, bodies tense in the expectation of being challenged from the reception desk behind us. It wasn't till we were outside on the pavement and breathing normally again that I realised we'd said nothing about this evening. I rectified that immediately. 'This evening?' I asked. My voice betrayed my nervousness.

'City Bar at seven?' he answered, equally tensely. *'City Bar a las siete?'*

'Yes,' I said. I thought of another thing. 'Give me your fucking number.'

He reeled it off – in English, and a little slowly. After all, words were his big thing: not numbers. I tapped his digits into my phone as he said them and then he did the same with mine.

We shook hands butchly, without hugging.

'Hasta las siete,' said Theo.

'Hasta la City,' I answered, and Theo gave me one of his best smiles as a reward for my first attempt at a pun in Spanish. Then he turned and strode off abruptly. I stood on the pavement and once again wondered what you were supposed to do in a holiday resort at six thirty in the morning.

EIGHT

I hadn't made an arrangement with Nat to spend any part of the day with him. But when I sauntered onto the terrace Bei Thomas for a coffee at around nine o'clock there he was already sitting at a table with his own *café con leche* in front of him.

'How did you get on?' Nat asked when I joined him.

'All good,' I said. I told him about the dinner we'd had and about my fiendishly clever idea of smuggling Theo up to my hotel room via the bar behind the reception area. I left it at that. It was probably as much detail as he wanted.

Nat grinned. 'Theo's nice. I really liked him.' He went on, as if it was the most unsurprising thing, 'I had a message from his sister.'

'A message from Marina?' I thought for a second. 'You didn't contact her first by any chance, did you?'

Nat moved his head from side to side a couple of times. 'Well yeah, I did actually.'

'But she must have given you her number.' Then I said the stupidly obvious. 'She's engaged to Alberto.'

'Well,' Nat said. 'It is partly business. I told her I knew someone who might be able to get the orchestra a gig in Calgary.' I looked at him in astonishment. Nat was a painter and decorator. I hadn't seen him as someone who could broker international symphony concert engagements. 'So I'm going back over there later.'

'To Santa Cruz?' I checked unnecessarily. He would hardly have meant Calgary – a place I associated with rodeos, stampeding bulls and horses, rather than with high culture. 'Well, have a great day,' I said, trying not to sound too astonished. I didn't offer to go with him. 'I'm seeing Theo later,' I continued. It was not a change of subject. 'In City Bar.' I jerked my head across the street towards it, shut and silent at nine o'clock in the morning. 'If we don't see you Theo will ask where you've got to. Do I tell him?'

Nat's face registered a moment of discomfort. 'Perhaps not just yet,' he said. 'I mean, probably nothing'll come of it.'

'Of course,' I said, and nodded. Though whether he'd been referring to the concert engagement or something else I wasn't certain.

After we'd finished our coffees and parted company I went back to my hotel, took a book and my sun-cream out to the pool area and lay on a sun lounger. There were worse ways to spend a day when one of your two regular companions couldn't spend it with you because he was cooped up in a classroom, and the other one was taking a bus thirty miles over the mountain to go and chat up the first one's sister.

Of course Theo did ask about Nat when we met up later. I lied slightly and said I didn't know where he was. We weren't close friends, I told him: simply bar buddies.

'I liked him,' Theo said frankly. 'I don't often go for guys who're slightly balding but I could make an exception for Nat.'

'Lucky for me he's straight then,' I said. 'Though he is a bit young to be losing his hair. He's thirty-two he told me. Two years younger than we are.'

'Same as my sister,' said Theo. That arrived like an unexpected punch in the belly. Where had it come from?

I said, 'Remind me about your family.' We'd gone through this the first night we'd met, I thought. Or certainly on the second. But we'd been drunk on both occasions. It would do no harm, I thought, to run through it again when sober. And it would stop Theo from unfortunately mentioning Nat in the same sentence as his sister again. At least for the moment.

It all came back to me as Theo retold it. His father had died when he was twelve. His mother still lived up in La Orotava. (When Theo pronounced the name of his birthplace it came out as Larotava.) He had his sister but no other siblings. Though he had no end of cousins and second cousins dotted around the island. That would account for the thicket of Gonçalves names in the phone-book.

Then it was my turn. I was an only child – Theo nodded as he remembered – and my mother was still alive and not all that far from Glasgow, in Stirling. 'But like you,' I finished, 'I lost my father when I was eleven.' Actually Theo had been twelve; but it hardly made a difference; it was something we had in common.

The other thing we had in common, apart from our age and gayness, was that we'd both broken up with a partner in recent months. We had exchanged that information two nights ago sitting right here at the bar counter. Theo revisited the subject now. It was fair enough. The subject might be sensitive but we knew each other better now. 'You know, when you and Harry broke up…' He began shyly, tentatively, as well he might but he'd paid me the compliment of remembering Harry's name.

'Yes,' I said, in a tone of voice that indicated I was OK with him going on.

'You told me when, but not why. Maybe I shouldn't be…'

'It's OK,' I said. 'We're getting to know each other. It's the kind of thing you need to know. We were together for four years. We're still good friends. Why did we split up? Details a bit complicated. Perhaps they'll keep for another time. Basically we couldn't manage to be faithful to each other. At first we thought we could live with that, provided it was on both sides. But we couldn't. Because it never can be quite the same on both sides. One of you plays around with one guy, the other one then thinks he needs to even the score by playing around with two. Then it's a question of what you do with the other people. How far you go; the way you feel...'

Theo was nodding all through this. Now he said, 'It was a bit the same with Mateo and me. We survived five years. But in our case it was Mateo who was the unfaithful one. I was always faithful to him. It got too much. In the end I said, enough's enough, and we agreed to part. We still run into each other from time to time. We're friendly enough when we do.'

Ouch. Mateo was the unfaithful one and Theo had remained faithful to the end, unlike me. That stung, but I didn't think Theo had meant it as a reproach; he was just stating the facts of the case. I said, 'I'd forgotten his name was Mateo.' Though I hadn't forgotten that Marina had told me Theo's partner had 'abandoned' him. I didn't raise that now.

'Yes,' said Theo. 'We could have been Theo and Teo but to avoid everyone getting confused we chose not to be. We were Matt and Theo.'

'Harry and I were the same age,' I said.

'Matt was twelve years older than me. He had an apartment of his own. He let me live in it free.' Marina hadn't told me those bits.

'You were his toy-boy,' I said, then wished I hadn't. I'd meant it as a joke but Theo didn't take it that way. His face darkened.

He said, 'That wasn't the case at all. He was older and so he had more money than I did. That was all.'

'I'm sorry,' I said. *'Perdonme.'* I put my hand on his nearer thigh and rubbed it in a familiar, sexy way. I didn't know if you could do this in broad daylight in a straight bar in Puerto de la Cruz but the situation was too important for me to care. 'I was only joking. I promise I didn't really think you were Matt's toy-boy. It was just a joke. Honestly. But I shouldn't have said it even so. *Perdonme.*'

I was rewarded for my humble speech of apology by one of Theo's most beautiful smiles. He was also quite accepting of my hand so publicly sitting on his thigh. Nobody around us seemed remotely fazed by it either. And I remembered that I'd drunkenly kissed one of the barmen here during my first stay. So I gave Theo's leg another rub and then for a further half minute I left my hand there. I had another question to put to him during that time. 'So where do you live now?'

'Two friends of mine from university took me in. One girl, one boy. They live together as a couple but are not married. Perhaps they will one day. I knew them both and we were all close friends. They have a spare room with one small bed in it. The room is small and with very thin walls. They know I'm gay but I don't think I could take anybody back there. To sleep with, I mean. That's why I haven't invited you.'

'I understand,' I said. 'I had wondered a bit but I wasn't going to ask you.'

Theo looked straight into my eyes. 'You are very sensitive,' he said. 'And sensible.'

'Thank you. Of course you can stay with me at my hotel for the rest of my stay.' But at once I thought I might have gone too far, saying something that was neither sensitive nor sensible. I added quickly, 'But only if you'd like that too.'

'I would, actually,' Theo said in a very serious tone and I was so relieved I almost cried.

I removed my hand from his thigh at that point. There seems to be a right moment for doing this and I felt I'd judged it well this time. I asked, 'Where did you meet

Mateo?' And as I spoke I realised instantly what his answer would be.

'I met him on the same bench where I met you.' I didn't tell him I'd had a premonition of what he'd say. 'He was – he is – a teacher at the British College here. He has a Spanish name and surname. His father's Spanish. But his mother is English. I was about to say, English like you. But of course Scottish isn't English: I do know that.'

'It's similar enough,' I answered graciously. I felt I needed to atone for my *Perfidious Albion* churlishness when talking to Marina. 'Harry's English too.'

Theo's eyes twinkled with mischief suddenly and I wondered what he was going to say. He came out with, 'So that's why your English is so bloody good.'

I laughed. 'You got it in before I did.'

A beer or two later Theo announced, 'Dinner's on me tonight. Do you like Chinese?'

'Yes,' I said. 'Like most people on the planet.'

We went to a restaurant I'd walked past a dozen times, halfway down the Camino San Amaro, the long slope that led to the Cabras steps. It was a pretty walk, between rows of cypress trees, past smart houses where crimson and purple bougainvillea tumbled blazingly over white garden walls. From the top of the slope the immense view of Mount Teide appeared. 'No clouds on the mountain tonight,' I said.

'That could be a good sign or a bad one,' said Theo gravely. 'When there is cloud piled up above Teide like an umbrella we say it's going to rain. When the clouds are lower down and the mountain has them wrapped around itself near the top like a scarf we say it's going to turn cold.'

I laughed at that. 'Does it always work?' I asked.

Theo wrinkled his nose. 'Sometimes yes, sometimes no. Fifty-fifty, I'd say.'

I wondered how many hundreds of years they'd been using that saying about Teide with its scarf and umbrella for. People had always had scarves. They were mentioned in Shakespeare. But umbrellas?

'When were umbrellas invented?' I asked Theo as we walked on down.

'I've no idea,' he said. 'You see them in nineteenth century paintings, but not before.'

'We could google it, I suppose.'

'Yes, but not now.' That was good of Theo. I needed someone like Theo to stop me endlessly googling things. We arrived at the restaurant door.

We were served by a camply charming waiter who clocked us as a gay pair as soon as he saw us, and talked to us accordingly in a pleasingly familiar way. After we'd eaten we meandered slowly back to my hotel and repeated our routine – bar, back way out to lift-well, beer on balcony, then bed – exactly as we'd done the night before. There was a rhythm to our life together now, even if the routines had only been in place for two days. I liked it enormously. I even enjoyed getting up early the next morning to get Theo off to school.

Actually we didn't get up quite so early this time. Theo had brought a bigger backpack with him. It contained overnight and wash things, a change of clothes and his school stuff for the morning. He showered and shaved in my hotel bathroom and, after I parted from him outside on the pavement, went off directly to his school. 'Last working day today,' he said just before we said *hasta pronto*. 'Tomorrow and Sunday we can be together the whole day.' Then, just as happened to me so often, a doubt entered his mind and he said cautiously, 'If that's what you'd like to do…'

'Of course I would,' I assured him. 'I'd like that more than anything.'

We turned away from each other, happy for the moment. I was more than happy at the thought of spending a whole weekend with Theo. But weekends themselves have endings. Theo would go back to school on Monday. And on Tuesday I would fly back to Glasgow.

When I went to City Bar to meet Theo again at seven o'clock I found him already there and deep in conversation with Nat, whom I hadn't seen for the best part of two days. I joined them happily enough but I was thinking, had Nat met up with Marina as he'd intended? Had he told Theo about that? And was I supposed to know about this? In other words, did Theo already know I'd kept him in the dark about Nat's interest in his sister?

I got no clues from either of them while we drank and chatted, and then Theo and I went off to eat. I was still happy that Theo and Nat hit it off so well, yet slightly worried by the interest that Theo took in Nat and the affectionate attention he paid him when the three of us were together. There were alarming moments at which I glimpsed a possible development – a sort of vicious triangle in which Theo transferred his affections from me to my Canadian friend, who in his turn went panting after Theo's sister, leaving me to pine unrequitedly for Theo. But then I would tell myself to get a grip and cast my imaginings back into the darkness where they belonged.

We spent that evening, Theo and I, planning our weekend together. Actually, since it was Friday night it already was the weekend. And we were already basking in its spacious luxury. Later we sat out on my balcony talking until the small hours and in the morning lazed in bed till nearly ten.

Theo took me on a walk out of town. We passed beyond the patch of waste ground where the Calle del

Aceviño stuttered to a stop and where our by now mythic bench stood. We took a footpath that tunnelled beneath the main road out of town and burrowed its way among deep and dense plantations of banana palms. We were still walking parallel with the cliff edge, and the sea was in sight for much of the time among the undulations of the banana groves. After a sea-blue and frond-green mile or two our track descended to the bottom of a gorge where a dried-up stream bed met the sea. We went down via alternating slopes and flights of steps. We were not alone on our walk. Energetic tourists passed us at intervals in twos and threes: Germans mostly, I guessed. And as we climbed down into the ravine we could see more of them coming and going on the continuation of our path as it led up the other side. 'Elderly hikers,' Theo observed. 'Determined to make it to the top without breaking wind.'

I laughed happily. When people make a mistake with a foreign language it's really only funny when they're very fluent in it, just as it's funny when educated people make mistakes in their own. Doctor Spooner's absurd coinages are remembered as funny principally because he was an Oxford don.

'I got that wrong, didn't I?' said Theo with a grin.

I said, 'I think you fell between two stools. There's "without breaking stride" and there's "without getting out of breath", or puff, or "being winded" – though I'm not sure if we still say that these days.'

'Breaking wind means...?'

'Farting. Or burping. It can be either end.'

'Of course,' said Theo. 'I did know that once. Matt must have told me.'

I said, 'Did Mateo like words too?'

'Of course. It was one of our things.'

And now, I thought, it was one of ours.

'When someone farts noisily,' Theo went on, 'we say *Este culo quiere algo.*'

I laughed because I found I could translate the sentence easily. 'That arse wants something.'

'Exactly.' And I felt Theo's hand give my own backside a cheeky pat as if to remind us both it was still there.

The sun shone on us from a blue sky that was split apart by the thunderbolt flights of swifts that screamed summer as they sliced beside our ears. Our way wound through a farmyard. We crossed paths with a boy of about twelve who was carrying a kid goat in his arms. The goat was black and shiny and the boy was nearly as dark. The boy frowned out of chocolate eyes as we passed him and the goat did likewise because goats' faces, even in their earliest days, are set in a perpetual frown. After we'd passed on I was left with the impression of dark velvet pelts, both the goat's and the boy's.

We dropped down again to El Bollulo cove, where there was a bar and restaurant beside the beach, and we had a perfectly ordinary lunch there. That was a symbol of the day as a whole. Ordinary. Perfectly ordinary. And in the ordinariness the perfection lay.

During the switchback return walk I told Theo how I had discovered the Selvagem Islands while flying home after my last visit. He had to think for a second, confronted with an unfamiliar pronunciation of a name that he would naturally have known. Then he said, 'Ah, the *Islas Salvajes.*' That light-bulb moment of his triggered another one in me. 'I see... The Savage islands.'

'Perhaps Wild Islands translates the idea better,' suggested Theo.

'Yes, of course. Like *sauvage* in French. Even wild flowers are *fleurs sauvages.*'

'It's the same in Spanish. *Flores salvajes.*'

We both loved the way that languages, like nations, and like individual people, didn't live in isolation; they were intimately connected with others of their species by intricate and surprising pathways and owed their existences and their character to others. We went on finding words that linked up between languages, while beside us the sea expanded across the horizon then shrank away below it as our path crested the summits of the cliff-edge hills and dropped into the ravines between. We went on to words that were onomatopoeic, or simply sounded beautiful. 'I love the word *escuchacorchos,*' I told Theo. The Spanish word for corkscrew. 'You can almost hear the sound of the cork coming slowly up out of the bottle's neck.'

Theo said, 'Trust you to know that one.'

'It's a sign of a misspent youth,' I said. 'Like being good at darts and snooker.'

'I like your word silver,' said Theo. 'It's not onomatopoeic exactly because it doesn't imitate a sound...'

'I know. But you're right. It somehow seems to express the gleam of light.' I'd never had that thought before. It had taken a Spanish guy's love of the word to bring it to me. Though not just any Spanish guy. It had been Theo. 'You know, I suppose...' I went off at a tangent, showing off because I was happy. 'There are some English words that sound most truly like themselves in a Scottish accent.'

'Such as?'

'Well murder for one.' I did an exaggerated version of my own accent for him. 'Murrdurr.'

'Er... yes. I can sort of see that.'

'Another one would be...' Again I steered my accent towards very broad Scots. 'Deprraissed.'

Theo did laugh, but it sounded an uncomfortable throat tickle of a laugh, as though he hadn't liked that particular one. Unfortunately I couldn't come up with any alternative examples that might have cheered him up again and we walked in silence for a bit. Then he said, 'You can't see the Wild Islands from here, obviously, but I might be able to show you La Palma later.'

'That's a long way off, isn't it? A long way to the west?'

'Yes. It's the island where your Greenwich Observatory has its biggest telescopes. If Britain opts for Brexit we'll presumably throw them into the sea, I guess.'

I said, 'It won't come to that.'

'Anyway, far away though it is, the island sometimes shows itself at sunset.'

I liked the sound of that, I liked the poetry of it, and I said so. A moment later I heard Theo humming softly, a cheerful tune with mouth closed, and I knew that he was happy again, as I was.

When it was getting close to sunset Theo took me to the viewing point at the top of the Camino San Amaro and we looked out to sea. 'With any luck La Palma will appear,' said Theo optimistically.

'No sign of it yet, though.' The western horizon appeared vague and hazy in the sinking sun's glare. There was no sign of any other island along its immense flat line. The orange fireball sank behind a thin line of cloud. The cloud was so wispy that it made no apparent difference to the brightness of the light. And then the sun touched the sea. At that moment two low dark humps appeared.

'You see,' said Theo. 'La Palma, fifty miles away.' I was touched that he'd troubled to convert a distance he must have stored in his head in kilometres into something easier for me to appreciate.

'It looks like two islands,' I said.

'Two areas of mountain. There's lower ground in between but it's not very easy to see from here.' I had a momentary image of the two of us viewed from behind, pointing out to sea towards an island that was almost impossibly far away. We'd look like a picture from a brochure advertising gay-themed holidays. And then the last diminishing segment of the sun went down behind the sea, and the island vision vanished as quickly as it had come: as if someone had pressed the off switch.

'That was wonderful,' I said. Because it had been. 'But why don't we see La Gomera? Isn't that nearer?'

Theo pointed leftward to the western headland of Tenerife, the landmass on which we stood. 'Round the corner. You'd see it from Los Gigantes. Los Christianos...'

'All the south-west coast resorts, I suppose.' Except for the airport the southern half of the island, the hotter, drier half, was foreign territory for me. 'I've seen Gran Canaria from the eastern side.'

'You can. Quite easily when the weather's clear. The others are too far away to see. Fuerteventura and Lanzarote a hundred miles to the east. I don't think you could see those even from the top of Mount Teide. Then, well west of La Gomera is El Hierro. The smallest island of the lot.' Theo paused before he added, 'I think it's the most beautiful of all the Canary islands. I own some property there.'

It shouldn't make a difference when someone you're beginning to fall for announces that he owns property on a remote and beautiful island in the sub-tropics. But somehow it does.

NINE

We ran into Nat in City Bar later that night. I thought he might be a bit off me because I'd been neglecting him. But his smiling greeting showed that wasn't the case. All the world loves a lover and Nat clearly wasn't feeling hard done by because I was spending my daytime with the man I slept with rather than with him. But it was not until Theo had to disappear down dark stairs to visit the toilet that I was able to bring up the subject that had been on my mind. 'What's the news on Marina? Have you seen her? Does Theo know?' Selfishly I was more anxious to know the answer to the last question than to the others.

Nat nodded. 'Yes, I did see her that day. We talked about a concert in Calgary. I told her I could talk to one or two people back there.' He took a slurp of beer. 'Actually I don't think there'll be much I can do. I don't really know those people very well. Basically I've simply painted their houses. I came clean about that and she didn't seem too surprised. I think she may have seen through my ruse.' His eyes smiled at me.

'I wondered if she might.'

Nat went on. 'But I went over there again today. We had lunch.'

'Wow,' I said. Then, 'Does her fiancé know you're seeing her?'

'I'm not sure if seeing her...'

'All right. Having lunch with her.' I was suddenly impatient. Theo would be back at any second. 'Look, does Theo know?'

'No,' Nat had just time to say, and then Theo was with us again and hopping back up onto his bar stool. Nat asked him brightly, jerking his head towards me, 'How's his Spanish coming along?'

I answered before Theo could. 'We haven't been speaking any Spanish. His English is so good. That's what happens when you meet another English teacher.'

Theo drew himself up on his stool. 'Next time he comes we shall speak only Spanish.' He turned to me and grinned triumphantly.

Neither Theo nor I had yet broached the subject of any foreseeable next time. Sometimes these things are easier to do in the presence of a third party. A kind of 'through the chair' way of doing things. The important sub-text would keep for another time. For the moment I responded just to what lay on the surface of Theo's announcement. 'That's going to put a strain on things,' I said. 'My Spanish is…' I tried to finish appropriately. Compared to Theo's English my Spanish was nothing. 'My Spanish is like a baby's.'

Theo said, *'Mi niño,'* and looked at me. Again there was one thing on the surface and something else beneath it. Nat and I both laughed at the little joke. But I caught Theo's look. And the way he'd called me his baby.

Bells clanged. They followed us to the bus stop that Sunday morning, and they followed our bus as we climbed out of Puerto. It was difficult not to feel a residual sense of wrongness as we religiously ignored the thousand-year-old summons. Theo and I glanced at each other at the same moment but it was I who voiced the question. 'Do you ever still go?'

Theo screwed up his face for a second. 'No. Family occasions sometimes. Baptisms… Though you use another word…'

'Christenings.'

Theo nodded. 'Weddings and requiems.'

'Funerals. Same as me.' Theo and I lived two thousand miles apart but we had inhabited the same monolithic Church.

We could have walked to La Orotava. It was little more than an hour away. But it was a nearly vertical hour, and the fact that you could see the place from the coast didn't signify. You could also see the twelve-thousand-foot summit of Mount Teide, and there was no question of our walking up to that. Besides, we weren't only going to La Orotava. We were continuing on up the hill a few miles past.

La Orotava didn't look too promising from the bus. A hillside of modern villas in tidy gardens and a bus station among office blocks in the centre. 'The bus misses the good bit,' Theo reassured me. 'You'll see it this afternoon.'

Somehow the villas disappeared below us and we were winding up a forest road. A curious rock formation appeared in the distance across the trees. A cliff face hundreds of feet high that was made up of even more hundreds of vertical pillars of basalt, it was called Los Órganos, the organ pipes. It could only have been called that: nothing else came so immediately to mind.

'Do you drive?' I asked Theo suddenly. I didn't know why I hadn't asked him this before.

'Yes, but I don't have a car. Mateo had a car. I used to drive it. But now…'

I asked, 'Where is Mateo now?'

'Inside my head most of the time,' Theo answered. 'I find I take him everywhere I go.'

I said, 'It's exactly the same for me. With Harry, I mean. I get the benefit of his thoughts about almost everything I do. Benefit or otherwise.'

Theo chuckled. 'I know exactly what you mean,' The wonderful thing was that I knew this was true.

The bus decanted all its passengers at a place called El Portillo. It wasn't really a place at all, but a mountain pass where hiking trails branched off among the trees.

There were only about three buildings there, the main one being a restaurant and bar. We headed there.

The air was cooler here at six thousand feet than it had been in Puerto. That didn't matter. It had been a hot morning down there, and the sun shone just as brightly here. The other thing about the air was what it carried with it: the warp and weft of birdsong; the turpentine fragrance of pines; the freshness of mountain sky. I felt a pang of happiness at simply being here. Here with Theo. I wondered if I would carry him in my head all the time from now on. The way I carried Harry. The way Theo carried his Mateo.

We ate an omelette and downed a beer. We set off down a narrow path that lost its way among the trees. After a while we stopped in a narrow clearing, removed each other's shirts and uncomplicatedly did what lovers are meant to do in such a setting.

Then we caught the bus back and wafted down the pine-clad hill. I asked if there were squirrels in the forests. Theo said no. The fauna was a bit restricted. Swimming and flying things predominated. Mammals, for rather obvious reasons, were not well represented – except those species that had been introduced, on purpose or by accident, by man. Theo finished, 'But squirrel is a beautiful word.'

I agreed. If the word silver gave an idea of reflected light, then squirrel conveyed an idea of the animal's liquid movements through the trees and of its body language in general. 'What is it in Spanish?' My misspent youth hadn't involved knowing the Spanish word for squirrel.

'*Ardilla.*' Theo pulled a face. 'Not quite sure that cuts the mustard the way squirrel does. It's beautiful in Italian, though. *Scoiattolo.*'

'And in French. *Ecureuil.* Which is really the same word as the English, though. Over the centuries they've simply dropped the S.' I remembered that I knew the word in German too. 'The German name has a different root, but it's still expressive and beautiful...'

'Eichhörnchen,' said Theo unexpectedly.

'I didn't know you spoke German.'

'I know a few words.' He boldly grabbed my thigh for a second. 'Sign of a misspent youth.' He looked at me mischievously.

We passed the distant Organ Pipes again, glimpsing them briefly across the forested gorge. I was so happy that I almost expected them to burst out in a fanfare of jubilant noise.

Theo was right about La Orotava: the bus got nowhere near the best bit of it. But we did. Nat had described it well. It was wonderfully picturesque, with steep streets and little tree-freshened squares. When you turned and looked downhill the streets picture-framed the distant sea. The big old houses had white plaster facades that were pierced with big wood-framed windows. The ornate Canarian balconies were also of carved wood, in surprisingly brilliant shades of brown. The best houses were almost the size of palaces. I asked Theo jokingly, 'Were you born in one of those?'

'No such luck,' he said. 'In a bit I'll show you where.'

The Orotava valley had grown rich centuries ago on fruit and wine and sugar cane. The mansions we were looking at attested this. 'It was a wealthy place,' I said unnecessarily.

'And La Orotava was at the centre of it. Puerto was just that, a little port, a hundred years ago. The place where the goods were loaded and unloaded and where fishermen set out to sea. The money was up here.'

I found I wanted to ask something. 'How did the islanders feel about Spain back then? Did they feel a part of the mother country – the place you call *La Peninsula*

– or did they see themselves as an oppressed colony?' I could see Theo thinking about this rather than answering immediately. I found I could put the question in another way. 'When Scotland became a part of the United Kingdom three hundred years ago most people embraced the idea. They saw they'd become a part of a growing imperial power. They could influence its decisions and share in its spoils. Scots have been at the heart of British government and industry ever since. Our present Prime Minister is Scottish and so were the two immediately before him. There've been loads of others. But with Ireland it was different. They joined the Union unwillingly. They didn't identify with the rulers of the empire but with the subject nations. After a revolution or two they got out. Except for the north, which caused a problem by wanting to stay in. The north of Ireland's more passionate about the Union than the English or the Scots have ever been. I wondered what the situation was here.'

By now we had stopped in the middle of the pavement. Theo had turned to face me. By chance his figure formed the central feature of a striking panorama. The streets ran downhill behind him and there was an infinite expanse of blue ocean above the rooftops. Only his head rose above the horizon and was framed in the other miraculous blue above it.

His face wore the most serious expression I'd yet seen there. 'You can't compare Ireland and Scotland to the Canary Islands. Their relationship with England is more like Catalunya's and the Basque Country's with Spain's Castilian heartland. Here the Spanish arrived as conquerors in the fourteenth century. The poor islands of Fuerteventura and Lanzarote gave into the invaders without a struggle but the more powerful islands – Tenerife especially – fought for a century. Of course we lost the battle.'

'We?' I knew to tread carefully when people used the W-word when talking about nationality.

'The Guanches.'

I shook my head, smiling dimly. 'You'll have to remind me.'

'The native population of the Canary Islands. Related to the Berbers of North Africa. They suffered the unspeakable... The annihilation of our language, our culture. It was pretty much the annihilation of a people. Most of the few families that remained alive were shipped off to the Americas as slaves during the following centuries.'

'Oh God, I'm sorry.' I had nothing else to say. I wanted to ask how come, if he identified himself as Guanche, he was still here when all the rest had perished or been cruelly exported, but this was hardly the moment.

We strolled around the edges of the town's botanical gardens, a sea of waving palms. Theo pointed up a steep and narrow street of terraced cottages. Grass grew so thickly in this lane that the floor of it was a striking green. 'Up there is where I was born,' he said. He didn't say any more and we didn't stop. There was no walking up to the door and knocking, introducing ourselves to whoever lived inside these days, or cupping our hands on the ground-floor window panes and peering in. We went on past, while I acknowledged Theo's sound-bite with an *Ah, I see.*

'You know,' I said when we were back on the bus, heading down the precipitous road back to Puerto, 'this Scottish, Irish, cup half full, half empty thing. It's not that different from what we're going through at home just now.'

'Brexit, you mean,' said Theo, nodding. He hadn't needed to be told what I was referring to. Then he looked sideways at me anxiously. 'I'm assuming you...'

I put his mind at rest. 'I'm a European,' I said. 'Same as you. Although...' I heard a bit of a sigh escape me, 'A few people I know – people I'm friends with – think differently.'

'It's fair enough,' said Theo in a tone of voice that said, broadminded, me.

'It won't happen, though,' I said to reassure him. 'In Scotland almost everybody will vote to remain. England's more divided, but even there I'm pretty sure reason will prevail.'

'I hope so,' said Theo. 'It's like when you're a kid and you threaten to run away from home to upset your parents. But then you realise, lying awake before you go to sleep, that it's not such a good idea.'

'It's not so different from what's happening in America,' I suggested. 'All this Trump nonsense. But voters are adult. They squawk and protest but generally they get it right on the day.'

Theo said, 'Hope so, anyway.' Then he stood up from his seat. We were back in Puerto and rapidly approaching the bus stop at La Paz.

Nat was a sensitive man. That was no doubt one of the things that had drawn me to him in the first place. When we met him in City Bar a little later he allowed the dynamic to be subtly different from that of the past couple of evenings. He was content to be on the sidelines. We were not a trio after all, his demeanour and body language seemed to be saying, but a couple who were due to be parted in under forty-eight hours with himself as the outsider. A very welcome outsider, but inescapably that was his role now. And Theo for his part, happy to be quite forward, almost flirtatious, with Nat on the previous occasions, seemed ever so slightly to distance himself from that forwardness. The emotional static this evening was entirely between Theo and me.

Ours were the two wavelengths that vibrated in unison. Nat gave us a graceful, understated wave when Theo and I went off to eat. And he'd left City Bar by the time we returned to it much later on.

Theo returned to the subject of Brexit. To my surprise, when we were getting into bed together. 'Of course a lot of your people are really bothered by the migrant crisis. But that isn't a European thing at all, or not much. It's a piece of world history unfolding in front of our eyes. We have it here.'

'Of course you do,' I said, remembering. I felt almost guilty that I'd forgotten about the seemingly endless stream of African migrants who washed up on the Canary Islands' eastern shores and had to be dealt with just as they had to be in Italy, mainland Spain and Calais. In the last couple of years the Canarian aspect of the migrant crisis had fallen out of the British news. 'It's fear of the outsider,' I said as I peeled off my socks, preparing to join Theo beneath the duvet. 'All down the years. Jews. Gays. Muslims. Poles.'

'Poles?'

'Not here. I meant in the UK. And yet it's better, isn't it, to live in a country that people want to come to rather than one they want to escape from?' The words came out so easily I felt I couldn't have just thought them up on the spot. I guessed I'd heard them somewhere.

The morning came with the wrench of Monday. Early dawn. Theo going off to school. A curt goodbye on the pavement outside my hotel at an ungodly hour. 'See you this evening,' I said. Neither of us was going to say the obvious: that it would be our last one together before I flew back to Scotland. The last evening we'd be spending together in any future we could foresee.

Theo looked very directly at me. There was an eagle-like fierceness in his eyes I hadn't seen before. 'Yes. See you this evening. But I won't be staying the night with you.'

I felt everything crumble suddenly. 'Why, Theo?'

'It would be too emotional. For me anyway. I couldn't handle it.'

'It'll be difficult to handle,' I said, 'but let's try and handle it anyway.' I couldn't hide the feelings that I was trying to cover with sensible words. I was begging Theo to stay one last night with me.

'I won't be able to hack it.' The look in Theo's eyes shifted from proud fierceness to misery. 'We'll have to say goodnight out here on the pavement. That's the best I'll be able to do.'

I wanted to say, And then? When…? Where…? But I couldn't say those words. All I knew was that Theo wanted to say them, and couldn't say them, too. I said, 'Seven o'clock then. City Bar.' And we turned away from each other as smartly as soldiers and I went back into the hotel.

We managed to be very British that evening. Theo especially. There were no Latin-style displays of emotion from either of us. Me, I was British. Theo… He'd lived with a half-English guy for years; perhaps some of the temperament had rubbed off on him. Though it wasn't in evidence most of the time. Perhaps he kept a store of it saved up. For difficult moments such as now.

There was no sign of Nat in City Bar. In a way I was glad. I could have messaged him but I didn't. After all he could as easily have messaged me. I didn't comment on his absence and neither did Theo.

I asked Theo about the property he owned on El Hierro, wondering why I hadn't done this before. I'd been intrigued when he'd briefly mentioned it but then we'd had a sunset to watch and gone on to talk of other things.

Theo told me now, 'It's just a tiny *casita* – a cottage, I suppose you'd say – with a little bit of land. In one of the hamlets around Valverde.'

'Valverde's the capital?' I hazarded.

'If you can call it that. Nothing's bigger than a village on El Hierro. The whole island only has eight thousand people.'

'I'm interested. How come you own a house there?'

'Big absentee landowner and property speculator, that's me.' Theo laughed. 'No. It's been in the family for ever. It was lived in by an aunt of mine who died childless. Spanish inheritance law is a nightmare. Everyone in the family gets a proportion of a relative's house when they die. So I don't really own the place on El Hierro. It's simply been agreed that I do the small amount of work involved in managing the place, so the rest of the family don't have to bother about it, and pocket what's left of the rent as my reward.'

'And who lives there?'

'It's rented to ... to a peasant family, I suppose you'd say.'

'Do you ever go over there?' I had a sudden romantic vision of Theo and me sailing a small boat together across the sixty miles of sea that lay between us and El Hierro. I had difficulty pushing the image away.

'Once or twice. But the people look after it well. The rent goes into my bank like clockwork quarterly.' I must have given Theo a certain look. It made him chuckle. 'It's a tiny amount. Not worth marrying me for.'

At that point I managed a chuckle too, though it came out nervously. Why did he have to come out with that? I called to the barman and ordered two more beers. I screwed up my courage and did it without saying please. The way Theo had been trying to teach me to.

96

We walked down the steps and through the town. I treated us to a final dinner at El Regulo. I could hardly forget that I'd eaten my previous last meal in Puerto here, two months before. Found I'd lost my debit card, and Theo had saved me from starvation the following day. I reminded him of the story now. He nodded across the table at me. 'All this because of a lost debit card,' he said. He didn't say what he meant by *all this* and I couldn't bring myself to ask him.

We ate a hearty rabbit stew and then a fragrant dessert that seemed to be made mostly of foam. With Theo's previous agreement I paid the bill. Then we were outside. Darkness had fallen while we ate but the lamp-lit streets were warm. Within seconds we found ourselves in the Plaza del Charco. Well here we go, I thought, and heard myself sigh. 'You don't want to walk all the way up the hill with me, only to have to walk all the way back down again on your own.'

'You don't want to have to walk all the way *up* on your own,' said Theo. We'd stopped walking and were standing facing each other near the line of taxis.

'It seems I must. As you're not going to spend the night with me.' I put a hand on his upper arm. 'For reasons I entirely understand.'

'We'll see each other again one day,' Theo said in a voice that had become a growl.

'Yes,' I said. Then we hugged each other stiffly and for a second kissed each other's lips.

'Go with God,' Theo said quickly, then turned and stomped off across the square.

'*Hasta la proxima,*' I called after him. This time I watched him go.

In the departure lounge was a huge model of the island of Tenerife. It was big enough to show the island's few skyscrapers, its two airports, and its coiling motorway in addition to the enormous centrepiece of Mount Teide. Actually, as this model made clear, the whole island, the size of a small British county, was Mount Teide. Its upper slopes were a vast natural pyramid, its lower, gentler inclines were ancient lava flows, now tree-grown in the northern part; half scrub, half desert in the south.

The model reappeared an hour later. It was framed in the porthole I was sitting next to and this time it was real. At first it was too big to fit inside its meagre frame and I had to be content with just the east coast of it. Then the top of Teide appeared, thrusting upward through a Polo mint of cloud. We passed the docks of Santa Cruz and the northern airport as we rose. No sign of Puerto: we were the wrong side.

I screwed my head round as far as it would go, pressing the bones of my head against the pane of the porthole. The whole of Tenerife now fitted in the frame, then La Gomera and La Palma too. The tops of the three islands floated on a white surface that was part cloud, part sea. Most of their bulk was hidden beneath this surface now; they floated like black icebergs. Try as I might I couldn't find distant El Hierro. The Ancients had written of the Fortunate Isles, somewhere out on the western edges of the known world. Islands beyond the sunset. The Gardens of the Hesperides. These days many people believed that the Fortunate Islands were actually the Canary Islands, accidentally discovered by bold navigators thousands of years ago. I found myself believing it now.

At last the cloud swallowed the two smaller isles and only Teide showed. It was small now, though: a tiny black triangle, lost in an ever growing, infinite sea.

TEN

Kids are endlessly curious about most things. An exception is the lives of their teachers outside school. If they meet one of their mentors in an extraordinary situation – walking along a street, say, or in a supermarket – they really do find this overwhelming, a matter for genuine astonishment. This only begins to change when they get to about the age of seventeen, by which time they're pretty much adult and ready to leave school anyway. So it was no surprise that none of the people I taught asked me what I had done during half-term. Except one. Who had turned eighteen and whose name was Chris. The big surprise was that he did ask.

'I went to Tenerife,' I told him.

'You're kidding,' Chris said. 'Nobody goes to Tenerife during a half-term. It's a summer holiday place.'

'It can be a winter holiday place too,' I said.

'Only for the old and infirm.'

'That must be my case, then,' I said. I strode off; I had a class to get to.

'Don't message me from the airport,' Theo had said. He meant my departure airport, Tenerife South. 'You can let me know when you get to Glasgow if you want.' I did want. And I wasn't the only one who wanted it. I did know that. Theo's answer pinged into my phone about thirty seconds after mine was sent. He'd known what time I was supposed to be landing. Had he been waiting for my message, phone in hand; waiting for me to touch base?

We'd talked about keeping in touch but rather vaguely. We'd message each other, of course, but … how often? I knew that after a while those things fell rather naturally, if often disappointingly, into place. Did Theo do Skype?

I'd asked him. I'd rather hoped he'd say no and, rather shyly he did say it. 'Neither do I,' I'd said. On the few occasions I'd used Skype I'd found it even more unsatisfying than the telephone. Did you comb your hair before doing it? Choose your background carefully? You couldn't make real eye contact. Above all, you couldn't touch. We used the expressions *keep in touch* and *be in touch* every day. But we usually meant almost every sense, every avenue of communication, except touch. But that first exchange of messages had been nice.

Then, after a few days a definite routine set in. We'd exchange a minimal message at lunchtime, then a slightly longer one in the evening. Sometimes I wrote the first one, sometimes Theo did. But if I wrote first and Theo's answer hadn't come before I went to bed I'd go to sleep unhappy. What was he doing? Who was he out with so late? What was so important in his life this evening that he couldn't find a minute to get back to me? It would have been easier in our parents' day in some ways. Post a letter, then resign yourself to waiting days before the answer came back. Frustrating, no doubt, but more relaxing.

I took my English Highers class to see Arthur Miller's The Crucible at the King's Theatre. There was an upside and a downside to these school theatre trips. The bad news was that you had to be alert and vigilant: on duty, in disciplinary mode; it was an extension of the day's work. The good news: you saw a good show, if you were lucky, without having to pay for your seat. A visit to the King's was in any case a treat. The theatre had one of those wonderful turn-of-the-last-century Italianate interiors, with horseshoe-shaped dress and upper circles and wraparound ambience. At least I thought the experience of being inside this gilt and plush confection was a treat. My charges didn't seem to notice it. Or if they did they never said.

We didn't use the school minibus for trips into central Glasgow. We took the train and then either the Clockwork Orange or a local bus. When we were going to the King's we simply walked from the Central Station up to Bath Street.

These days, for health and safety reasons, it took two members of staff to supervise a school trip involving a dozen or so kids. (Though in my own schooldays one accompanying adult had been deemed enough by the authorities and had seemed more than enough to us.) So along with me came a colleague, Kirsty, who taught French and whom I liked. 'I'll treat you to a drink in the interval,' I told her as we took our seats.

'Won't that be setting a bad example to the woozles?' Kirsty said.

'Some of them are already eighteen,' I protested. 'The younger ones already take their chances when they go to bars and pubs. None of them are under sixteen. They're all technically adults in most respects...' I was going to go on, but Kirsty laughed.

'I was joking,' she said. 'Just a wind-up.' She patted my knee lightly. 'Of course we'll have a drink.' She leaned over to a section of our party that was in the row in front. 'What did Mr Allen tell you? All phones to be switched off. Yes, that means you, Keira. Now, please.' The lights went down, the offending phone was neutered, and the curtain went up.

A number of our party were to be seen in the bar at interval time. Boys, mostly, though two or three of them had a girl in tow each. Most bought themselves soft drinks. A few went for alcoholic stuff. Kirsty and I clocked that and then generously pretended we hadn't. There was a bit of a queue at the counter. Only one woman was serving; I remembered from past visits that two was the usual complement. Then someone shouldered his way through the little crowd, lifted up the flap in the counter and shuffled behind it with a crate of bottled beer in his arms. He put the crate down, said 'Sorry,' to his female colleague, then turned towards the counter and faced the queue. At that moment Kirsty and I had just reached the head of it.

'Yes?' the newly arrived barman said, beaming a wonderful smile towards the pair of us. He was a handsome black guy, resplendent in dark trousers, white shirt and black bow-tie.

I said, 'Gosh.' The barman was Maxwell. We recognised each other at the same moment.

'Jonty!' Maxwell said.

'Good to see you,' I managed. 'Um... Two gins and tonics.'

When Maxwell had served us, Kirsty and I moved away from the bar into the dense little throng. 'Catch you later,' Maxwell said as I led the retreat.

'Yes,' I said, at first hoping that he wouldn't catch me later, then half a second afterwards hoping that he would.

'Someone you know, obviously,' said Kirsty, trying but failing not to sound curious.

'He used to work in one of the bars at the airport,' I said, trying to make a smokescreen like a cuttlefish squirts ink. 'Probably still does.'

'Doing a bit of moonlighting,' said Kirsty, nodding understandingly. My eyes were still full of the sight of Maxwell, resplendent in bow tie and dress shirt. I took a gulp of gin and tonic to try and banish the image but it didn't work.

Only minutes later the bell began to chime, calling us back to our seats. The crowd in the bar immediately began to thin out. I didn't get away quickly enough. Maxwell lifted up the flap in the bar counter, came out through it and made a beeline for us. 'Can we talk later?' he asked me, ignoring my companion. 'I need to see you.'

'Hang on,' I said, and found I'd half raised my free arm as if to ward him off. 'I'm actually at work.' I indicated Kirsty. 'This is a colleague of mine, Kirsty. We're here with fourteen school kids…'

'See you back in the stalls,' said Kirsty, extricating herself with gentle tact and joining the last few people to funnel out. I was left with Maxwell.

'Sorry if that was a bit…' said Maxwell, pulling a sorry face. 'Only I've had to change my job and I don't really have anywhere to stay tonight. Then I suddenly saw you and it was like … it was like it was somehow meant. I couldn't come and stay at yours tonight?'

'Oh bloody hell, Maxwell. I don't know. It wouldn't be very…'

Maxwell gazed into my eyes. 'Please,' he said. 'I need your help.'

'I have to escort the kids back to Paisley,' I said.

'That's where you live… I'd buy my own ticket.' He touched my forearm very lightly. Just for an instant.

The final call to return to our seats came over the PA system. 'You should have phoned me if you were in a jam.' I wasn't very proud of myself for saying that.

'I don't know what I'm going to do.'

'Meet me in the foyer at the end of the show,' I said unhappily. 'We'll take it from there. Now I've got to get back to my seat…' Without thinking I gave his bum a pat as I turned and left. A half second later I felt but did not acknowledge his answering touch.

The Crucible was not a bad metaphor for my state of mind as I tried to concentrate on the second half of Miller's masterpiece. If Maxwell really didn't have a home to go to I could hardly ignore him in his plight. But take him home with me? On a train with half the

Highers English group? Perhaps I could persuade him to sit in a different carriage... Thoughts of Apartheid came unpleasantly to mind. Kirsty whispered to me, choosing a moment when the on-stage action had reached a conveniently high-decibel moment, 'Are you all right?'

'It's that barman,' I whispered back. 'He wants me to take him home with me tonight.'

'You know him that well?'

'Sort of,' I whispered sheepishly. 'I rather wish I didn't. I've got to talk to him in the foyer afterwards.'

'Wow,' said Kirsty almost silently. The play had moved into a quieter scene and we watched it for a time in silence. But a few minutes later Kirsty whispered to me, 'I can take the woozles back on the train by myself. Don't worry. You stay behind and sort yourself out.'

'Are you sure? That's very generous. It would be ... useful. What'll you tell the woozles about my disappearance?'

'I've got from now till then to find out.' We re-focused our attention on the scene in front of us.

Maxwell was transformed by jeans and a hoodie when I spotted him at the edge of the emptying foyer. A lone stationary figure beside a hurrying stream of people. I trod water and let the English group overtake me. At least I tried to. I motioned discreetly to Maxwell to wait before moving through the crowd towards me. But some of my charges – mine and Kirsty's – wanted to talk immediately. What did I think of the production? What was Miller's motivation for writing the piece? Chris in particular was eager to hear my opinions. Kirsty came to my rescue. 'Come on now, lads, we've got a train to catch.'

'So's Mister Allen...'

'Mister Allen's had some news from home he needs to deal with. He'll come along later.' She turned to me.

'Take your time. I'll deal with this lot.' We didn't call each other Jonty and Kirsty in front of the woozles.

I stayed put, watching as Kirsty rounded up our charges like a sheep-dog. She even got Chris to leave my side without further protest, though he did cast one or two puzzled glances back at me before disappearing through the exit. I let several seconds pass after the last stragglers from our party had left the building. Then I moved through the thinning procession of other departures to where Maxwell waited.

'OK, Maxwell,' I said. 'It's good to see you. And you can come home with me if you want to. But what's all this about? Are you really homeless and jobless? You wouldn't be able to stay with me for ever.' I thought I needed to get that in quickly even if it did sound brutal.

He gave me a smile that had many layers to it. 'Cheers, Jonty. I'm happy you came here.' He made a move towards the exit but I stopped him.

'We need to wait a few minutes. Can't go tailing my school-kids through the streets to the station. And we need to get the train that leaves after theirs does.' I looked around me. 'Is there a bar we could go to?'

Maxwell frowned and for an instant reminded me of Theo.

'There's a pub opposite the stage door. I suppose we could go there.'

I said, 'Could we get out that way?'

Maxwell said, 'We could try it.'

So we walked back into the stalls, now deserted except for usherettes checking brusquely for left-behind items, and Maxwell led me towards the pass door. He had to ask someone for the code to get through it, but then was given it without hesitation, slightly to my surprise. But then he had that kind of face, Maxwell.

I was briefly passing through a realm I'd never before visited. I had time only to look about me quickly, at very large and very small spaces, tall stacks of flattage, and corridors that led to places from which came quiet, broken fragments of the conversations of stage managers and actors. Then we were out in the street, with Maxwell pointing to the pub opposite.

'He's putting the rents up,' Maxwell told me when we'd each got a pint glass in our hands and were standing in the crowded bar with them. 'He wants us out so he can convert the house and do something else with it.'

'He can't do that,' I said. 'You must have an assured tenancy agreement?'

Maxwell shook his head. 'No such luck. It's all cash in hand and no paperwork. It's made it cheaper.'

I sighed. 'Not in the long term it hasn't. And what about the airport job?'

Maxwell winced. 'I was a bit too generous with the customers.' I had no idea what he meant by that. I decided I didn't want to be enlightened. I was annoyed with him for barging back into my life like this but at the same time I wanted desperately to hug him. Unfortunately we weren't in Del's but a city centre pub and this was Glasgow so I couldn't.

We drank up our pints, not saying much but looking searchingly at each other. Eventually I said, 'I reckon the coast's clear now at the station. We can get going.' I saw Maxwell's hand and thoughts move instinctively towards his wallet. 'It's OK,' I said. 'I'll get your ticket.' Then my phone pinged in my pocket. I took it out. It was a late-night message from Theo.

How was the play? As they asked Mrs Lincoln. There were times when Theo could be a bit too clever for his own good. *Very well done,* I messaged back. *On way home now. Message when back.* Maxwell and I were now out in the street. Maxwell looked at me with curiosity but wasn't going to ask.

'I should tell you I'm sort of seeing someone,' I said. 'Spanish guy. My age. Lives in Tenerife. On Tenerife.'

'How can you be seeing someone who lives in Tenerife? It must be a thousand miles away.'

'Two thousand actually. But yes.'

'Be like me having a boyfriend in Nigeria.'

'To within a hundred miles or so, I'd guess,' I said. 'I take the point. But life makes its plans for you without thinking what's convenient.'

Maxwell said, 'I suppose you can still sleep with me tonight.'

Theo and I hadn't got as far as this. No promises of mutual fidelity had escaped our lips. I took a leap of faith. Not just in Theo but in myself. 'No, I can't. Sorry but I'm on a promise.' Though a promise to myself only. And made in just the last two seconds. 'There's a nice comfy bed on the mezzanine.'

'What's that when it's at home?'

'You'll enjoy it when you get there,' I said. 'I promise.'

He kissed me as we sat next to each other on the train. In Glasgow nobody had ever done that. Or not to me at any rate. The train was quite crowded and it was late at night. But there were no jeers or other unpleasantness. Everyone pretended not to notice although it was quite clear that they all did. Perhaps Maxwell and I had blown their fuses. They were not only having to deal with two men kissing in public but with the fact that one of us was black. There were not that many black guys in Glasgow. Two examples of otherness in the same train compartment: it was proving difficult for our fellow passengers to deal with. The population's prejudices hadn't been fine-tuned for this. Our kiss might have been greeted with a lack of violence and with silence. But it was by no means an approving silence or a condoning lack of violence.

Of course Maxwell was impressed by the place I lived in. Even the outside of it. It was of a similar size and shape to the White Tower at the Tower of London, though happily with more and bigger windows. Inside was a great atrium with a glass roof to it, such as you'd see in a prison. Galleries ran round it – four floors of them – and all the individual flats led off the galleries. Although it was pitch dark outside Maxwell hurried towards the big windows and peered out of one of them. 'Fuckin' amazing,' was his reaction.

He hadn't paused to remove his backpack or his coat. It was only now that I was viewing him from behind that I realised the backpack was a very small one. 'What about all your stuff?' I asked him. 'What's happened to it?'

He turned to face me. 'Gotta go back for it in the morning. I could do with a van really.'

I felt like someone who's fallen through a trapdoor that they themselves have opened. 'Yeah,' I said, 'but you can't bring it all here. I said I'd put you up for the night. You'll have to sort out something more permanent...'

For answer Maxwell walked towards me and slowly wrapped his arms around me. Then he equally slowly kissed me, and I kissed him back of course, and I enjoyed it. Couldn't not do.

I pulled my lips away from his just enough to be able to say, 'We'll talk about it in the morning.' Luckily the next day was Saturday. There'd be time to do that. 'Have you eaten?'

Of course he hadn't. I made some toast and opened a tin of sardines. Maxwell opened his backpack and surprisingly pulled two beer cans out of it. He gave me one of them. The gesture reminded me achingly of Theo.

ELEVEN

I didn't have a van. But I owned a car. My Ford Fiesta, mostly used for the short daily trip to school and my weekend supermarket run, was parked in the cavernous residents' garage below my block of flats. The Fiesta was pressed into service that next morning to fetch Maxwell's things from Govan. We did it all in one trip, filling the boot brimful, and stacking the back seat and the back foot-wells so high as to reach the roof and make a view from the rear window impossible. I relied on the wing mirrors for the drive back from Govan. It was a place I'd never driven right into before but Maxwell was able to guide me through the final intimate bits.

'For one week,' I said. 'It can't be longer.' He wasn't so insensitive as to ask the reason for the time limit so I kindly supplied it. 'Theo wouldn't like it.' Theo whom I hadn't told that Maxwell was moving in with me in the first place. I was thankful that we weren't Skyping each other. I had a vision of trying to talk to Theo with Maxwell tripping over the wiring of his sound system, now sprawling lethally across my living space, in the background.

In the evening I took him to The Bull in Paisley's New Street. I thought it would be reasonably anonymous. Harry and I had gone there sometimes, but I hadn't been in on my own since we'd parted. It was a cosy place of snugs and crannies, with dark oak panelling and beams in the walls. It was more like an English pub actually than like most of the ones we had in Scotland, and perhaps that was one of the reasons Harry had liked it. Maxwell had told me he didn't know it. I looked around us as we came in from the late spring light to the relative darkness. There was nobody in the crowded place whom I recognized. I was glad in a way. It meant I wouldn't have to explain Maxwell. But it was also a slight disappointment. I was high on my companion's good looks and mildly exotic appearance; I would have liked to show him off to somebody.

He looked round the pub's welcoming interior and nodded approvingly. As I handed him his pint of Belhaven he said, 'I should be buying you this. After all your help today.'

'When you grow rich,' I said. 'Don't worry about it.' I wondered if Nigerian children sang Oranges and Lemons.

In a way the pint I'd bought him was a thank-you to him for going to bed so meekly on the mezzanine last night. I didn't know if I'd have withstood a determined onslaught on my resolve to be faithful to Theo. It helped that I had to write my nightly message to Tenerife before I went to bed and that Maxwell saw me doing it. I thought there was probably nothing quite so effective in cooling the ardour of two people than one of them phoning or messaging a third party at bedtime. Even so, I hadn't mentioned Maxwell in what I wrote.

We found a snug corner and sat in it, at right angles to each other, around a table. Our knees could touch if they wanted to and sometimes we let them. Maxwell asked suddenly, 'Have you had much sex since I last saw you?'

I laughed. 'Quite a bit. But out on Tenerife. And only with Theo.'

Maxwell stared into his beer glass. He was using two hands to keep it anchored to the table, as if it might struggle free like a captive animal or bird. 'Not much luck my end.'

'Mmm?'

'Only quick stand-up stuff if you get me. I've only actually been to bed with one bloke since our last time.'

'Our only time,' I corrected primly.

'He was nice enough looking,' Maxwell told me. 'But he was a very devout Muslim. We went to his place. Got undressed… Then he said he had to pray before we got started. It was that time of day or something. That put a bit of a damper on it. In the end he said he found he couldn't. Couldn't talk to God, I mean, when he was sexually excited. Naked with a ramrod hard-on.'

'I can imagine.'

'He said he'd have to say his prayers later. So we got on with it. Even so he made me rinse my mouth with mouthwash. Said he didn't want the smell of alcohol.'

That was something I hadn't thought of. I'd never been to bed with a devout Muslim. 'I guess … like passive smoking.'

'Guys always go for us lot. They're curious about our cocks. They expect us to have big ones. It's such a cliché.'

'But no more than the truth in your case.' This became one of the moments when my knee decided to rub itself against Maxwell's.

He took a swig from his beer glass then put it back in its arm-lock on the table. He looked at me and grinned. 'So tell me about the guy you used to live with. What did you say his name was?'

'Harry.' I must have spoken his name twenty times today. Almost as many times as I'd mentioned Theo. But how to answer Maxwell? Tell him that in my late twenties, at the age that Maxwell was now, I'd put all my emotional and existential needs into one basket, a basket called Harry, and that Harry had done the same with me? That four years along we'd carelessly let the baskets drop and seen their contents dashed before our eyes?

I'd been in relationships before. They hadn't involved the commitment of a joint mortgage, civil partnership or marriage. Not that Harry and I had gone down the marriage road ... though we had discussed it as a future 'maybe'. But we'd moved in together. Done more than that. We'd bought a flat together, with parental help. The flat, the very, very nice flat, that I'd helped Maxwell move his belongings into today.

Harry and I hadn't met on a park bench. We'd met in the hallway of another flat: one I'd been sharing just off Great Western Road in Glasgow. We were three lads and two girls. I was the only gay one. Then one of the guys was moving away. Groan. Who do we get to replace him? Do we have to advertise? But the soon-to-be leaver, anxious to please, said he had a friend who might be interested in taking his place. The friend was English, a civil engineer who had recently started a new job in Glasgow, and was the same age as all the rest of us. Late twenties. He was a pretty responsible sort of guy. Could he bring him round one evening to meet us?

In general it's Scottish guys who become top-notch engineers and then go off to work in England. But no cliché holds true all of the time and this instance was clearly an exception. It was pure chance that the evening he came round it was I who opened the door – five floors up, and there was no lift of course – to Harry.

He wasn't remotely out of breath. A lean, fit, dark-haired guy who'd come straight from work. He carried the knapsack in which he'd presumably packed his lunchtime sandwiches. His trousers were tucked into the top of his biggish work-boots, and he carried his building-site safety helmet. He was a knockout. 'Come in,' I said. My voice sounded as though I and not he had just climbed five flights of staircase. 'I'm Jonty. You're obviously Harry.'

Throughout the informal interview that followed I was on tenterhooks lest one of my flat-mates might take against him. But that didn't happen, and a week later Harry moved in with us.

I took my own looks and personality for granted. The face that presented itself to me in the mirror every morning was ordinary at best, I thought, and on hangover mornings a positive eyesore. I could never get to grips with the evidence, presented several times during my life, that it had a different impact on other people. Harry told me, some weeks later, that he'd been as knocked out by his first view of me in the hallway as I had by my first sight of him.

In a flat that was full of straight flat-mates neither Harry nor I paraded our sexual orientation boldly at first. It came out gradually, drip by drip, like juice exuding from an overripe peach.

At the end of his first week in the flat, early Friday morning, we coincided in the kitchen. I said, 'I was thinking of dropping by Del's this evening. Don't suppose you'd like to join me.' I kept my eyes glued on the cup of instant coffee I was stirring. I dared not look at him.

He could have said something camp and prickly like, 'Didn't think you'd know a place like Del's. Nice boy like you.' But he didn't. He said, 'I'd like that. Haven't yet plucked up the courage to go in there.' My eyes remained cast down towards my coffee but my spirits burst upward through the ceiling.

In Del's that night we had eyes for no-one but each other. We were back home before midnight. We went to bed together in Harry's room and had sex loudly, not giving a flying fuck what our flat-mates might think of us, or say to us in the morning.

They didn't say anything actually, but regarded us with fond and tolerant amusement. A few days later they were delivering their quiet congratulations. Eventually I moved all my stuff into Harry's room – it was bigger than mine by a small margin – and somebody new moved into mine. It was an economical adjustment as well as a cosy one.

A year later the development and construction company Harry worked for got hold of the old cotton mill building in Paisley, gutted it and turned it into flats. Workers for his company were offered very favourable purchase terms. Harry took me to look at the work in progress and at the wonderful views out over the countryside from the upper floors. I was as happy with the place as I was with Harry. I found myself concluding that we would be together for ever – a bizarre follow-on from falling in love with an apartment, but I guess not that rare – and we told our parents of our plans. Where would we have been without the Bank of Mum and (in Harry's case) Dad?

Didn't the Confucian saying go, 'If you want to be happy for a year, get married'? Harry and I hadn't got married. But we'd done what married couples do and bought a place to share. And we were happy for a year. For more than year.

I told Maxwell all this but I left the story there. He already knew that Harry and I weren't together now, and was bright enough to work out that if we had been he wouldn't be staying on the mezzanine. He'd probably heard as much of the When Harry Met Jonty story as he needed or wanted to hear. 'I've never really lived with anyone,' he said. 'Not seriously or for long. Never really belonged to someone.' He paused, then added, 'Though of course I'd like to.' As he said that I felt his knee brush lightly against mine. Later I took him for an Indian meal, and we had prawns.

I lay in bed nursing a troubled heart and mind. Maxwell wasn't exactly on the other side of the wall. There was a bathroom, a storage cupboard and the boiler room in between. But even that didn't make him all that far away. It was disturbing to have such a beautiful house-guest, lodger, flat-mate or whatever his relationship to me was, lying just a few feet away in the bed on the mezzanine above the kitchen. It seemed a waste of a beautiful cock, one whose details I could picture in my mind's eye and remember in the nerve endings of my skin. It was only too easy to imagine Maxwell pleasuring himself with it now: it was something I'd actually seen him do. It would all have been much easier if Maxwell hadn't wanted to sleep with me. But he did want to sleep with me: it was a fact that he'd made me repeatedly aware of in the hours before bedtime in various subtle, and some less subtle, ways. And it wasn't at all a one-way street. I would very much have liked to sleep with him.

I had a message to write to Theo. His evening one to me had explored the possibility that some English words might have come directly from Spanish. OK, they were Latinate words, and most Latinate words in English had arrived either through French – in the period of the Norman Conquest and the Angevin Empire – or later on during the expansion of international scholarship and science at the time of the Renaissance and the Enlightenment. But Theo thought that some Spanish could have arrived in England without stopping off elsewhere in the way. He pointed to the similarity of the English word morsel to the Spanish *morcilla,* which meant black pudding or blood sausage. After all, we always used morsel in the context of food, and usually with the adjective tasty in front of it. Unlike the French, who used their word *morceau* to describe a small piece of pretty much anything, English speakers never said a morsel of paper or a morsel of soil. At least Theo thought we didn't. Was he right in that?

Theo suggested two possible direct routes for the transmission. There had been several marriages between

English kings and queens and Spanish royalty. The English court had seethed with Spaniards at several times in history. And then, as everyone knew, the Armada had got wrecked on the western coasts of Scotland, Ireland and the Cornish peninsula. (Which, as I knew, accounted for the unlikely presence in those parts of the British Isles of people who looked remarkably like Theo.)

Before replying to Theo's interesting thesis I did what he hadn't done and looked up the word morsel on the internet. There I found the following, quoted from Webster's 1913 (and therefore out-of-copyright) dictionary:-

From French *morceau*, from Old French, *morsel,* from Medieval Latin *morsellum* ("a bit, a little piece"), diminutive of Latin *morsum* ("a bit"), neuter of *morsus,* past participle of *mordeo, mordere* ("bite, nibble, gnaw"), from Proto-Indo-European *merə* ("to rub, wipe; to pack, rob").

I loved the interconnectedness of all this, but there was a disappointing lack of any reference to Spanish black puddings. At least the link to food was there. Bite, nibble and gnaw. That was what you did with black pudding after all.

I copied and pasted the wet-blanket information into my reply to Theo. I added that, just because *morcilla* hadn't been mentioned by Webster, Theo wasn't necessarily wrong about it. I hoped that would cheer him up a bit.

It had been unusual for Maxwell to have a Saturday night off from the theatre. But there is always a reason for an exception to a rule. In this case the reason was that he had to work the following day, Sunday, instead. I thought this was just as well. His absence from my life, even for a period as short as eight hours, would give me a moment to breathe. I drove over to my mother's house near Stirling for the day. Most people who have juggled the experience of a complicated love or sex life with the immoveable existence of a mother would know that amounted to exchanging the frying pan for the fire.

'How was Tenerife?' mum asked me almost as soon as I arrived. Despite the fact that we'd had several conversations on the phone in the fortnight since my return. But I knew what she was getting at. I had never mentioned Theo to her and somehow that was an omission she seemed to be aware of.

'Good. I told you.' But her face told me she needed to know more. Before I'd gone to Tenerife the second time she'd scored a bulls-eye by asking if I had anyone out there. I said, 'I've sort of met somebody out there,' but found I wasn't looking her in the eye.

'A British ex-pat?' she asked. I could read her mind; after all, I'd known her for over thirty years. She was thinking: second home; expensive villa on the cliffs somewhere; wealthy contacts and friends.

'No,' I said deadpan. 'He's a local boy. Teaches in a local school. He lost his home when he split up with his boyfriend. Has a small room in a flat with some kind friends. He doesn't have a pot to piss in actually.'

'Jonty,' my mother protested at my coarse directness, 'please!' She shook her head fractionally. 'I still can't think why you didn't hold on to Harry. Somebody with charm, good looks, and a bit of money to his name.' She gave me one of her looks before I could answer, then said, 'No. Don't come out with "Money isn't everything". You know exactly what I mean.' And of course I did. I was her son.

She had cooked a small joint of topside, with Yorkshire pudding, roast potatoes and – just coming into the shops – new broad beans. She always gave me a good meal when I went to see her, even if it meant her having to live on leftovers for the rest of her solitary week. I sometimes wished unselfishly that she might find someone to fall in love with and so marry again. Then selfishly hoped she wouldn't.

Her own thoughts were evidently similarly preoccupied. When we were washing up together she came out with them. 'I still wish you had stayed the course with Harry. He was good for you.'

'I know. But it didn't work out that way.' After a pause, 'We were both selfish, I suppose.' That was as close as I could get to admitting to my mother that we'd both had affairs.

'You're supposed to stay the course with someone if you've committed yourself to them. Like dad and I did. I had to go out on a limb for you. To stand by you proudly when you and Harry got your flat together. I still had friends who disapproved.'

'Catholic friends...'

'And Catholic family too.'

I wasn't going to say I didn't see myself as sheltering under that particular umbrella; it was a tricky subject between us. My mother hadn't been a regular attender at church since about the time I left university a dozen years ago; but that hadn't stopped her from invoking the Church's support for her moral high ground stances when arguing about things with me. She decided to do so now. 'We're supposed to set an example in things like marital fidelity. Even these days. If Catholics can't do that then I don't know who can. Before you know it we'll be leaving it to the Muslims to teach us right and wrong.'

'Oh dear,' I said, then giggled suddenly as I remembered Maxwell's story about the Muslim lad he'd gone to bed with wanting to say his prayers before getting started.

'There's no need to snigger,' said my mother patiently.

'I wasn't,' I said, like a child. 'Well, not at that, anyway. I was remembering something someone said to me. A young Nigerian guy who's come to stay till he sorts himself out.' I added, 'He's staying on the mezzanine.'

My mother turned to me with the pained expression I remembered from my early infancy: the one she turned on me when I'd done something wrong in her eyes. 'Jonty. You've finished with Harry, who was supposed to be The One for you. You're half-seeing someone in the Canary Islands. And now you've got someone else living with you. You're not an experimenting teenager any more. You're thirty-four. Don't you think it's time you took the big things of life a bit more seriously?'

'I do take them seriously,' I pleaded. 'Only life's always more complicated than we think it's going to be.'

My mother turned away and started plonking the wiped-dry cutlery into drawers. 'Where did you meet him anyway?'

'Who?'

'The Nigerian.'

'In a bar in Glasgow,' I said. At least that was true.

My mother sighed. 'Do you want the rest of the joint to take back with you when you go? There's too much for me on my own.' Half under her breath she finished, 'Now it looks like there's two of you to feed.'

I thanked her for the offer of the cold beef and accepted it. Mothers need you to say yes to their endless stream of small presents. But heavens knew what she was going to live on during the coming days. Mind you, she did have a job still. Office work at the local hospital, until she retired in a few months' time. Perhaps she'd eat in the canteen.

TWELVE

I turned some of my mother's cold roast beef into a
sandwich for Maxwell when he came home at midnight.
He said he'd eaten but he sounded as though he hadn't.
And he watched me making the sandwich, and then ate
it, like someone who hadn't. 'Next week,' I told him,
'you're spending your free time looking for a more
permanent place to live. A room on your own in a flat-
share,' I suggested. Thinking of my own experience.
'And find a full-time job.' I'd already established that
his work at the theatre was only part-time, evening work.
He'd had a full-time post at the airport. He'd need a
proper job when he started having to fork out for rent
again. Needless to say, I wasn't charging him anything
for his tenancy of my mezzanine.

'I hope we can sleep together one time before I move
out,' he said, looking sideways at me as he munched his
sandwich. I thought that was a truly masterly piece of
blackmail. Heads he stayed with me, tails he had sex
with me. My trouble was that both possibilities were
equally alluring and, in reality, not mutually exclusive.

'You'll need a key for tomorrow,' I told him, pointedly
ignoring his cunning bit of knavery. 'You won't be
awake when I leave for work and you'll probably have
gone to work yourself by the time I'm home again.' I
went off to my bedroom to find him a spare set and was
rather relieved that he didn't get up and follow me in
there. I returned and dangled the keys in front of his nose
like a bunch of carrots in front of a donkey. 'You've got
to promise you won't trash the place. And I don't want
you bringing back any randoms in my absence. If you
want to bring someone back you'll have to introduce me
first.'

He looked at me with eyes the size of saucers. 'Why would I want to bring anyone back with me?' he asked.

'You might want to have sex with them,' I said baldly.

'So might you.' He guffawed lewdly.

'I happen to be on a promise, if you remember. Anyway, I'm putting you on your honour.' What honour? I wondered. Boy scout's? Officer and gentleman's. 'On your honour as a fellow Catholic,' I came up with. It seemed I'd picked up some unconscious lessons from my mother. At any rate we shook hands on it.

'Bit worrying about Brexit, isn't it, sir?' That was Chris, catching me on the way into his English class the next morning.

'You mean the opinion polls south of the border?'

Most of Scotland was firmly united in wanting to remain in the European Union. That included Unionists as well as Separatists. Chris wasn't making insolent assumptions about my politics in guessing that I shared his own opposition to Brexit.

'It's a protest,' I said. 'It happens with the polls before every election.' I remembered what Theo had said and quoted him without acknowledgement. 'It's like threatening to run away from home when you're a child. When the time comes you think differently about it. The English will think differently once they get inside the voting booths.'

'Hope so,' said Chris. Then, 'Did everything sort itself out all right on Friday night, sir?'

'What are you talking about?' I was genuinely puzzled.

'When you couldn't come back on the train with us. Miss McCleesh said you'd had some news from home that you needed to deal with. I just hoped it all worked out, sir.'

'It did,' I said. 'It wasn't anything major, but it just had to be sorted. Thank you for asking.' I made a move to enter the classroom but Chris stopped me.

'Did it have anything to do with that young barman?'

I was within a split whisker of saying 'What young barman?' but miraculously managed not to. I said, 'You could say that.'

Chris looked down and said, 'Sorry. I was being nosey.' I realised that for the first time we were talking not as teacher and pupil but as two adults.

'It's OK. But I don't bring my private life to school with me. I'm sure you can understand that. It's not professional. It's just that sometimes things trip you up.'

'I understand, sir,' Chris said, and I could see that he did.

'Then perhaps you can treat this conversation as private?'

'Of course, sir. Obviously.' Chris turned away from me and went bouncing through the door into the classroom where the others were already gathered. I followed him in. A moment later we were facing each other, Chris and his peers expectant around the big table, I primed and ready to deliver what I hoped might be interesting insights into English literature. My eyes met Chris's and I saw that I was looking into the eyes of someone who had grown up suddenly and carried new responsibilities upon his shoulders. I was looking into the eyes of someone with whom I shared a secret.

I told Maxwell about the incident much later that day. He came back from work, or from whatever he'd been doing after work, around midnight. I was just coming out of the bathroom, naked as it happened, on my way to bed. I reached for a towel and quickly tied it round me. 'Have a beer before bed?' Maxwell asked me, simultaneously shucking off his backpack and diving into it.

'No thanks. But I'll sit with you for five minutes while you do,' I took the opportunity to tell him about the Chris conversation then.

'It's hardly a big deal,' said Maxwell dismissively. 'There's no law against hobnobbing with theatre barmen.'

'That's hardly the point,' I said. 'Although technically I did break the law in letting my colleague take the kids back on her own without a second responsible adult. They're very strict on that these days. But it's not that. It's the gossip thing. You must remember from when you were at school. Kids love nothing better than to find out something about their teachers that they can gossip about, spread around the classroom. You might not know that teachers make great efforts not to give the kids any cause for gossip.'

'I still don't see...'

'I don't tell the people I teach that I'm a gay man. Straight teachers don't talk to the kids about their girlfriends. If they're married they say so and that tends to be the end of the conversation. But if they're not their lives are considered fair game, and if there's any hint that they might have unusual interests – that includes being gay – then the rumour machine goes into overdrive.'

'Yeah, I suppose you're right,' said Maxwell. He gulped from his beer can. 'Looking back... Yeah, I remember all that.' He gave me a conciliatory smile and I thought at that moment that he looked gorgeous. I only just managed to stop myself from saying so.

A few minutes later I got up, saying I was off to bed. Maxwell smiled up at me and wished me a courteous goodnight, but he didn't get up to embrace me or give any other sign that he would have liked to accompany me. It had been past midnight when Maxwell had come in, and the theatre bar had been closed a good hour and a half before that. I made a lazy guess that he'd enjoyed someone else's brief company at some point in the interim. Perhaps in what he'd have termed a 'stand-up job'. In a toilet or a dark alley. Well, why not? He'd wanted to come to bed with me the previous nights he'd been with me and I hadn't let him. I could hardly object if he transferred his sexual interest to someone else. It wouldn't have been reasonable to feel jealous. And yet I did feel jealous. Insanely jealous.

Theo's next message was mostly about the decline of the English adverb.

You Brits just keep copying the Americans, he complained. *These days I'm always reading 'Go direct' instead of 'Go directly.' 'It's been spelt wrong' instead of 'It's been spelt wrongly.' 'Real good,' for 'Really good'...* Theo went on at quite some length, offering a lively selection of examples.

I wrote back. I had to agree with him. I too was in mourning for the loss of the English adverb. *You're right. It does come from America, like so many things, good, bad and indifferent. I put it down to the immigration into America of German-speaking intellectuals during the nineteenth and twentieth centuries.* Many of these highly educated and highly qualified people were of course Jewish. But I didn't put that into my reply. I didn't want Theo to have the smallest grounds for thinking I might be the kind of person who would blame the Jews for the state of things. *Because the German language doesn't observe the difference between adjectives and adverbs – they sound the same and they look the same on paper – it was only natural that these immigrants should apply that to their adopted language too. And because they were among the top communicators of their generations they were copied by the rest of the American nations. And now, of course, by us British...*

On the other hand, I went on, *those same people were pretty fussy about the use of the subjunctive. And that stuck too, especially in America. While we're quite happy to write 'It's essential that the door is shut' even in quite a formal context the Americans will always go for 'It's essential that the door be shut'. Just as – I guess – you'd use the subjunctive in Spanish.*

I was guessing, of course. I'd tried to make myself improve my Spanish following my return from Tenerife, but then term had started, and Maxwell had turned up, and I hadn't got very far with it. I certainly hadn't got anywhere near the subjunctive.

I was enjoying batting ideas about the English language back and forth with Theo. I could imagine us in middle age – years down the line – as two pedants of the kind who write to the newspapers about declines in standards of grammar and pronunciation at the BBC and other places. At moments there seemed an appealing cosiness about the idea. But at other times it could seem decidedly unattractive. It was certainly a world away from the thrill of a midnight park bench pick-up, and from the rapture of those few nights we'd spent in bed together.

Chris button-holed me as I was leaving the school to go home a couple of days later. He was out on the pavement in front of the gates, one of a small knot of classmates. 'Mr Allen. Sir. Have you seen what's on Twitter?'

'No, I have not,' I said. For a terrified half-second I thought there might have been something about Maxwell and me. But the look on Chris's face and his school-mates' faces told me that wasn't the case. They looked genuinely upset by something. Back in control again I said, 'And I hope you weren't on it during any of your classes.'

He took no notice of my mild censure. 'Jo Cox has been assassinated.'

'Who's Jo Cox?' I asked him.

He looked at me as if I'd confessed to not having heard of David Cameron or Elvis Presley. 'She's a Labour member of parliament south of the border,' he explained with indulgent patience. 'Supporter of the Remain campaign. She was killed in the street by someone who was pro-Brexit.'

'How awful,' I said. That's usually the best we can do when informed of the violent death of someone we've never heard of.

It seemed that everybody knew more about Jo Cox than I did. Even Theo, whose message that evening told me how sorry he was. Evidently I had not been spending too much time on Google – as I had imagined, and as Theo had complained – but too little. Maxwell, when he came home around midnight, couldn't stop talking about the awful occurrence. 'It won't do the Brexit cause any favours,' he said. Though when we went our separate ways to bed a little later he changed the subject. 'Got the evening off tomorrow. Thought I might head out to Del's. Want to come with me?'

'I might,' I said. 'Have you made any headway with finding somewhere to live?'

In the morning the Jo Cox murder was the talk of the school, among teachers and pupils alike. Thankfully nobody on the pro-Brexit side had come forward and said the murder was a good thing. There was a touching coming-together of all sides, pro and contra Brexit, and from across the political spectrum, to condemn the barbaric or lunatic act, and campaigning, with the referendum less than a week away, was temporarily suspended as a symbol of respect and solidarity.

'She was ever so good,' Chris told me on the way in to class. 'One of the few politicians who gets the species a good name.' Chris was evidently among the huge majority of people who knew more about Jo Cox than I did. 'It's having a massive impact on the opinion polls south of the border. They're coming back to the Remain idea.'

'That's not a very sportsmanlike way to look at it,' I said. I was actually feeling quite guilty about the fact that opinion had shifted back again to where I wanted it to be – given the cause of the shift. But I said, 'Don't worry. It's shifting back anyway. You'll see when the results are in next week. The Brexiteers are all noise. They'll collapse in the privacy of the voting booths. South of the border as well as with us.'

Unexpectedly I got a message from Nat, still enjoying his month in the sun. It began in the Spanish way but then relapsed reassuringly into Canadian.

Hola. Que tal? How you doing? Are you still in touch with Theo? I saw him last evening. He walked past the entrance of City Bar, heading in the direction of your old hotel. He glanced towards the entrance but only for a second. I waved but he didn't see me. He was in sunshine, me in the dark interior. Perhaps better that he didn't spot me. I'm still seeing his sister a bit and not sure if he knows this. Don't know if you told him.

Still nice weather out here. How's Glasgow?

Take care

Nat

So sorry about Jo Cox

That shook me up a bit. Clearly Nat's main aim had been to check whether I'd told Theo about himself and Marina. He'd want to know how to play it if the next time Theo walked by City Bar he didn't go straight past but came on in. But what was Theo doing in that neck of the woods? He might have been going in the direction of the hotel where he'd clandestinely shared my bedroom night after night, but that direction also led on towards the waste ground where I'd first discovered, and then re-discovered, Theo sitting on a bench in the darkness. Nat wouldn't have known that.

So was Theo routinely haunting that old cruising ground and hooking up with men there? I was hardly in a position to cast stones: I who was, unbeknown to Theo, sharing my flat with Maxwell.

Then there was the business of Marina. Whatever Theo might think of her seeing a Canadian – seeing him a bit, as Nat had put it; though how could you 'see someone a bit'? – he'd be pretty pissed off if or when he discovered that I'd known all about it for weeks and not told him.

It wasn't at all clear to me whether Maxwell and I were going to Del's together in the spirit of two friends companionably on the pull and who would each go home with a different stranger at the end of the evening, or like an established couple, to see and be seen together and to get high on the buzz of it all. I've written *in the spirit of* and *like*, because there was no question of our actually belonging in the second category, or of me belonging in the first. Maxwell was welcome to pull some youngster and go off with him – he could even bring him back to my place provided I'd vetted him thoroughly first and approved – but I would not be following suit. It wasn't simply that I still wanted to be faithful to Theo, or at least to the idea of Theo: I simply wasn't in the mood for anything else. Even if, as I'd inferred from Nat's message, Theo had gone back to the cruising-ground bench. Though it was only an inference, from the throwaway fag-end of a remark that was really about something else.

All such nuanced, finely-tuned thoughts went out of my head the moment we walked in through the rainbow-flagged door in Virginia Street. For the first thing I saw in front of me was the back views of two very young lads, presented to me as they leaned over the bar deciding what they would have to drink. They belonged to Chris and another boy from the school, whom I had taught when he was younger but no longer did.

Oblivious, Maxwell made his way to the bar – in my eyes he seemed to sprint there – and called back over his shoulder, 'Jonty, what do you want?'

There was no shortage in Glasgow of men called Jonty, but Chris seemed to have a clairvoyant's perception of which one was being addressed. While his companion, whose name was Jimmy, glanced towards Maxwell, Chris swung right round towards me, ignoring Maxwell, and gazed full into my face.

Chris was a slender willowy eighteen-year-old, about the same height that I was, though threatening to overtake me in that respect some time quite soon. His face was on the small side but strong-jawed. His hair was thick, wavy and dark. His eyes were an attractive blue: open and frank. They were usually quite wide and round. But I'd never seen them quite as wide and round as this. I read his shock in them, but also a kind of fascination with the sudden turn things had taken. And the thought, easy to discern there, that he had no idea what he was going to say. That thought was easy to discern because it chimed with my own at that moment and that was probably equally legible in the expression on my own face.

I found my tongue first. After all, I was the adult. I decided in a nano-second that I must treat Chris and his companion like two friends I knew from another context.

'Hallo, Chris,' I said, doing my best with a smile that was being a bit reluctant to break out, 'I haven't seen you in here before.' I nodded towards his companion. 'Nice to see you, Jimmy.' I turned towards my own companion. 'This is Maxwell.' I'd given names. Provenance could sort itself out. Then I did what everyone in this situation has to. 'I'll get them, Maxwell. What are you lads having to drink?'

THIRTEEN

Chris shifted his attention from me to Maxwell. It was probably less uncomfortable for him. 'You work at the theatre,' he told him, as if he might not yet know that.

It sounded like Maxwell could be an actor or a director or something, and his answering smile reflected that. 'I work in the bar,' he said.

Chris said, 'Saw you the other night.'

Jimmy hadn't been on that theatre trip. I'd taught him English for a year a little while back, but then he'd gone on to do his Highers in maths and sciences, I thought. Except for an occasional fleeting hallo in a corridor our paths didn't cross. Now he turned to me suddenly and said, 'Is he your boyfriend?'

I looked at Maxwell as a kind of reflex. Before I could get my *No, we're just good friends* out Maxwell looked back at me and spoke. 'Well, am I?' he said.

'Sometimes,' I heard myself say weakly.

Nobody wanted to be difficult when it came to drinks. We got a pint of lager each and I forked out.

'It's our first time here,' Chris told me chattily. It seemed he'd fully recovered himself. 'Are you... I mean, are you often here?'

'From time to time.' I was relaxing too now. I had quickly realised, and I saw that Chris had too, that we were all equally compromised. That meant that if we were all clever enough we could all be equally safe. *If* we were all clever enough...

I heard Maxwell ask Jimmy, 'So do you go to school with Jonty, then?' Though technically correct this was an unusual way of putting it.

The eighteen-year-olds had well-developed social skills, I was pleased to notice. After a minute more of chatting with Maxwell and me about nothing very much they withdrew politely, not too abruptly, with reiterated thanks for the drinks, and disappeared into the crowd around us.

'You handled that well,' said Maxwell. 'Mr Cool, I said to myself. It could have been difficult but you sorted it.'

'With your help,' I said. Though I wasn't sure what he'd actually done to help. Just been himself, I supposed. Just been black and beautiful and charming. And reassuringly exotic. There weren't any other black faces around the place tonight.

The last time I'd been in here with Maxwell I'd straddled his thigh in a corner and we'd got each other's cocks out and played with them. There was no question of our doing that tonight. Whether or not I was still on an unspoken promise to Theo, Chris and Jimmy were still somewhere about the place and there were limits to what you could do in the context of a gentlemanly truce. My mind boggled at the thought of Maxwell and me groping each other publicly and Chris or Jimmy catching us at it.

Then I realised that Chris and Jimmy would be having the same thought. They might or might not want to misbehave in this anonymous public space but the option wouldn't even be available to them while Maxwell and I remained on the premises. We spent a few minutes aimlessly watching the people around us and passing admiring or derogatory private comments; then Maxwell said, 'Not quite sure what we're doing here. Wouldn't we be better off at home in bed?'

And there, an hour and a quarter later, a knee-pressed-against-knee train journey later, was where we ended up.

Theo's next message announced, *It's time we upgraded your Spanish a bit, don't you think? I'll be writing a few things to you in Spanish from now on. You*

can, of course, reply in whichever language you prefer.
Theo was nothing if not a teacher. I replied that I was
fine with that but he wasn't to expect too much from my
pathetic Spanish. In the meantime (of course I didn't tell
Theo this) I had my hands quite full with Maxwell.

Once we'd spent half an hour beneath my duvet it
seemed absurd that we hadn't done this earlier in the
week. And when we woke up together in the morning,
our nerve-endings alive with the memory of a hundred
half conscious caresses and gentlenesses in the night, I
had no reason to change my mind. Maxwell had very
sweetly said he wanted me to fuck him this time round,
had lain submissively on his back and smiled up at me
while I did so in a semi-trance of awe and alcohol. (We
hadn't tumbled straight into bed on our return. There had
been a half-full bottle of whisky in a kitchen cupboard,
and now there wasn't.) In the small hours Maxwell, after
a moment's groping for the packet of rubbers atop my
bedside locker, had returned the compliment.

The question now was how the weekend would play
itself out. OK. a one-night's stand had returned for an
encore. That wasn't new in my experience. But it had
involved the person with whom I was, at least
temporarily, sharing my living space. I had only one
previous experience of that.

Four years ago. Harry and I had had to get up for work
the morning after we'd first slept together in the flat
we'd found ourselves sharing. There hadn't been time
for much more than a grunted See you later. And in the
course of that day I was too occupied, perhaps just as
well, with the demands made on me by the job of facing
class after class of pupils, to have much time for
introspective analysis of what had happened and how I
felt about it. In the evening Harry and I were the first
two to return to the flat – the teacher and the building-
site engineer – and we were rather pleased about that.

We made ourselves mugs of tea and, without saying much except with arms and hands and lips, took them back upstairs to bed. Later, so as not to have to spend too much of the evening crossing paths with other flat-mates we went out to a Chinese restaurant to eat. And by the time we'd returned from there, well, it was pretty much time to go back to bed. With Maxwell it would be a bit different. It was Saturday morning now and we had the whole weekend ahead of us.

I made us a brunch of *huevos rancheros,* which is a Mexican version of scrambled eggs. The exact recipe varies from household to household but it normally involves tomatoes and red sweet peppers as well as eggs. Eggs are eggs and tomatoes are tomatoes, but the taste of them together in the same mouthful is something quite different and especially delicious, as everyone who has ever eaten a British breakfast well knows. It's because of something in the tomatoes that, in combination with other things, creates the flavour the Japanese prize highly and call *umami.* I had a vague idea that the something was actually naturally occurring monosodium glutamate.

At any rate the *huevos rancheros* were a pronounced success with Maxwell, who said they did something similar in Nigeria but he hadn't had it for ages. Then I told Maxwell we needed to get on with the task of finding him a more permanent place to live, and a more than part-time job. We would comb the internet and read the local press. Maxwell wasn't too excited by this prospect and I had to make a bit of an effort to jolly him into it. I felt like a parent who was planning to send his child to boarding school. It was a case of having to be cruel in order to be kind. But I knew I was being cruel in order to be kind to myself.

We looked at the internet and made notes, both as to local flats and to one or two maybe jobs. Then we went down to the public library and looked to see what was on offer there. It was a new experience for me. New since my days of looking for university vacation work at any rate. This wasn't the way that school teachers found jobs. It was while we were learning our way around this new information source that Maxwell informed me he wouldn't be coming back to my place tonight because he had a date. But he'd be back with me on Sunday night.

Apart from the surprise of simply hearing this I had mixed feelings about it. Maxwell hadn't actually been begging me to sleep with him during the previous week but his Labrador eyes had been doing that job on his behalf. Now we had spent a night together, and his body language told me he'd been as happy with the experience as I was, and as we'd both been on that first occasion months back. I wasn't exactly flattered to learn that he was going to spend the coming night with somebody else. On the other hand, wasn't I was actually in the throes of trying to move him out of my apartment and my life? I had no right to feel aggrieved that he'd taken the initiative in that, and was removing himself voluntarily from my private space at least for tonight. I should have been pleased and relieved by that. But I wasn't.

In the afternoon I supervised his drawing up of a short list of phone numbers and email addresses to contact. Then I told him to get on with the business of doing that. He was an adult; I wasn't responsible for him; I wasn't going to do all his work. I had other things to do. There was a long message from Theo to translate.

I could get help from online dictionaries if my phone and my laptop were in the same place. I also had a pocket Collins dictionary, Spanish-English, somewhere about the flat. I'd taken it on trips to Spain in the past. I rummaged around in a box of half-junked books and came up with the little red pocket volume. Now I had two sources of translations available. To make assurance double sure, as Macbeth says.

This first Spanish missive from Theo appeared at a first reading much as I imagined the world would look in the eyes of someone with quite advanced cataracts. I got the general drift of it, somehow, without knowing what half the words meant. I went through it again with the dictionaries; this was quite a time-consuming process, but eventually worth it. Little by little its focus sharpened up. Theo told me what he'd been doing that day (now yesterday: when the message had arrived, at nearly midnight, I'd had rather a lot on my plate). He went on at some length about the weather. He'd googled – taking a leaf out of my book? – the weather in Glasgow and couldn't help noticing the difference. He didn't envy me the current Scottish climate. Then he wrote, *Siento mucho que necesites un poco de calor. Te lo envio. ¿Lo acceptas?* Again I got the general drift but I had to use the dictionary in order to be sure I wasn't getting the wrong end of the stick about the sentiment behind it. At last I had a workable translation that seemed accurate. *I have a strong feeling that you need a bit of warmth. I'm sending it to you. Do you accept it?* Given that Theo had written that around half an hour before I'd got under the warm duvet with Maxwell I found myself a little uncomfortable with it.

Maxwell said he'd made as many phone calls as he could, and written enough emails, for one afternoon. He'd got some encouraging leads, both job-wise and on flat-shares, and would be pursuing them during the coming week. Meanwhile it was time he went off to work. Had I remembered he wouldn't be coming back tonight? I said it hadn't slipped my mind completely, and he said he'd see me, probably, some time late on Sunday night.

I wasn't too sorry in the end to find myself alone that Saturday evening and night. I wandered down to The Bull, chatted half-interestedly to various slight acquaintances there – people I'd lost touch with since Harry's departure – had something to eat and wondered what I'd write back to Theo. In the end I managed to cobble together something that gave an idea of what I'd been doing, without mentioning Maxwell, or that fact that I'd embarrassingly bumped into two of my pupils in a gay bar. I eventually typed it on my laptop while lying in luxurious isolation in my double bed.

Maxwell didn't come back on Sunday night. Nor did he phone or text to say where he was. In a way it didn't matter. He wasn't my boyfriend, and I was trying quite hard to engineer his disappearance from my life. But at another level I missed him. And in a more pragmatic spirit I couldn't help regretting the fact that he was roaming footloose around Glasgow with, in some pocket of his backpack, a set of keys to my apartment. I could have messaged him, obviously, but I found that my pride drew the line at that.

Monday morning brought one more care with it than it usually did. I would find myself teaching Chris. Confronting Chris. This had never been a source of anxiety before; he was an easy person to deal with. But after Friday night... The knowledge that he would be equally nervous in advance of meeting me again, if not more so, didn't make it any easier to think about.

I didn't cross paths with him before we met in class in the double period between mid-morning break and lunch. And when I entered the room he was already ensconced, among the others, at the big table around which we usually sat and worked. But no sniggers, titters or funny looks greeted my arrival, from which I deduced that Chris hadn't gone public with his new insight into my weekend social life. As the class progressed Chris's eyes met mine often, just as they always did in the normal course of things. But I could see that this morning he was trying to gauge from my face what thoughts were going on behind it. I tried to reassure him with occasional smiles, but finely-tuned ones: I was careful not to smile too much at him, or too collusively. By the end of the session he was visibly more relaxed and because of that I was.

After I left the room at the end of class I loitered deliberately in the corridor, walking slowly, allowing the group to overtake me and giving Chris a chance to catch me on my own if he wanted to. He did.

'That was nice seeing you the other night,' he said. He'd had some time to prepare this.

'It was nice seeing you too,' I said blandly.

Chris's face, which had been open and sunny during that exchange, suddenly tautened with worry. 'I don't know what to say now,' he muttered.

I took a small leap of imagination. 'You might want to ask me if I was going to tell the world exactly where we bumped into each other. In which case I'd tell you that of course I haven't and of course I won't. And then I might ask you to do me the same favour.' I stopped, and wondered what would happen next.

Chris's relief was immediate. I could see the tension leave his legs and shoulders, and his eyes glistened for a moment. 'Thank you,' he said. 'I won't tell anyone, I promise. Neither will Jimmy. We both know the stakes.'

It was my turn to feel the mini-stab of unshed tears. I saw Chris glance to either side for a nano-second to check there was no-one in hearing distance. Then he said, 'Jonty,' as if trying the name for the first time, and a flicker of a smile tweaked the corners of his mouth. I put a hand on his shoulder for an instant; I couldn't stop myself. 'Chris,' I said. Then he put his hand on my shoulder for an instant. It was a moment of wonder; it suddenly equalised us. We were two grown-ups now. Or two kids.

FOURTEEN

There was no sign of Maxwell on Monday night. But there was a long message in Spanish from Theo which I decoded with the help of the dictionaries. He wrote about the changes in the weather; about the progression from spring to summer, and how subtle this was, unlike in Britain. For the climate of the Canary Islands had been dubbed *eterna primavera* – eternal springtime – by no less a travel writer than Christopher Columbus. Set in the tempering environment of the Atlantic Ocean and a little way north of the Tropic of Cancer the islands enjoyed a seasonal pendulum swing that was gentle rather than extreme or abrupt. Theo wrote of singing blackbirds and the succession of the bright flowers. His style was almost poetic. I seemed to see a different side of him when he expressed himself in Spanish and was no longer the pedantic English teacher getting hot under the collar about the decline of the adverb or split infinitives. At the end of the message he wrote a short sentence that I had to look up. *Te echo de menos.* It turned out to be 'I miss you'. The Spanish words seemed more resonant somehow than the English.

I sent a reply of some sort, in English. It lacked any poetic quality. I did write 'I miss you,' though, and meant it. But the English words, as I typed them and looked at them, seemed to lack the power of *Te echo de menos.*

Maxwell reappeared without warning, almost startlingly, at eleven o'clock on Tuesday night. He didn't volunteer any information about where he'd been. I asked him if he'd made any progress on the job and accommodation fronts. He said, 'No, not yet.' He reached in his backpack and hauled out a can of beer for us each. We drank them. Then he came and slept with me in my bed.

Chris made a point of catching me and talking with me at some point every day now. Neither of us referred again to last Friday or to our Monday's moment of frankness. It was the referendum that preoccupied Chris during these days. At least, that's what he thought it was. 'It's all going against us, isn't it?' he said.

'Hold tight,' I said. Senior statesman that I was. 'It's just opinion polls. People striking a pose.'

'Yes, but south of the border…'

'The English won't let us down on the day,' I said. I was still trying to make up for my Perfidious Albion moment with Marina a few weeks back. 'Anyway, it's not as if you can't do something about it. You're eighteen. You've got your voting papers, I take it?'

'I applied too late,' said Chris with a downcast look on his face.

I had to laugh. 'What it is to be young.'

'I posted a load of stuff on Facebook…'

'Unfortunately that doesn't quite amount to a vote. Perhaps I'll have to try and register a vote for both of us.'

Chris's face brightened. 'Can you do that, Jonty?' He brought out the J-word with a certain self-consciousness. But it was the sweet innocence of the question itself that tugged at my heart.

'No,' I said. 'Sadly that was a joke.' I gave my watch a reflex glance. 'Better be getting along. Time we were both in class.' There was nobody to see us in the corner of the corridor in which our paths had crossed. I gave Chris's shoulder a man-to-man pat. The broad grin he gave me in response to that was worth ten return shoulder claps.

'When will you vote?' Maxwell asked me on the Thursday morning. We'd slept together again the previous night.

'On the way in,' I said. 'There's a handy primary school they've closed for the day just near where I work. You?' I thought for a moment. 'I suppose you do have a vote?'

'Of course,' he said. We'd discussed the referendum question from time to time – who hadn't during those days? – and I knew that Maxwell was as much of a European as I was. After all, he had an Italian stepfather. I just hadn't known whether, like Chris, he would be ineligible to express his opinion in the polling booth. 'I'll find a moment.' He stopped then and said, 'Oh shit. I'm on the voting list in Govan. I'll have to go over there and do it.'

A moment's weakness made me say, 'If you haven't done it by the time I'm back from work, and if you're here, I'll drive you there.'

Maxwell gave me one of his sweetest smiles but it turned to a frown a second later. 'Would I have time to get from there into the city centre in time for work?'

I couldn't back out now. I said, 'I'd wait for you to vote and drive you on into the centre. Drop you at the door. In Bath Street.'

'You are lovely,' he said, and gave me a smacking kiss.

I returned the kiss; there was just time for that. But I said, 'Though if you're not coming back here tonight, if you don't mind, I'd like my keys back.'

'Oh, I'll be back tonight,' he said. 'Don't worry.'

I had to go, if I was going to vote before I got to work. I said, 'See you later then,' and left the flat, with Maxwell, my spare keys in his pocket, in sole charge of the place.

There was an atmosphere during that day like you feel in the hours before a thunderstorm. It grew as the time passed like a build-up of static. The rush of sympathetic feeling, of solidarity, that had gushed in the hours and days after the murder of Jo Cox had ebbed away. The polls were grimly forecasting a renewed swing towards Brexit. 'It'll be all right,' I told Chris to cheer him up. And to have an excuse to say something to him, of course. These days I was feeling a need to see and talk to him often, and I knew that he felt something similar. But as for the referendum vote, by now I was whistling in the dark. I was no longer certain that it would 'be all right'. Ideas had been let loose in the last few days that would be difficult to put back in their boxes. One was the idea that it might be all right, in certain circumstances, to send our immigrant populations back to where they came from. Poles to Poland. Maxwell to Nigeria. And following on from that would come the idea that the likes of Chris and me, the likes of Theo and me, the likes of Maxwell and me, could also be exported. Back to where we came from. It had happened before, after all. Only two generations ago. Exported into eternal darkness. Via the death camps.

Were my thoughts running mad? Was I getting things out of proportion just a little perhaps? Seeing threats that didn't exist? I didn't think I was.

Startlingly, because the timing was so weird, I found a message on my phone from Nat. *Hola desde Canada. I'm back now. Still in touch with Marina. Don't know what will happen there. Didn't get to see Theo before I left. Guess the two of you still in touch. Hope your Brexit thing works out for the best. Best Nat.*

I sent back a brief thank-you, saying *keep in touch.* I finished: *re Brexit, watch this space.*

But that surprise was nothing compared to what I got from Theo in the lunch break. It took me a while to translate it because I didn't have my pocket dictionary with me, and kept having to switch screens to get an online translation source. Here is what I eventually made of it.

I dream of you almost each night. Do you dream of me, or is that just a wishful hope? Usually my dreams of you are beautiful. But last night I seemed to see you in bed with someone else. A beautiful black guy. But dreams are crazy things. They tell us things about ourselves that are difficult to understand even after we have dreamt them and pondered them. I hope you have voted – I am sure you will have done by this time – and that it all turns out all right. Then, again, 'I miss you.' *Te echo de menos.* Theo signed off with Spanish kisses and hugs.

I looked at my watch. I had just two minutes in which to compose myself before class.

I had high hopes of Maxwell's not being around when I got back to the flat after work. But there he was. And so I got the still warm car out again and drove him to Govan, following his directions through the back streets. I sat in the car and entertained gloomy thoughts while he was inside the polling station. Then I drove him through the rush-hour traffic into central Glasgow, realising he'd have got there quicker if I'd put him onto the Clockwork Orange and wishing I'd thought of that in the first place. I had a sense of everything in my life that I'd felt certain of falling suddenly apart. That included, of course, the person I'd thought I was.

Maxwell didn't come back that night. I wasn't too surprised by that. But the news came in throughout the small hours. It got grimmer and grimmer. In England only London and the university cities seemed to have voted in favour of remaining a part of the home continent. Wales was rapidly abandoning the ship... I struggled to get my head round this. Those parts of the

UK that benefitted most when it came to receiving shares of Europe's pooled wealth seemed to be the most ready to turn their back on it. What were the expressions? Biting off the hands that fed you? Cutting off your nose to spite your face? I thought ... but then I was biased ... it was only in Scotland that we were getting it right.

I couldn't stay up all night with the TV's endless reporting of the results. I went to bed eventually. And when I woke up in the morning no miracle had occurred. Despite Scotland's overwhelming desire to continue to be a part of the European Community, the Kingdom as a whole (I couldn't bring myself to think United Kingdom) had voted out. Not even Maxwell's vote had been enough to swing it. And he hadn't re-materialised in the night.

On the way to school I tried to think about what I would say to Chris. I'd been completely wrong in my mature judgement of how the vote would go and I would have to tell him that. It wasn't an admission that any teacher would want to have to make to a pupil of his.

In the event we got it over more easily than I'd expected, and perhaps more easily than he had. Chris said, with the confidence and knowingness of a much older person, 'There'll be another independence referendum after this. You see if there isn't. Nicola Sturgeon will never let London get away with this.'

I could imagine Chris's father having come out with this over whatever passed for breakfast in their household but I wasn't going to let him know that. I said, 'We'll see. Some very strange things happen in politics.' I hoped he'd find that a sufficiently adult response.

The day passed surreally, like the day that follows the death of someone you've loved. In the staff room and the canteen nobody knew what to say or how to behave. Some were boisterously angry and noisy, others subdued and quiet. I experienced the day as if it were a watershed, a defining, dividing, moment in my life. It seemed to draw a line, months after we'd parted, under the life I'd shared with Harry. That past was now not merely past but irretrievable. While the future was something I couldn't begin to guess about. I'd met someone wonderful on a fairytale island two thousand miles away. I'd started to fall for him and he for me. But distance begets distance. The weeks had passed and I'd accidentally got involved with Maxwell. Maxwell who lived with me, and slept with me sometimes, but then absented himself for days on end, spending his nights in places he didn't tell me about, with people he clearly didn't want me to know about.

Meanwhile Theo, if I'd interpreted Nat's message correctly, had gone back to haunting the cruising ground on the verdant outskirts of Puerto de la Cruz where we'd first met. I could comfort myself a little with the thought that I had done nothing since my return from Tenerife that Theo wasn't doing too. We wrote nice things to each other, and missed each other and said so, but clearly that was as far as Theo and I could go.

And now, to confuse my thoughts still further, I was beginning to find I had feelings for Chris. For someone I'd been teaching. That was always a scary place in which to find yourself. Chris was not a child, of course, but a man of eighteen who would be leaving school in less than a month's time. We would no longer be in a teacher-pupil relationship. Nevertheless I had a strong (and I thought healthy) feeling that the pursuit of any kind of close friendship with Chris, whether or not he was spoken for by his friend Jimmy, was not something into which I could or should plunge myself.

The day reeled groggily from morning through afternoon to end of school. I was glad when it was over and I could take my whirling thoughts home with me and sort them out in something like peace. Maxwell wasn't in when I got back to the flat and not for the first time I found myself feeling relieved by that.

It wasn't just my own thoughts I had to deal with now. A message from Theo had arrived during the day. I hadn't been able to bring myself to read it while I was at school, in all the turbulence of the day and of my mind. A message from a man who wrote lovely things in poetic Spanish and said he missed me... I needed to deal with his latest thoughts and words when I was at home alone. I changed out of the chinos I wore for school and put on a clean shirt and a pair of jeans. I made myself a cup of tea and took it into the living-room where, through the two long windows, the sun streamed in. There I made space and time for my friend who wrote from Tenerife.

His message read: *Ayer tarde estuve en nuestra banco.* 'Yesterday evening I was sitting on our bench.' Our bench! *Te sentia muy cerca.* I thought I'd got this right: 'I felt you were very near.' The next sentence was: *Te anoré aparecer al atardecer...* There were two words I didn't know among those five. But somehow I knew that this was one of the bigger messages I would receive during my life. I didn't want to close the window on Theo's message in order to go to a dictionary app. My pocket English-Spanish dictionary was on the table; these days it was always. I turned its cigarette-paper pages with fingers that threatened to tear the little book apart. *Anorar – to long, to yearn.* So: 'I longed for you to appear.... *al atardecer.'* I loved words. Even if I didn't understand them. I somehow knew that this strange Spanish one was a talisman of great power. That it was full of beauty and magic. That when I extracted its meaning from the dictionary in a few seconds' time it would have the power to change my life. Again with shaking hands I scrabbled through the pages. And there it was, this spell so powerful that it needed two English expressions to encompass it: at dusk; at sunset. *I longed for you to appear at sunset-dusk.* I broke apart.

FIFTEEN

I couldn't write. What would I say? I couldn't phone. No words would come, I knew. I would only break down and cry. And then so would he. I needed to see him. Face to face. He didn't do Skype. But Skype wouldn't have been any good. It would have been like seeing someone through prison bars. We talked of seeing people face to face, but that wasn't what we really meant. Face to face was a polite code for holding hands, clasping fingers, caressing forearms, feeling the other's breath upon your cheek, catching the other's scent almost subliminally, exchanging pheromones, hugging tightly, squeezing the breath out of each other, kissing, tasting the sweetness of the other's tongue…

I looked at flights. Today's had already gone. Tomorrow's, Saturday's, would not leave till 15.20, arriving at Tenerife South at 20.05. The returns flight left on Sunday morning at 9.05. That would give me barely twelve hours on Tenerife, including the transfer between the airport and Puerto de la Cruz – over an hour each way. But it was purely academic; the flight was full.

I checked out flights to Tenerife North. There was one that left Glasgow at 8.45 tomorrow morning. But you had to change, and hang about, at Heathrow. You didn't get to Tenerife till 10.35 pm. The return flight on Sunday, with a long wait at Madrid, involved a journey of another twelve hours. And that flight too was full.

My father had had a friend or acquaintance (a French guy, in the fur trade, don't ask) who, when he occasionally decided he needed a holiday at short notice, would simply go to the airport, look at the departure boards and choose a destination that took his spur-of-the-moment fancy. He'd go to the relevant airline desk, take out his chequebook... That had been a very long time ago. I was pretty sure you couldn't do that now.

But pretty sure wasn't enough to stop me trying. I ferreted around my bedroom and found a small man-bag I very rarely used. Into it I put my passport, my wallet and my phone. And the bag of euros, coins and a few notes, that I kept in a drawer. I added my wash-bag, checking I'd included deodorant. After a moment's thought I added a pair of clean underpants. Then I re-checked the wallet. It contained not just my debit card but my credit card as well. As the Irish said, to be sure, to be sure. It was a warm evening. I didn't bother with a jacket. I just walked out of the door.

Glasgow airport was just a short bus-ride out from Paisley. From the flats on the other side of my building you could see the planes. I was there in less than ten minutes.

Once inside the terminal building it wasn't very obvious what people who hadn't booked tickets were supposed to do. Unlike at a train station or a cinema. I wandered round for a while until I spotted a young woman in the uniform of the airline that was flying to Tenerife South tomorrow afternoon. I told her I wanted to buy a ticket and she looked at me as if I'd made an indecent proposition in the crudest terms. But then she relented and pointed me towards a help desk that was tucked away where nobody would easily find it. 'I doubt very much they'll be able to help you, though,' she warned.

'It's very unusual,' said the beautifully made-up woman behind the desk. She took my passport and inspected it minutely. She tapped at her keyboard pessimistically, shaking her head. 'No,' she said when she looked back up towards me. 'The first information you had was right. That flight is full.' She must have read a lot from the expression on my face; because then she said, a bit uncertainly, 'This afternoon's flight has been severely delayed. It won't be leaving for another couple of hours. I think it wasn't quite full. I don't know if…'

'Oh yes,' I said, 'I'm OK to go today.'

'What I was going to say was, I don't know if they'd let me… Look, I'll have a try.' She picked up a phone.

It cost hundreds of pounds. I'd been expecting that but even so I nearly fell over when she read the numbers out. I messaged Maxwell. *Won't be back tonight. If you there look after the place for me. Don't take any bad money.* He might not understand the last part but I didn't care. Three hours later I was watching the sun set from 27,000 feet above the Irish Sea. I had no idea what I would say to Theo when I arrived. But I had plenty of time in which to think about this. We wouldn't be touching down till one a.m. How I would make the sixty-mile journey from the south airport to Puerto at that hour I had no idea. I decided I wouldn't think about that. The drinks trolley arrived. I asked for my first gin and tonic of the five-hour flight.

We were the last flight to land that night. They'd kept the airport open late especially for us. That was nice of them. On the other hand they didn't look particularly pleased about it. We landed passengers walked in a bewildered sort of way through the arrivals halls. A bit like people who'd spent a whole evening on the piss. Which was no more than the truth for some of us. We were not only sixty miles from Puerto but a good ten or fifteen from even the nearest of the south coast resorts. Some people had airport transfers arranged, or booked as part of their package. Others had rental cars to pick up and were waiting anxiously to see whether the office was still open, and even more anxiously preparing to begin a drive on unfamiliar wrong-side roads in the dark of night. The rest of us would have to hope for taxis. (The

Spanish verb *esperar* fatalistically translates both hope for and wait.) But at this hour there were unlikely to be many taxis about. Grimly apprehensive we piled up the escalator and spilled out into the balmy midsummer night. The air was still, and scented with palm and plumbago flower.

I heard a shout from across the car and bus and taxi park. 'Anyone else for Puerto de la Cruz?' It came from a little knot of people I could dimly make out, huddling around one of those taxis that are the size of minibuses.

'Yes!' I shouted back. I ran towards the little group, repeating my shout of yes. There might have been others with needs greater than my own. People with walking frames, families with babies or small kids. For the moment I blocked them out of my conscience and consciousness. I needed to get on that minibus.

In the end we filled every seat. There were a couple of babies, and young and not-so-young children sat awkwardly on their parents' laps. So my conscience was assuaged and after a few minutes' further thought I decided I had nothing to reproach myself with. We headed out along the motorway, the invisible sea to one side, the invisible mountains to the other, and nothing but our lonely headlights to show the way ahead of us.

Most minibuses have an odd seat or two that are not side by side with another one. I had made a dive for one of those as soon as I climbed on board. So I was able to spend the journey alone with my thoughts and staring through the dark window, while the babies cried, the children bickered rebelliously and their parents assured them again and again, untruthfully, that we would soon be there.

And yet for me, in the subjective time bubble of the moment I found myself in, it was ironically true. How slowly taxis travel when you know where you want to be and know what you're going to do when you get there, and the meter turns faster than the road wheels. But how quickly a long journey seems to pass when you have no idea what you will do when the doors finally open and you and your worries about the immediate future are tumbled out into the midnight street. So it seemed that we were skirting the suburbs of Santa Cruz in almost no time, then cresting the spine of the island alongside the unlit north airport, while the scent of pine forest crept in through the air con vents. A moment after that only, as I perceived time just then, we were stopping outside a hotel in the La Paz district of Puerto de la Cruz, not far from the one I had twice stayed at in the last couple of months.

There and then I paid my share of the fare we'd all agreed before setting off – it wasn't very much, as there were so many of us – and I was the first to hop out. I didn't want to stay on board while the taxi made its trip around town to other hotels in areas I didn't know, or hang about while buggies and baggage were disentangled at the back. The air was full of the night scents of hotel gardens that had been warmed by the sun all day. I breathed deep snorts of it for reassurance, willing its floral smell and warmth to give me confidence. I walked away from the taxi and the other disembarking passengers quite purposefully in a direction I was familiar with. Towards City Bar. I had no idea, though, what I would do, where I would go, after that.

I hadn't expected City Bar to be open, and of course it was not. It was well past two o'clock, and City Bar was just that: a bar, not a club. I carried Theo's street address in my head these days and I knew roughly where to find it: a couple of blocks inland from the Plaza del Charco, down in the oldest part of the port. I could walk there in twenty minutes or so. But having done that, was I actually going to ring the doorbell and wake up not just

Theo but also the people with whom he lodged? I carried on anyway, down the slope of the Camino San Amaro, past the dark and shuttered Chinese restaurant, then down the Cabras steps.

The Cabras steps too were devoid of life, the bars closed, the African hucksters and handbag-sellers gone. But down in the town below there were things going on. Two nightclubs were powering away, their open doors spilling light and throbbing bass beat out into the street, while little thrums of youngsters argued the toss with the bouncers at the doors. I thought about going into one and killing some time. But I looked at the lads and girls around the doorway. They were Chris's age, not even Maxwell's, still less Theo's and mine. At thirty-four I was already too old for this. Inside I would have stuck out like a spare dick. And what was the point anyway? I'd had enough to drink on the plane; I didn't want drugs pushed at me; I hadn't come here for conversation … except with one person.

I found Theo's address easily. In fact it found me. I looked up at a street name in the tangle of streets between the Plaza del Charco and the bus station and there it was. I walked along this street and the numbers descended in an orderly, inexorable fashion – thirty-nine, thirty-seven, thirty-five – like a doom-laden, awful countdown to judgement day or some other no-going-back decision moment.

I stood in front of the doorway. It was recessed, beside a shop window. The shop front had a grille over it but through it I could make out a display of trainers and sports clothes. If I'd understood the geography and the numbers rightly, Theo and his friends lived on one of the two floors above.

I looked up at them. No lights were on. One window, directly above the doorway, stood open, one casement was opened inwards, snagging a pale curtain. Absurdly close to it a drainpipe ran up alongside.

I'd had some experience of climbing drainpipes. For dares when I was at school. But that had been some time ago and I was heavier now. I'd never climbed up to an unfamiliar window at three in the morning in a foreign town. I needed to assess the situation carefully.

First I looked at the doorbells. There were two and, unusually, they were clearly marked. The number of Theo's apartment was written beside the bottom one. That meant I could forget about the upper flat. There were two windows on Theo's floor that I could see: one open, the other closed. There might have been two or three more windows at the back.

It was a hot night. You wouldn't go to bed leaving the living-room window or the kitchen window open, surely, yet leave your bedroom window closed? It seemed highly probable that the open window belonged to a bedroom. Theo had told me the flat had two of those. The other bedroom might be next to it at the front – with its window closed – or else it might be at the back, quite possibly also with its window open, but from where I stood that could not be seen and, anyway, was irrelevant. I wasn't an expert in probability theory but I reckoned that the chance that the open window I was looking up at was Theo's was close to fifty percent.

The next question was a practical one. Would I be able to get up to the open window by means of the drainpipe … if I decided I even wanted to? Casement windows look easy at first glance. But if they open outwards in the direction of the drainpipe it's almost impossible to bypass them unless you're a real expert – which I wasn't – and if they swing the other way then there's a second, fixed casement between the drainpipe and the climber which also presents an obstacle to amateurs like me. But this one opened inwards, unlike most such windows in

Britain, and its hinges were on the drainpipe side. If I managed to get up to it I could, at a stretch, peer in through the opening without letting go my hand- and foothold.

I thought about my footwear. Trainers, with pretty flexible soles. My luggage: a small over-the-shoulder man-bag. OK, I could do it, I thought. But did I really need to? It would be easier all round simply to hang about till it was morning and then ring the bell in a civilised way. But the next thought was an obvious one. What would Theo want me to do? What would he expect of me?

The answers to both questions were immediately obvious. I didn't need to think about them for even one second. I pulled the strap of the man-bag across the top of my head so it hung diagonally from the opposite shoulder and shouldn't fall off; I clasped the (pleasantly warm) drainpipe firmly, and started to climb up it.

There is a story called The Lady or The Tiger, in which a bold young man asks a king for the hand of his daughter in marriage. The king's answer is unusual, not to say sadistic. He arranges a public spectacle. Two pavilions are set up. In one is concealed the princess, in the other a tiger is confined. The young man is confronted with a choice between two doors. The outcome of the young man's quest will depend on which door he decides to open... I found myself in his position now. I'd made my decision and would have to live with its consequences. Even if it led me to the bedroom of a young couple I'd never met.

I felt a bit clumsy as I went up. I'd done this more easily as a teenager. Perhaps I was still a bit drunk from the plane. Though if I hadn't been perhaps I wouldn't have been bold enough to tackle the climb at all. It probably took no more than fifteen seconds but it felt as long as a voyage through space. Then I was almost there, my head just inches below the open window's sill. And at that point I knew the room inside belonged to Theo.

When you are very intimate with someone, or when you are in love with them, you are sensitive to every way in which they present themselves. Their humour, their way of speech, their movements, their looks, the feel of their skin... Their personal smell. For no matter how often you shower or change your clothes, that clings to you, unnoticed by most of the people you come in contact with, but picked up almost magically by those who care for you most. That, after all, is how your dog, whose eyesight isn't brilliant, can pick you out in a crowd and make a beeline for you. And that was how, at a distance of a few feet from his sleeping form, and still a few inches from his window, I knew I'd found Theo.

I had to release my hands' grip on the pipe, first one and then the other, while still clinging limpet-tightly to it with my feet and knees. Only when I'd got some of my body's weight over the sill, folding myself, head down, into the room, did I release the drainpipe from the anxious embrace of my legs. I let them kick their way up the wall behind me and then they followed me in as I rolled forward, headfirst, onto the cool tiled floor beneath.

I landed lightly but not lightly enough to not wake Theo. I heard his startled voice call out in the darkness, '¡Joder!' That's Spanish for fuck and it sounds infinitely more guttural and challenging when it's shouted at you than it looks written down.

It was dark in the street but there were lamps at least. There was no light in the bedroom; from my upside-down vantage point I peered into complete darkness. I sensed without seeing Theo's leaping out of bed in attack-is-the-best-form-of-defence mode as I tried to unroll myself from the floor. He was on me in a second: a bare-footed – and thus happily ineffectual – kick in my ribs; a very much more forceful bang to the side of my head with the flat of his hand.

'It's Jonty, Theo, it's me, *¡soy yo...!*' I only just managed to make this into an urgent hiss rather than a frightened shout.

The assault stopped as abruptly as it had begun. '*¿Que...?* What the fuck are you doing...? Get up...!'

'I'm trying to...'

Between us we got me to my feet, then Theo pressed his completely naked body against my clothed one and it felt wonderful. 'I'm sorry I hit you,' he said.

'It's OK.' I didn't have time to say any more. Theo's lips were against my mouth, and then his tongue was inside it, alongside mine.

It was like being a child again. In bed with your best friend. Trying not to make a noise as you played with each other, discovered each other's bodies and hearts. Neither of us came during those short midsummer hours before the sun rose. We had erections, both of us, and we paid attention to those, but neither of us came. Nor did we speak: there was too much to say. Theo had told me that once, many years ago, he had asked his partner Mateo what the exact difference was between the English terms hug and cuddle. Unwittingly following one of the precepts of creative writing courses, Mateo had gone for 'show, don't tell,' and as a result my Theo had quickly got the idea comprehensively. As he demonstrated, though not for the first time, during this short night.

Theo had told me the bedroom walls were paper-thin. I wouldn't have been surprised if the alarm of my arrival had woken Theo's hosts and they'd come banging on the door, or barging through it, to see if he was OK. But it seemed we hadn't woken them. Or if we had, they'd chosen to lie still, wondering a little, rather than marching in to protect the life or property – or virtue – of their friend.

I was accustomed to the early midsummer dawns of Scotland. Grey light before four a.m. and sunrise at half past. One of the joys of winter holidays in the Canaries is that it doesn't get dark at three p.m. But in midsummer the situation is reversed. To my surprise, when Theo explained the situation later, it was not until nearly seven that light pierced the sky, the sun rising about quarter past. Then the midsummer *atardecer* came at just after nine p.m. In my part of Scotland the sun stayed in the sky till after ten o'clock.

I slept through that day's sunrise, unsurprisingly, and Theo awoke me with a kiss, in the fashion of fairy-tale princes everywhere. When my eyes were open and focused he said, 'Shall we go out and get a coffee?' I remembered that up in La Paz the cafés didn't open till about nine. But here we were in the un-touristed workaday centre of the town. Anyway, Theo would know where to go.

'Sure,' I said, showing willing by sitting up with him in the single bed and thinking about putting my feet to the floor. 'But can I...? Before we go?' I had no idea whether we'd be coming back here after our coffee, or ever again. I hadn't been to anything like a bathroom since I'd got off the plane.

Theo got the message before I'd finished delivering it. He looked up at me from the pillow and smiled. 'Of course. I should have told you where...' He did so then.

We had coffee and rather chewy croissants at a place in the street from which all the island's buses left. Theo kept breaking off from our eggshell conversation to say, shaking his head, *'¿Por que eres aqui?'* Why are you here?

I had no answer. I knew why I'd come, of course I did. I'd come to confess that I had a young guy living in my flat and that I'd three times slept with him. But I could no more come out with that now than... No strong enough comparison came to mind. Even flying was an easier thing. I'd done that just ten hours ago and suffered no mishap. But then the words just came out of their own accord. 'I came because you wanted me.'

My sleeves were rolled up. The sleeves of the shirt I'd put on in Paisley yesterday evening, and which I'd still be wearing when I arrived back in Paisley tomorrow night. Theo's hand alighted on my bare forearm. He said what at once became obvious to me that he'd say, though I hadn't thought about it till now. 'I love you, Jonty.'

And so I said the thing that now became equally obvious. So obvious that I fear I waste the reader's time by writing it. 'I love you, Theo.'

SIXTEEN

It was difficult to know where to go, what to do, after that. The moment for praising Theo's prescience in dreaming of me in bed with a younger, black guy had passed and was unlikely to return in the near future. But here we both were, with the person we wanted to be with, on a sunny street in Tenerife, and that seemed more than enough for now.

There was a practical issue, though. I'd slept with Theo, pressed against him pleasantly tightly in his single bed, but I wasn't a guest in his house. I hadn't been introduced to his friends who lived there; and though I had my toothbrush in my backpack I had nowhere to go back to in order to clean my teeth or any of the rest of it. I didn't know where I was going to – where we were going to – sleep tonight. I broached these subjects now. It was a bathetic descent from the ILUs of a moment ago.

We cobbled together a compromise that we could both live with. I would do my ablutions in the café's toilet. Theo would go back to his place to do his. There he would tell his friends that a foreign friend had come to Tenerife unexpectedly, and ask them if I could share his room tonight. He didn't think they'd say no, but if they did then the two of us would find a cheap hotel room.

I made the best of the café's cramped backstage facilities and its rather basic plumbing, then came back out and treated myself to a second coffee while I sat under the awning on the pavement and waited for Theo. After a few minutes I saw him at the end of the street, hurrying towards me, bouncing along. I got the impression he was happy about something and I hoped it was something to do with me. As he got closer I could see he had a bulging backpack on, much bigger than mine.

'We're OK,' he said even before he sat down with me. 'You can stay the night with me. I didn't mention last night and they didn't ask about the rumpus. I thought, let sleeping doggies lie.' (Was that the way he'd learnt the phrase, at school, or from Mateo? I rather liked it that way.) 'I thought we might go to the naturist beach beyond Bollullo. If you'd like that...' He gestured towards his backpack, now on the ground beside his chair. 'I brought two beach towels anyway.'

'I couldn't think of anything better.' It was true. What happier way to spend our one day together than getting naked in the sun? Except...

Theo seemed to read my mind. 'We'll get some sun-cream for you on the way. Factor thirty for you.'

'I'm normally OK with factor fifteen,' I protested mildly. 'We do have sun in Scotland too occasionally.'

'It's not the same as out here,' he said authoritatively. He laid his brown arm on the table alongside my milky one. 'You see? As proved by the evolution of centuries and millennia.' I couldn't disagree.

We walked in our own footsteps of a few weeks ago. Out of town and up the Cabras steps to La Paz, and then along the switchback cliff path – between green bananas and blue sea – to Bollullo. As we passed through the farmyard I looked for the boy with the baby goat we'd spotted that last time but he was nowhere to be seen. I reminded Theo. He snorted. 'Kid boys with kid goats... There'll always be another one. They're like London buses here.' He must have got that, at least, from Mateo.

'I guess you're pretty upset by the referendum vote,' was his next conversational move. I said I was. 'It said on the news that people were attacking immigrants in the streets, writing insults on … how do you say? … Polish people's doors.'

'It's horrible. But that would be in England. That won't be happening north of the border. We don't have quite as many immigrants as they do. Except perhaps in Glasgow.' I thought for a moment. 'Glasgow does have its fair share of Poles.' But I thought about Maxwell then. 'And others too.'

'I heard that a gang of … do you say tugs….?'

'Thugs.'

'Thugs were going round London last night chanting, "First get the Poles out, then the gays."'

I hadn't heard that bit of news. Now I did, it sent a chill down my spine. 'Thugs. I suppose they're not confined to London. We probably have a few in Scotland too.'

Theo nodded. 'All over the world. Even in Tenerife too,' he acknowledged broad-mindedly. He changed tack. 'Will Scotland demand an independence referendum again now?'

'Now, yes,' I said. 'People are angry and feel betrayed. But things may settle down.'

'What is the problem with England, then?' asked Theo. 'Don't they like working with other countries? Or do they only trust the Americans?'

'A bit of both, probably. They always had a thing about outsiders. Ever since the end of the Middle Ages, when they got cut off from their French empire. They opted out of the Catholic Church at a pretty early stage of the Reformation. At least their king did.'

'Was that the one with eleven wives?'

'I don't think it was quite that many. And to be fair, he didn't have them all at the same time.'

We had reached the restaurant at Bollullo Cove where we'd had some lunch the last time round. We didn't stop there now but went on up the cliff beyond. At that point

I felt Theo clasp my hand and give it a firm swing or two. I marvelled a bit at that. 'Have you ever walked around Tenerife hand in hand with a man before?'

'No,' said Theo. 'Not even with Mateo.'

'I haven't walked holding hands with anyone. Not since I was a small child anyway.' It seemed an extraordinary and wonderful thing, this childish contact with a fellow adult man. I wondered what would happen when we passed people coming the other way.

At the top of the cliff the path entered a region of tall scrub and bushes that were so high that they arched and met overhead. Beneath our feet the earth had been so hollowed out by the passage of goats and humans over the centuries that we were walking in a narrow tunnel whose section was almost perfectly circular, like the tube-tunnels of the London Underground. Our feet went tripping over tree roots, and the sun's light came twinkling in through the thousand tiny holes in the leaf canopy above us like the sparkle of sea waves or the glint of stars.

Nobody came the other way. Our resolve to walk hands together went untested until the tunnel came to an end in a bursting disc of daylight and we found ourselves climbing upwards over rocks and boulders. We had no choice then but to let each other go, and clamber, using our hands for balance, on our own. A thought came into my mind. 'How do you say in Spanish, "They lived happily ever after."?'

'They lived happily and ate partridges,' said Theo.

'They ate partridges?!' I nearly lost my handhold. I laughed at the sheer unexpectedness of the translation.

'You need to hear it in Spanish. *Vivieron felices y comieron perdices.*'

'Of course,' I said, realising. 'It's a rhyme.' It rhymed more than neatly. The second line emerged from the first like a drawer within a drawer in some exquisitely crafted piece of cabinetry. I knew that in historic times in Spain, in Moorish times, partridges were the food of sultans and kings: the ultimate luxury. I thought now how nice it would be to live on partridges: to spend a lifetime eating them with Theo.

We reached the summit of our rocky climb. Below us lay an empty, secluded cove of black volcanic sand. It wasn't quite empty actually. Three or four naked couples lay about on it; whether they were same-sex or opposite-sex couples was not easy to see at this distance. Our way down to the beach was short now, and all downhill. But that didn't make it easy. At least, it didn't make it easy for me. The path ran down the actual face of the cliff in a steep diagonal. At some points there were railings between the path and the sheer drop to the beach below but for some longish stretches there were no railings at all; you had to rely on your self-confidence and sense of balance to stop yourself falling giddily into the sea.

Theo must have heard my sharp intake of breath. 'What's the matter? Are you not OK?'

'Whooh! It's a bit… For me.'

'It's OK. Let me go in front of you. Put your hands on the tops of my shoulders and hold tight; press your chest against my backpack and we'll walk together. Look at the back of my head or at your feet. Don't look at anything else.'

'If I fall you'll fall.'

'You won't fall. Neither will I. *Confía en mi.*'

I linked onto the back of him the way two short trains couple up to make a long one, and we started off. The view would have been nice but, following Theo's instructions, I didn't dare look at it. I made do instead with the sight of my trainer-shod feet and his glossy black curls.

It was only about a minute and a half. But it was a time out of time, just as, less than twelve hours ago, had been my journey up Theo's drainpipe. Perhaps it would feel similar if you spent an eternity eating partridges. At the bottom, on the black sand, we uncoupled and Theo turned round to face me. 'Well, that was all right, wasn't it?'

'It was fine,' I said, struggling a little with my voice.

'You, a climber of drainpipes in the middle of the night… I thought you'd have no trouble with that.'

'In the end I didn't, if you notice. Here I am.' I spread my arms and hands as if about to take a bow. 'The drainpipe… I'd had quite a bit to drink on the plane.'

'We've only got water for the way back,' said Theo, mock-frowning.

'I'll be fine on the way back. I'm perfectly OK with going up.'

It was Theo's turn to put his hands on my two shoulders, this time from the front. He smiled. 'Do want to get your kit off?'

I bet he didn't teach that expression to his pupils. In fact I was surprised he knew it at all. Perhaps I'd taught it to him.

We'd invested in a fairly big squeezy-bottle of sun-cream on the way out of La Paz. It had travelled in Theo's backpack. Now, as we stood on our spread-out beach towels he took it upon himself to rub me all over with it, paying particular attention to the delicate bits of me that least often saw the sun. And when I was lying down he leaned over me and reapplied it to a few bits he thought he'd missed.

'Do you need any yourself?' I queried.

He laughed, and grinned so broadly that his teeth sparkled in the sunshine. 'Look at me,' he said. I did.

We were staring up at the sky through closed eyelids. Even so, we remarked to each other, the light was pretty bright: a kaleidoscope of plum red, gold flecks and violet. We competed to see who could identify the largest number of colours, and name them in English. Then Theo made me try and do it in Spanish, which was brain-knottingly hard. He had to give me a lot of help. Curiously the regular beat of the waves, the incoming growl, the liquid break and the withdrawing rasp, seemed to alter our perceptions of the colours we saw through our eyelids and from time to time made us want to reclassify and rename them.

Then Theo said, 'Scotland, England, Britain. Most people here think lazily that Britain and England are the same place. I know they're not, of course. Since knowing you I've had to think more precisely about that. That Scotland's not a part of England and never was. But how did the ... what do you call it, the Union? ... come about?'

'I'm not a teacher of history,' I said, 'but I do have a bit of an idea. Most people know, if only from films like Braveheart, that England spent half the Middle Ages trying to annex Scotland just for the hell of it. Men fought and died bravely, on both sides, for centuries, but England never conquered Scotland, for all its size and strength. There was an English king, Edward the First, I think, who was actually nicknamed Hammer of the Scots, *Malleus Scotorum,* and he wasted most of his reign and assets trying to do just that. Crush Scotland and make it his. He decreed that when he died his flesh should be boiled off his bones and the bones carried at the head of his successors' armies when they tried to invade Scotland, for good luck. Much good it did them.'

'Where are the bones now?'

'Fuck knows,' I said. 'But you know what? And there must be a lesson about peace and love here, because what actually happened in the end... I mean on the one hand they were beating the shit out of each other but on the other, well, the two dynasties, English and Scottish, were forever intermarrying, just as both of them were intermarried with the Spanish and the French. And one day it all kind of worked out. An English king, Henry the Seventh, married his daughter to the son of the Scottish king James the Third. The English bride was called Margaret Tudor, the Scottish prince became James the Fourth. Two generations down the line the English queen Elizabeth died childless and, bingo, the king of Scotland – by that time James the Sixth – inherited the lot. England, Wales, and theoretical claims to France and Ireland too. It's a lovely irony. England couldn't take over Scotland by force, but Scotland won England and Wales in an inheritance.'

'And that was the beginning of the United Kingdom?'

'Not quite yet.' I opened my eyes and glanced diagonally down my slightly reddening chest towards Theo's crotch, where his bronzed cock lolled, half stiff, as if waiting for the end of the story and for what would happen after that. 'James – in England he was James the First – wanted it, but the people weren't ready for it, and neither were the two parliaments. He went off to London happily, like a school-kid going to university, and promising the people of Edinburgh he'd soon be back. Actually he never went north of the border again.'

'Probably the weather,' said Theo knowingly. He might have had a point.

'Scotland never quite forgave him, or the Stuart kings that followed him. They may have been pleased their kings had inherited the bigger kingdom, but they felt betrayed in a way. As if they'd been dumped for a richer bride.' I felt, rather than saw Theo nodding his understanding beside me. 'On the other hand King James did create the prototype of the Union Jack. It's actually named after him.'

'James...?'

'James being the same name as Jack.'

'Of course,' said Theo. 'I remember. I did know that.' I saw through that one but didn't challenge it. I tweaked his cock instead. 'So what did happen?' he asked.

'The Stuarts weren't as successful at running England as they'd been at managing Scotland, though they reigned over both countries, plus Wales, for four generations. Anyway, a hundred years after James went off to London, Scotland nearly went bankrupt over a failed colonial project in North America. England had to bail them out… It was like a sort of semi-friendly takeover in industry. That was in the reign of the last of the Stuarts to actually sit on a throne of any sort.'

'Queen Victoria?'

'Queen Anne. You've jumped ahead about five generations, I think. Anyway, that's the long and the short of it.' I thought then that if all lessons could be taught and learnt while you lay naked on a beach, stroking a loved one's cock in the sunshine, how much more effective would be the teaching, and the learning, process.

'Maybe,' said Theo, 'it's time to put a bit more sun-cream on you.'

'Already?' I asked.

Theo rolled right round until he lay on top of me. 'I didn't mean all over you this time. I was thinking of one special place.' I could feel the ridge of his erection pushing into my belly. He leaned sideways and reached for the sun-cream, then, after he'd anointed his fingers with it he reached down and into my buttock cleft. It became clear which special place he meant.

'I'll be back out here again in no time.' Our post-coital euphoria had given way to talk of my ever so imminent departure. We were sitting on our towels, still unclad in the sun. I'd never been fucked on a beach before, in the presence of a small number of people who sat scattered no more than a hundred yards away. But our activity didn't disturb or much interest them, and their distant presence did nothing to diminish my appetite for Theo or his for me. I'd expressed concern about the presence of so much sand nearby. Theo had reassured me. Not only were we on a protecting towel; there was no wind; Theo had done this before with Mateo without mishap he told me; then as now he had used a truly extravagant quantity of sun cream. I'd worried for a moment that he wasn't going to use a condom; that, silenced by my moment-by-moment increasing love for him, I'd let him go ahead like that and have to take a test when I got back to Scotland. But that imagined scenario vanished when he reached into his backpack and pulled out a packet of the things. He'd prepared in advance for this eventuality. It was more than I had done.

Theo said, 'You'd better be back out here in no time.'

Theo's school term would end in just over a week's time: a few days after mine. I was already making private plans to come back out to Tenerife then, spending money I couldn't afford or didn't really have.

'I promise.' I took his hand.

The beach wasn't exactly filling up but there were more people on it by now than there had been when we'd arrived. 'Perhaps it's time for a change of scene?' suggested Theo. 'Get something to eat and drink at some point.'

'Yes,' I said. Together we stirred, we helped each other to our feet, and started to get back into our clothes. Somehow, tomorrow morning I would be getting up, leaving Theo's warm bed, at five o'clock. The hours that lay between now and then had the sudden focus that comes upon a beautiful dream in the moment when you realise that you are waking out of it and will never have that particular dream again. Every second of what remained was going to matter, to be counted down, to be stored and treasured in our memory.

'Are you going to be OK climbing the hill?' Theo meant the first upward path, the one that climbed the sheer cliff face, the one I'd had trouble with and where I'd had to hold on to him.

'I'll be fine. Going up's OK.' And I was fine. I led the way proudly, not even needing to touch the rock wall at my side. Though I was prudent enough not to turn my head towards the other side, towards my right, towards the sheer drop to the sea. Nor did I turn round to look at Theo who was following me protectively, not touching me, but just a metre behind. I didn't need to see the smile he was wearing, the many-layered smile. I knew it was there. The smile that said, among so many other important things, that for the moment – just for that moment – he was proud of me.

SEVENTEEN

I didn't twist round in my seat this time, trying to fix my eyes on the receding black cone of Mount Teide among the clouds. I looked forward resolutely, peering ahead as we climbed, looking out for the Selvagem islands, if I could spot them through the blue weather holes.

I thought back to Theo's self-identification with the Guanches. That surprising thing he'd come out with as we'd walked round La Orotava a few weeks ago. How did he know he was a Guanche? He had the chestnut brown complexion all right, and the chocolate eyes. But then so did most Spaniards from the Peninsula. Though how, for that matter, did I know I was a Scot? My milk-white, now slightly sun reddened complexion? When we'd laid them on a café table side by side our arms had looked strikingly different. Theo was clearly not from northern stock, and I was clearly not a Guanche or a Berber or even descended from the invading, plundering hordes from Medieval Spain. And yet...

Then there was Maxwell. He whose fingers when interlocked with mine resembled black piano keys, ebony and ivory alternating, so strong was the contrast. Yet he'd voted in the referendum. Voted the same way as I had. We were fellow Europeans, fellow Scots indeed. And if you judged him by his accent, by his pronunciation of English words, he was more authentically Glaswegian than me.

I'd sometimes watched the TV programme, Who Do You Think You Are? Various celebrities, most of whom I'd never heard of, were given the opportunity, and a BBC budget, to delve into their ancestry. Often with surprising results. Some traced tragic branches of their family trees into the dead ends of the concentration camps. One English TV actor turned out to be descended from an English king, Edward I or Edward III, I didn't remember which. The point was that none of us really did know who we were, and without spending a fortune were unlikely ever to find out. Theo might indeed have come from Guanche stock. Maxwell might well have colonial European blood in his veins, or royal blood for that matter, while I might be ... well, anybody at all.

These days you could google stuff on planes without causing them to fall from the sky. I decided to start looking at a couple of people whose genealogy was impeccably charted and well known. I started with Elizabeth the First. I didn't mean the great English lady of Shakespeare's day but the present Queen of the UK and Commonwealth. For though she was Elizabeth the Second in England and other places around the world, north of the border she was still, through no fault of her own, Elizabeth the First. But for the moment I had to give way to force majeure: I tapped Elizabeth II into my phone.

When people north or south of the border wanted to say something derogatory about the royal family they always began with, 'Of course they're bloody Germans.' That was pretty rude to the Germans too, when you thought about it, as it implied that being German was about the worst birth defect you could possibly have.

OK, everybody knew that German blood flowed in the veins of the House of Windsor. But there was plenty else there as well. Everyone also knew that Prince Philip, the Queen's husband, was sort of Greek. Perhaps everyone except me also knew that his name was registered as Philipos Andreou when he was born on the island of Corfu. It was only now that I discovered this.

That the Queen's mother was Scottish... Everyone knew that. That her father was a Scottish aristocrat, the 13th Earl of Glamis. Though perhaps not everyone would remember the number 13. But I'd never given any thought to her mother's nationality. That was English, apparently. And the baby who'd gone on to be The Queen Mother for about a hundred years had been born in England (some said, in a horse-drawn ambulance en route for hospital) and her birth registered in Hertfordshire. The present Queen's grandmother Queen Mary had been half English, half German; her great-grandmother Queen Alexandra Danish. Et cetera, et cetera. And those people who sneered that the family were all German had forgotten, if they'd ever learned, that Elizabeth would not be on the English throne if she didn't carry the genes of the Scottish Stuarts.

And that the first Stuart king of England wouldn't have been promoted from Edinburgh to London if he hadn't had English blood in his veins, come to that.

I looked out of the window, and at the time on my phone. I'd missed the Selvagem Islands by several minutes. While Madeira, I was pretty certain, would pass by on the other side. Only a cloud-studded expanse of open Atlantic Ocean lay below. I decided to investigate the Scottish Stuarts' family tree while I had the time, and was in the mood.

Not everybody's family was as international as a royal dynasty, not everyone's background as intricately intertwined. For many ordinary people living in wee villages before the advent of the steam train and the pedal bicycle, the gene pool had been very small. Yet that hadn't been the case for all Scots. Even before the industrial revolution created enforced as well as voluntary mobility, coastal towns had always seen their share of foreign births and marriages. The wrecking of the Spanish Armada had produced some interesting results in the Western Isles. Results with Theo-like eyes and hair...

Just hours ago I'd explained to Theo how the Stuarts came to the English throne because James IV of Scotland was married to Margaret Tudor of England – thanks to the shrewd matchmaking of their respective fathers, Henry VII and James III. But now I learned (though I'd probably been taught it at school) that James IV, most successful and patriotic of Scottish kings, who died for his country on Flodden Field, was half Danish by birth. While his father James III was half Dutch – his mother being one Mary of Guelders.

I ignored the intriguing questions of who Mary of Guelders's mother and grandparents might have been, as all genealogists have to discipline themselves to do, and concentrated on the direct line back through the Scottish royals. James III was the son of James II... This was getting to be like that book in the Bible in which people with outlandish names begat yet more people with outlandish names, except that I was going in the other direction – and that for about five generations the names were all the same. James.

James II of Scotland had a Scottish enough father (James I, surprise, surprise) but his mother was as English as they came. Her name was Joan Beaufort, her father the first Duke of Lancaster, John of Gaunt. That same John of Gaunt whom Shakespeare felt was English enough to attribute these words to.

> *This royal throne of kings, this scepter'd isle,*
> *This earth of majesty, this seat of Mars,*
> *This other Eden, demi-paradise,*
> *This fortress built by Nature for herself*
> *Against infection and the hand of war,*
> *This happy breed of men, this little world,*
> *This precious stone set in the silver sea,*
> *Which serves it in the office of a wall*
> *Or as a moat defensive to a house*

> *Against the envy of less happier lands,*
> *This blessed plot, this earth, this realm, this*
> *England.*

You couldn't get much more English than that. I didn't have to look the lines up. They were in my head already. I was a teacher of English, and they went with the territory. I was pretty sure that if asked to, Theo would be able to recite them too.

Yesterday we'd stayed out all day. Yesterday. A word that had no meaning now. I could feel no yesterday in me. No tomorrow, no today. I found myself inhabiting simply an enormous aching Now.

We'd looked for the sunset. From the viewing point at the top of the Camino San Amaro. I saw for the first time that this little cliff-top square, with a tree in its dusty centre had a name of its own. It was the Plaza Mirador de la Paz, according to a plate on a wall. (And here was another lovely word. *Mirador.* A place for looking out from, an admiring place.)

The sunset happened of course. It always does. And it was visible – a commoner case here than in Scotland. But this evening it was not a splendid one. Rather it was subtle, muted. There were mists across the distant sea and the sun's orb had a veiled look to it, like the yolk of an egg beginning to poach among films of whitening albumen. The island of La Palma did not appear. But Theo was there, and I was there. We were there together at sunset, sitting on the low wall, our feet dangling over the romping fall of the land below towards the sea two hundred feet below us. Together at sunset. *Al atardecer.*

Behind us stood the small church of San Amaro, a little white box with unpainted granite quoins, with a roof of red canal tiles and a miniature bell tower at the side. Theo said, 'My grandparents were married there.' I wondered if, in an unimaginable future of changed perceptions and changed laws, Theo and I would also be married there.

We spent much of the evening in a place where we both felt at home: in City Bar. The familiar spot seemed somehow different now. But as usual it was we and not the place that had changed. We were a couple in ways we hadn't been a couple before. That was reflected in the greetings, the welcomes, we got from the staff whom we already knew. They seemed to know that things had changed, and in what way, without being told or having to ask.

Except for the bar staff there was no-one in the place that either Theo or I knew. If Theo had friends in Puerto – as he must have – they didn't come to City Bar. The only other friend I'd made there, Nat, was back in Canada. I didn't mention him to Theo now. There was the awkward business of Theo's sister. I didn't mention her either, didn't ask after her. And since Theo mentioned neither of them... I decided it was better to let sleeping doggies lie.

Apart from his sister I had met no-one who belonged in Theo's life. One of the ways we get to know a new person, get to trust them, begin to understand who they are, is by triangulation: discovering them through their other friends and the way they relate to them. But Theo still presented himself to me without human background or scenery. His context was an inanimate one: the rocks of Tenerife, blood-red sunsets, blue and silver sea. He merged with my image of the island itself. *This little world, this precious stone set in the silver sea.* Dear John of Gaunt; dear wonderful Mr Shakespeare; there were other precious stones, other little worlds, in silver seas you only dreamt of.

I'd thought I would perhaps get to meet the friends Theo lodged with at least, but it was late when we returned to the apartment and they'd gone to bed.

Spanish people – already gone to bed! It must have been later than I'd thought.

There was a miraculously early bus that left the town for the south airport at half past five. The bus stops – replacing the bus station, now demolished, that I remembered from earlier visits with Harry – were just five minutes from Theo's front door. He walked down with me, getting up with me at five, returning the compliment I'd paid him a few weeks ago, getting up and seeing him on his way, goodbyes on the pavement outside my hotel, when he had to go to school.

'I'll be back in a few days,' I told him madly. 'As soon as term ends. As soon as I've sorted things.' Sorted Maxwell was perhaps what I meant.

Theo frowned his Theo frown. 'Are you sure you can afford it? All this travelling?'

I smiled early-morning bleakly. 'I don't know. I don't care. I'll come anyway.' Then, wildly, 'Or you come to me.' I didn't ask him if he could afford that. I was pretty sure the answer would be no.

And then the bus came: a pair of searchlights in the warm jewelled darkness. We hugged, kissed briefly, then I was climbing the steps, un-jacketed, un-luggaged except for my man-bag. *'Hasta pronto,'* we exchanged. Glimpsed each other hurriedly through the window as the bus swept me away from the pavement. Away from Theo. Away from Puerto.

I glanced out through the porthole and to my surprise saw a coastline inching towards us slantwise. We'd got further than I'd thought we had. The lacy fringes of the sea were teasingly covering and uncovering the golden beaches of western Portugal. Down there... Down there a Sunday morning was in mid-yawn. The stayabeds were still in the place they wanted to be. The churchgoers had been and done that, or were heading out to a later Mass, crossing paths with their earlier co-religionists now eating *pasteles* and drinking espressos on the café terraces. The roads… I peered carefully. Sunday drivers were out, in small numbers, their cars moving almost imperceptibly, like greenfly on leaf veins before the Monday morning infestation really took off. Down there… Down there was the place that Theo called the Peninsula, though he was usually thinking of the Spanish eighty percent of it when he referred to it. I forgave him. Like him I seldom gave a thought to Portugal, except when I was there or, as now, flying over it.

Back on Tenerife now all the same things were happening as here. Churchgoers, Sunday workers, people on family visits, Saturday night revellers catching up with themselves, all doing their thing. Theo himself… It was one of the great unknowns of human experience: what people did when you had left them and gone away. When you had said goodbye and begun your journey to somewhere else, and they turned away from you, back to the empty doorways of their empty homes. As my mother did each time one of my visits to her came to an end. As Theo had done just a few hours ago.

Puerto de la Cruz was good for sunsets. It didn't do sunrises in the same way. There was a mountain blocking the view. But this morning I had crossed the island in the end of night-time darkness. The eastern sky was lightening as we descended from the island's spine. And as we approached the southern airport the sun came up like a slow-mo rocket, a blazing ball alongside the silhouette, the basking whale hump, of Gran Canaria thirty miles away. Venus still lingered, holding out for a few more seconds in the vastness of the thrush-egg sky. I knew the Spanish word for sunset-dusk. It filled the expanses of my mind. *Atardecer.* But I realised now that I hadn't learnt the Spanish word for dawn or sunrise.

EIGHTEEN

Mid-afternoon, midsummer, mid-Sunday. The streets felt oppressively quiet as I made my way from the airport bus stop to home. As I turned my key in my lock I prayed that Maxwell would not be inside. He wasn't. And everything else was. Everything in its place, and no squalid mess in the kitchen. I gave silent thanks to Maxwell for not being there and, if he had popped back during my absence, for treating the place with respect at least.

There was a message from my mother on my house phone. She knew I had a mobile and she had one of her own but seemed somehow not to trust the medium. If she wanted to contact me she would always use my landline. Her message told me she wanted to know simply if I was OK. I normally phoned her during a weekend. This weekend, for reasons obvious to me but not to her, it had slipped my mind. I called her back and said I was fine. I'd been busy seeing friends. I'd drive over to Stirling and see her in a few days, as soon as term came to an end. I reminded her that we'd spoken as recently as Friday morning – though that had been a hurried moment, just to exchange the information that we knew the result of the referendum and were both equally horrified. That that sort of phone-call didn't count when it came to sons keeping in touch with their mothers was evident in her tone of voice when we said goodbye.

For the rest of the afternoon and evening I stayed at home alone. I had my thoughts for company though, and there were plenty of those to keep me entertained. I listened to music, and watched TV, but those things seemed to overcrowd my already full-to-bursting mind. Around nine o'clock I was beginning to think of popping out to get a takeaway. And then I heard the scratch and rattle of a key in the door. A moment later Maxwell was with me in the living-room.

He looked slightly startled at seeing me. 'You didn't say when you were coming back.'

'Well here I am. Look...' I'd been sitting on the sofa. I found myself standing up, turning and facing him. 'You won't be able to go on staying here.'

'What?' If Maxwell had been carrying a suitcase rather than a backpack he would have dropped it on the floor.

'After tonight, I mean. Obviously you can stay tonight...' I stretched my arms out in a way that said, look how reasonable I'm being.

He stood his ground, a foot or two away. 'What's brought this on?'

'I can't go on living with you. I mean, what I mean is, I can't go on having you living here with me. It's not as though you're just a lodger. I've slept with you – when I shouldn't have done, because I was supposed to be committed to someone else. And I'm even more committed to him now...'

'You what? You want to turn me out into the street because you've fallen in love with this guy in the Canary Islands? That's crazy. And it isn't fair.'

I felt my facial muscles tense. 'I can't live with one person and be in love with another one. Nothing crazy about that.'

Maxwell snorted. 'Half the world lives with one person and is in love with a different one. Anyway, I thought you sort of loved me.'

'Maxwell...' I had to stop. I had never said to anyone *I don't love you.* I didn't think I could ever be prepared to hurt someone that much. And anyway I'd always have the suspicion that the disavowal wasn't entirely true.

He jumped into the space I'd left him. 'Because I love you.' His hands, which he'd left hanging at his sides, moved slightly but his arms didn't follow through. He made no attempt to reach out to me.

I groaned silently. 'Don't say that. Please. OK, I know we've slept together. Of course I'm fond of you...'

'You're the greatest person I've ever met. I've always wanted an older man to love and ... to nurture me. You...'

'Me? I'm hardly any older than you!' I felt myself punctured – more than punctured – it was more like the high-speed blow-out of a car tyre. I tried to carry on. 'If you love me – if you loved me – why were you going out at nights, sleeping around, picking up God knows who?'

'To make you jealous, I suppose.'

'For fuck's sake!' Then I watched, horror-struck, as Maxwell's handsome strong face scrunched up like a sponge and poured with tears. For a second or two we just stood there. Then I reached out and touched his arm uncertainly. 'Let's sit. Put your backpack down.'

He did that, shrugging it to the floor. Then we moved awkwardly towards the sofa together: he forwards, me backwards, as if we were carrying an invisible piece of furniture. We sat down heavily at opposite ends, angled towards each other but not touching. At that moment I burst into tears.

Maxwell watched me in silence, unflinching, until after a dozen slow seconds I calmed down. Then he said with some emotion, 'You're a hypocrite, you know.'

'Why?' I asked, stung. 'What's hypocritical about me?'

'While you away, there was a gang going round London – somebody told me – saying, "First get the Poles out, then the gays." That's England, that's Brexit for you. We agreed. We were on the same side. You and me were.'

I nodded. 'Someone told me about the Poles thing, the gay thing, too…'

'But now you're just the same. The same as those English… England for the English … Brexiteers. You want to get rid of me. An inconvenient African in your life. He's had his uses; now he doesn't any more.'

'Maxwell, it wasn't like that with us, as you well know.' I spoke urgently, almost angrily, though mainly in order to prevent him from interrupting me. 'I've put a roof over your head for two weeks now, without asking for anything in return. OK, I've slept with you – but it wasn't just me that wanted that – and it certainly wasn't a quid pro quo. You wanted to sleep with me too. I've tried to help you as much as I can with finding a job and a place to stay when you leave here. But you haven't done anything for yourself in that line. You haven't followed up the leads I found for you. I told you right from the start that your staying here could only be temporary. I told you on day one that I was involved with Theo.'

He sniffed back tears. 'What does it matter? You're just clever with words. But you're an English teacher so I suppose you should be.'

'And you're clever with words too. You make out you're a penniless beggar with nowhere to go. But you own your own house in Nigeria. Or say you do. You've got a mother with a nice house in Italy…' I saw him shake his head. 'OK. Married to a man with a nice house in Italy. But either way you're not somebody with nothing at all.'

'OK then,' Maxwell said, and I saw his face tense up just as mine had done a few minutes earlier. 'If I've got so much going for me in Nigeria … if everything's a bed of roses for me over there … and if it's all wonderful in Italy, like you seem to think it is…'

'You showed me a photograph…'

'Then what am I doing here?'

'You thought a house in the north Italian countryside was a nice enough background to yourself when you wanted to impress me all those weeks ago.'

The taut panels of his face buckled and collapsed again. He shed another stream of tears. I sat and watched him. I was trying hard not to start crying again too. At last he was able to look out at me from his wonderful eyes, challenging me to say something else to him. I rummaged in my head for words but none came to hand. Eventually I said, 'I was just going out for a takeaway when you came in. Will you come with me?'

I expected a dusty answer but to my surprise he nodded his dripping face and said that he would. I couldn't help it: a pang of wanting him ran through my heart and bones. He said, 'Can we get our usual? That thing that has prawns in it?'

We sat and ate our meals in front of the TV, which was on, and we pretended to watch it. It gave us an excuse not to talk about anything. When bedtime approached I said, 'Obviously I'm not going to chuck you out into the street with nowhere to go. In a couple of days, when term's over and I've got time, I'll help you find somewhere. I can't get you a job so easily, but I can stand over you while you write emails. Make sure you do that. And weed out the Nigerian spellings.' He smiled at that, though in a wintry sort of way. It was something I'd gently teased him about during the time he'd stayed with me.

We used the bathroom separately, both of us primly shutting the door while we were in there. Then Maxwell went up to bed on the mezzanine and I went to my bedroom. A message had arrived from Theo; I took my phone to bed with me so I could read it properly, like a dog retiring to its basket with a gnawy bone.

Theo's message was in Spanish. It was full of love and of lovely firework phrases that flared in my mind. He described his feelings, watching the tail lights of my bus recede down the night-time street. Then his lonely walk home – at that point tears sprang to my eyes – and his wait for the night to end and for dawn to fill the sky. He imagined me seeing the sunrise over Gran Canaria. He described it exactly as I'd seen it myself, while I thought longingly about him. And now of course I learned what the dawn was in Spanish. *El amanecer.*

I tapped a message back in English. With feelings of guilt that were irrational but still strong. It wasn't my fault that Maxwell was sleeping on the mezzanine. At least he wasn't in my room. And Theo would hardly have wanted me to make a fellow human being homeless. But still, Maxwell was there.

I finished my message in Spanish at least. I wrote that I was Theo's for ever now. From dawn to sunset-dusk I would belong to him. *Desde el amanecer hasta el atardecer.*

The alarm went off at a quarter to seven. The final Monday of term. I could hardly believe I'd slept for seven hours. I didn't feel as though I'd slept at all. On my way to the bathroom I looked up towards the mezzanine. There was no-one there. Nor was Maxwell to be seen anywhere about the apartment. His backpack had gone, his bathroom things and a few of his clothes: about a backpack-full. What remained was mainly his sound-system and computer, and the foot-entangling chaos of wires. No note from him. The set of keys he'd had from me had been left baldly on the hall table. It was that, oddly enough, that hurt most of all.

Classes were finished. There was no teaching to do. The final two days of term were admin days, with a sports morning followed by final assembly in the

afternoon. I wouldn't be meeting Chris in a classroom
setting again. But I saw him from time to time around
the school. Before the eventful weekend just gone we'd
been eager for each other's company, finding excuses to
stop and chat in corridors, or by the gate or in the
canteen. I wasn't so sure how I was going to feel about
that now, or how I would feel about Chris now. But my
feelings didn't get put to the test this Monday. Chris
made no effort to seek me out or to cross my path on
purpose accidentally. If I saw him at all it was at a
distance and he seemed to be in a hurry to be somewhere
else each time: somewhere that coincidentally lay in a
different direction from mine. If something had changed
for him that made him less keen on stopping and talking
with me, then so be it. I thought it was perhaps just as
well. Tomorrow we would be saying our final farewells;
it was probable that our paths would never cross again.
Perhaps Chris was simply getting in practice for that
soon-to-be new state of things. If so, I thought it sensible
of him. People of my age, teachers especially,
sometimes forgot that the young people we taught could
on occasion be wiser than we were. I would take a leaf
out of Chris's book of wisdom and not make too much
of an effort to run into him.

There was a leavers' do that evening. It was a party for
the youngsters only. We teachers weren't expected to be
there. I did stay quite late in the staff room, though.
There was still quite a lot of paperwork to be completed
before the term finally ended. And quite a few other
teachers shared the staff room with me. As it happened I
eventually left at the same time as Kirsty, the French
teacher whom the kids knew as Miss McCleesh and who
had been with me when I'd run into Maxwell at the
King's Theatre. As we approached the school gates I
asked her if she'd like to have a quick drink with me
before we made our separate ways homeward.

There was a bar quite near the school gate. It was so near the school gate that our pupils never went in there, and our colleagues gave it a miss for the same reason. We were fairly certain that we could go in now, just this once, without being noticed – everybody else being totally caught up in the coils of end of term – and without running into anyone we knew once we were inside. We were proved right on both counts.

Kirsty opted for a half of lager when I offered her something and I went along with that too. I wanted her to know that I wasn't thinking of getting settled in. 'What happened with that young man?' Kirsty asked as soon as we were seated at a table in a corner out of the way.

'Which one?' We both smiled.

'The … um … black guy from the theatre bar.'

'Maxwell,' I supplied. 'He's been living in my spare room, on and off, ever since.' I thought that spare room sounded more definite than mezzanine when it came to giving the message that we didn't sleep together. 'Actually I gave him his marching orders last night. They didn't go down too well.'

'Has he got somewhere else to go?'

'I'm not going to just chuck him out, obviously. I promised he could stay a few more days and I'd find a place for him as soon as I had the time. But this morning when I got up I found he'd already gone. Left his set of keys behind … bless him … but he's also left a load of stuff. Computer and so on.'

'So he'll come back for that at some point.'

'Yes,' I said. 'I imagine so.'

Kirsty gave me a long look, presumably thinking how to put the next bit. Then she said, 'If he's left important stuff behind he's sending you a message. It's that he doesn't really want to leave. Actually, that night … I thought the two of you looked lovely together. Are you quite sure you…?'

'He is lovely,' I agreed. 'But the thing is, I'm sort of seeing someone else. I already was when I first met Maxwell. And I definitely was by the time we met him that night at the King's.'

'Then why on earth did you let Maxwell go and live with you? What does the someone you're sort of seeing think about it?'

'He doesn't know.'

'Doesn't know you share your home with another man? Where does he live? The moon?'

'Tenerife, actually.'

'Ah, I see.'

'It does make it rather difficult.'

'On all sides, I imagine. Will you try and contact Maxwell? Or wait for him to come to you?'

'Play it by ear,' I said. 'He hasn't got a key now.' A thought struck me. 'At least I hope he hasn't. Would he have had them copied? I don't know now.' I came to a stop.

Kirsty leaned towards me. 'If he hasn't had them copied he'll need to turn up when he knows you're in, or else fix a time… You can message each other I suppose? Phone?'

'I can message him,' I said, 'but it doesn't seem to work the other way.'

Kirsty gave a small sigh. 'It'll all work out in time, I guess.'

'Of course it will,' I said. 'Just don't quite know how.'

'We never do. Anyway, time I went. Or there'll be questions.'

'Like, are you sure Jonty's gay?' I suggested.

Kirsty gave me a cheerful smile. 'I'm pretty sure he is.'

I thought about trying to contact Maxwell when I got home. But it wasn't urgent. If he wanted to, when he wanted to, he would contact me. I hadn't thrown him out; he'd left of his own accord. I wasn't in love with him. He was not a child but an adult.

Meanwhile I had my apartment to myself. Or rather, to myself and Theo. I felt his presence all around me now; that was a new development; it hadn't been the case up to now. I sent him some pictures of the place on Snapchat, wondering why I hadn't thought to do this before.

He wrote me a lovely, almost poetic, message in reply. In Spanish. But dealing with the language was getting easier for me now. I only had to look up a quarter of his words these days; no longer two thirds of them. He asked how soon I could get back over to Tenerife once term was finished. His own term would end in just a couple more days. Before replying I checked my bank statement. I'd sort of guessed, though I hadn't wanted to look to see it confirmed. But yes, it was as I knew it would be: I was overdrawn.

NINETEEN

I hadn't given any thought over the years to Chris's sporting prowess, or even to whether he had any sporting prowess at all. I'd been his English teacher, that was all; I wasn't a sports coach; I'd never seen him (and certainly never thought about him) in the gym or on the sports field. None of that had changed during the last few weeks of our closer connection. If I'd seen him taking part in events and races in past years while I politely watched without really seeing, I had no memory of it now. But this morning... Well, I could hardly help noticing him.

The main sporting event days had been a couple of weeks earlier. This morning was a kind of display put on by the event winners. Chris wasn't in everything by any means. He clearly wasn't a sporting star of the highest magnitude. He ran the hundred metres sprint and came a respectable fourth. He threw the javelin and got nowhere. He wore the tightest pair of white shorts imaginable. They were so tight that I thought they couldn't possibly be good for him. On the other hand they were pretty good for me. His legs, which I'd never seen unclad before, were slender and colt-like, but beautifully proportioned. They looked a bit like mine had looked at his age.

You had to ignore the physical charms of the young people you taught: the woozles, to borrow Kirsty's sweet Winnie-the-Pooh word. That was a matter not just of moral high-mindedness but of self-preservation. Put one foot wrong in that direction and your next career move would be stacking supermarket shelves. Put more than one foot wrong and you'd land in Barlinnie. But I had ceased to be Chris's teacher some days ago and would be saying a formal goodbye to him in a few hours. I allowed myself to admire him this morning from the respectful and respectable distance of the spectators' seats. It was the least I could do, my covert stare through sunglasses bouncing like a cricket ball towards his white figure across an acre or two of greenness.

I didn't speak to him during that morning. It wasn't till the end of the afternoon assembly, after the awards had been distributed among the deserving, that the long round of goodbyes began. I found myself giving Chris's friend Jimmy a farewell shake of the hand. We hadn't spoken since the night we'd met in Del's, when he'd been with Chris and I with Maxwell. Nor had I seen him in Chris's company since then. But that was just at school. I had no other knowledge of how their friendship played out beyond the school gates.

'You off to uni in the autumn?' I asked Jimmy uncertainly. I didn't teach him these days; I knew nothing of his future plans.

'Strathclyde ... er ... if I get the grades. To read Chemistry.' I was pretty sure that the hesitation in his first sentence had resulted from indecision as to whether to pop sir into it, or Jonty, or Mr Allen. I thought his eventual choice to leave the gap empty had been a wise one.

'I'm sure you'll get your grades,' I said. I didn't ask him what grades they'd asked him for. The conversation could have gone on for ages and there were loads of goodbyes to be said, especially to my more recent pupils, and rather more time would have to be spent on them.

Chris appeared suddenly, amidst a bunch of his English Highers classmates. We were all saying goodbye together, shaking hands. Evidently I wasn't going to be granted a private audience. I've heard it said that people who get to meet the Queen become tongue-tied and (if they're not on friendly terms already) can't remember a word that has been said on either side when they try to recall or recount the moment afterwards. It was not unlike that with Chris and me that afternoon. I remember we shook hands. I remember my own voice saying, 'Edinburgh.' I remember it saying, 'Don't worry about the grades; you'll get them.' The sight of Chris's jaw working as he spoke to me, pumping my hand in a rather too prolonged handshake, was etched on my mind, but when I went over it later I realised that I had no recall of a single word he might have been saying. And then it was over. Term was over. Chris was over. *Sic transeunt gloriae mundi.*

There was no sign of Maxwell when I got home. It was a relief actually. His stuff remained untouched where he had left it. I thought about trying to contact him, as Kirsty had suggested. Not this evening though. I was happy to have the place to myself again. To myself and Theo.

I'd bought a frozen shepherd's pie on the way home, and some up-market purple broccoli that would only take a few minutes while the shepherd's pie cooked in the microwave. I thought that after I'd eaten I might wander down to The Bull to celebrate my new end-of-term freedom with whoever I might run into down there. Even if that happened to be Maxwell.

I'd had my meal, and the last two inches in a bottle of red that I had left over, and was about to do my minimalist wash-up when my phone rang. It's funny how, in retrospect, you remember all the unimportant, boring details of what has happened just beforehand. I told myself it must be Maxwell, who never rang me. But the name on the screen was Theo. Theo who also never rang me.

'Theo, di me,' speak to me, I answered. *'Mi cariño.'* I'd never called him that. He'd never called me that. But I knew it was roughly equivalent to my darling.

Theo wasted no time in bandying endearments. He started straight in, in English. 'You knew all the time and didn't tell me...'

'What, Theo?'

'My sister's disappeared to Canada.'

'I didn't know... How would I?'

'With your friend Nat. Alberto, her fiancé... He's distracted. You don't know how seriously we take these things here. She's shamed his manhood.'

'I'm sure...'

'And you knew and didn't tell me. Our mother...'

'Theo, I know nothing about this. I promise.'

'Your friend had been seeing her for weeks. You knew that.'

'Theo... he's not a friend exactly. Someone I met in a bar...'

'Like I'm someone you met on a bench. In a place where gay men go smoozing.'

'Cruising.'

'You knew what was happening. You said, you did, nothing.'

'There was nothing I could do, for God's sake. As for saying... OK, I didn't tell you. Partly because Nat asked me not to. Partly because I didn't take it seriously. If I'd thought for a moment that Marina might break off her engagement... Oh God, Theo, I'm sorry.'

'Listen, Jonty, we live three thousand kilometres separate. We have to trust each other. Much more than with people who live just near each other. If I can't trust you with little things, how can I trust you with the big things?'

I felt everything rise up inside me as if I was about to vomit. Or cry. Or something. 'Theo, you can trust me. You must trust me. Trust me with the big things.'

'How can I? After this.'

'Theo, you can. Look, I'll come straight over.' With a lurch I remembered my negative bank balance.

'I won't have time for you. My mother needs me. She's in... oh what's the word? Inconsolable.'

'I'll come over anyway.' Theo wasn't to know that the anyway referred to my bank balance.

Theo's voice became a growl. Dog-like. 'Don't come. Because I won't see you. Don't come here. I won't see you. I don't want to see you. Ever.' The line went dead. I knew, I could see, as clearly as if I were there with him, that now Theo was crying. I waited a couple of stunned, numbed minutes and then I called his number. There was no answer.

I called him three more times that evening, Messaged him as well. I told him that he COULD trust me, that I WAS to be trusted. But I got no reply. I stopped doing it at about nine o'clock. It wasn't that I gave up on him. But if he wasn't in the mood to reply then he wasn't in the mood to reply. I knew how I would feel if I were being bombarded with unwanted messages. He would think me a nuisance and a pest, not just perfidious. I was also getting a bit drunk by then and realised that if I went on messaging him while getting even drunker it wouldn't help very much.

I had gone to the Bull. It was better than staying at home alone, sober and brooding, in the flat that now had neither Harry nor Theo nor Maxwell in it. I stood at the bar and leant on it as I drank. It's a pose that allows you to think you're in command of your surroundings and of your life, in a way that sitting at a quiet table on your own with just a phone for company does not. One or two people came and chatted to me. I behaved civilly to each of them. One guy I was hardly aware of knowing said that he hadn't seen Harry for some time and asked how he was. 'We split up a few months ago,' I said.

'Oh, I'm sorry to hear that.'

I shrugged in a man-up sort of way and said, 'Well, these things happen in life.' To my relief he wandered off and went to talk so someone else.

I tried to phone Maxwell but his phone didn't seem to have the facility to enable me to leave a voice message. It just rang out, and rang on till it stopped. I sent him a Whatsapp message instead. I told him that he didn't need to stay away. Repeated my promise that he could stay with me until between us we found him somewhere else. And I said that if he already had found somewhere else he had only to call or message me to arrange a convenient time to come and pick his stuff up. No answer came back. I wasn't remotely surprised by that.

I phoned my mother. I asked her if I could go over to Stirling and have lunch with her the next day. 'Of course,' she said. 'Of course. What would you like? I passed the butcher's today and they had some lovely looking pork chops.' I said I thought pork chops would be brilliant. 'Have you been drinking?' she asked. I reminded her that my term had ended earlier that day. She said that of course she knew that. How could she have forgotten that? She didn't need to add that she took my answer to her question as a yes.

I thought I was probably still in shock, not just hung-over, as I headed out along the familiar road to Stirling: the chain of motorways than circled Glasgow, then headed up past Cumbernauld. I tried to make sense of Theo's extraordinary behaviour. But how does anyone do that except by reference (compare and contrast) to their own? I simply would not have spoken to Theo the way he'd spoken to me. I wouldn't have felt the thing in the way he did. All right, I didn't have a sister. I didn't have a fierce southerner's feeling for the honour of family. I didn't have a hurt, outraged Spanish mother to deal with. A mother who felt violated by the turn that events had taken. I wasn't Spanish. (Or Guanche.) In the end I simply wasn't Theo.

But did Theo have the remotest idea of the pain and anguish, the tearing apart, the loss, and the feelings of rejection and un-lovedness that he'd caused me? It's when we are hurt most grievously that we manage to hurt others the most, almost without noticing.

I didn't share any of this with my mother. Of course she asked after the other people in my life, feeling her way like a blind person towards people she had never met or even seen pictures of. What was happening with the man who had come to stay on the mezzanine? she wanted to know. He'd recently moved out, I said. Found himself somewhere else. That wasn't a lie exactly; he obviously had found himself somewhere else, even if it was a shop doorway or a dry spot under a bridge. My answer wasn't a lie. But it was pretty shitty.

She wanted to know if I was still in touch with whoever it was out on Tenerife. I said we were still in touch but that things had cooled off a bit. 'Well, thank the Lord for that,' she said. 'I've been afraid you were going to tell me one day that you were going to up sticks and move out there. I've been lying awake at night thinking about it.'

Oh fucking hell, I thought. I too had been lying awake thinking about that possibility. Although in a rather more wishful-thinking kind of way than, evidently, my mother had. The new knowledge that if I did move two thousand miles away this would be a major catastrophe in her life did nothing to cheer me.

She didn't know I'd been out to the Canaries as recently as last weekend, and I didn't enlighten her. Though I did catch her eyeing my face very carefully several times as we squared up over the pork chops. Eventually she said, 'You've been out in the sun.'

'Yes,' I said. 'Yesterday was the sports winners' morning.' She nodded impatiently, to say that there was no way she wouldn't know that. 'You couldn't escape it. For a lot of the time I sat full in it.'

'You must have had more sun Glasgow way than we did,' she said, taut-cheeked, like Billy Connelly doing an Edinburgh lady. We called it a draw at that point and neither of us said more on the subject.

Later, as we sat in her small garden I found there was something I wanted to ask her. 'I've been thinking about some of my friends' racial roots. They're complex affairs in many cases. I came to wondering about us. I mean, how Scottish are we as a family?'

'Scottish on both sides,' my mother said. There was some satisfaction in her voice. 'You know that.' Then her face showed signs of a faint unease. 'Of course I'm talking about the generations we know about. Your grandparents. My grandparents. Your father's grandparents.'

'But before that. What do we know about before that?'

My mother made an uncomfortable little movement in her garden chair. 'Well, I don't know. If you go back far enough... Well, anyone can find anything. You've seen those Who Do You Think You Are? programmes. People discover all sorts of things about themselves if they go back far enough. We might find if we went back far enough that we had an ancestor who was black.' She laughed at the absurdity of that, then glanced quickly at her bare, milk-white forearms, to reassure herself of the sheer improbability of it.

'Actually,' she said a moment later, as though remembering something that was a wee bit inconvenient, 'on my mother's mother's side there was a little branch that was English.'

'Could be worse,' I said with a straight face.

'There were some photographs. I guess I've still got them somewhere. Very old ones. They must go right back to the beginnings of photography. They're in that what d'you call it … octopus ink.'

'Sepia,' I said. 'I think it actually came from cuttlefish.'

'I'll have a rummage around before your next visit. See if I can find them for you to have a look at.'

I had one more go at messaging Theo that evening. No reply came back. I didn't try to phone him. If he'd wanted to talk on the phone he'd have said so, or else rung me himself. I sat at home watching the telly and pondering the irony that before term ended I'd been juggling so many things and people that I'd hardly had time to think; while now that I had all the time in the world on my hands I had nothing to do with it. My life was suddenly empty. Like when you're having a bath and you accidentally catch your foot in the plug chain and almost before you know what's happened all the water has run out of it. At least I wouldn't be rushing back to Tenerife any time soon. My overdraft could heave a sigh of relief about that.

Next day I unplugged all Maxwell's equipment, sound system and laptop, and stacked it up in the hall where it would have to wait till he came to remove it. In the evening I took the train into Glasgow Central and walked up to Bath Street.

I walked through the theatre foyer towards the stairs that led up to the bar where Maxwell worked. Before I got to the foot of the steps I was stopped by a grey-haired woman in glasses and a smock uniform. 'May I see your ticket?'

'Sorry,' I said. 'I haven't come for the show; I wanted a word with someone who works in the bar up here.' I pointed reasonably. 'Maxwell.'

'Ooh,' said the usherette, with a perplexed look on her face. 'I don't think I know a Maxwell. But I can't let you go up. You'd need to ask the duty manager for that.'

'Of course,' I said. I looked around the foyer, now crowding up with an incoming audience. 'Is he about?'

'It's she tonight. But I'm afraid she's not very handy just now. She's had to help to man one of the bars. One of the staff hasn't turned up.'

'Which bar would that be?' I asked. Again I pointed up the stairs. This time the gesture was meant to represent a question mark.

'Yes, that's right,' said the woman.

'I see,' I said. 'I wonder if in that case you could possibly pop up and ask?' I wasn't hopeful. My interlocutress didn't look like someone who popped anywhere.

'Terribly sorry,' she said (when we Scots say terribly sorry we always sound more terribly sorry than anyone else does), 'but I can't leave my post.'

I felt my blood start to pump hotly, angry at this brick wall of Kafka-esque logic. But I kept my tone level as I said rather crisply, 'Then in the circumstances could you make an exception just this once and let me go up and speak to the manager myself? I'll only be a minute.'

'Well I suppose...' began the woman, but I had dodged past her and up the stairs before she could finish the sentence.

It was evident as soon as I came in sight of the bar that Maxwell was not at work. Happily my arrival coincided with a lull and I was able to lean over the bar and speak to the duty manager at once. I'd had no difficulty picking her out. She had a look of authority about her, an authority that extended beyond the bar counter. And the other person on duty there was male anyway. 'I'm sorry to trouble you,' I said. 'I was looking for Maxwell. But it doesn't look like he's here tonight.'

The manager was a woman of about my age with straight chestnut hair. She peered at me carefully. 'That's right. He's not. May I ask who...?'

'I'm a friend of his,' I said. 'I've been putting him up at my flat for a bit. But he disappeared three days ago, leaving his door keys and most of his stuff.'

The woman shook her head. 'We haven't seen him – he hasn't come into work – since Saturday night.'

'I see.'

'You have his phone number, I imagine?'

'Of course,' I said. 'But he's not picking up.'

The manager sighed. 'That's also been our experience.' Then she frowned. 'Well, leaving aside the inconvenience to us, I hope he's all right.'

'So do I. Look, I know one or two other places he might be. I'll try them and let you know if...'

A moment or two later we were swapping phone numbers. 'Does he have family?' the manager asked. Her name was Ellen.

'His mother lives in Italy,' I told her. 'His father's dead.'

'At some point someone may have to report him missing. I'm not sure if there's an obligation on employers. I'd have to look it up...'

'There's rules about it in schools. Sorry, I'm a teacher. Duty of care and so on. But that's kids. Maxwell's an adult. So I don't know...' It was at that point that I realised this might be a bit serious.

I walked on over to Virginia Street. It was still early evening. I didn't really expect to find Maxwell in Del's.

I just thought that someone in there might know where he was … or what had happened to him. As soon as I walked in I saw an unmistakeable figure, rear view, standing at the bar. There was a forlorn look about him. I had the impression he wanted to engage the barman in conversation but that the barman was too busy to play. I wasn't sure whether he swung round towards me before I called his name, or whether I called his name first. 'Chris.'

For half a second the look on his face was strained, unhappy. Then it brightened, quick as a spark, into a smile of happy recognition and greeting. He made a move towards me, wagging his whole body like a puppy. 'Jonty!'

I hugged him.

He clutched at me as if I'd gone to his rescue when he thought he was drowning. In response I held him even tighter. Then it was like I was drowning and that in that moment he was the whole world to me. Everything I had and everything I hoped for suddenly channelled into him.

We let each other go and stood eyeballing each other from about a foot away. 'You're not with Maxwell,' Chris said. How had that thought popped into his head so suddenly? And he had remembered the name Maxwell.

But then I found myself doing the same thing. I blurted out, 'You're not with Jimmy.' That wasn't a very discreet way to begin with a so-very-recent ex-pupil. At least I had a good excuse for remembering the name Jimmy. I'd taught the boy a couple of years back, and had spoken to him the day before yesterday. I glanced around very rapidly, moving only my eyeballs while my face stayed trained on Chris's. I took in his barely started pint of lager on the counter and the fact that there were (at this early hour) some empty tables. I said, 'I'm going to get myself a drink. I don't know if you'd like to...' my voice became childishly diffident '...sit at a table?'

'Yes.' It came out very quietly.

I became a schoolmaster for a moment. 'Then go and find one.' And he did.

We didn't begin with Jimmy or Maxwell. We talked about the routine, just ended, of the last days of the school summer term. About the strangeness of them for Chris, this year when it was the last one. 'You get a weird feeling,' he said, 'during the final few days, like someone's blowing up a bicycle tyre inside you. And then in the days that come afterwards ... well, like now ... you feel you're kind of floating. Floating above everything that's gone before. Like oil above water.' His eyes had been sparkling into mine as he spoke but now he dipped them like a pair of headlights. 'Not that it would have felt the same for you, I guess. Not that you'd remember.'

I said, 'It was exactly like that for me. I might not have put it into words so well as you just did. But I do remember.' It was my turn to dip my headlights.

'So what's happened to Maxwell?' Chris asked a few minutes later. Three quarters of a pint had damped his inhibitions. 'You said he was your boyfriend sometimes. Is that still the ... situation?'

I laughed at his brazen nosiness; I revelled in it. 'Yes and no.' I shook my head, a weary reflex. 'It's a very long and complex story. I do have a rather more serious boyfriend. You don't want to know about...'

'In Tenerife, right? Or am I being...'

'Oh bloody hell, Chris. No, I don't mean... I mean you're right about Tenerife. That just surprised me. But that's another complicated story. Which you won't want to...'

'I do want to.'

I sighed involuntarily. 'You really do not. Maxwell's gone missing. I came here to try and find him.'

'Wow.' I could see from the light in Chris's eyes that my private life – that thing that woozles normally can't even imagine their cardboard cut-out teachers owning – had morphed into a rich and amazing adventure in his imagination: something from the pages of Defoe or Agatha Christie.

I said, 'I don't suppose you've seen him?'

'Me? No way. I haven't been in here since that night. The night we met in here last time. I haven't seen him around town either.' Then Chris's face took on a pained, strained look. 'Do you need to go on out and look for him? Or do you have time to tell me the story?'

I smiled. 'I've time to tell you the story.' How little Chris knew about being thirty-four! He couldn't guess that rather than combing the streets of Glasgow hopelessly I would happily stay here and tell him twenty stories. After a moment's indecision I went to the bar and bought us each a fresh pint of lager. Chris had come through his first one more or less unscathed. He was eighteen and I'd seen him with a pint glass in his hand before now. I reckoned I wasn't being irresponsible in buying him a second one.

And then I told him the story. Reasonably briefly. Where and when I'd met Theo. ('Where exactly did you find him?' 'On a park bench. It was all fairly civilised.') I mentioned the fact that we'd pretty quickly gone to bed together but didn't go into details. I was pretty sure that Chris would neither expect nor want them. I told him how I'd lost my phone and then met Maxwell... ('Just over there.' I pointed.) I went through the whole thing, trying to focus on the salient bits rather than irrelevant or too intimate details. I left out the bit about Maxwell referring to me as an older man: it seemed unnecessary. I didn't mention my worries about my overdraft, and I spared him a lecture on the depth, complexity and confusion of my feelings. I only told him how my discovery of the Spanish word for sunset-dusk had somehow changed everything. He nodded his head vigorously at that, understanding very clearly that this single glimpse into my soul was representative. He was a young man of great sensitivity and understanding, with a gift for empathy beyond his years. He was someone who understood the importance of words, the talismanic power of them. *Atardecer.* After all, he'd been my pupil.

TWENTY

'Have you contacted Nat?' Chris asked. He was evidently also quite practical.

'No,' I said. 'I really can't imagine what I'd say to him.'

'Well you could let him know that his selfish behaviour has caused a split between you and your boyfriend. It's his fault, not yours, that Theo is angry with you.'

'OK,' I said, 'but I can't see what good it would do to point that out to him.'

'It might make you feel better.'

I chuckled. 'OK. I'll think about it. I'm still not sure how I could word it.'

'And isn't it time to tell the police that Maxwell's gone missing? Three days now…'

'I talked about that with the theatre manager. She's looking into it. It's hardly my responsibility.'

'Couldn't you at least contact his mother?'

'I don't have an address or a number for her.' I'd already told Chris that she lived with her new husband in northern Italy.

In the enthusiasm generated by his second pint of lager Chris got his phone out. Not to be outdone I got my own out. Between us we looked into the question of how to report a missing person. 'It says the police spend a whopping fourteen percent of their time on missing persons cases,' Chris said. 'Why do they always say persons, not people?'

'It makes them sound more important, more official,' I said facetiously. Chris wasn't the only one whose second pint was getting to him. 'Seriously, I think it's a legal thing. A person as a legal entity.' Chris seemed pleased with that. He nodded appreciatively at the word entity.

We put in a further minute or two of research on government websites and then I found myself phoning the local police station. I wouldn't have done this if Chris hadn't goaded me, perhaps shamed me, into it.

They asked me if I would go and see them, and fill in a form, at the police station in the morning. In the meantime they took as many details as I could give them, including the fact that Maxwell's mother lived in Italy. They said that they would look into it.

We put our phones away like two swordsmen sheathing their weapons. I saw Chris eyeing my nearly empty pint glass. He said, 'Can I get you another lager?'

I was certainly up for another. I wasn't sure if Chris was. I said, 'Have you eaten? Are you going to?'

'I told my parents I was going to Jimmy's.' That was an intriguing answer, though it wasn't the answer to my question. 'Yes, but have you eaten?'

'No.'

'Then perhaps we ought to…'

'Oh, let's have one more here first.' He sounded very grown-up as he said that. Someone who could handle three pints. Someone who probably had done.

'OK,' I said. He was eighteen; I wasn't in charge of his stomach. 'But I'll get them. I get a salary. You don't yet.' He probably didn't have an overdraft yet either. But that's the way things are when you go out drinking with a younger person. The way things always have been.

I bought the drinks and walked back with them to our table. I had a view of him watching my return from the otherwise empty table. The sight was heart-stopping. I put the drinks down on the table and said, 'After we've had these we go and eat something. That's an order. But don't worry. I'll be buying.'

I saw Chris blush slightly. But he smiled through it, took his glass in his hand and said, 'Thank you, Jonty.'

I said, 'Cheers Chris,' and he tapped his glass against mine and said, 'Cheers Jonty.'

The next thing he said was, 'I need to get a job for the summer,' and an idea popped into my mind even as he was saying it.

'I can think of a possibility for at least a day or two,' I said. 'I'm thinking of Maxwell's bar job at the theatre. They could probably do with a stand-in. I'd put a word in for you if you were interested.' This was third-pint talk, I realised.

'Could you?' Chris's face lit up. It seemed he was third-pint interested. At that point my phone rang in my pocket. I took it out and answered it.

It was someone calling from the police station. After checking my identity they told me that Maxwell had left the country. He'd flown out of Glasgow, bound for Turin, on Sunday. 'You told us his mother lived in northern Italy,' the voice said.

'Yes. I don't remember the name of the village. But I know it's in Piedmont. Turin would be his local airport.'

'Then the evidence would seem to point to his going home to his mother, wouldn't you say? Or do you still want to go ahead with registering him as a missing person?'

'No,' I said, feeling a bit abashed but trying not to let Chris see it. 'It looks like you've found him. Thank you,' I remembered to say. 'I do appreciate that. I'm sorry for troubling you.'

'Not at all, sir,' said the person at the other end and the call ended.

'Well,' I said, looking at Chris brightly, 'you probably got that.'

Chris had. 'Sounds like he's gone home to his mother.'

I nodded. 'That's about the size of it. Now I'd better…' I realised as I began the sentence that I could kill two birds with one stone here. I gave Chris a meaningful look. 'I'm going to phone the manager of the theatre.'

A couple of minutes later I'd spoken to Ellen and given her the news from the police station. Before she could wind up the call I said, 'If you could do with someone to man the bar for a few days, till ... well, till whatever ... I could recommend someone.' We spoke for another minute. Chris made an impatient gesture, wanting to take the phone and speak directly to Ellen but I overrode him with a raised hand and a shake of my head. I told Ellen that Chris was a highly responsible eighteen-year-old. That I'd been his teacher for three years ... and so on and so on. I didn't tell her we were currently sitting in a gay bar together and that the young man whose virtues I was extolling was now into his third pint of lager. Had I allowed Chris to talk to her I knew that would have become only too apparent. We ended the call with an agreement that Chris would go round to see her at eleven o'clock tomorrow morning. I peered carefully at Chris as I suggested that particular time. I didn't think he'd be able to give a good account of himself much earlier.

I put the phone back in my pocket. Chris and I looked at each other across the table. 'Thank you, Jonty,' Chris said. Then, in a respectful tone, 'I think you're wonderful.' At that point I saw his lower lip tremble. I knew the reasons for that would be complex. Not mainly about me; that was certain.

I decided it was time to change the subject. I picked a risky one, and perhaps I shouldn't have done. I knew I was being intrusive. But we were on third-pint terms now. 'So what's happened with Jimmy?' He didn't have to tell me if he didn't want to.

Chris's lips tightened. He said, 'We're still friends. I wanted more than that. He didn't.'

'It's often that way,' I said softly. He didn't acknowledge the remark. Perhaps he didn't hear it.

'He may not be gay. I mean we did stuff. Sex stuff. But now he wants to stop that.' Chris shrugged. Covering his hurt with a dismissive gesture. 'Besides, I'm going to Edinburgh in the autumn and he's going to Strathclyde.'

'You may not be gay, Chris,' I said. 'You're only eighteen. You've still got a lot more to discover about yourself.'

Chris looked at me challengingly. 'When did you know? How old were you?'

'OK.' I'd asked for this. I couldn't deny him. 'I had experiences with boys as a teenager...'

'With girls too?'

'No,' I said. 'Only boys.'

'Same with me.' He muttered that quietly but I heard him clearly. Then he said more loudly, 'You went to Edinburgh, didn't you?'

'Yes,' I said. 'Edinburgh University. Where you're going.' I ran on. 'I dated girls. I wanted to keep my options open. Not box myself into a corner.'

'Is that advice you're giving me?' He smiled knowingly.

'Yes,' I said. He would have a whale of time with lads at Edinburgh. I knew that. Just as I had done. Up to a point he would forget Jimmy. I wasn't going to tell him this, though. All in good time, I told myself. Let those things be his own discoveries. 'It didn't work out with girls in my case. Doesn't mean it won't in yours.'

'It worked out with guys, though?' Chris checked. I nodded. 'And then ... we used to say at school that we thought you lived with a guy. Perhaps it was just rumour...'

'It may have been rumour. But it was true. I lived for years with a man called Harry. He was English. Still is, obviously. And he's a lovely guy. But we split up six months ago.'

'Jesus,' said Chris. 'Is that what life's like? Gay life anyway? An endless series of break-ups? You and Theo. You and Maxwell. You and Harry. Me and Jimmy.'

'It needn't be,' I said. 'I've known gay couples, getting on in life, who've been together forty years or more.' It was true. I did. Only not very many. 'Come on.' I found a businesslike manner. 'Time we got something to eat inside you.'

We went to an Italian place just a couple of blocks away. I wasn't going to spoil him by buying one of the expensive main meat or fish courses. I wasn't going to spoil myself by buying one of the main meat or fish courses either. I said, 'Pizza? Pasta?' and hoped he'd take the hint. Which he did. He went for a pizza that had almost everything in it but wasn't too expensive, and to make him feel comfortable I copied him. It was actually very nice – and extremely big. Each one, when it arrived, was the size of a small cocktail-tabletop, and in order to fit both of them on our small table we had to let the plates overhang our laps a bit, like Alpine snow shelves that threatened to tip into the condition of avalanches.

I wasn't going to order a bottle of wine. I thought that would be dangerously incautious. I suggested we had a glass each. But I wasn't able to steamroller him this time, as I'd managed to do over the main course. He made a little wide-eyed moue of disappointment and said, 'Or if we went ahead and had a whole bottle then you could drink most of it?' This conversation took place in front of the waiter, whose face told me he knew I was being taken for a complete mug. I too realised I was being taken for a complete mug. But I found I didn't care a bit. I went ahead, to quote Chris, and ordered a bottle of something. Something strong, red and Sicilian.

We talked about the big news of the moment. It was still Brexit of course. Nicola Sturgeon had, as expected, demanded a new referendum on Scottish sovereignty and independence. A Scottish MEP had got up in the European Parliament and made a moving speech along the lines of: Scotland did not lose faith with Europe when the chips were down; now Europe must keep faith with Scotland. This had fallen on deliberately deaf ears. The Spanish delegates had looked particularly uncomfortable. Their discomfort was all too transparent. If Europe could cut deals with Scotland, bypassing the UK and its institutions, what havoc might not be wreaked if Europe started cutting deals with the parts of Spain that didn't see themselves as Castile-Spanish? Catalunya? The Basque Country? The Canaries...? Chris and I chewed this tough bit of gristle over and managed to feel quite mature and sensible while we were doing it.

Chris said, 'I was too young to vote in the Scottish Independence referendum. But I'd probably have voted to stay in the Union if I could have. I know my parents did.' I nodded. I had also voted to remain a citizen of the United Kingdom. In almost everyone's case there had been a bit of a battle between heart and head. Overall, head had won on the day. I thought, by the way, that Braveheart was a good name for a popular film. It would never have sold under the name Bravehead.

'I think,' Chris went on, 'that if we get another chance to vote on Independence I'll vote for it. Out of sheer bloody-mindedness.'

I said, 'If you want to vote for Independence, that's fine. Go for it. But do it for a good reason. Not out of bloody-mindedness, which is just another word for spite. That's what a lot of the Brexiteers did in England. And that's why we're in our current mess.' I caught myself sounding like a teacher and knew I'd better stop myself.

I told him my theory about the naming of the Braveheart film instead.

He smiled at that. 'I suppose you're right. Fantasies about a glorious past are one thing. Real politics is something else. Real politics is about real pockets.' (I wondered where he'd read that.) 'It's about everyone's standard of living in the end, isn't it?'

I said I thought it was.

'And it's going to put an end to the Erasmus Programme. At least it is for us Brits.' He scowled as he said that.

'It might do,' I agreed. It was deeply unfair, I thought, that intelligent youngsters who had voted to remain in the European Union would now probably be deprived of their opportunity to study in continental European universities by a small majority of people who were too old to benefit from it. 'The trouble is that the people who've voted out have never heard of the Erasmus Programme and wouldn't approve of it anyway. They'd say it was giving an unfair advantage to people who already had a good start in life…'

Chris rose to this, outraged. 'By having rich parents? That's not remotely true. Look at…'

'I didn't mean by being rich,' I said gently. 'I meant by being bright.'

He calmed down visibly and thought about this for a moment. I could see him gradually working out that I'd been paying him and his generation a compliment. 'The trouble is,' he said eventually, 'that sometimes people just go and behave like lemmings.' Then a moment's anxiety clouded his face and he looked at me narrowly. 'Do you know what a lemming is?'

I just managed not to smile. I was often charmed by teenage uncertainties as to which areas of knowledge were inaccessible to adults. I thought this one a cracker.

I nodded seriously. 'Yes, I do know what a lemming is,' I told him. 'Good analogy.'

We came on to the other issue of the moment. The candidature of Donald Trump in the upcoming elections for US President. Actually there was nothing to discuss about his candidature: he was a candidate. It was the possibility of his winning the election that was exercising our fearful imaginations. By now he was the only Republican still in the running. He was therefore in with more than a remote chance. But I tried to be reassuring.

'Don't even think about it. Lightning doesn't strike twice. It's unprecedented that there should be two world-class tragedies, each of historical proportions, in the space of six months.' I was sixteen years older than Chris. I'd been his teacher. Those things helped give me the confidence to say that.

'What about Hitler and Mussolini, then?' Chris argued.

'Not in the space of six months,' I said, now sounding like a teacher who is not quite sure of his facts. I was conscious that it was sixteen years since I'd studied the history of the period. Chris, on the other hand, had taken an exam in it during the past month.

'Well that's true,' Chris said, nodding. 'Mussolini 1922, Hitler 1933.' I was relieved to hear him say that. What's more, this seemed to vindicate my belief that Trump could never come to power. QED. My argument was conclusive.

'Just think,' I said. 'All those women at the top tables. Hilary Clinton in Washington, Angela Merkel in Berlin, Theresa May in London...'

'Not forgetting Nicola Sturgeon,' Chris very properly reminded me.

'It'll be tea and sandwiches at Number Ten.'

'And they'll take it in turns to bring the cheesecake.' Chris laughed at his own flash of cleverness and I joined him. Then he said, 'Why did you and Harry break up?'

'Oh dear.' I felt awfully old suddenly. And I wondered if Chris was old enough. Old enough or experienced enough to understand it. I took an imaginary deep breath and went for it. 'OK then. I'll tell you a story. It was like this, if you like. There were two people who lived in a very beautiful garden and they were idyllically happy. Happy with each other. Happy with their surroundings. In the most beautiful part of the garden there was an apple tree with lots of apples on it…'

'I think I know how this ends…'

'But there wasn't a serpent. They picked the apples themselves, in each other's plain sight. Sometimes they shared an apple between them, taking a bite each then passing it back again…'

Chris seemed to shrink and shrivel in his chair. 'Stop. Stop now. Please don't go on, Jonty.'

He hadn't needed to say that. A glance at his face was enough to tell me I'd gone further than he'd wanted. Though he had asked the question he hadn't wanted the answer. Or anyway, not that answer. 'I'm sorry, Chris,' I said. But sorry Chris didn't seem to be enough at that moment. I mumbled, 'I'm sorry, sweetheart.'

He'd been on the edge of tears, I knew, but now I saw him overcome the reflex with a steely mastery of his emotion. I admired him for that, but it also unnerved me. 'Does it always end like that?' he asked. It was a question but there was a stern judgement embedded in it like a pebble in a snowball.

'I don't know,' I said. 'I told you I knew some gay couples who'd been together thirty, forty years or more. But who knows what volcanic upheavals they've experienced along the way? Who knows what compromises they've had to reach? I've never had the temerity to ask anyone that directly. It would be like asking your parents if they'd ever thought about splitting up.'

Chris nodded. 'I see,' he said. 'Yes. That makes sense.' It might have made sense to him but he didn't sound very happy about it. There wasn't a lot of joy in being Bravehead.

'So...' I began, then stopped. But he seemed to know exactly what I was hesitating on the brink of saying, as he came out with the thing himself.

'So what about your man in the Canaries?'

'I don't know,' I said. 'As you've seen, it hasn't got off to a very good start.'

'Because of Maxwell, you mean?'

'Because of Maxwell, and because of the fact that I haven't told him about Maxwell. I wanted to. I intended to, then we both surprised each other by saying I love you ... and it was sort of too late.'

Chris nodded vigorously. 'It's a big thing to say, isn't it. Saying I love you to someone.'

The way he said that made me fairly sure that he'd actually said that to someone other than his parents and family pets in the course of his short life. I found myself rather awed by that. 'Yes, it is,' I said. I was glad I'd only called him sweetheart.

There was a moment's hiatus. Chris took a swig of his wine and I followed his example in a sort of reflex that might have been born out of courtesy or out of habit.

Then he asked, 'What's it like to live with another person?'

'Big question.' I was buying time with that, the way a teacher does in class. 'In some ways it's the same as when you live with parents or brothers and sisters.' A thought struck me; later I would investigate it. 'There's all the give and take of bathroom share. Who gets to do the chores, whether you want to watch TV together, or separately, or not at all...'

'But there must be more to it than that.'

'There is, of course...'

'I don't just mean sex...'

'No, obviously you don't.'

'I wondered whether it's like... You know, in Wuthering Heights, when Heathcliff bribes the sexton to remove a panel from Cathy's coffin, and a panel from his, so that when he comes to die and is buried next to her they'll be joined in death.'

'Yes,' I said. 'But don't you find that passage a bit gruesome?' I was playing devil's advocate now though. I found it one of the most deeply moving episodes in the book.

'I agree, it's gruesome. But isn't it really a metaphor for something else? That's really what I was asking you. When you live with someone, I mean really live with someone, the way our parents do, the way you and Harry did... I wondered if it was like that. That the panels between your beings get removed somehow and you become ... you know how it says in the Bible ... you become one flesh. One mind, one heart, one soul if you like.'

I didn't know where I was going to find words, or even voice, to answer that. He read my storm of feelings in my face. 'I'm sorry. Did I...?'

That gave me just time to compose myself enough to speak. 'Don't be sorry,' I said. I saw his hand move towards mine on the table. Then he placed his fingers on top of mine on the table top.

After a moment he said, in a changing-the-subject sort of voice – though it was also a three-pint-and-half-a-bottle-of-wine sort of voice, 'Have you never sometimes been scared that everybody, yourself and the whole rest of humanity, is living in boxes like Heathcliff's coffin and Cathy's, but that everybody else's box is opened up to everybody else's – like with Cathy and Heathcliff? That they're all somehow joined up? But that yours isn't. That you're the only person who lives in a totally isolated box?'

For a second I could hear the tick of my heart, the hiss of my blood. 'When I was your age, or younger … yes, I did sometimes think that…' I could hardly believe I was managing to get my words out.

'Otherwise, how can we ever know what another person feels or thinks? When you say the sky is blue and I say the sky is blue, how can we possibly know we mean the same thing?'

'We can't,' I said. 'We can look at a picture together, or at a bright blue shirt, and we can agree that's the colour of the sky… We agree it matches our image of the sky's blueness, but we can't really know. One of the oldest questions in philosophy is what makes you you and me somebody else.'

'And vice versa,' Chris allowed generously.

'But we can't really know what another person feels or thinks. Except a little bit, in art, perhaps. In listening to music. Reading books…'

'That passage from Wuthering Heights…'

'And as you suggested, in living with another person. And in that situation…' This came to me in a sort of flash; I'd never had the thought before – unless I'd read it somewhere and buried it. 'It's only through knowing another person that we can know ourselves.'

'Only in knowing you can I know myself,' Chris said. Then he became flustered. 'Sorry. I didn't mean you in particular, Jonty. I think I might have read that somewhere.'

'It's OK,' I said. 'I knew what you meant.'

He wasn't still holding his hand over mine on the table top in that startling role-reversal gesture of comfort.

He'd withdrawn it after an appropriately judged couple of seconds. But now I found my hand moving across the table towards his hand. I shouldn't be doing this, I told myself. But all the same I did it. Changing our roles back again I placed my hand over his for a moment.

We came to the end of our pizzas. And of the wine. Perhaps I'd drunk slightly more of it than Chris had but there wasn't much in it. When the bill came Chris actually started rummaging in a pocket and burbled about paying something towards it. I firmly talked him out of that idea; actually it wasn't all that difficult.

When I'd finished paying, and left a small tip on the table, the moment arrived at which we would have to stand up. I would need to talk to him about setting him on his homeward road before we left the table. For a second we looked into each other's faces, neither making a move to our feet, each waiting for the other to say something.

In the event Chris found his words first. 'Where do you live exactly?' he asked.

'Paisley,' I said. 'Like you. I have a flat in the old mill.' Our pupils' addresses were not a secret. In loco parentis, duty of care, whatever, we had them on file. Of course it didn't work the other way round.

Chris said, 'I told my parents I'd be staying with Jimmy.' He spread his hands on the table top: the tension of the moment. 'Obviously I won't be doing that...' He looked searchingly into my eyes. 'Could I come back to your place?'

I said yes. What else was I going to say? I said yes for fuck's sake.

TWENTY-ONE

'You're an only child, aren't you,' I said.

'How did you know? Oh of course, you'd have all that stuff on your files about us.'

'We do have, as it happens, but I wasn't remembering anything from there. I haven't been spending my spare time researching you.'

We were sitting opposite each other on a late train out to Paisley. Our knees weren't touching. On the other hand I had bought his ticket for him.

'Then how did you know?'

'I was guessing,' I said. 'When I was talking earlier about living at home with brothers and sisters it went through my mind that you probably didn't have any.'

'Yes, but why?'

'I'm an only child too. Takes one to know one. Not sure what made me guess that. Just some kind of instinct.'

'Can you guess when other people are gay? I mean you personally, Jonty.'

'Sometimes,' I answered. 'I very often get it wrong though. Even with my age and experience.' I smiled to show him I was mocking myself a little. Sometimes young people needed guidance in this area.

'What about the people you teach? Can you guess about us lot?'

'I try not to let myself do that.' I was speaking truthfully. 'Apart from the fact that I might guess wrongly I kind of feel it wouldn't be appropriate.'

'Would you have guessed about me?' he persisted. 'I mean, if you'd allowed yourself.'

'I honestly don't know. I don't think I thought about it till I saw you in Del's that night with Jimmy. Even then I didn't think too much about it. People your age go through phases. They experiment in all directions.' I stopped, hearing myself. 'Of course you know that. I don't need to tell you.'

It's funny how when you know a train route thoroughly, even at night you seem to know where you are; you recognize your home patch of darkness. Patterns of trackside lights, I supposed, memorised subliminally, along with the individual sounds the points made when you went over them, and the sensations of speeding up and slowing down. At any rate I was able to say with conviction as I got to my feet, 'Come on, we're back in Paisley.' Chris seemed surprised by my announcement although he too must have known the route well – at least in daytime. Perhaps he'd dozed for half a second.

He wasn't disoriented by the walk back to my place from the station. He seemed almost familiar with it. The mill was quite a landmark; everyone knew it.

Earlier he'd phoned his parents and told them he was staying the night at a friend's house. That he'd met someone who'd put him in touch with someone else who would interview him for a part-time holiday job at the theatre in the morning. He'd be back home at lunchtime. The person at the other end – I took it to be his mother – must then have asked him about clothes for the interview, because he smoothly said that the friend he was staying with would lend him some.

I listened to Chris's end of this conversation in a state of anxiety that bordered on the feverish. I was terrified he'd put a foot wrong at some point: give away the wrong kind of information; trip over words in a way that pointed only too clearly to his state of intoxication; finger me as the person he was staying the night with. But he did none of those things. He breezed through it like a star candidate doing an oral exam in a foreign language and heading for an A double-plus at the end of it.

But amidst my anxiety I found space to dwell on one word he'd used. Friend. He'd said it twice during the conversation. OK, he'd had to say friend: who else would his parents let him stay the night with without questioning it? However drunk he was, he wasn't going to say he was going home with his ex-teacher. Now as he walked through the streets beside me, prattling happily for the moment about nothing really, I felt almost ridiculously elated, and privileged by his company.

Still I found a moment for a pang of introspection. What was I taking him home for if it wasn't to have sex with him? And if we weren't going to have sex together then what was I going to do with him? It would hardly have been kind to him to uncork another bottle of wine. And sit and share it. Not when he had an interview in the morning, plus his parents to deal with at lunchtime. Perhaps we would simply sit for a final half-hour with a cup of coffee. Like people did at uni. As Chris would soon discover.

'Hey, it's big when you get up close to it.' Chris threw his head right back to look up the wall of the massive building while I got my key out. Then we were inside and Chris liked the place better moment by moment. He loved the aviary-like space of the atrium, the great openness of it and the greenhouse-type roof above it, even though that looked up at this hour only into the night's opaque darkness. He even liked the four flights of the staircase. He liked my hallway, once I'd unlocked and we'd walked into it. He saw Maxwell's stuff still stacked on the hall table and fingered it gingerly. 'Maxwell's?' he asked. Like 'Doctor Livingstone I presume', it was hardly a question. I just nodded.

And then he loved my living-room. 'This is wonderful.' He chuckled. 'Those massive windows.' He walked to one of them and peered out of it. The curtains were still open: I'd left the place in daylight. I walked over and stood by his side. I pointed to the lights of one or two obvious landmarks so that he could get his bearings, but he tired of that game after a dozen seconds. He span round towards me, gave me a great bear hug and kissed me.

I didn't resist him. I joined in the hugging and the kissing. I loved the beery, winey, pasta smell of him. I hadn't kissed an eighteen-year-old since I'd been an eighteen-year-old. This didn't just bring back memories; it was an entirely new and different, and wonderful, experience. And if I hadn't kissed anyone quite so youthful in all those years, then I certainly hadn't been to bed with, or had sex with, anyone that youthful. As the years piled up around me it became less and less likely that I would ever do so again

We'd stopped kissing. We rested in each other's arms, unmoving, like animals caught in traps that they can neither understand nor escape from. We were prisoners of the moment and of each other. We felt each other's breaths on our cheeks, felt each other's chests expand and contract in time with them, and felt each other's racing heartbeats, faster than the breathing, not in synch with it. Through his jeans I could feel the sturdy little ridge of Chris's erect penis pressed hard up against me. I could feel my own, standing up right next to it. I could feel it pressing into him as he let his body weight slide against me. And if I could feel that – then I knew he could feel it too.

He did more than that a quarter-minute later. He lowered one of his hands down my back and cupped one of my buttocks with it. I let him. After a moment's hesitation I did the same to him. He took that as his cue to make the next move. He brought his hand round to my front, squeezing it between our bellies, and squeezed my cock through my denims. If I hadn't had so much to drink I might have come at that point.

Of course I followed suit. Who doesn't? Seconds later we'd got our hands down behind each other's waistbands (his was looser and easier than mine was) and had grasped the warm delicate skin of each other's dicks. Unsurprisingly they were both wet.

One of us had to stop this at some point. I was the supposedly responsible one, the older one, the one who could drink three pints of beer and half a bottle of wine without changing my patterns of thought and behaviour too much. So I did it. But I'd seldom done anything with as much reluctance in my life.

I unclasped his cock and pulled my hand out of his trousers. 'Sorry,' I said meekly, 'but we can't do this. You know we can't.'

He did know. His release of my cock and his taking his hand out of my jeans (a bit of a cat burglar's escape) was the evidence of that. He didn't try to speak. I tried to speak for both of us. 'I've told you my problem with Theo is that he doesn't trust me. I've told him that I can be trusted and should be… Oh shit…'

'I understand, Jonty,' Chris said. We were holding each other loosely around the waist, our chests and faces now drawn away from each other's, a few inches apart. Our crotches no longer pressed together but stood an inch away.

'The other thing is, you'd feel awful in the morning. I might feel bad but you'd feel ten times worse…'

'I understand,' Chris repeated, in exactly the same tone of voice. A flat tone of voice that nevertheless concealed peaks and troughs of feeling and thought. I knew that because it was the same for me.

'Come on.' I patted his shoulder manfully. 'We'll get you a bed sorted out. Talk about interview clothes in the morning.' I released his waist, which obliged him to release mine, and stood back from him, about to turn away. But he stayed standing where he was. Only his face puckered into a wry grin that might have hidden tears behind it – a cloud that almost spits at you on a summer day – and said, 'I don't suppose we could have a nightcap first?'

It would be a small price to pay for a lucky escape, I thought. Or even a reward for being almost good. I found a bottle that had a little whisky in it. We sat on the sofa and drank it. We talked about the music of J. S. Bach, which Chris was just acquiring a taste for. I found an old CD of the Brandenburg Concertos and we listened to it. Then I made up his bed on the mezzanine, lent him a toothbrush and deodorant, and we went our separate ways towards bed. We did have one final goodnight kiss, though. We thought we could run to that.

I fetched out my own interview suit. We were the same height and build. Even the appropriately formal pair of shoes I found him fitted. Clean white shirt and tie. I did find it quite an emotional experience, seeing this beautiful, much younger guy dressed in my own clothes. It was almost as if he'd taken on my personality and character and was inhabiting me, not just the shell I sometimes wore. The moment was dented only slightly when he said, a smidgin of embarrassment in his voice, 'You don't have a belt I could use for the trousers?'

'I'm sure I can find one,' I said, keeping my voice neutral. 'My waist's thirty, though.'

'Mine's twenty-eight,' he said deadpan.

Earlier I'd woken him, with a cup of tea, on the mezzanine. He'd sat up in bed (unselfconsciously? brazenly? Who know these things? I doubt that he did) and showed off an attractive pair of long arms, a hairless unblemished ivory chest – surprisingly big nipples, I couldn't help noticing – a taut tummy and a perfectly circular belly-button that was like the inlet/outlet of a toy balloon. I liked what I saw but thought it wiser not to tell him so. He asked if I had any paracetamol. I told him aspirin would be better for him and went and got him two. By the time I came back with them he was out of bed, in underpants though nothing else, and I didn't comment on this pleasing tableau either. I threw him my spare dressing gown – I was already clad in my other one – and it was in dressing gowns that we sat on the living-room sofa, drinking coffee, eating toast spread with Dundee marmalade, and admiring the distant view from the window. Outside was a bright and sunny morning.

By the time we set off the aspirin had taken effect and Chris, showered and be-suited, was quite chatty in the car. As chatty as anyone on their way to a job interview can be, that is. He'd never had an interview for a job before. Interviews for university places had been his only experience of them to date. 'Think of it as a dummy run for when you do interviews for real jobs in a few years' time,' I told him. 'You don't get good at anything without practice. Even if you don't get the job it'll be a good learning experience.' I thought it unlikely that he wouldn't get the job. Going for a vacancy that's being temporarily filled by an overworked manager, and with an availability of now, is usually a dead cert provided you're polite and don't fart while you're sitting there. I didn't tell him any of that, though. I didn't want to make him complacent. I just said, 'You're in with a pretty good chance.'

I drove him all the way through Glasgow city centre to Bath Street. He hopped out when I pulled up at the theatre's front entrance. I wished him luck and we squeezed each other's fingers for a second before he shut the car door and I drove off. I couldn't just leave him there and go home, though. He was wearing my suit for one thing.

There was a public car park right next to the theatre but it was a small one and it was full. I drove around town for a bit, stopping off from time to time in parking spaces that should really have been paid for, then moving off again if I saw a warden coming. Half an hour passed surprisingly quickly. I couldn't imagine Chris would be longer than that. I was right. When I dawdled along Bath Street at just after eleven thirty, there he was, out on the pavement, peering for me among the traffic.

We set off back to Paisley. Chris's mood was sky high. 'I start tonight,' he said. 'It's only for a couple of weeks. The theatre closes for a month then. The expression we use is "going dark". But that's really all I want. We're off on holiday after that. Me and my parents, that is.'

'Where are you going?' I asked. For a ghastly moment I thought he was going to say Tenerife. But he didn't.

'We're going to the Dordogne.' He explained, 'It's a river in the south of France.' Again I thought how sweet this was: his perception of the things that someone of my age might not know.

I drove him back to my flat. I lent him my bedroom to change in – back into the clothes he'd been wearing the previous night. He didn't bother to shut the door while he was doing this and, though I left him in peace, I was rather charmed by that.

Then he phoned his parents. He'd got the job (he told them what it consisted of, how long it was for, and what the money was) and said he'd be with them in half an hour. His friend would be dropping him off. This didn't come as a surprise to me: we'd already agreed on the arrangement.

As I was driving him towards the opposite end of Paisley it went through my mind that if students and school-leavers took holiday jobs as a matter of course to buoy their finances up then why shouldn't a teacher – one who had a long empty holiday ahead of him, plus an overdraft – do the same thing? I wondered if the theatre would have any casual backstage work. I still had Ellen's number. I should be in her good books now, since I'd supplied her with a replacement for Maxwell. I decided I would phone her and ask. I didn't tell Chris I was thinking this.

We'd already swapped numbers. Snapchat, Facebook, the lot. We'd done that last night when we were both drunk. We probably wouldn't have done had we left it to this morning. The cold light of circumspection and all that. But what was done was done. I thought now, perhaps it was just as well that we'd got drunk.

Chris made me pull up a few doors short of his parents' respectable semi-detached house. 'Thank you for everything,' he said, turning towards me. He flashed me the most gorgeous smile then, and followed that by leaning in towards me.

We kissed briefly, doing the best we could to hug each other for a second within the constraints of the car seats, the gear lever, and my seat-belt. 'Meet up soon, I hope,' Chris said as he opened the door. My heart leapt at that. I couldn't have said it, wouldn't have dared to say it, myself.

Though I was brave enough to say, 'We sure will.' And, 'Let me know how you get on with your first shift.' It's easy to be bold when someone has been bold before you. Like walking down the cliff-face following Theo, my chest against his backpack.

'Talk soon,' said Chris.

I mimed a telephone against my cheek and said, 'Good luck.'

I drove off, feeling like I was dreaming everything and that at any moment I might wake up. I wondered if I would soon be Chris's work-mate at the theatre, and if I was, would he like that? I'd promised Theo he could trust me in the big things. That would include being faithful to him, of course. But he'd told me he didn't want to see me. Ever. Days had passed since he'd said that and he hadn't come back to me with any change of heart. I wondered what the protocol was. Everyone agreed that you didn't have to stay faithful to an ex. And then I told myself sternly that Theo and I were having a lovers' tiff, nothing more. He was anything but an ex.

Thinking of that brought my mind back to Maxwell. Should I feel bad about handing his part-time job to someone else so quickly, on a plate? No. I had nothing to feel bad about. Maxwell had walked out of his job without explanation, just as he'd walked out of my flat. He hadn't shown any sign of wanting to come back – unless I counted his belongings, stacked on my hall table. If he came back... But that would be a new and un-guessable situation. If it came to pass I would deal with it then. I wouldn't waste time thinking about it now. I started to think about what I would say to Ellen when I phoned her, as soon as I reached home, to ask about a possible temp job for myself.

When I got back to the apartment I found a message on my house phone. It was from my mother, of course. She had found her grandmother's ancient photos of our distant English ancestors and she thought I really ought to have a look at them. Could I pop over for lunch in a day or two?

Her message made it sound almost urgent, which it obviously couldn't be. I also felt that it couldn't be all that interesting. I'd seen umpteen sepia-tinted photos of lower middle class Victorian English people. Nevertheless I called mum back dutifully and we arranged that I'd go over to Stirling for lunch on Sunday, three days from now.

Then I focused my thoughts on the call I was going to make to Ellen at the theatre. I guessed that backstage wouldn't be her department; she was a manager of the front of house. Even so it was important to make a good impression. I needed to sound eager for a bit of holiday work but not desperate for it. When I felt ready – that was after I'd made myself a cheese sandwich and drunk a cup of coffee with it – I called her.

I got her at once, which I felt was a good start. I began by telling her how pleased Chris was to be starting his new job. That gave her the opportunity to say what a charming and responsible lad he seemed. An opportunity she took. She was sure he'd handle the job fine, she said. I couldn't help asking what would happen if Maxwell returned unexpectedly and wanted his old job back. 'He'd find the position no longer vacant,' Ellen said. 'We go dark in a couple of weeks anyway. September's two months away. We could see how things stood then if he was still around, I suppose. But he'd need a pretty good explanation for why he left us in the lurch like that.'

'Yes, I suppose he would,' I said. Actually I thought Ellen was being quite generous in even considering the possibility of taking him back. But then that was Maxwell. One look at you from those puppy-dog eyes and you found yourself powerless to resist. 'There is another thing… While I'm here. I was wondering…' I came clean about the fact that I too was looking for a summer holiday job. I threw in the word backstage, and added that I was sure it wasn't her department…

She cut me off. 'They're always looking for casuals for strike and get-out nights. A very high turnover of people… There'll be two of those before we close in three weeks. The first one would be this Saturday. Listen, I can't put you through on this phone but the person you need to speak to is Roddy Cairns. I'll give

you his number. Tell him you know me and that I told
you to phone…'

'Well, wow, thank you very much…'

Ellen gave me the number there and then. A minute
later I was phoning it.

Roddy Cairns was so Glaswegian that even I had a job
to understand him. But after a few moments of
acclimatisation I was able to catch that he was indeed
looking for extra casual labour on Saturday night. He
could do with two people actually. So did I know
anybody else…?

I thought quickly. 'There's a young lad starting work
in one of your theatre bars tonight,' I said. 'He might
want to earn a bit of extra after his shift on Saturday
night. I can't speak for him, of course. But I could
message him and get back to you…' At once I found
myself looking forward to that. Chris and I might find
ourselves working shoulder to shoulder in two nights'
time, dismantling a set and loading it onto lorries…

'Or I could simply toddle up to the bar tonight and see
if he's interested myself,' I heard Cairns say. 'What did
you say his name was?'

Roddy Cairns's sensible proposal was obviously meant
kindly, to save me trouble. It had the additional merit of
giving him the chance to get the measure of Chris face to
face. Nevertheless it registered with me much like a slap
in my own face. And Roddy Cairns hadn't asked me to
go in and see him. That too was probably meant nicely; I
wouldn't have to traipse into the centre of Glasgow
specially to meet him for a two-minute interview. He
had already asked me in the course of our short
conversation if I was confident with basic hand tools and
didn't suffer from colour-blindness; I'd said yes to the
hand-tools question and no, I wasn't colour-blind. He'd
left it at that. Presumably if I came recommended by

Ellen then that was good enough. Still, his kindness to me had accidentally robbed me of a good excuse to message Chris, and of any excuse at all to go into Glasgow this evening or tomorrow evening and see how he was getting on in his new job.

I found myself wondering what pretext I could find for getting back in touch with Chris so soon after our parting at midday. But did I need a pretext? A simple 'How's things? Good luck tonight' would be perfectly natural and OK, wouldn't it?

I wondered how his day was going. What had his parents asked him about the friend he'd stayed the night with and who had lent him an interview suit? Would he have said quite simply that the friend was none other than Mr Allen from the English Department, whom they'd occasionally met? Or would he lie, and say it was Jimmy, or someone else?

The more I thought about this the more I began to see myself in a different – perhaps not so pleasant – light. How would Chris's parents view last night? True, I hadn't gone to bed with Chris or had sex with him. True, I wouldn't have been breaking any laws if I had done. Or any code of professional conduct. I was no longer his teacher but ... as someone says to Hamlet, *Indeed, my lord, it followed hard upon.* It was becoming clear, the more I thought about it, that Chris's parents would not be overjoyed at last night's events if they came to hear about them. And that they might already be less than overjoyed if Chris had told them even the half of it.

I decided I wouldn't message Chris today. I wouldn't doorstep him at the theatre tonight. I would wait until the morning. Then I could message him with a 'How did it go?' And see how he replied to that. In any case I'd be likely to see him on Saturday night, when I went in to do the strike and get-out – whether he was working alongside me on that or not.

In the evening I took myself down to The Bull. I imagined Chris starting his shift – just as Maxwell used to – at six o'clock, with bottling up. At around seven o'clock I imagined him serving his first customer of the evening. I kept fingering my phone and it was all I could do not to press the buttons – like a nuclear code – that would explode us into each other's lives again. I kept imagining him being about to message me. But he did not.

Later I imagined him changing out of his penguin suit and dicky-bow. Going home. On the train? Or would one of his parents have come to pick him up? I walked the short distance home and still neither of us had contacted the other. Then around eleven o'clock my phone rang. I was startled by its loudness. I whipped it out of my pocket. The little screen showed me Theo's name. A second later I heard him speak.

TWENTY-TWO

His Spanish accent always came as a shock when I hadn't heard his voice for some time. When I was with him, because of the quality of his English and the content of what he said with it, I somehow never noticed it. Now he said urgently, all in one breath, 'Jonty. Matt's died. I think I need you, Jonty.'

For a moment I couldn't think who Matt might be. Had Theo meant Nat? But I felt knocked back, as if by a sea wave, by the force of emotion in Theo's voice. In the split second it took me to process the moment I had time to notice that he had called my name twice. That he'd said I need you. An INU, I realised for the first time in that long short moment, spoke even more strongly than an ILU and went even more quickly to the deepest reaches of the heart. I also realised that Theo was struggling against tears as he spoke. It didn't matter for the moment who Matt might be. I said, 'I'll do anything, Theo. Just tell me what you want.'

He said, 'Could you come over here? Matt's mother's desperate.'

It sounded as though Theo, rather than Matt's mother, was desperate. Though perhaps they both were. By now I'd had time to realise, or to remember, that Matt was Mateo, Theo's former partner, the older man whose car Theo had driven, in whose home he'd lived. I didn't tell him I'd had a job remembering who Matt was. I said, 'I'll come as soon as I can. I don't think I can make it tomorrow. I've things to sort. I'll come out on Saturday if I can get a flight.' My mind ran to my overdraft, but then I had the happy thought that my month's salary would have been paid into my account this morning – it was June 30 – and would have cleared it. At least for the present.

Theo muttered broken thanks. I said, 'Theo, how did he die? I have to ask.'

'It was a … in Spanish *embolia pulmonar.'*

I threshed around. 'I think … pulmonary embolism. Dear God, I'm sorry. He was only…?'

'Forty-six. He was at the gym. Finished his session. He was back in his street clothes and just walking to the door. Suddenly he was breathless and with big chest pain. They called an ambulance. Thought it was a heart attack. They got him to the hospital. But he was dead within a few minutes of arriving there.'

'Jesus!' Of course I was thinking, there but for the grace of God go all of us. 'Listen, Theo – *mi niño* – I have a couple of things on at the weekend. I'll need to cancel them. I can't do anything tonight. I'll get straight onto it in the morning, then I'll book a flight. Even if I have to take a train to London to get it. And I'll phone you at every step. Now … tell me how you are. Have you got a drink?' There was a bit of irony in that perhaps: I wasn't sure what caused pulmonary embolisms. But I was pleased to hear him say yes, he had a beer in front of him.

We talked for some time. It was difficult to remember afterwards what we talked about. But I did remember that we didn't mention Marina's disappearance to Canada. Or Nat. Nor did we revisit our last phone conversation; the one during which Theo had told me angrily that he never wanted to see or speak to me again. We didn't discuss the question of how I might have felt about that. Or of how I might have behaved in the aftermath.

After we ended the call I sat looking at my silent phone for a minute as if mesmerised by it. That tiny contraption of metals, plastics and chemical elements had moments earlier contained Theo. All I had of him was contained in that wee box. I was impatient now. I wanted to get out to the airport, as Maxwell had done, in the middle of the night. I wanted to be with Theo, to comfort him as he now needed to be comforted. I wanted him to comfort me too, I realised. He wasn't the only one who'd got hurt recently.

I remembered how he'd placed his copper-coloured arm alongside my milky one on the table of a pavement café the last time I'd been with him on Tenerife. That difference between us was a symbol of our deeper difference: I was a northern European; he came from the far south: Guanche, Spanish or whatever else. It wasn't just a matter of geography; there was the question of our very different temperaments. Theo and I had said we loved each other. Did that mean we were in a relationship? If so, did that mean we'd want to live together? Apart from all the mountainous obstacles in the way of that – of which the two thousand miles of heaving sea between us was just a start – how could you – how could I – ever share a living space with someone who could decide in an instant that he didn't want anything to do with me, and then change his mind a few days later without a word of explanation?

I gave up trying to think about that and went to bed.

I didn't sleep very much. I was awake and alert at six o'clock. There were people I needed to contact urgently. I was angry and frustrated that I couldn't phone them yet. But I could get onto a travel website and look at flights to Tenerife. To my surprise there was one seat left on this afternoon's direct flight from Glasgow. I booked it, together with a return flight a rather arbitrary eight days hence. There was no reason not to. I might have to explain my sudden departure to a couple of people, and apologise for letting them down at short notice, but there was no way I needed anyone's permission to travel: no way I wasn't going to go out to Tenerife.

I held off till seven thirty before calling Theo. The Canary Islands and the UK shared a time zone. It was still only seven thirty a.m. where he was. But I was pretty sure he wouldn't be sleeping very much. I told him I hoped to be in Puerto by about nine o'clock that evening. 'Meet you in City Bar,' he said.

That was a bit disconcerting. It was over a mile away from where he lived. 'Do you think I need to book some accommodation?' I asked. He would have heard the hint of dismay in my voice.

'No. You're fine to stay at my place. If you don't mind the single bed.' That wouldn't be a problem. Provided he was in it. 'I just would like to meet you in City Bar, if that's all right.'

'It's fine,' I said on a surge of relief. 'I'll give you a more up-to-date arrival time later. Are you sure you're all right?'

'I am now,' he said. It was one of the loveliest things he had ever said.

I managed to wait till eight o'clock before calling mum up. 'Look, I'm sorry to ring so early. And I'm sorry, but I'll have to cancel Sunday. I've got to go to Tenerife.'

Her response was less than understanding. 'No-one's got to go to Tenerife…'

I gave us both a little time by taking a deep breath. 'My friend over there's having a difficult time. He needs me with him to help.'

'And only you can do this?' Many years had passed since I'd last heard so much steel in my mother's voice.

'Yes, apparently. His ex-partner has died and he wants me with him. The ex-partner's mother, who is British, is beside herself with grief.'

I was astonished at what my mother said next. 'Oh bugger Tenerife!' I'd never heard her come out with anything remotely like that in all my life.

'I'm sorry but…'

'I've got a leg of lamb for Sunday. Now what am I to do with it? It cost an arm and a leg.'

Nerves, I suppose, made me guffaw loudly.

'What?!'

'Sorry, mum. It was just the expression you used. Leg of lamb. Arm and… Look, I'm really awfully sorry, but I can't do anything about this. Couldn't you freeze it? Or invite a friend or two round to eat it? And when I'm back – which will only be a week from now, I'll buy another leg of lamb myself … and a bottle of wine … and I'll bring it round … and we'll…'

'It won't be the same,' said my mother stonily, and then the line went dead.

My heart felt heavier than I could have believed possible when, two minutes ago, I'd dialled my mother's number. It wasn't about the lamb of course. I did realise that.

I didn't think I could dare to contact Chris before nine o'clock. I made myself some toast and marmalade, and coffee; but it all tasted like cigarette butts in my mouth.

At last I messaged Chris. *Major thing come up. This pm I have to go to Tenerife. I need to talk to you urgently first. Phone me asap.*

To my great relief a message came back a minute later. *Phone u in 20. Hope ur ok.* The content of the message was an even bigger relief. It helped to smooth my feathers after my mother's ruffling of them. Even so, the twenty minutes were a penance. But they passed at last, and then my phone rang, and it was Chris.

I felt I needed to take control of this. 'Chris, I need to know if you're OK. Then I'll explain that my life has changed suddenly and I need your help. But first ... are you all right?'

'Yes and no,' he said. 'I mean I'm not in trouble or anything. I told my parents a white lie about where I was the other night and they seemed OK with that. It's just that...'

'I know,' I said. Although I didn't know. I only guessed. I leapt into the dark. 'You don't want to be pursued by a man in his mid-thirties. I understand that, and I won't do that. But I'd like us to stay friends. And ... I need your help...'

He agreed to meet me in The Bull at twelve o'clock.

He did look a bit whey-faced when he turned up. I offered him a drink and he accepted. But he carefully specified only a half. I was beyond caring, though. I ordered a full pint for myself.

'I behaved a bit out of character the other night,' he said after we'd clinked glasses. He didn't look me in the eye as he said it.

'So did I. But it's one of the things about growing up. Things happen. You get through them. You stop feeling embarrassed by them because you learn that everybody else is in exactly the same boat...'

'Is that your lesson for today, Jonty?'

'Yes it is, Chris,' I said. And then I laughed. And then he giggled, and looked into my eyes again, and smiled that wonderful smile of his. We held each other's gaze for a good few seconds, setting the seal on our discovery that we were still friends and that, for now at any rate, everything was all right between us.

I pulled my spare keys from my pocket and plonked them on the table we were sitting at. 'Like I said, I have to go to Tenerife. I'm heading off to the airport as soon as we've finished our drink.' I'd seen him clock the small suitcase and backpack on the floor beside me when he came in, though he hadn't commented. 'Theo needs me…' I saw Chris nod his head firmly. He understood. He knew I didn't need to say more than that. But I did anyway. 'The man he lived with for five years has died suddenly. He's upset, and the guy's mother is in distress.' Chris went on nodding almost impatiently. Clearly this was all too obvious to have needed spelling out.

'The thing is, although I'll only be gone a week, there's loose ends to tie up. Maxwell might appear at any moment and need to get into my apartment to get his things out. Can I give him your number so that he can contact you if he does come back? And you let him into the place?'

'Of course,' Chris said, and I saw him glow a little with the knowledge of being trusted with such an adult responsibility. He picked the keys up from the table and, after shooting me a little question-mark of a look, to which I responded with a tight nod, put them into his pocket.

'The other thing is … and I should have asked before… How did it go at the theatre last night?'

'It was fun. Hectic in short bursts. But most of the time… Oh, someone came to see me. Mr Cairns from backstage. With a very thick accent. He was asking me… Was it you, Jonty, that told him I might be looking for a bit of extra cash?'

'Yes, it was. Roddy Cairns offered me some work on Saturday night. Doing the…'

'The strike and get-out.' Chris found the words more quickly than I could. 'I said I would.'

'Good for you,' I said. 'But I'm going to have to let him down. I thought we might be working together but…'

'That would have been fun.' Chris laughed boyishly, forgetting for a moment the complications of the subtext. 'Oh, I see. You're wondering if I can find someone else.'

'Exactly that,' I said. 'Of course I'm going to phone Roddy in a minute and make my grovelling apology. But it would be more than helpful if you were able to find him a replacement.'

'Maybe Jimmy…' Chris looked doubtful. 'Don't worry. I'll find someone.' Then he gave me a puzzled look. 'Why were you looking for backstage work?'

'I needed the money,' I said. 'I've overspent a bit. All these trips to Tenerife.'

He nodded wisely. 'Of course. I understand.'

I didn't tell him the other reason why I'd wanted to get a job in the theatre in which he was working. That particular penny would drop of its own accord in the coming days or months.

At the airport I bought a book. It was called The Unfolding of Language. Written by a man named Deutscher. I'd read a review of it some time back. I thought it might make a nice present for Theo. Something non-Mateo-related that we could have fun talking about.

If you sat on the right-hand side of the plane, as I did that afternoon, it was an island-hopping flight. The day was exceptionally clear. No clouds were in sight for once; the atmosphere was without haze or thickness; everything was pin-sharp. The Isle of Arran and the almost-island of Kintyre came into view almost at once. Then there was the northern edge of Ireland. Kintyre, reaching out like a finger, seemed almost to touch it.

So near a place was Ireland. I'd never crossed the water to it. That seemed remiss of me now, almost wilfully negligent, when I'd been to so many other, much more distant places. We brushed the coast of

Northern Ireland just south of Belfast, over Strangford Lough. Which is the same as the Scottish 'loch' but spelt differently. There must be some ancient tribal reason for that. Perhaps I would find it in Guy Deutscher's book.

The coast receded from us for a time, but then we turned inland over Dublin and spent twenty minutes crossing the Republic overland (it looked as green and pretty as it was supposed to: painted daily by leprechauns, people said) before finally heading out over the Atlantic just south of Cork. How come I was so knowledgeable about the geography of Ireland so suddenly? I'd recently downloaded a new phone app with a moving map on it. It told me where I was, minute by minute.

Little more than forty minutes to cross this island of Ireland. Another precious stone that was set in a silver sea. And yet it had managed to get divided. One half of it was staunchly European; they used the euro just like in Tenerife. Though that half hadn't wanted to stay in the UK and had a revolution and a civil war to prove the fact. The other half was more than attached to the idea of the UK. It was more attached to the idea than any other part of the UK was, even including the English. Now the referendum was going to drag that northern half of the island out of Europe, although the majority of its population had voted to remain a part of it. It seemed that Northern Ireland, which by substantial majorities wanted to remain a part of the United Kingdom and a part of Europe, could have one or the other – but not both. I looked back at the receding shoreline of Ireland and wondered, like a naïve teenager, how people could make such a bloody mess of so beautiful an island.

The next island would not appear for another four hours. I sort of knew that, and my app confirmed it. I started reading Deutscher's book about language.

I found wonder upon wonder in it. I already knew that languages weren't static: they changed over time. That was why my pupils found Shakespeare difficult. And why I found Chaucer difficult. Now, as the book explained and elaborated the process I began to think of language itself as a sort of island or landmass. Time and use eroded it on one side while on the other side, as generations came and went, more new land was built up. New words. New grammar. New expressions. New ways of voicing thoughts. I remembered the anxieties that Theo had. But if the English adverb was disappearing like a vulnerable sea cliff, then disappear it would. No amount of wishful thinking on Theo's part or mine, no indignant letters to the papers, could halt the process. I looked forward to talking with Theo about this.

The sea is silver when you peer towards the sun at it, blue when you look at it with the sun behind you. My porthole looked west this clear afternoon and the sea stayed silver for hour after hour like a limitless bath of mercury while I ploughed on through my book and another small silver sea of gin and tonic.

We made a little left turn over the island called Porto Santo. (Thank you, map app.) Why did planes still do this, I wondered, in the age of navigation by satellite? Because that was the route they'd followed since the air routes were first laid out, I supposed. The way country roads wound and twisted for reasons that were sensible in medieval times but no longer apparent.

Porto Santo was the baby neighbour of Madeira, visible a few miles ahead. The Madeiran Archipelago was a sort of rehearsal for the bigger Canary Islands, but unlike them belonged to Portugal, not Spain. Presumably they'd fought over it at some point in the past. That both countries were now members of the European Union meant there was less likelihood of that being repeated in the next few centuries. The Pearl of the Atlantic was what people called Madeira. It certainly looked good from thirty thousand feet. Green, like Ireland, and semi-mountainous; its capital sprawled around a sun-trap bay on its south coast.

No sign of the Selvagem islands this time. And no sign of Tenerife in the distance: I was the wrong side of the plane for that. But the western Canary Islands came gradually into sight as we made our descent. La Gomera, very close by. La Palma further off. And then in the far distance, one final precious stone, and Theo's favourite. El Hierro, a chip of jet adrift on the sea of mercury. My first ever sight of El Hierro, where Theo owned a house.

Theo was already sitting at the bar when I arrived, a Dorada in front of him. He jumped off his stool when he saw me and we embraced breath-knockingly among the other customers.

'It's OK. You can kiss him if you want to.' That's what I heard the barman say, laughing, from behind the bar. He was the one whom I'd kissed drunkenly on a previous occasion. So Theo and I did kiss, though only for an instant and a bit self-consciously. Then we disentangled ourselves, Theo climbed back up on his stool and I got onto the stool next to him.

'New colleague,' said the barman, and presented a shaggy-haired rangy guy of about thirty. 'He's called Julian.' In Spanish that came out like Hooligan. A beer appeared in front of me and the two barmen withdrew to serve other customers.

'Thank you for coming,' Theo said quietly.

'I had to. Obviously.'

'You've arrived at sunset.' Theo pointed out into the street where the sun was still just catching the tops of the buildings opposite.

'You see!' I said jocularly. But inside I was suddenly almost crying. I looked into Theo's face searchingly. It seemed composed and calm now. 'You seem to be surviving. I'm so sorry about Mateo.' That was true. I was sorry. But I also felt somehow guilty. His death had very conveniently brought Theo and me back together. I patted my lover's knee affectionately.

'It's a shock. But time had passed since we split. I still loved him but I was no longer in love with him. If that makes sense?'

'It makes perfect sense. You don't need to explain it.' It was the way I felt now about Harry.

'It's his mother. She needs someone to pour her heart out to in English. I'm taking you to see her in the morning.'

'But you speak perfect English...' I stopped myself. I was about to say that surely Theo, who knew her, would do a better job of comforting Matt's mother than I, a perfect stranger, could. That he hadn't needed to summon me. But God moved in mysterious ways, and so, evidently, did Theo.

He looked at me cautiously. 'I'm sorry. About ... you know.'

'It's OK,' I said. 'Water under the bridge.' He didn't look entirely convinced yet. I repeated it. 'It's OK. *Mi niño.*' I smiled encouragingly and after a second he cautiously smiled back at me. I rumpled his shiny black curls roughly.

TWENTY-THREE

Señora Perez Ramos, Mateo's mother, lived a good way down the west coast, some distance past Los Gigantes, in the sunnier, drier southern half of the island. We took the bus and it took its time getting us there, along roads that were largely made up of hairpins as they negotiated the rugged skirts of Mount Teide.

Señora Perez Ramos lived in a smart modern villa with a garden, in the middle of an enclave of many similar properties. Some, including hers, had sea views. Theo rang the bell and Matt's mother came to the door, a tall elegant woman with honey-grey hair. She might have been five years older than my own mother but no more; she must have had Mateo when she was very young. She must also have wondered what on earth I was doing here. I was absolutely sure, though I hadn't told him so, that I'd been asked to come out here entirely for Theo's benefit, not for hers. But she welcomed me inside along with Theo with a smile, asked me to call her Claire (as Theo did already) led us out through French windows onto a vine-shaded terrace, sat us down, then went back inside to make us coffee. I looked around at this lovely setting, peering out at the sea from underneath the vine-leaf awning, and remembered vividly my return to my own fine apartment the evening I'd lost my phone and Theo with it. I imagined Claire looking around her nice villa these days as I had looked around my apartment that broken-hearted evening, and wondering what the point was.

I asked Claire, once initial pleasantries were over, and we were talking about what had happened, if she planned to stay on in Tenerife or return to England. That was presumptious of me, perhaps, as I didn't know her. But it seemed to me that this was part of the role I was expected to play today. Claire probably knew as well as I did that I was here in response to needs of Theo's not hers, and seemed ready to play along; at any rate she seemed comfortable with the question. I thought it rather splendid of her to allow Theo his share in a grief that she might have been forgiven for wanting to monopolise.

She looked at me carefully. 'I've thought about it. Of course I have. And with all this Brexit thing a lot of ex-pats are feeling pretty insecure. But I took Spanish nationality years ago. If the worst came to the worst and the British who live here got kicked out in tit-for-tat expulsions they wouldn't be able to get rid of me easily. But actually I don't really have an English home to go back to.' She gave me a pale smile. 'I'm not talking about money. Within reason that wouldn't be a problem. I could sell up here and still buy something reasonable.' Her nostrils flared slightly as she said that. 'But I have no family over there any more. Distant cousins, nobody close. My sister and her husband live in Canada.'

Oh no, I thought. Theo and I had managed to get through an evening, a night and a morning without mentioning Canada, or Nat or Marina. Now Canada had gate-crashed our coffee-party. Theo and I tried not to exchange glances but couldn't quite manage it. We looked at each other then looked away very quickly.

'And here?' I had to ask her. I felt I was expected to.

'Friends. No family. Well, Javier's family – my late husband's family.' Theo had already told me that Claire was a widow. A widow with just the one son to succour her. And now she'd lost him.

Grief can be contagious. Claire's manner was brisk and friendly. There was no breaking down as she talked to us, no display of violent emotion. She kept her upper lip stiff, as we British people were supposed to. Yet the grief was palpable. It came to us like waves through the sun-warmed air around the terrace. The more we talked

– Claire, Theo, Jonty – the more strongly the waves hit me. They were like the big deep waves of the Atlantic that, from where we sat, we could hear distantly. Claire's had been the same situation as my mother's; the same as Theo's mother's now was. Widowhood with just one son to knock around in it. OK, Theo's mother had also had a daughter. But now she hadn't. The daughter had disappeared to Canada. Theo's mother just had Theo. My mother just had Jonty. Now I was face to face with a woman who had just lost that, and for all her outward show of bravery I could see that her life had become meaningless. The implications of this discovery of mine, of this new knowledge, were enormous. Incalculable. For me. For Theo. For me and Theo. And I knew, as if the thought had been written on his forehead, that this discovery, this new knowledge, and the understanding of its implications, was shared by Theo.

We took Claire out to lunch. That is, we made her come out with us to a nearby bar-restaurant. But it was she who picked up the tab. She was, after all, better-off financially than the two of us put together. Though only financially.

The three of us took a short walk to the edge of the sea and Theo and Claire talked about Mateo. In a light and anecdotal way. They didn't discuss the manner of his death or its implications for Claire's future or for Theo's. I guessed they'd got the core-shocking thing, the death of an only child and an ex-partner, out of the way on the phone in the days before I arrived. The implications for the future, whose waves and ripples were only beginning to reach them both, were still, I guessed, too big and immediate to deal with in conversation.

In the afternoon there were visitors. I was glad to see that. Bereavement is a busy experience; it came back me now, remembering how frantically occupied my mother had been in the days that followed the death of my father. I'd been glad of that back then, even as an eleven-year-old. Now I was glad of it for Claire.

A brother-in-law arrived and he and Claire spoke together about funeral arrangements in rapid Spanish. Usually a Spanish funeral took place no more than two days after the death, Theo had told me. In which case I would have already missed it. But there was another uncle, who lived near Málaga and would be travelling here by ship from Cadiz, which took three days. He couldn't fly, apparently: something to do with his ears. Because of him the funeral had been postponed by a few days. The uncle who was now here discussing all this clearly knew Theo well; he was friendly with me, treating me like a family member. I felt absurdly flattered. But the man was big and boisterous. I didn't follow all the twists and turns of their conversation. Was this man, I wondered, a little bit inclined to bully Claire? I wondered what it was like to have in-laws who came from a different culture, spoke a different language from your own. I dared to wonder if I would be finding out for myself one day.

'She shouldn't be on her own at night,' Theo said to me while the older pair were talking. 'What do you think?'

That slightly startled me. 'You think we ought to offer to stay the night here?'

'I think so.'

'Then whatever you say. I'm here for you.'

'And Claire,' Theo reminded me a bit severely.

'Of course for Claire,' I meekly toed the line.

Other callers came and went, there were many phone calls. In between them Theo put his proposal to Claire. Would she like us to stay the night with her? She seemed surprised at first but then suddenly glad. She accepted gratefully and I realised that Theo had correctly read her needs. That impressed me and made me proud of him. I also thought it was very honourable and decent of both of us to have made the offer but I worried that if we spent one night here we'd have no excuse to leave again before the funeral. I wondered if I was ever going to get any time alone with Theo. But I resolved to remain decent and honourable, at least for the time being.

That resolve wasn't put to the test, happily. Salvation came in the form of a phone call from Canada. Not for Theo, not from Marina. It was Claire's phone that rang. It was from her sister who lived in Toronto, Claire told us when the call was over. The sister was coming over. Flying to Amsterdam then coming on to Tenerife. She would arrive tomorrow evening and stay ten days here. Claire beamed happily as she shared this news. That was a relief to Theo and me. Albeit a slightly guilty one. The terms were clear and no negotiations were needed. We only needed to stay the one night with her.

And staying the one night here had other benefits. The house was large and modern, the garden and terrace spacious. Claire cooked a great evening meal for us. She was more than accepting of me as Theo's new partner. (It occurred to me that many mothers in her position would not be.) The spotless room she gave us had a double bed in it – unlike Theo's bedroom in Puerto.

'Do you often stay overnight at your own mother's?' I asked Theo when, for a few minutes before dinner, we were alone together on the terrace.

'No,' he said. He paused. 'I don't really feel I need to. She's only up in La Orotava. I go up to see her most weekends anyway. And if she comes into Puerto we meet for a drink or a coffee.' He gave me a tight little smile.

'It's about the same with me,' I said. Although the tight little smile had put a wee question-mark in my mind I was reassured by Theo's answer and a little less guilty. I elaborated. 'Although she doesn't come into Paisley very often. Stirling's quite a bit further away than La Orotava.'

'Well, obviously,' said Theo.

'I meant further away from Paisley.'

That was as far as we went into that difficult subject that evening. The double bed was wonderfully comfy. The following afternoon we took the bus back along the winding road to Puerto between the mountain and the Atlantic.

The funeral was still a couple of days off. My return to Glasgow another two days later. On one of the days in between we made the ascent of Mount Teide.

The first part of the journey was familiar. Up through La Orotava, into the forest, past the Organ Pipes rock formation, and a stop at El Portillo. Last time here we'd wandered a little way down a hiking trail and had sex among the trees. There wasn't time for that now: the coach was waiting. And anyway, we hadn't been out of bed that long. As we got higher we passed spectacular views back down to the coast. There was Puerto with its unmistakeable handful of tower blocks and its breakwater, looking uncannily like – and the same size as – it did on the big scale model of the island at the airport. There was La Orotava, a sprawl of orange rooftops, nestling at the foot of its fertile valley of farms and orchards. We climbed on, or rather our bus did, and left the trees beneath us. And then we left the scrub beneath us and came upon a world of rocks and stones and lava.

We took the cable car for the next-to-last bit. It was expensive, but at least it was operating that day. Theo said that, because of changeable weather conditions it was liable to closure at short notice; there were days when it didn't run at all. I'd asked him when he first brought up the possibility of this morning's adventure if he'd done the cable car ascent before. 'Yes,' he'd said. 'With Mateo. I was a bit afraid of the cable car,' he'd admitted. 'But Matt said nothing could happen to me if I was with him.'

Theo repeated that to me now, as we hummed quietly out of the bottom station and sailed up through empty air above the rocky incline. 'But now it's my turn,' he added.

'To do what exactly?'

'Look after you. Matt was twelve years older, remember. Now I'm the older.'

I laughed. 'By a fortnight!' But still I flushed with pleasure. Theo evidently saw his relationship with me in the same terms as he'd seen his relationship with Mateo. The age thing was immaterial. Mateo's death, even though not the death of a current partner, must have given him cause to reflect on the matter.

All around us the sea and its partial cloud cover rose, blue and white marbled, above the craggy horizon, and seemed to continue climbing with us. It felt strangely companionable. 'Do you still keep in touch with Harry?' asked Theo suddenly.

'Not very often,' I said. 'Two or three times since we parted company. He doesn't know about you for instance. But Mateo … you know … has made me think about him. I ought to talk to him. Tell him about you for a start. I feel I want to. Because of … you know. Is that all right with you?'

'Obviously.' And rather to my surprise he then kissed my cheek, right in the midst of all the other people in the cable car. The way we'd used to do in lifts, though only when we were alone in them.

The top station grew big ahead of us and then we burrowed into it. Doors clunked open and we got out.

The view, which had been improving metre by metre on the climb up here, got even better now.

I started to set out along the path but Theo caught hold of my arm and pulled me back, letting the other occupants of the cable car go on and up ahead. Then he looked at me and said very earnestly, 'When you split up with Harry ... what, six months ago? ... did you leave him or did he leave you?' A moment's anxiety clouded his eyes. 'Sorry if that's too...'

'No, it's fine. I haven't told you. You haven't asked me before. We found we were leading separate lives. Almost more like flat-mates and friends than... Then his company wanted to put him on a job south of the border. He didn't need to live in Scotland. We agreed to part, on friendly terms. We got the flat sorted out with a solicitor. It's now all mine. Of course there's a big mortgage to pay....'

'You still manage to afford your trips to Tenerife though...'

'Of course,' I said bravely. 'Number one priority.' I realised this was the first time we'd dipped our toes into the subject of our finances. I asked, 'But what about you?'

'It was amicable, like with you. But there was nothing to split up where property was concerned. I was just his house guest in a way. I couldn't put up with the way he wanted to carry on. I just walked out on him.' He caught a look on my face and so went on, 'I mean I told him I was going. And I'd made the arrangement with Jose and Elena. He knew I had somewhere to go. Like with you and Harry it was friendly. We said we'd stay friends. We kept in touch. We met a couple of times. But I haven't seen him ... I mean I hadn't seen him ... since I met you.' He stopped.

'I'm sorry,' I said. 'I understand.' I remembered that Marina had said Matt had abandoned Theo. Yet here was

Theo telling me he'd walked out on Mateo. Clearly, if Matt had abandoned Theo it hadn't been in the material, concrete sense of the word. I really would need to speak to Harry soon.

You couldn't go right up to the rim of the crater without a permit. But a couple of other trails led upwards from the cable car's top station, to different viewing platforms just below the summit. Ours, once we'd scrambled for twenty minutes to get up to it, gave us the westward panorama. It was after midday and the sun was beginning to turn the sea silver. The clouds seemed to have thinned even in the last few minutes. Or perhaps they'd been more to eastward. At any rate, out to the west lay the dark iceberg tips of La Gomera and La Palma. Theo said, 'I'm trying to see El Hierro.'

I tried too. 'I can't.'

'Nor me.'

'I saw it from the plane the other day.'

And then he quoted it, as I had somehow known all along he was going to. 'This precious stone set in the silver sea: this earth, this realm... I'm not sure how to finish it now. Since you're a Scotsman.'

I was in love with Theo, I was in love with the moment. 'Oh what the hell,' I said. 'It's a shared stone. England and Scotland – Wales too – share an island. It's all one place.' I thought of divided Ireland; I'd flown over it a few days ago. It looked like a single place to me. 'Why the fuck can't people learn to share things?'

Theo silently turned me towards him and thoughtfully, carefully, wiped my cheeks with his forefinger. 'It's views like this,' I explained. 'They always make me do that.'

Going down the mountain was almost as wonderful, almost as spectacular as going up. But with it came that slight melancholy, the sad adult knowledge that this was the second half of the experience – like the second week of a fortnight's holiday: there would be no third half to follow it.

'Alberto's heard from Marina,' Theo said. This came out of nowhere, as we were trudging from the lower cable car station to the coach stop. 'She's not coming back from Canada. She's staying with Nat. Going to live with him.' This was delivered in a voice as hard and stony as the ground we wandered over.

'I'm sorry.'

'It's not your fault.'

'At least that's something.' Somehow, after that we found we were both laughing. Though only for a moment. 'How's Alberto taking it?'

'He's quite a stoic actually. Not too badly. It's Mama. She's the worst one.'

'Oh dear,' I said. 'Mothers.' I had told Theo the leg of lamb story.

We walked back to the coach in silence. Then we were seated on it, knee to knee and enjoying that little domestic comfort. I said, 'Will I get to meet your mother? One day?'

'She'll be at the funeral.'

'Oh God,' I said. 'I meant in other circumstances.'

'Ah. I see.'

I waited for him to say more but he didn't. So I said, 'Well, I hope you'll meet mine one day.' Though I couldn't easily imagine those circumstances. His answer was something between a grunt and a snort.

'At least I've met your flat-mates now,' I went on, trying to be up-beat about all this. I'd met them several times in the last days. We'd all had drinks together in a café-bar one evening. Jose and Elena were a pleasant couple… No, they were more than that. They were welcoming and friendly. Elena was small and dark and had an infectious laugh; Jose, unusually for a Tenerifian, was tall, with blue eyes and fair hair.

But the most important thing about them from my point of view was that they seemed wonderfully normal, and treated Theo as though he too was. I found this immensely reassuring. They were the first other people in Theo's life, apart from Claire, that I'd met. They presented the first real opportunity I'd had to see him in any kind of social context. With his friends. Meeting Elena and Jose, I was able to see that he did have a context, he did have friends; and that those friends really liked him; they hadn't taken him in out of pity the way you might take in a half-wit cousin in a spirit of charitable obligation. I'd had it proved conclusively at last that my lover Theo was not the local madman, psychopath, or village idiot.

Theo loved the book I gave him: Guy Deutscher's The Unfolding of Language, that I'd read most of on the flight out. We delved into it together at many spare moments. After he'd digested quite a lot of it Theo admitted, 'I guess I've been too conservative when it comes to English. Perhaps we both have. Things like adverbs disappearing… *Go direct* instead of *go directly* and so on. *On the weekend* instead of *at the weekend*. In principle I know that language is always changing. That's why people find it difficult to read Cervantes and Shakespeare. But I think I fell a bit in love with the English I grew up learning.'

'I guess you cling even more tightly to it when it's not your first language.' This was a moment of realisation for me: it had never crossed my mind before now.

We were taking a walk through La Paz. Theo wanted to show me a house in which Agatha Christie had lived, and where she'd written two novels, before the Second Wold War. It was just two blocks seaward of City Bar and the hotel I'd stayed at on my first visits here but I hadn't known of its existence before.

'There,' said Theo. A street no more than thirty metres long ran towards the cliff-top from a larger residential road. The little street was called Calle Agatha Christie. On either side of it a large house lay, surrounded by gardens, hidden, except for rooftops, behind high walls. Across the T-junction was a very grand and imposing residence, like a Georgian mansion. The path up to its front door was visible through a wrought-iron grille. Lawns lay to either side.

'I see,' I said, looking around me. 'But which one was hers?'

Theo pressed his lips together and a pained look came into his eyes. 'Actually,' he said, 'I'm not quite sure.'

I laughed and gave him a pretend clip on the ear. A flock of wild canaries flew overhead, twittering. Green birds with striated brown backs. They were named after the islands; the islands weren't named after them.

Theo said, 'Of course when Agatha Christie lived here La Paz wasn't built on. It was all orchards, scrub and pasture. And where the Cabras steps are now was a real dirt goat path down the cliff-side.'

Then he changed the subject slightly. 'I had another thought, some time ago. It wouldn't have struck me without knowing English. But some of your irregular verbs don't change in different tenses. *I put,* present. *I put,* past, *I've put,* perfect. The same with *hit, hit, hit; cut, cut, cut;* and a handful of others. We get along fine without changing them, so why couldn't it be the same with all the others? Instead we have to learn *become, became, become; speak, spoke, spoken;* and all the rest of them.'

'Yes, I see,' I said. I did know that non-native speakers of English had trouble with that little lot. There were about a hundred of them. 'I like your idea, though.' It was a new one for me. I picked it up and ran with it. 'If it works with *put, put, put* in English, then we could probably do without verb endings in Spanish.'

Theo shot me a mischievous smile. *'Tuve, tuviste, tuvo, tuvimos, tuvisteis, tuvieron.'* That was the conjugation of the simple past tense of one of the commonest verbs in any language: have. *Tener* in Spanish. Theo knew only too well that I always tripped up over that one.

'It's been tried,' I said. 'It's called Esperanto. Everybody knows it's the easiest language in the world to master. It's got about three rules and no irregularities. Yet nobody speaks it.'

'That's because it doesn't belong to anyone,' said Theo. 'There's no-one who loves it like a mother-tongue: no-one to cherish and protect it.'

'I guess you're right.'

'Even so, it would be nice if verbs didn't change in English. *Wish, wish, wish; want, want, want.* It'd be so simple.'

'But they're regular verbs,' I objected. There's no difficulty. All you have to remember is the *-ed* ending in the past tenses.'

'And the *s* in the present. He want*s*, she wish*es*. Causes no end of difficulty for the kids I teach.'

'Hmm.' Perhaps I had an easier time of it, trying to awaken people's interest in Shakespeare and Dickens.

'Wished, desired, wanted. You pronounce a *t* at the end of wished, a *d* at the end of desired and an *id* at the end of wanted. Your kids pick that up from their parents. Mine don't. I have to teach it to them. Same with write and wishes. Writes just has an *s* but wishes has an *iz* at the end of it.

'Wow,' I said. I'd never given any thought to that before. And me an English teacher. Perhaps it would have been different if I'd had children.

'Matt's place wasn't far from here,' Theo said then.

'Oh. I didn't know.' I'd never given a thought to where Matt's place might be. A flat belonging to someone's ex. It wasn't something you bothered with. But I thought about it now. 'What happens to it? Did he own it? Was he there on his own?'

'He did own it. He didn't have a new boyfriend the last time I saw him. Happier to flap from flower to flower.'

'Flit, actually...'

'And no-one's come out since he died to say they were...' He got stuck there.

'I understand. He didn't have a new boyfriend as far as you know.'

'The house will belong to his family now In fiendishly complicated proportions. Like the property on El Hierro.'

We'd turned back now and were heading towards the café Bei Thomas. It was five o'clock in the afternoon. A bit early for City Bar.

TWENTY-FOUR

I heard Theo talk to his mother on the phone several times during those few days. Except that he was speaking Spanish he sounded exactly like I did when I was speaking to my own mum on the telephone. Perhaps every man does.

'How old is she?' I asked.

'Sixty-one.'

'Roughly the same as mine… Oh, actually… Oh my God. Next week's her sixtieth birthday. I haven't planned anything. Haven't even got her a card…'

'You said you'd buy her a leg of lamb,' said Theo naughtily.

'I think there needs to be something else.'

'Which day?'

I told him and he did a quick calculation. 'You'll be back in Scotland in three days. You've still got time.'

'It's also … because she's sixty … she's due to retire.' I reminded Theo about her job at the Forth Valley Hospital. 'One of those admin people that everyone loves to hate.'

Theo nodded. 'It's the same here. Everyone hates the hospital managers. They feel the money should be better spent. At least people will be able to stop hating her now.'

'She's hardly a manager,' I said quickly. 'More secretarial. But she gets a pension anyway.'

'She'd better keep quiet about that then. Or people will start hating her again.'

'Nobody could hate my mother if they knew her,' I said. 'As you'll find out when you meet her one day.'

I thought I'd lit a bit of blue touch-paper there, but nothing happened and Theo said no more. But I got to meet his mother, at Mateo's funeral, the following morning...

The funeral Mass was held, to my surprise, at the tiny church of San Amaro: the little whitewashed building near the mirador up in La Paz from which Theo and I had seen the sun set over La Palma; the church in which his grandparents had got married. It was just round the corner from Bei Thomas and City Bar, and just along another little road from the house where Agatha Christie had lived and written. Whichever house it might have been. Theo and I walked up the two hundred and twenty-five steps from the town. We wore suits and black ties: Theo's were his own; mine were borrowed from his flat-mate Jose ... and we'd tucked up the rather long trouser-legs with safety-pins. A few minutes after we'd arrived on the pavement outside the church Theo's mother joined us – she'd come down on the bus from La Orotava. There was no mistaking her as she came down the road towards us.

Sixty-one she might be but she was still beautiful. In her lace-trimmed black dress and mantilla she looked like one of the proud Madonnas that are carried aloft in the religious processions of Córdoba or Sevilla. Her bearing was regal, and she looked like Theo – though it might be more accurate to say that I could see where he got his looks from: the big dark eyes, high cheekbones and slightly arched eyebrows. She also looked painfully alone.

Theo introduced me. I said, *'Encantado, Señora...'* and then stopped because I wasn't sure how it worked with Spanish family names. Was she Señora Domingo or Señora Gonçalves, or was she, like her son, a Gonçalves Domingo?

While I hesitated wretchedly she said, *'Llama me Anastasia.'* She smiled gently and extended her hand. I took it and found myself bowing slightly as I did so. Then we went inside.

We sat in the second row. Theo arranged us so that he had me on one side of him, his mother on the other. Then we stood. A group of teenagers dressed in ancient costumes struck up a strange sad fanfare on a medley of instruments and the coffin was brought in. Following it came Claire, draped as voluminously in black as Theo's mother was but looking wracked today. Gone was the chin-up, soldier-on, composure of the days we'd spent with her. She looked like someone who had slept little the previous night and wept a lot during the course of it. Alongside her walked a woman who looked like her: the sister from Canada of course. I felt a sense of relief that the sister had come all this way to be at Claire's side. And gratitude. Though I knew that some of that relief was not for Claire but for Theo and me. Behind the women walked Mateo's uncles and aunts and a cousin or two, infinitely black and infinitely dignified. No-one does death like the Spanish do.

The coffin followers filtered left and right into the front pews. As Claire came level with us her eyes sought out Theo. She gestured to him to move into the front row with the rest of Matt's family. But the space was small; Theo was squeezed in between his mother and me. He leaned past his mother to take Claire's hand, which he kissed. But then he indicated, touching his mother's hand, that he was in the place he had to be. But he didn't touch his mother's hand only; he touched mine too. The touch ran deeply into me and moved me. Claire passed on, her in-laws behind her likewise, and they took the seats in front of us.

I heard Theo's mother say quietly, but in a voice vibrant with the deepest feeling, 'Nothing in the world is more terrible than to lose an only son; nothing more difficult to bear.' She said it in Spanish but I understood every word. Who was she speaking to? To Theo? To herself? To the consecrated house in which we stood now? To the Being it was consecrated to? It seemed to be the cry of religion through all the ages. From Abraham sacrificing his son, to the God of Christianity giving up his son-self to be crucified for men's sins, to Mary standing beneath the cross and weeping as He died. I no longer believed in the theology of it all but those images were still branded indelibly on my heart and mind. They reached deep into the core of our psyche and told us something of what it was to be a human being.

There was a full Mass, of course. Brought up as a Catholic I was used to this. Hearing it said in Spanish for the first time I was struck by how like Latin it seemed. I'd heard Latin Masses occasionally over the years. My parents, and Theo's, would have heard it in that language every Sunday when they were small children; and so would all the generations before them, going back fifteen hundred years. Once I whispered to Theo, 'Are you OK?' and he turned to me, nodded and smiled. If this was a weird experience for me, then it must have been weirder for him, as well as a hundred times graver and more emotional.

The door at the back of the church stood open throughout the service and so the sun streamed in, of which I was glad. At last the Requiem was over, the coffin was borne out of the church while the teenage band struck up another peculiar air – though perhaps it only sounded peculiar to me – and we all filed out, with relief diluting grief, into the life-affirming air.

We watched as the black car spirited the coffin away, and the following car went after it, taking Claire and her sister up the hill to some crematorium I didn't know where. Then we moved a couple of doors up the little road and into one of the biggest cafés there, where they were ready for us with drinks and food that by now were more than welcome.

Theo was very good to me. He didn't let me be alone, adrift among strangers in a Spanish-speaking milieu. He took me wherever he went, introducing me to those he knew under the umbrella of the all-covering word *amigo,* friend.

I asked him who the teens were who had made up the band. They were British children of ex-pat residents, he told me. They were Matt's ex-pupils from the Colegio Británico where he'd taught until a week ago. I didn't need to go in search of them, it turned out: they had clearly heard there was a Brit among the little crowd and, instead, came and surrounded me. They were excited to talk to a strange newcomer who spoke English; I was relieved not to have to speak to everyone in fragile Spanish. They were seventeen- and eighteen-year-olds. Chris's age. It seemed they knew Theo had been Matt's partner; one or two of them had actually met him before. I couldn't pick up on whether they knew the pair had split up during the past year. None of us was going to bring that up now. I was accepted simply as a friend of Theo's.

Either someone had told them, or they worked it out somehow, that I was an English teacher too. 'Come and teach us,' said one of the lads light-heartedly. 'We'll need a replacement for Mister … for Mateo. To teach A level.'

Another one, a girl, was Scottish. She said, 'You do Highers, though, don't you. Not A levels…'

I said, 'It's not so very different. Same language, same literature. We even let the English share our island with us.' They laughed in the polite, and rather nice, way that kids have when they like the teacher more than the joke he's made.

I made sure to talk to Claire when I had a chance to, after she had returned from the crematorium. I met her sister. She was staying a further week with her. 'Good,' I said.

'Not such good news after that, though,' said Claire. 'My English next-door neighbours who I... They're here actually...' She pointed vaguely into a little knot of people. 'They're planning a move back to the UK. It's the Brexit thing. It's unsettled them.'

'And you don't know who you'll get instead.'

'It's not just that. They're *friends.*' I said I understood. I did understand. Very well.

Then Theo's mother came up to me. I was too much in awe of her to think of her as Anastasia, even if that was itself a pretty awe-inspiring name. We talked a little about general things. Then, shocking me because I was so unsuspecting, she said – in Spanish but I followed her – 'A holiday romance can be a lovely thing. And you've been good for Theo. You've helped him to get over Mateo... Until...' Just like Claire had done a few minutes earlier she waved vaguely around the black-clad gathering. 'Until this tragedy. This has hurt him all over again.'

I said I understood very well.

Anastasia's voice grew vibrant with intensity. 'But you can not take Theo away from here. Canarians do not thrive in northern climates. His place is here.'

I knew what was hidden in that. The pebble in the snowball. She meant, his place is here with me. I wasn't so ill-mannered as to say I knew she meant that. In any case she knew I knew. But my spirits, already subdued by the occasion, low in the water, now sank beneath the waves.

The eating and drinking didn't go on very long. We were not celebrating the conclusion of a long innings, a life completed and fulfilled. We'd come together to mark the cutting off of a life that was barely halfway done, and every minute of this day must have been an agony for Claire. The choked words that Anastasia had uttered in the church were true.

As the gathering was breaking up, spilling out onto the pavement in a tangle of goodbyes, an English-looking man came up to me. He looked about ten years older than Theo and me. I saw him through the eyes of someone who worked in schools; his appearance said Rugby coach to me. Which is exactly what he turned out to be. He was also the head of English at the college whose pupils I'd been talking with earlier.

'You're Jonty,' he said and shook my hand. He smiled. 'You've been pointed out to me and I thought I'd like to say hallo. I gather the kids were telling you we'd need a new teacher following Matt's...'

'Yes,' I said.

'We'll be advertising, of course. Don't know if you've any plans to move out here yourself...'

'I'm not sure...'

'I just thought I'd mention it. Saw you chatting to the kids and ... well, first impressions and all that. You seemed a likely lad. So if you wanted to apply...'

'Gosh,' I said. I was careful to use no stronger an expletive. First impressions and all that. 'But you'll be needing someone at start of term. I'm not sure...'

'There'd be ways of solving that, I'm sure. If it came to it. Look, may I give you my card? And I don't know if you'd like to give me your email...?' We did the little exchange. Then my new acquaintance, whose name was David and whose accent I'd come to realise was slightly Welsh, scooped up his little band of musicians and their instruments, and led them away up towards the bus stops, taking his leave of me with a friendly wave.

Theo had missed that little exchange. He couldn't be at my side for every minute, obviously, and had understandably left me to it when I was safely cocooned in English speakers' company. But he came up to me now, amidst the goodbyes, and I told him what had happened. He just had time to say, 'Wow, *guapa,*' before his mother arrived hard on his heels. It was her moment to take her leave. After nodding politely, perhaps anxiously, to me, she asked her son if he would go to her place for supper this evening. He said – I understood every word and every nuance – that this was his last evening with me. She then, rather grudgingly I suspected, suggested we both went up to La Orotava to spend the evening with her.

Theo answered that he would go to her for supper tomorrow, but that he really wanted some time alone with me. He would bring me to see her next time I was in Puerto. (I couldn't help noticing, and delighting in, that throwaway *la proxima vez,* next time.) This was accepted at last. Theo would walk to the bus stop with her, he said. He turned to me and, with a look in his eyes that I knew only too well, asked if I'd mind waiting for him for five minutes here. I said of course I would, and Anastasia and I exchanged a farewell and a handshake that was civil but no more.

I watched them go up the little slope together, towards the Calle del Aceviño where the City Bar and the café Bei Thomas lay to the left and the bus stops to the right. They disappeared from sight in the direction of the bus stops.

How well I knew the little deals that only sons had to cut with their widowed mothers, and that all mothers had to cut with their sons. Having spent a couple of hours in the close vicinity of Anastasia I couldn't but feel that Theo had been quite brave. Filial but firm. But it didn't augur well for whatever kind of a future – if any – that there might be for us.

We ate at El Regulo. I'd returned my safety-pinned suit to Jose, and Theo and I were relaxed in shorts and T-shirts. We hadn't talked about when or where we might see each other again. Theo didn't seem in a hurry to bring the matter up. He'd had enough to think about with the loss of his ex-partner. Did he think of me now as his current *novio?* He hadn't said so in those exact words, though it was in the endearments we exchanged, the looks, the caresses, the sex we had. It was in the poetic, yearning words he wrote to me.

I brought it up over dessert eventually.

'You know, when people have said the things to each other that we have, there's a kind of next step, isn't there?' It sounded crass in the extreme. I didn't need Theo's facial expression to tell me so. But I went on. 'You know what I mean.'

'Yes,' he said emphatically. 'I do know what you mean. And I want it too. I'll say that just in case you think I don't. But...' He shrugged and raised his eyebrows.

'OK. I've met your mother. You haven't met mine...'

'I haven't forgotten the leg of lamb.'

'Exactly. But we can't live in their pockets. I've as good as been offered a job out here.'

'El amor encontrará un camino,' he said unexpectedly. That's 'love will find a way'. But he said it in the tone of voice that said it wasn't always true.

I said, 'We'll make it find a way.' There was silence for a moment and then my phone rang. I mugged a look of apology at Theo and got it out of my pocket. It gave me Chris's name. I felt a frisson of something. My important moment with Theo had been hi-jacked by a phone-call. 'Sorry, Theo,' I said. 'I have to take this.'

I put the phone to my cheek. 'Hallo Chris. What news? I'm just having dinner with Theo.' Whatever he was going to say he needed to know that. Or rather I needed him to.

'Maxwell came back for his things. We worked the strike and get-out together on Saturday. We spent the night at your place.' Tiny pause. 'I hope that was OK?'

'Yes of course,' I mumbled distantly. The way people in shock do. 'Where's Maxwell now?'

'Gone back to Italy.' Another wee pause. 'I'm still at your place, though.'

Keep calm, I thought. 'That's fine,' I said. 'But ... any particular reason why?'

'I had a bit of a falling out with my parents. About being gay. Well, not really about being gay. They accept that. But about getting in with Maxwell, and with you.'

'You brought me into it?!'

'You were already there,' he said, which was not unreasonable. 'They're a bit old-school. They think a person should only be involved with one person at a time.'

'I'd agree with them.' I felt I needed to spell it out for the benefit of Theo who was sitting opposite me, wide-eyed with curiosity. 'I also think a person should only be involved with one person at a time. Look, I'm back tomorrow night. Will you still be there?' The answer was a nervous sort of Mmm. 'We can talk then. Are you finding your way around the flat OK? Eating properly?' He told me that he was. 'Then see you tomorrow night. But if you're back home with your parents by then, even better, and we'll talk soon. Take care. Bye now.' I ended the call.

Theo and I looked into each other's astonished eyes for a moment. Then Theo said, 'Who the fuck was that? And who's Maxwell?'

The next part of the evening wasn't particularly happy. As we walked grimly back to Theo's place I told him the whole story about Maxwell, and the whole story about Chris. It wasn't easy to make it clear that the three of us were not entangled in some three-way relationship.

'But you had sex with both of them. Even if it was separately and not together.' It's amazing how people always want to home in on this question before you've had a chance to explain the bigger picture properly. By now we'd climbed the stairs and were standing facing each other in Theo's small bedroom.

'I've never had sex with Chris,' I said. 'We had an innocent goodnight hug the night he slept on my mezzanine. It went no further than that, I promise you.' Well, we'd grasped each other's cocks a couple of times, but I didn't go into that. Theo had enough to deal with.

'But Maxwell...'

'OK. Yes I did. But...'

'You...'

'Let me explain. You and I had made no promises about being exclusive, or about anything. I actually thought you were picking up random guys on the bench...'

'On *our* bench? Why would you possibly...?'

'It was something Nat wrote in a message to me on some other subject.' I hoped Theo wouldn't ask me what the other subject was and, thank God, he didn't. 'I misinterpreted things. He said he'd seen you walking past City Bar, going towards...'

Theo's face screwed itself up the way I had once seen Maxwell's do. 'And that bit of evidence was enough to prove... My God, Jonty, what kind of a person are you? I don't know you. I don't know you at all.' By now he was in tears.

I tried to be calm and north-European. 'You do know me. You know me very well. I'm someone like you.' I reached out to touch him but he backed away. Now I started to cry.

Theo said, 'I'm going to bed now.' He pulled his T-shirt off.

'Then so am I.' I took my T-shirt off too.

'But not with me. Go find yourself a hotel.'

'Oh for God's sake, Theo.' But I looked with dismay at the single bed. It was way too small for two people who were having a row.

'You're not faithful, Jonty. You can't be. It's not in your nature to be. You're just like Mateo.' Tears ran down his cheeks. They were in his voice too. 'You're a lovely guy but I couldn't live with you.' He was sitting on the side of his bed now, naked except for socks and shoes. I still had my shorts on. Just in case I did have to go out and find a hotel. 'Oh fuck.' He was struggling with one of his trainers.

'What?'

'Fucking knot…'

'Let me…'

'No. Stay away from me.' He held up one hand as if warding off something ugly and evil, while struggling uselessly with the knot with his other hand alone.

I made a huge effort, the way you make a huge effort to keep a small boat afloat when it's being battered by huge waves. 'I'm going to count to ten, then I'm walking over to you. I'll help you with the knot. Then if you still want me to I'll go and get a hotel.' I counted out loud. I did it in Spanish. *'Uno, dos, tres, cuatro, cinco, seis, siete, ocho, nueve…'* I thought it would have more impact that way. I said, *'Diez,'* and walked towards him, wondering what would happen now.

I knelt at his feet and he didn't push me away. I hoped so desperately that I could untangle that shoelace that I almost prayed. Perhaps, without knowing it, I did pray. At any rate it came undone after a few seconds. In silence I pulled the shoe off, then the sock. He let me. Then I turned my attention to the other shoe and did the same. Still kneeling on the floor I looked up at him.

His face was expressionless. Perhaps mine was too. We stared at each other for several seconds more. Then Theo began to smile, and after another second it became the most beautiful smile I had ever seen.

TWENTY-FIVE

When I stepped off the airport bus in the centre of Paisley the first impression on my senses was the smell of Scottish meat pies baking. It made the most powerful possible statement about being home, about being in Scotland, about being where I belonged. There is no smell of baking anywhere in the world that is anything like it. No cooking smell is quite as wonderful; not the scent of baking baguettes that wafts in the early morning through the streets of Paris; not the smell of frying garlic and onion, shortly before lunchtime, that drifts round Spanish towns; not the sizzling rabbit aroma of the Majorcan countryside... I could go on. If I was even toying with the idea of transplanting myself into Canarian soil this one wonderful scent would make me pause. I wondered whether, if he ever came here, Theo would like it the way I did. If a Scottish meat pie could ever come to mean as much to him as it did to me.

We'd parted on wonderful kiss-and-make-up terms. The aftermath of a lover's tiff. Endorphins, is it? Hormones? I can't remember. But the sublime feeling of being more in love than ever is perhaps the best state of being in the world. Theo had already been naked when I'd un-knotted his shoe-lace. I'd simply run my hand up his shin, then over the summit of his knee and we'd taken it from there. We hadn't had a lot of sleep: I'd had to get up early to catch my plane.

Now I threaded my way through the streets between the bus stop and the old mill. When the handsome building came in sight, with the river and its green banks in front of it I saw that someone was sitting on a bench by the water, apparently contemplating the stream. When I got closer I saw that it was Chris. A lone figure on a bench. Echoes... He got up when he saw me; we walked towards each other and hugged cautiously. Chris said, 'I didn't want you to find me actually inside your place when you arrived.'

'You didn't need to worry about that. It might have been raining.' But I was touched by his sensitivity. 'You can stay as long as you like.' We made our way indoors. 'But how are things with your parents?' I risked a joke. 'Do you think you'll ever see them again?'

'I'm going home to them tomorrow night. We've spoken on the phone. Things are more or less OK. In the meantime...'

'In the meantime it's OK. You can stay tonight. I've just said so. Tomorrow I've got to drive to Stirling to have lunch with my own mum. Until your parents die you still have to go on negotiating these things.'

Chris laughed, almost happily. I'd spoken to my mother by phone while I was still on Tenerife. We'd made up, and made this arrangement for Sunday. Now I had a new thought for Chris. 'Come with me if you want to. If you're not going home till the evening. Don't be knocking around all day on your own.'

'Well...'

'We can talk about it nearer the time. We don't have to do everything now.'

I unpacked my things while Chris made tea. The flat was by no means a tip but it had an unmistakeable look of having been lived in. I admit that I did turn back my duvet. There was an unmistakeable and enviably large indication that my bed had been occupied too.

'How did Maxwell seem?' I called to Chris through the half-open door.

'In good spirits. He's a lovely guy. He sends you his best wishes... Sorry, I should have said before. And he said to thank you for everything. That you'd been a wonderful friend.'

Well, that was nice to know. It was also nice to know, from the evidence on my bed-sheet, that Maxwell hadn't been too unhealthily preoccupied with the search for an older man to nurture him.

I joined Chris in the living-room. 'And you say he's gone straight back to Italy?' I'd noticed the absence of his belongings from the hall table as soon as we'd walked in through the door.

Chris handed me my mug of tea. 'His step-father's found him a job in his company. Milk and no sugar. Is that OK?'

'That's fine.' I wasn't going to ask what sort of a job it might be. That Maxwell had a job at all was wonderful enough news.

A little later Chris and I went out for a meal. I took him first to The Bull for a pint or two, but not three. Then we went to an Indian restaurant. 'Choose what you want,' I told him. 'It's on me.'

He opted for the thing that had prawns in it. 'I had this with Maxwell once.'

'I'm sure you did,' I managed to keep a straight face but Chris still saw he was being teased. He smiled at me.

'Can I sleep with you tonight?' Chris asked when it was bedtime.

Perhaps that final red wine nightcap had not been a good idea.

'I don't know… I don't think…'

'I didn't mean have sex with you. I just meant share a bed, like friends do. Comfort. Company. You know.'

'I know.'

He smiled angelically. 'Honestly, I don't want to have sex with you.'

'No, obviously.' I tried not to show that that had hurt me. There were plenty of people in the world who didn't, or wouldn't, want to have sex with me. Over the years a few had had to make that clear to me by subtle or less subtle means. But nobody had put it in those exact words. Till now.

Even so it was a lovely experience. We slept naked, back to back. I'd taken a surreptitious gawp at his full-frontal self in the seconds before he jumped in under the duvet. Of course he'd had a quick little look at me. Neither of us was erect. Just halfway there.

We behaved ourselves. Back to back and no reaching out of exploring hands around and behind. Our only concession to naughtiness was a little rub of buttock against buttock after we'd put out the light and said goodnight. Then I listened to his breathing slowing into the rhythms of sleep, thinking I should make the most of that because, with Chris, this moment was never likely to come again.

In the morning I phoned my mother. 'Is it OK if I bring a young friend? Just a friend. But I'll bring a bottle too.' I didn't have to bring a joint of lamb. Having only flown back into the country a few hours ago I was excused that. We'd sorted this out already on the phone. 'We're both invited to Stirling,' I told Chris. He tried to make the I-can-take-it-or-leave-it face of a bored teen, but I could see he was pleased, perhaps even relieved. Few people say no to a free cooked meal.

Then a message arrived from Theo. We'd spoken last night on the phone. He'd been fine about Chris staying over. But his message this morning – it came in the form of an email – wasn't really a message at all. It was a poem.

Chris watched me reading it as I stood in the living-room. It was very private, and yet it was too good not to share. I had to use the dictionary a bit as I went along, but I translated it for him. He was awed, almost shocked, by Theo's words to me. He said, 'To have something like that written to you ... written about you...' He stopped and looked me straight in the eye. 'Actually I'm jealous if the truth be told. I can't believe anyone will ever love me that much. Love me enough to write like that about me.'

The aching twang of those words. An echoing twang in me.

'Believe me, Chris, they will. Sweetheart, they will. And very soon.' I laid a hand on his shoulder. If it hadn't been for the immense gravitational pull of Theo that *they* would be me, and that *soon* would be now.

He very wisely turned his attention back to the poem as a work of art. 'It's almost like Shakespeare,' he said. 'You know, like you taught us, the ideas in the sonnets are like holograms, layer beneath layer. And he – I mean Theo – does the same.' He wrinkled his nose. 'Though can you really say the sky unfolds?'

'You can if you're Spanish,' I said. 'And remember, unfolds was just my feeble translation of a Spanish word. There's a connection in Spanish between the idea of folding and the idea of prayer. It's not really translatable.'

'I see.' He sank down onto the sofa. 'It's a lovely poem anyway.'

I messaged Theo back. I said I didn't have the words to thank him for what he'd written to me. I'd try to thank him in other ways. Then I told Chris it was time we got ready to go.

Chris returned to Theo's poem in the car, on the motorway. 'You know we talked once about the coffins of Heathcliff and Cathy? The way the removable panels between them were a metaphor?'

'You said they were a metaphor,' I corrected. 'Clever boy. You pointed that out to me.'

'Reading that poem of Theo's I thought, that's done the same.'

'Not quite with you now. Sorry.' I was passing a lorry with a loose and flapping tarpaulin. Chris was only getting half my attention.

'I mean, a poem like that, that is directed to you, that is about you... It breaks down the panel, the wall, that separates his identity from yours. It makes you like one person. You and Theo.'

'Thank you,' I said. 'I guess that's true.' I felt honoured and very humbled by the knowledge that Chris thought it was so. 'In a way that's also true of Shakespeare's sonnets. Don't you think? Each one may have been addressed to one person in particular – some to a woman, some to a man – but they open up the barrier between his heart and yours.' I stopped. I wondered if I'd gone too far. I'd never have said this to a class of boys and girls.

'Oh God, you're right, Jonty. That's so true. I never thought of it before.' And then he said the most wonderful thing I ever heard him say. 'There's not much of a barrier, actually, Jonty, between my heart and yours.'

I had no answer to that. No words that could have come out without tears. I put my hand on his knee and gave it a chaste squeeze. Then wonderfully he did the same to me.

By the time we reached my mother's house we'd talked of many things. Chris knew all my doubts and fears about my future, and I knew all of his. My mother, after greeting us with smiles, kissing me, and shaking Chris's hand, gave us a wary, searching look. It was the look we give to any pair of arriving visitors who have clearly had deep discussions in the car on the way to our door.

The lamb leg was good. Really good. I guessed it was the one that mum had bought over a week ago, and that

she had stuck it in the freezer as I'd suggested she
should. I wasn't going to ask. As Theo would have said,
it was a time to let sleeping doggies lie. Mum and I
talked sweetly together about plans for her birthday in a
couple of days' time. She was having a few people
round. I said of course I'd be coming. She asked, would
Chris like to…? I answered for him. He was going back
to his parents tonight, and they were about to go to
France on holiday… Chris said very nicely, 'I'll see if I
can get away.'

I saw him taking in his surroundings as my mother
helped him to more roast tatties. The small dining-room
with its second-generation furniture; the picture of my
dead father, in his naval officer's uniform, on the wall.
The out-of-date bourgeois cosiness of it all. Then he
started in quite suddenly.

'You'd get enough from this place to get something
really nice on Tenerife.'

Mum laughed, I was pleased to see. 'I'm not planning
to move to Tenerife.'

'Well, not if Jonty doesn't get the job out there. But if
he does … it might be nicer to live out there near him
than to have to keep flying back and forth from here to
there.'

Mum looked at me. She wasn't laughing now. 'Job…?
In Tenerife?' She was trying not to show panic in her
face or in her words but it was there. She was my
mother. I knew.

'It's only a remote possibility,' I said. I told her about
my conversation with the head of English at the Colegio
Británico. I made light of it. Nothing would come of it. I
wouldn't be giving much thought to it; she wasn't to
take it seriously.

But Chris would not let go. 'There's this lady, Claire.
Jonty was telling me… The house next door to hers is
coming up for sale. She's a retired English woman

who's lost her only son. Very cultured and nice. She's going to be lost without her neighbours as friends.'

Part of me wanted to kick Chris under the table to shut him up. But it would hardly have been fair. After all, he was only relaying my own words, passing on the thoughts I'd shared with him in the car. It was just that the bull-in-china-shop way he was doing it would not have been my preferred method of going about things.

'It's all pie in the sky,' I interrupted in the end. 'They'll want someone to start at the beginning of term. I'd have to give half a term's notice…'

Chris turned to me. 'Why don't you contact the head tomorrow and see if he'll do a deal?'

'Cart before horse. Nobody's offered me a job yet.'

'Jonty, they will. You know they will.'

I felt I was being battered by the storm of Chris's energy, his teenage optimism. I know my mother was feeling battered by it too. It struck me that sometimes it could be an advantage to have a bouncy, hopeful teenager do your dirty work for you.

Mum looked at me. She said – the words came from a face as enigmatic as the Sphinx's – 'What's this house like? The one next door to your friend Claire.'

I told her all I could about it. How lovely the setting was. How nice the gardens were. How near to the sea. 'It's actually quite a bit nearer to Puerto de la Cruz than Stirling is to Paisley.' I threw that in casually. I didn't say that the journey in between lay over the lower slopes of a mountain and was made up largely of hairpin bends. We hadn't nearly reached that stage.

Chris nodded towards a painting on the wall. It was a beautifully executed water colour of a blue and white house in the Kasbah of Tangier. He asked about it. Mum told him, 'It was painted by a friend of Jonty's father. They were in the navy together. Stationed in Gibraltar. Just across the strait from Tangier. That's where that house is.' She added, half bashfully, half proudly, 'The friend was a professional artist...'

'Of course,' said Chris. 'I can see that clearly. I'd love to go to Morocco one day.'

It crossed my mind that Chris might have a bright future as a negotiator ahead of him. In international affairs, say, or brokering trade deals.

After lunch we sat in the small garden, where there was sunshine. After a little while my mother said a bit nervously, 'Do you remember, there were some old family photographs I wanted to show you?' Her eyes flicked towards Chris. 'Though I'm not sure if it would be...'

Chris said at once, 'I love looking at other people's family photos.' He said it with the brightest sincerity, and gave one of his most brilliant smiles. Even I believed for a moment that he meant every word. But anyway, what else were we all going to do for the next hour?

I said, 'Bring them on,' and mum went into the house to get them. Chris and I didn't say anything as she left. We just mugged complicit smiles.

When my mother came back she was carrying two manila envelopes. One had written on in – in presumably my grandmother's neat hand – Old Family Photos. The other bore the words: Very Old Family Photos. Dutifully we went through them. Old Photos first. We would save the Very Old Photos till the end.

There were faded snaps of family groups in the nineteen-twenties. Of houses in what must have been suburbia but still, back then, looked like woodland glades. Unknown relatives sitting on beaches in deckchairs. An elderly man (my great-great grandfather maybe?) sat in the sun in a three-piece tweed suit, plus-fours, thick socks and laced-up boots. He wore a tie around his neck and a trilby hat – to indicate the casualness of the situation, no doubt. He was after all on holiday. His wife sat in the deck-chair next to him, dressed in an ankle-length frock that seemed to be made of curtain velvet. She had a big hat with a feather in. Around them children played in the sand, swaddled in white from head to toe. They must all have been sweltering.

Each photograph bore a stamp, on the back, of some local professional photographic studio. The locations were instructive. Weymouth. Hastings. Folkestone...

At last we broached the second envelope. The one containing the Very Old Photos. Together the three of us peered closely at the studio portraits of people in the nineteenth century. The women in wasp-waisted bodices and pleated dresses than ran down to near the floor. The boys in knickerbockers and Eton collars. A lap-dog that looked like the HMV dog sitting on the knees of a miserable-looking boy. Men with beards. Dark beards. Dark-skinned men with big, sensitive eyes. Swagged velvet curtains in the background. Shabbat candles on the table to the side.

It was Chris who said it, of course. Out of the mouths of babes and sucklings. 'They're all Jewish, aren't they.' The emperor's new clothes. We looked for the photographer's stamp. It read, Ezekiel Bros., Mile End.

I heard my mother's voice say, a bit haltingly, 'Following the pogroms in Eastern Europe in the 1880s a lot of Polish Jews settled in London's East End.' She shrugged. 'I don't need to tell either of you that. But it seems that we're partly descended from them.'

There was a second's silence while Chris and I digested the news. Then, 'I think that's great,' I said cheerfully. 'England and Scotland being good Europeans – and America of course – doing their bit for humanity back then. Give me your tired, your poor, your huddled masses yearning to breathe free.'

'Yeah,' said Chris. 'And look at the situation now.' Then he must have decided to lighten the tone. He looked at me with a great big grin. 'I'd never have thought you were Jewish, Jonty. Knowing you as I do. No sign of it last night when I looked at you.' Then he realised what he'd said and in whose company. I saw the shock of it steal over his face, and then he blushed to the roots of his hair, and so did I. Amazingly, incredibly, but thank God it was so, the implications of the remark completely passed my dear mother by.

Later in the day I drove Chris back to his parents' home. 'Do you want me to come in with you?' I volunteered as we pulled up a few metres short of the door.

He twisted sideways in his seat and looked at me. 'No, I'll be fine. Like I said, I discussed everything with my mother on the phone, and spoke to dad too. Everything will be fine. And they know I don't sleep with you at any rate.' He gave me a wicked smile. 'At least not in that way.' I found myself hoping that Theo would also see it in that way. There were perhaps a few things that Theo wouldn't need to be told; there are some situations whose nuances you can't perceive unless you're there. Theo already knew that Chris had stayed the night in my apartment, and that he'd be having lunch with my mother and me. He'd been OK with that, and it seemed like enough actually.

'Any problems at all – you just call me. Talk to me. And if you want me to come and get you, I'll drop everything and do it.'

'I know you will, Jonty.' He hesitated a second and the uncertainty was in his face. Then he came out with the thing he wasn't sure if he could say. 'Sweetheart.' I felt as though he'd tucked a rose into my buttonhole. His face became decisive again. 'Thank you but I'll be fine.'

'But if you did have...'

'Then I would. I promise you. My first port of call.'

'Good luck then.' We kissed across the gear lever briefly. Then Chris got out of the car. He turned back and waved when he had his hand on the gate, like someone in a 1940s film. Then he disappeared from view. I hadn't started the engine yet. I did now. After a moment's thought I reckoned that he'd be OK with his parents. If he was anything like as good at dealing with them as he'd been at dealing with mine. And with me.

That evening I called Harry. 'That's nice,' he said. 'I'd been meaning to call you. But ... you know.'

'I do. Listen, there's something I need to tell you. I'm kind of involved with somebody new...'

'That's great. Oh hey! I mean, really lovely. Tell me: who is he?'

'I'll tell you in a minute. But that's not why I'm calling. The thing is, he split up with his long-term partner within the last year...'

'Sounds familiar...'

'Two weeks ago the ex-partner died.'

'Oh no. I'm ... er ... sorry. Was he... I mean, was he a lot older than we are?'

'Ten years or so. He died suddenly of some sort of embolism. A blood clot on the lung. But the point is... Theo – that's my new guy – felt really bad because they hadn't talked recently. He hadn't had a chance to say goodbye. That's why I felt I needed to ring you.' I had to pause before I went on. 'You see, I needed to tell you that just because people split up it doesn't mean they've stopped caring about each other. It doesn't mean the end of loving them.'

'Oh, my angel.' There was a moment's silence from the other end. 'Oh, Jonty, it's lovely to hear those Scottish vowels again. But there's something I need to tell you too. I'm also seeing someone new. I wasn't sure how to tell you because you were still on your own. That's why I didn't phone or message you. But ... no, let that wait. First tell me about yours.'

I did.

'Spelt T-A-O? T-A-Y-O?'

'Spelt T-H-E-O.'

'So will he be moving in to the mill?'

'Unlikely. There's a wee chance – I mean a really wee chance – that I might be offered a teaching job out there.'

'On Gran Canaria?'

'Tenerife. Keep up. But there's about ten other completely unconnected things would have to happen to make it possible.'

'Angel-face, don't be defeatist. Those things will happen if you want them to. Make them happen. Faint heart ne'er won fair male.' Harry went on to tell me about his new man, an English guy who worked for the same civil engineering company. Also named Harry.

'Isn't that going to be very confusing for people?' I asked.

'What do you mean going to be? It already is. It's a positive nightmare.'

I told him how nice it was to hear his southern English vowels.

'I'm just thinking, suddenly, about another thing. We – I mean the company – have got a big new contract in Glasgow. Harry and I may both be moving back up to Scotland for a couple of years. I just wondered if – I mean if you get this teaching job out there – there'd be any chance we could do a deal over the apartment...'

'In the mill?' I felt my heart accelerate with the surprise of all this. 'I'm sure we could. If, if, if, of course... But we'd need a clause in the tenancy agreement to say that Theo and I could stay on the mezzanine from time to time.'

'Angel,' Harry said again. 'Look, I need to go now. But we'll keep in touch over this. See how things go. I'm sure the job will work out fine.'

I thought of something. 'Just one more thing. You know that vote we had – the Brexit thing. Which way did you vote in the end?'

'I voted Leave,' said Harry tersely. 'No doubt you, being a good Scottish boy, voted Remain.'

It's said that when people think they are about to die they get a chance to review their entire life in a mind-bogglingly short space of time. Something like this happened to me now. I saw the whole argument I might have with Harry over the phone: the one we'd had so many times before. He would talk about red tape slowing down the procurement of materials in the construction industry, the undercutting of prices by unfair competition from Eastern Europe. The breathtaking intransigence of Angela Merkel and the bloody-mindedness of the executives of the Commission. I would fulminate about the impending loss of access for the UK's youth to the Erasmus scheme, the danger of a return to pan-European wars in the centuries to come, the derailment of a thousand year's natural progress of history. We'd all be poor...

I said, 'Well, it takes all sorts to make a world.'

'I do love you, little angel,' I heard Harry say.

'I love you too, Harry.' We ended the call.

TWENTY-SIX

Sunday had been a day and a half. So had Saturday. So had Friday. I didn't wake up till half past nine that Monday morning, and I wouldn't have done that if the house phone hadn't rung. It would only be mum. But I got out of bed groggily and answered it anyway.

It wasn't mum. It was the Colegio Británico calling from Tenerife. It was the Welsh Rugby player, the head of English, who I'd spoken to at the funeral. They wanted to interview me. Would it be possible for me to attend in ten days' time? If I would be prepared to travel by the cheapest possible means they would pay my fare. I did a quick mental check to make sure my mother's birthday would have come and gone before then, then said yes – there being nothing else of importance in my diary – and we agreed a time.

I made myself calm down and make a cup of tea before phoning Theo. 'I don't believe it,' he said. 'No, I don't mean I didn't believe they'd want to see you. I mean I can't believe you've phoned me. I'd just picked up my phone – maybe a second before you rang – to call you. I have amazing news.'

'What?' I asked stupidly.

'Matt's apartment… You know how it belongs in bits and pieces to his whole family.' He stopped tantalisingly.

'Yes.'

'I've just opened a letter from Claire. It seems she's persuaded the family to let me live in it for my lifetime. I'd have to pay the upkeep and the rest of the mortgage. But still…'

'Oh bloody hell.' My thoughts seemed to freeze. I could only find meaningless words. 'My God. That's incredible. Oh wow.' Then my thoughts unfroze again and I told Theo about Chris's conversation with my mother, and the possibility of her moving next door to Claire…'

'Hang on,' said Theo. 'Aren't you running a bit ahead here?'

'Maybe,' I agreed. 'But you have to blame Chris, not me. Oh, and another thing. Mum showed us some old family photos yesterday. It turns out I've got Jewish ancestry.'

'I think I need to make another espresso,' said Theo.

I called my school. There was a skeleton office crew in the holidays. They gave me the head's private number. He was on holiday in France, they told me. Perhaps it would be wise to wait till ten before calling him. By then it would be eleven o'clock over there.

I did wait till ten, and the time came round very slowly even though it had only been ten minutes away when I was talking to the school. But at last I rang the number, and the head picked up straight away. I told him about the Tenerife job interview and the circumstances in which it had come about. This included explaining that I was involved with someone over there. Their term wouldn't start till three weeks after ours did, but even so…

I knew we were supposed to give half a term's notice if we were planning to leave. Of course my boss knew this too. He said, 'Why don't we agree that you're giving notice now? The time between now and September is roughly half a term. And you can un-give your notice in ten day's time if you've decided to turn them down.'

'Or if they don't want me.'

'Oh for God's sake,' the head said. 'Think positive, Jonty. Think of your new friend.'

I thanked him almost too effusively and ended the call. I'd never known the head be so relaxed and easy about anything. I thought it was a good advertisement for French holidays.

I spent the wait at Glasgow airport googling some facts about Scottish history. Perhaps the delay was just as well. I was pretty sure you had to pay for wifi access on the airline I was travelling with. I found out a lot of things I'd either never known or else learnt at school and then completely forgotten; if the latter, then it wasn't exactly a ringing endorsement for my profession.

When at last we did get going I spent most of the flight simply looking out of the porthole. It was cloudy most of the way and the Selvagem Islands – the Jonty Islands as I thought of them now – were nowhere to be seen. But at least the clouds were free. I thought about what I was going to say at tomorrow's interview. I thought about what the future was going to do with me. What would it be like to share a life with Theo, a man I'd only known in the context of foreign holidays? His mercurial, southern changes alarmed me. Living with him would be like riding inside a barometer in the hurricane latitudes.

Tenerife itself alarmed me too. All very well for holidays, but actually to live there…? Taxes? Paperwork? Health insurance with Brexit looming? I was running ahead, though. I probably wouldn't get the job anyway. But Harry's words came back to me. Faint heart ne'er won fair male. And those of the head of my school. Think positive. Though shouldn't that be, think positively? Theo would have said so.

My mother's birthday had gone rather splendidly. She'd had a few local friends round for drinks in the garden – mercifully the sun shone that day – and there was a buffet. To my surprise Chris had phoned me the day before and asked if he could take up mum's invitation and come along with me. I picked him up and drove him there most happily. At one point during the proceedings we both overheard my mother saying to another woman of about her own age – it must have been in answer to that standby retirement-party question, what are you going to do now? – 'It's just possible that I'll be moving to the Canary Islands. Jonty's got a job interview out there next week...' We didn't hear any more; another conversation got in the way; but we exchanged meaningful smiles. I'd taken Chris straight back to his parents' house afterwards. They were off on holiday the next day. Flying to the Dordogne. They weren't likely to run into the head teacher down there. He and his family were in Provence, he'd told me. I thought that was just as well.

We broke through the clouds and were landing suddenly. When we were down and waiting for luggage at the carousel I messaged Theo to say I'd arrived safely. We'd arranged to meet, for old times' sake, in City Bar. I said I'd be there in about an hour and a half.

But when I emerged from the customs channel and was confronted with that array beyond the railing of taxi drivers and holiday couriers, I was astonished to see my name on a piece of paper being held aloft by one of the people in the little throng. Mr Jonty Allen. I looked above and beyond the paper. There was the grinning face of Theo.

'Theo! How did you get here?'

He smiled very smugly. He said, 'I brought the car.'

'Car? What car?'

'My car. Matt's car. That came to me along with his home. Which is where we'll be spending tonight by the way. Didn't I tell you about the car?'

The paper with my name on scrunched between us as we gave each other a quick hug. Dead men's shoes, I thought. Dead men's jobs. Dead men's apartments and dead men's lovers. Now dead men's cars.

As we crossed the car park Theo's key-fob found it for me, parked beside a row of oleanders. Its lights flashed on for a second. It was an Audi. When we were inside it and doing up our seat-belts Theo asked me, 'Are you nervous?'

'About your driving?'

'No. About tomorrow.'

'Everyone's nervous before interviews.'

'Listen, they won't be phoning many people up in England – sorry, Scotland – and offering them the plane fare to come over for an interview. Not even a low-cost fare.'

'I don't know,' I said. 'They might be paying the others to come on British Airways.'

'Ha-ha. You know what I mean. You've as good as got it.'

I remembered driving Chris to his interview at the theatre. Provided he was polite, I'd thought, and didn't fart while he was sitting there... 'Well, I guess it's good to think positively.' I was careful to use the adverb; I wanted to make Theo happy. By now he was accelerating out of the roundabout and onto the slip-road towards the motorway.

Theo drove very expertly. He drove like any Canary Islander, used to mountain roads. It'll be enough to say that we got to Puerto very quickly. We were in City Bar before sunset.

We greeted the staff there like old friends and Hooligan poured us two Doradas. As we were drinking them Theo said – surprising me, but it was probably to take my mind off my interview the next morning – 'I've been googling Scottish history. It's very instructive.'

I said, 'You're supposed to be breaking me of my addiction to Google, not getting into it yourself.'

'Oh, it's just an occasional thing with me. I won't get addicted.'

'That's what they all say. But...' I told him that, coincidentally, I'd been googling the same subject in the Glasgow departure lounge.

Theo sipped his beer. 'It seems that, throughout history, the Scots have always felt the English treated them as poor relations.'

'Well, to be fair to the English, that may have been because Scotland actually was a poor relation. Through no fault of its own though, and only in economic terms. England was born with a silver spoon in its mouth. Not just a silver spoon, but a copper spoon, a tin spoon and a bloody great iron one. That's why the Romans came there, and that's why they didn't try too hard with Scotland. Scotland had some of those things, but only in small quantities. It was different later, when coal became important, but by then the pattern had been established, and the perception. England rich, Scotland poor.'

'Though not poor in talent...'

I said, 'You only have to look at me to see that,' and Theo chuckled.

'All those Prime Ministers; engineers who built the British Empire; writers, poets, artists...'

'And yours truly,' I reminded him a second time.

'But you do go on a bit,' he chided me, 'about what a happy Union there's been between the two countries since 1707. You've never told me about the Jacobite uprisings. Bonnie Prince Charlie. Flora MacDonald...'

'Hmm,' I said. 'All history is complicated. Ask the history teachers in your own school...'

'I have done,' said Theo, deadpan.

'Most of the reasons that James VII and II was deposed were things that happened in England. But his daughters Mary and Anne who reigned after him (Mary was already conveniently married to William of Orange) were still Stuarts. It was only after their deaths that James's male descendants focused their attention on

Scotland, exploiting the Highland Clans' tribal loyalties. Most of the educated classes in Scotland, and most of the Lowlands, had accepted the Hanoverians as the ruling dynasty. They knew which side their bread was buttered.'

'Like the Brits who voted Remain in your referendum.'

'Exactly. They put aside nostalgic dreams of past glories…'

'What about the Butcher of Culloden, though? He didn't do a lot for the future relations between the two countries.'

'I agree. The King's younger son, the Duke of Cumberland. He was far too ferocious. And because of him there are still a good few Scots who can't stomach the English. But I've thought about this. Cumberland wanted a quick and decisive victory. He couldn't afford things to go any other way. But he ended up doing far more than he needed to. He did what Churchill did when he firestormed Dresden and Hamburg. He did what Truman did when he nuked Hiroshima and Nagasaki.' I spread my arms and hands in the universal not-my-fault gesture. 'It's hard to know what's proportional when you yourself, your family and everything you hold dear are in imminent danger of being butchered. There was a war on. Those things happened.'

'They happened,' said Theo, 'and wars only happen, because we start seeing some people as "the others" instead of being fellow members of the same community.' He clearly felt he'd said enough at that point. He broke off and took a good slurp of Dorada.

'Amen, my little Guanche,' I said.

He raised his glass and grinned at me. 'Cheers, my little Jew-boy.'

'Careful,' I said. I looked around anxiously at the multi-ethnic, mainly English-understanding customers at the bar. 'You can't say Jew-boy these days.'

'It's just two words which are perfectly acceptable…'

'It's just that you can't put them together. For some reason they then become disrespectful. Anyway…'

'Yes. You're right. Let's drop that.' He looked at our glasses, which were nearly empty. 'Would you like to see the place where you'll be staying…? Or do I mean living? We can come back here later if we want.'

We only had to drive a couple of blocks. Theo had told me I'd probably seen the place when walking around La Paz, but I hadn't given that much thought. The place where my boyfriend's ex lived had not preoccupied me. But now we stopped outside it, opened the gate into a garden, and were walking up the path. I saw that it wasn't an apartment in a block of other apartments that we were approaching: it was a fair-sized detached house. I felt like Chris must have done when he saw my old mill building for the first time. I said, like Chris, 'It's big, isn't it.' But perhaps I wasn't talking about the house.

Yes, I must have walked past it, but without giving it a glance. It was in a tidy, quiet residential road of nice villas. It wasn't unlike the kind of place where Claire lived. Though this house wasn't as substantial as Claire's, to me it seemed plenty big enough. For a start there was the garden. From what the street-lights told me, that consisted of an expanse of mown grass, a couple of tall palm trees with flower beds around them, and a few other flowering shrubs.

Theo unlocked and in we went. When Spanish people use the word *casa* they mean a home – it doesn't have to be a house. Home is where the heart is and it can be as small a broom-cupboard as you like. But this was in every sense a house. And Theo had walked away from it when he left Mateo. It had been a big thing to walk away from; I hadn't realised quite how big. If Theo could walk away from it once he could do so again. I'd need to treat him better than Mateo had. The house, its size and its quality, were telling me this. With rather heavy emphasis.

'Built about fifteen years ago,' Theo said. I looked about me. Most of the ground floor was open-plan, which gave it a spacious feel and look. All was clean and tidy. Everything looked ... that catch-all English word ... nice. The kitchen was only divided off by a breakfast bar at waist height. The walls were white-painted, with some features picked out attractively in bare brick...

That all this might be mine, or part-mine, depending on the result of a job interview, was a dizzying thought. I found the idea was bringing me close to tears. I tried not to think about it. Instead I grabbed Theo and kissed him.

'Three bedrooms upstairs,' Theo said once we'd un-coupled. 'Two bathrooms...'

'One each.' I somehow managed to laugh.

'I haven't actually... I mean, I haven't really moved in yet. I was rather waiting for... But now here we are. Though it'll be a bit like camping out at first.'

'At first...?' I thought Theo was getting ahead of things. 'I haven't got the job yet.'

Theo laughed and ruffled my hair. 'Oh thou of little faith...'

We went out to eat. Just two blocks away. We had a dish called *bacalao encebollado*, which is salt cod in an onion, tomato and sweet pepper sauce, with cumin added. It was seriously delicious and more-ish. And about as far away from a Scottish meat pie as you could get, much as I would always love those.

Eventually (how else could this chapter end?) we went to bed. We exchanged ILUs, then had sex, then did the

ILU stuff all over again. Then Theo asked, 'Are you nervous?'

'About tomorrow? You already asked me. I said yes. It's still the case.'

'I meant about the future. With me. Does that frighten you?'

'Yes,' I admitted.

'Good,' said Theo. 'Because I'm frightened too.'

'In which case, maybe we're in with a chance.'

'Sleep tight,' Theo said, and put the light out. Then he said matter-of-factly in the darkness, 'You make me more myself.'

It was a quote from somewhere. So I quoted something back. 'Only in knowing you can I know me.' I'd got that from Chris. But right now Theo didn't need to know that. I cuddled him tight. I was going to get that job in the morning if I had to kill for it. Never in my life had so much been at stake.

TWENTY-SEVEN

A year has passed. A year and two months actually. At this moment I am standing at the rail of a ship, looking out at the jetty we are tied up to and the untidy busy-ness of the port beyond it. The sun is high and bright in the sky, and the sky is alive with gulls. This is Tenerife.

I have found myself on Tenerife. I have found myself here. I have found myself in Theo.

The Poet and the Pedant. That's my nickname for him. It's an allusion to a piece of music by Schumann: The Poet and the Peasant. Translated into Spanish the wordplay doesn't work at all. Not that it's all that brilliant anyway. It was quite a labour explaining it to Theo. But for some reason he liked it.

He came back with a bit of convoluted wordplay of his own. On Forster's famous 'only connect' quote. Forster had written, *Only connect! That was the whole of her sermon. Only connect the prose and the passion, and both will be exalted, and human love will be seen at its height. Live in fragments no longer. Only connect, and the beast and the monk, robbed of the isolation that is life to either, will die.* Theo simply replaced beast and monk with poet and pedant. They are both aspects of him, of course, just as monk and beast – in Forster's view – were warring aspects of the human psyche. But you can take words, Forster's words, Theo's words, my words, any way you want to. Only connect could apply quite well to any pair of human beings. To Theo and me for instance.

I think often of Chris's thoughts about Heathcliff and Cathy. About the isolation between one human being and the next that is symbolised by that plank of coffin wood. The plank that is removable after death, Heathcliff hopes. And of course the reader hopes that this complete union might be attainable even in life. And what else had Chris said? Only in knowing you can I know myself.

Some nearly impossible things have happened in the last year. I got the job at the Colegio Británico. I'm still in love with my temperamental Theo. My mother, after dithering a bit with worries about Brexit, bought the house next door to Claire's and, even more remarkably, they have become good friends, shoring each other up, bonded by their ex-pat status and by shared widowhood.

But if that sounds too good to be true, too fairytale – *vivieron felices y comieron perdices* – well, even more unlikely things have happened in the wider world. Vladimir Putin sailed his navy down the Dover Strait a year ago; that was his wry comment on the Brexit referendum; Britain now cut off from the continent in which for centuries it had played a major role. And nobody said a dicky-bird about it.

For the first time in nine years the United Kingdom has a Prime Minister who isn't Scottish. (Cries of shame.) And it's turned out that a large percentage of Americans believed that the attributes of a thug and bully – and an intellect whose force didn't even register on the Beaufort Scale – were the qualities that a national leader really needed. They voted into office the most perfect embodiment of these qualities that they could find. So you see, unlikely things can happen anywhere. For good or ill. And so I shouldn't be too surprised by the fortuitous chain of events my own life has given me.

But now Theo has a problem to deal with suddenly. It's arisen in just the last few days. The family of small-holders who rent his property on El Hierro have got into a dispute over boundaries with the family next door. (In their part of El Hierro that means half a mile away.)

Rather than resort expensively to firms of notaries Theo is going over to sort it out himself. Or at least to have a go at sorting it out.

When I say that *Theo is* I mean of course that *we are*. It's not something I'd let him do without me at his side. *Con tigo a mi lado,* as he says it in Spanish, looking at it from his point of view.

So we've driven down to Los Cristianos and put the car on the ferry. Armas line. We'll need the car when we get to El Hierro. Theo's place is in the middle of nowhere. Any anxiety I feel about what we shall have to face when we get there is outweighed by excitement. Travelling for two or three hours to the only Canary Island I've never seen except from the porthole of an aeroplane. It's not quite the Selvagem Islands, but El Hierro, the island that lies beyond the sunset, *al dentro del atardecer,* is the nearest I shall ever get to an island of my own. An island of our own.

We stand at the rail as the ferry casts off and begins to churn the sea. As we move beyond the harbour mole the town of Los Cristianos first takes shape and then begins to grow small behind us. I hand Theo a small scrap of paper on which I have written some words. Unlike him I can't write poems, so it isn't one of those. It is the following.

There are mysteries deeper and stranger than any dreamed up by Agatha Christie. There are complexities more mind-boggling than those in any language-full of irregular verbs. There are vistas grander and more wonderful than the star-filled sky at night. There are distances greater than the infinities of time and space. They lie in the discovery and exploration of another human being. Of any human being. They are called the human heart.

Theo reads this with a frown on his face. That famous frown of his. He says, 'Hmm.' Astern Mount Teide is growing grandly into the receding view; its peak appears to be reaching into the sky as if drawn up by an invisible thread. Theo cups his hand over my hand and together we clasp the ship's rail as the waves of the Atlantic begin their rhythmic push-ups from beneath.

****

About the Author

Anthony McDonald is the author of thirty-one books. He studied modern history at Durham University, then worked briefly as a musical instrument maker and as a farmhand before moving into the theatre, where he has worked in every capacity except director and electrician. He has also spent several years teaching English in Paris and London. He now lives in rural East Sussex.

Novels by Anthony McDonald

TENERIFE
THE DOG IN THE CHAPEL
TOM & CHRISTOPHER AND THEIR KIND
DOG ROSES
THE RAVEN AND THE JACKDAW
SILVER CITY
IVOR'S GHOSTS
ADAM
BLUE SKY ADAM
GETTING ORLANDO
ORANGE BITTER, ORANGE SWEET
ALONG THE STARS
WOODCOCK FLIGHT

Short stories

MATCHES IN THE DARK:
13 Tales of Gay Men

———

Diary

RALPH: DIARY OF A GAY TEEN

Comedy

THE GULLIVER MOB

Gay Romance Series:

Sweet Nineteen
Gay Romance on Garda
Gay Romance in Majorca
Gay Tartan
Cocker and I
Cam Cox
The Paris Novel
The Van Gogh Window
Tibidabo
Spring Sonata
Touching Fifty
Romance on the Orient Express

———

And, writing as 'Adam Wye'

Boy Next Door
Love in Venice
Gay in Moscow

All titles are available as Kindle ebooks and as paperbacks from Amazon.

www.anthonymcdonald.co.uk